The Dreadful Dawn

Claiming Destination, Volume 1

Colleen A. Parkinson

Published by Sepia Tree Publishing, 2026.

This is a work of fiction. Similarities to real people, places, or events are entirely coincidental.

THE DREADFUL DAWN

First edition. February 7, 2026.

Copyright © 2026 Colleen A. Parkinson.

ISBN: 979-8988642985

Written by Colleen A. Parkinson.

For Spaz

Thank you for not letting me quit!

Prologue

If little Rosa Maria Rodriquez could have seen her future, she would have been terrified.

Rosa was only seven years old and already had the misfortune to see dark things no child should ever see. Yet, endowed with an internal fountain of resilience, she had acquired the ability to discern what she could and could not control. Her older brother Mario told her it was the adults' job to deal with the bad stuff and it was her job to just be a kid. Therefore, she was actually in control of nothing, and she was smart enough to know it.

She had managed five jumps before her foot caught the rope. She had spent the morning trying to master the criss-cross and had only managed a little improvement. She paused and sighed impatiently, repositioned the rope to begin again, lined her body up with her shadow on the pavement, watched the shadow of the rope pass above her shadow head, and jumped as it descended toward her leaping shadow feet. Her left foot caught the rope, causing her to almost lose her balance.

Her mother tapped on the window to get her attention. When Rosa turned and looked at her, Mama moved the white lace curtain, grinned and waved. Rosa knew Mama was just checking on her as she always did when she played on the sidewalk in front of their small row house. The girl grinned and waved back. Mama let the curtain drop and Rosa untangled the rope and began again.

She managed eight jumps before the rope caught her again. This time, she dropped the rope and sat down on the cement step to catch her breath. She listened to the birds twittering from the elm tree across the road and the hum of traffic from Tenth Street, the main drag, about two blocks up. Her neighborhood was unusually quiet for a Sunday. However, it was the end of the month and most of her neighbors had already spent their benefit checks. That meant less money for booze and drugs, which meant fewer people drunk or high, which meant fewer fights. For obvious reasons, Rosa liked the end of the month time best.

The second of her two grown-up front teeth had emerged just three weeks ago. She ran her tongue over it, and then tested its anchor strength with her thumb and forefinger. This tooth was in there for good as long as she didn't do that *meth* stuff her neighbor Julio did. Her brother Mario had told her Julio's teeth had fallen out because of the meth. Rosa was determined she would never mess up her new teeth with drugs.

As if on cue with her thoughts, four of the local toughs, boys between nine and twelve years of age—old to her—loped in her direction from the bus stop a block up. They passed a joint between them, playfully shoved at each other, waved their middle fingers at the cars that passed by, shouted bad words and laughed uproariously. The boys were bored and looking for trouble. Rosa was not afraid of them. They knew her and were always nice to her because she knew well enough to keep her mouth shut about their activities. *Silencio* was the rule in her neighborhood.

When they came upon the mouth of the alley, they stopped and peered at something. At once, they eyed each other, grinned mischievously and sauntered together into the depths. Rosa heard the noise of fists, grunts, laughter, and growls.

Growls?

Was there a dog or something down there?

Rosa trotted over to the corner of the alley and looked in. The boys were kicking and beating a homeless man who had undoubtedly been sleeping off a hangover. Somehow, the man got to his feet and fought back, and his eyes were wild as he growled at his assailants. He threw three of them aside and zeroed in on the smallest one. The boy laughed at him and challenged him as the other boys egged him on. The thin and sun-baked man, longhaired, bearded, barefooted and clad in torn soiled clothing, snarled and growled. Drool spilled down his chin and caught in his beard. In the next instant, he lunged for the boy, tackled him to the concrete and locked his jaws around the boy's throat. The boy's screams of pain stopped when the man pulled back with a dripping flap of glistening torn flesh in the vise of his upper and lower teeth.

Two of the three boys the man had wrestled away stepped back in disbelief. The largest of the three drew a gun from his waistband and cocked it, aimed at the crazed man who growled and chewed as he threw himself over his victim for another bite. The boy with the gun cussed as he fired a bullet into the back of the man's head. The shot made only a faint zipping sound because of the silencer. The man fell dead onto the bleeding convulsing body of the boy he had bitten.

Rosa backed away from the corner of the alley as the three boys abandoned their dying friend and dashed off in a panic. They ran in the opposite direction and did not see her. She peeked once more around the corner at the two in the alley. The boy who had been convulsing was now motionless under the body of the dead homeless man.

She would not be able to describe it if anyone were to ask her to explain what just happened. Even if she could, she would refuse to discuss it because of the *Silencio Rule*.

The grating whoosh sound of her front window lifting caused her to suck in a guilty breath. Her mother's voice called tensely from the distance, "Rosa! Rosa, where are you? *Rosa!*"

Rosa walked quickly to the front of her house and faced her mother through the screen. "I'm here, Mama."

She spoke accusingly through the screen. "Were you over by the alley?"

Her admission would ensure a spanking. "No, Mama." She pointed at the struggling little rose bush beside their front door to her right. "I was looking at a bug on the bush."

"What was that I heard? It sounded like a scream."

"Oh, that was Ricardo and his friends. They were teasin' each other—havin' fun. They're up the block now."

"Well, you come inside."

For once, Rosa didn't protest. She swept the memory of the horror in the alley to the Place of Secrets in her mind. Confined to the Place of Secrets, the incidents remained separate from her emotions. That is what Rosa did with all her secrets.

"*Silencio,*" Rosa whispered to herself. "*I didn't see nothin'.*"

CHAPTER 1

WARNINGS

THE PAPER TARGET HAD four shots through the torso section (two in the heart), and one smack in the middle of the forehead. Natalie wasn't surprised at the improvement, but she still wasn't satisfied.

"Go again, Dad?"

Her father removed the ear protection from around his shoulders and set it on the table. The corners of his mouth subtly lifted as he scrutinized his target with eight perfectly placed shots to the heart. He turned his attention to Natalie's results and whistled softly with approval.

"I know I can do better." Her brown eyes were eager.

He glanced at his watch. "It's getting late. I've got Bible study tonight."

"One more!"

"We'll come back next Sunday. You did a good job. Real good."

The manager's voice boomed over the loudspeaker, "Reset targets. Two minutes."

Brian Danbury set his .38 gingerly into its case, gave the butt of the gun a soft caress with his finger, closed the case and locked it. He stood up straight, bent backwards a little, and stretched his back. He paused in that position which made the slight paunch over his belt flatten a bit until he relaxed. "You want that burger, don't you?" It was more a statement than a question.

Natalie had been accompanying him to the indoor firing range for about a year, and it had been their tradition to top off the afternoon with a snack at the coffee shop there. She had come to relish their father-daughter time together. He didn't treat her like a little kid anymore. These days he seemed intent on teaching her the things that would be useful in life, things that would be useful for someone who was about to leave the nest. He advocated self-reliance, self-discipline and firearms skills. Her mother had offered an opinion that it was a leftover from his days in the Marines. Natalie agreed, but also figured being a cop had a lot to do with it. She thought he might be grooming her to follow his steps into the police force. She knew he was pleased with her progress at the gun range. When he first suggested she learn, he was surprised at her instant enthusiasm. Mom simply shook her head and mumbled, "...takes after the old man."

"Okay." Natalie followed Dad's lead and cased her mother's .38. She asked hopefully, "Am I really doing good?"

He grinned at her. "I'm proud of you."

His reply made her heart melt. Unlike her mother, he always knew the right thing to say to make her feel better about herself. These days she was often moody and had a snappish temper that caused friction at home. One morning after another heated battle, she overhead her dad assuring Mom their daughter's roller coaster emotions would level out once that nasty puberty phase was over, and the sweet girl who liked to decorate cupcakes would someday reappear as if nothing had ever happened.

Still, Natalie was never a normal kid. She disdained the cliques at school, was unimpressed with entertainers and celebrities. She would rather read a book than spend endless hours in front of the television or computer, or on her portafone. She had no interest in most things girls her age found interesting, especially if it had to do with dressing up, dancing or boys. Boys were at once a pain in the ass and a mystery. The last boy to call her, *Nutsy Natsy* suffered a broken tooth, compliments of her hair-trigger temper and equally impetuous fist. A young women's self-defense class expelled her for being too aggressive.

She insisted, always insisted, her burger be cooked medium. Two slices of American cheese—thank you—and don't be stingy with the onions. The second bite left a bit of mayonnaise on her chin. She wiped it away with the back of her hand, still chewing.

They were the only customers in the place. The television was showing the world news, something about violent social unrest somewhere in Europe, and her father was watching it from the table as he absently nibbled on french fries. The news footage commanded most of his attention, just as it did when he watched it at home. Her parents had not discussed it in front of Natalie, but she had overheard enough to get the impression they were concerned about something to do with supply shortages, agricultural and other supplies that nowadays came predominantly from China, parts of Africa, and the Middle East. Those countries had surpassed America and Europe in economic power, and that was the impetus for yet another riot across the Atlantic as shown briefly on this afternoon's newscast. All this Natalie knew but, having apathy most teenagers have toward world events, little of it concerned her so long as it did not impact her existence.

The waitress refilled their coffee cups and inquired if there would be anything else. He grunted and waived his hand dismissively as he mumbled, "thank you." She tore the bill off her electronic pad once it printed and set it on the table with a nod and a slightly flirtatious smile. He never noticed. As she walked away, a commercial came on. He took a sip of coffee, a bite of what was now a barely warm burger. His brow furrowed as if a sudden worry crossed his mind. He had been uncharacteristically quiet since they entered the restaurant and the TV seduced his attention.

"Carolyn said her dad's talking about their annual trip," Natalie remarked. "Said he's been stocking up the motor home. Go figure. Gas near ten bucks a gallon."

"Really..." He still had that look of concern on his face, and he was only paying half attention to her.

"They're gonna have a garage sale, too." She thought garage sales were fun. It was a blast to nose around in other people's belongings. It was like getting a glimpse into their lives. She could tell a lot about people by their possessions. She seldom bought anything, just enjoyed looking and imagining what their lives were like and what they thought was important.

It made her think about the lottery winners who lived in the house whose backyard abutted her property. Their garage sale was a doozy. Not ritzy stuff as one would expect, but weird stuff: Old record albums from the seventies, heavy metal and psychedelic groups mostly; an electric guitar and amp that had seen better days; a polished wooden pipe that reeked of stale pot. There was a book about witchcraft, other books on eastern religions, left-wing politics and social outcasts she'd never heard of; a doghouse that stunk of dog and made her stomach feel queasy; Asian tapestries and elephant statues. Lots of other assorted junk. Natalie figured this stuff had probably found their way to this family through many other garage and rummage sales over the years, probably the flea market, too. To top it off, they were blasting some old heavy metal music from an ancient c.d. boom box, as if they thought it would impress somebody or draw a crowd.

The man and woman looked like worn out drug addicts. The man was heavily tattooed and thin as an anorexic, his face prematurely lined, and his remaining teeth stained and crooked. He offered beer, talked fast in a strange accent, was overly friendly. The woman had long straight hair dyed coal black. It didn't suit her at all. In fact, it made her skin look even paler in the bright afternoon sun. There were shadows under her eyes, as if she hadn't had a full night's sleep in years. Like the man, she was bone thin. She had a tattoo on her left bicep, an image of a steaming pile of feces with the words *"shit happens"* under it. The woman was quiet, an invisible wall around her like a shield against his incessant chatter. Occasionally she would smile wanly; then she finally rose from her folding metal chair and went into the house. He continued chatting, oblivious to her absence. The yard was unkempt and littered with cigarette butts. He added another butt to the décor, uncaring.

Their teenage son burst out the front door, a cigarette dangling from his lips. He was thin, of medium height, with long legs, a trim waist and broad tanned shoulders. This package was dressed in jeans and a sleeveless white undershirt, what Dad jokingly called a *wife beater shirt*. The outfit was appropriate for the surroundings. He seemed in a hurry to get away and avoided eye contact with anyone. With a toss of the cigarette into the graveyard of butts, he brushed by the shoppers, made way to his motorcycle in the gravel side yard and roared off for destinations unknown. Natalie's last image of him at that moment was the glistening sweat on his muscular shoulders and upper arms, and his brown hair catching the breeze as he accelerated the bike toward the eastern range of the mountains.

The father never acknowledged the boy. He just kept chattering away, telling stories about some of the objects for sale. Chattering away, like a squirrel on speed.

Those people scared the hell out of her.

"I'm thinking about renovating the house." Her dad's voice seemed far away, causing Natalie to snap back into the present. He wrapped his hands around the coffee cup, as if he was trying to warm his hands. Another glance at the TV, then his gaze rested on the coffee.

He still had that concerned look on his face, and Natalie could sense the wheels turning in his brain, his thoughts already far ahead.

She realized then that when he spoke, he had simply been thinking aloud.

It made no sense to her that he would want to change anything about their already perfect house. "How come?"

Dad shrugged as he replied, "Upgrades."

"What upgrades? Our house is fine."

"Houses always need preventative maintenance, Nat." He bit into his burger and chewed, not looking at her, but across the restaurant at the far wall, his face pinched in serious contemplation that had nothing to do with his food.

She wondered how he planned to pull off this project. He worked nights. Her mother worked twelve-hour days as a trauma surgeon. Natalie did not like the idea of dealing with a bunch of strange men in the house while her dad was sleeping and Mom was gone. In addition, how was Dad going to sleep through the racket? "With your hours and Mom's hours, how are you gonna work around a contractor's schedule?"

"We'd be doing the work ourselves."

"You're gonna trust me with power tools?"

He finally broke from his contemplations and met her eyes, gave her a slight smile, and confidently told her, "There's nothing you can't learn."

"Dad..." She didn't know what to think. She couldn't picture herself doing that kind of work. "Are you sure? Are we really gonna do this?"

"Thinking about it." The news broadcast resumed and again drew his attention.

The female anchor was talking about a disease of some kind that had spread into Central Asia and Europe and was now appearing in parts of South America, Canada and the United States. The disease was something new and it was resistant to antibiotics, antiviral medicines and everything else doctors had been throwing at it. Now it was morphing into a highly contagious monster that seemed to be affecting its victims faster than when the disease first originated. The newscaster ended the segment with assurance the CDC was investigating.

It annoyed Natalie the news media did not describe the symptoms of this new disease. How would anyone know if they had it or if someone they knew had it?

Brian took a deep breath. When he exhaled, it impressed Natalie he was expelling a grave worry from his soul. He ran his hand through his thinning hair. Sadness and concern replaced the light in his eyes as he turned his attention away from the news broadcast and lifted his coffee cup.

He nodded subtly and said more to himself than to his daughter, "Yeah... I think we'll go ahead with the renovation."

HER MOTHER, BEVERLY, was cooking dinner and had already set the kitchen table when they arrived home. She was an excellent cook, and made good use of her little potted herb garden on the kitchen windowsill. She had taught Natalie about the use of herbs in cooking. In addition to her expertise with herbs, Beverly often combined her love of cooking with her skills as a surgeon and, in the happier days before that nasty puberty thing hit, had shown Natalie how to cut up a chicken with surgical precision. She even made a medical lesson out of it, showed her daughter the intricate muscles and arteries, identified the various organs (which made yummy gravy), explained bone formation, etcetera. The only question her mother could not answer was *which came first, the chicken or the egg?*

Tonight's dinner was... spaghetti. Natalie had grown tired of spaghetti. However, it was a work night, and Beverly saved her culinary masterpieces for her days off. She spent her days off preparing succulent side dishes while Dad fired up the barbeque for an early dinner.

Brian greeted his wife with a hug and a kiss on the cheek. It wasn't often enough these days they had the time to spend together. He buried his nose in her dyed blonde hair, enjoying the fragrance of her shampoo. It had taken a while for him to get used to her as a blonde. Sometimes he wished she would dye it back to its original light brown, simply because that was the real Bev. Even though she had put on a little weight over the years, he still found her incredibly sexy. As a playful afterthought, he patted her behind, which elicited a giggle and a whispered, "Save it for later, Casanova."

Natalie returned the firearms into the gun safe. She had caught their little love moment out of the corner of her eye, but pretended not to notice. She hoped someday she would find someone who would love her like that. Yet, she doubted it would ever happen for her. She felt she couldn't compete with the other girls her age that had already developed figures and had mastered the art of makeup and hair styling. Natalie saw herself as pathetically small breasted and had no real interest in the girly things learned at pajama parties and school restroom conferences. The girls at school never included her in these things, having dubbed her "weird" and "a snob". They didn't realize her standoffishness was more due to social anxiety than weirdness and snobbishness.

The only friend she had was Carolyn who lived next door, and Carolyn was as much an outsider as Natalie. One thing they did not have in common was Carolyn's attraction to the lottery winning couple's teenage boy. The girl made it a point to ogle him whenever he was in view, and made silly hormone drenched comments about his "fabulous body." So, maybe someday Carolyn would settle down with the white-trash-with-bucks, motorcycle riding rebel with no name, (who didn't know she existed), and Natalie would end up emotionally bonded to a house full of stray cats.

"Nat, come and eat."

Natalie turned and saw through the kitchen entrance the spaghetti and salad were already on the table. She realized she was still full from that afternoon's meal. Dad, however, had only had some french fries and three bites of his cheeseburger. Natalie figured he kept it in mind there would be dinner at home, even though Beverly knew they always stopped by the coffee shop after shooting practice. Regardless, the time around the dinner table was important to her parents. Natalie decided she would take small portions and eat slowly. When her appetite returned later that night, she would snack on the leftovers. Over the years that seemed to be her mother's plan, since they all seemed to be on different schedules most of the week. Beverly nodded impatiently at her, and she came and sat down. They joined hands, bowed their heads, and Dad said grace.

"How's the study going?" Beverly directed this question to Brian.

"Coltan's the only one who stayed with it." He didn't look up from his spaghetti that he was twirling on his fork so the strands wouldn't hang down too much. It was another quirk of his Natalie had grown accustomed to. Sometimes she found herself unconsciously emulating it.

"Well, at least there's one. The Lord didn't say we would win over everyone."

The forkful of spaghetti was only halfway to his mouth when he paused and looked up, the fork in mid-air, "He's the only one who ever completes the assignment before study time."

"Will they release him soon?" There was maternal concern in her voice and facial expression.

"He goes home tomorrow. I pulled some strings and got him community service." He finally ate the forkful of spaghetti. His next words came through chewing, "We'll continue with the study."

Beverly shook her head and sighed. "Is he planning on going

back to Reyton?"

"No. He'll be staying with his parents. For a while, anyway."

"What about his job and his place in Reyton?"

"He lost the job."

"Why? He was doing so well. Is that why he—?"

"He won't talk about it. All I know is he got into an altercation over a girl. The girl's parents had him fired." He looked seriously at Beverly. "I'm worried about him."

"He's come through far worse than this." She seemed to know what she was talking about. It made Natalie wonder if her mother knew this kid personally or only knew of him through Dad.

"I don't like the idea of him going back to his parents." Brian had forgotten about his meal by this time. Natalie studied his face, recognized the contemplation in his eyes, the wheels turning again as he considered an idea. "I'd like to bring him around now and then. Maybe if I had done that a long time ago, this wouldn't have happened."

What...? Natalie exclaimed silently.

Beverly eyed her husband with a wee bit of doubt. "This last incident concerns me. It's like he took a step backward."

"Kids like him do that sometimes. I've seen it before. If he'd stop being so stubborn and learn to ask for help. He knew he could've come to me. I think he was afraid, thought he would disappoint me."

"So, he gets into more trouble. Didn't he think *that* would disappoint you?"

"He wasn't in any condition then to consider how it would affect anyone else. You know how kids can be." He picked at the cooling spaghetti with his fork, his thoughts taking precedence over his stomach. "He still needs us, Bev."

"I know, honey." She considered it only for a moment before agreeing with her husband. "Whatever is best for him—you go ahead."

Natalie didn't like this idea. When would they consider what was best for her? There was the fact this stranger named *Coltan* was doing time in Juvenile Hall, and then there was the fact she feared losing much loved and needed attention from her dad. It was bad enough he had been spending so much of his personal time leading Bible studies at the Hall, and then privately with Coltan, whoever he was. Over the past twenty months, Dad had spent less time at home and more time away. It made her feel she wasn't as important to him as she used to be, and she couldn't understand why. Moreover, just when things were finally starting to get back to normal, Dad drops this into her lap. However, she was determined she would not relinquish any more of his time and attention to anyone, especially this loser of a boy. As a way to squash this plan, the obvious scenario came to mind.

"What if he steals something?" There was no hiding the harshness in her tone.

There was a glare in her father's eyes. "He won't steal anything."

"How do you know that? What if he goes after the guns?" She set her jaw in a *so, there* manner.

"He won't go after the guns." His firm tone told Natalie he was *absolutely* positive.

Natalie still wasn't warming up to the idea, but she knew better than to argue with her father when he already made up his mind.

Beverly had characteristically stayed silent. She had come to learn her interference would only set Natalie off on a defensive tirade that would end with a slammed bedroom door. This time, however, she saw a chance to gently teach a Biblical lesson.

"Before Jesus ascended into the clouds, what did he tell the disciples to do?" She put her hand over Natalie's.

"Go out and bring others to Him." Natalie knew where this was leading. She was suddenly downcast at the thought Jesus was disappointed in her for being so selfish and cynical.

"That's right." Beverly smiled at her. "This is what God wants. And, yes, the world is full of people who do bad things, and some never come to the Lord. Some are like the thorns the seeds can't grow through. We believe Coltan is the fertile soil the Lord described."

Natalie searched her memory, but couldn't remember anyone named Coltan at her school. Maybe he had spent more time in Juvy than in school, and he was probably an illiterate moron because of it. Most of the kids at Juvenile Hall were just like that, a bunch of stupid, throwaway loser-delinquents nobody wanted.

Brian gave her his full attention. "What are you worried about, Nat?"

"Well, if you're gonna bring him around here... What's he gonna be doing here?"

"Studying. Helping me out with some things. Work."

"Why's he in Juvy?"

"You know I can't talk about that."

"Was it something bad?"

"The only person he hurt was himself. Besides, he wouldn't be here alone with you. I'll be here. I'd never put you in danger. You know that."

"How often would he be here?"

"Now and then. He wouldn't be living here, if that's what you're worried about." Natalie offered no comment. Brian added, "He's actually a nice kid—more than he lets on. I know he wants to do better, and he's quite capable. You have nothing to worry about." He shifted in his chair and put his arm around her shoulders, "The Lord has impressed it upon me this is the right thing to do. The Lord doesn't want to lose that boy. He's got plans for him."

At that moment, Beverly's portafone chirped. She took it from the counter and answered. Her expression slowly turned to one of concern, then alarm. Finally, she said, "I'll be right there." She turned to Brian and Natalie. "They need me at the hospital. Bus crash.

Multi-trauma. Medi-Vac inbound. Natalie, will you be okay by yourself till Dad comes home?"

"Yeah." Natalie was used to this.

Brian wasn't surprised. It was the nature of their respective career beasts to call them away from the dinner table. However, something in his gut told him this bus accident would turn out to be unique in some way. He was eager to get details about the crash, and he knew the details he was looking for wouldn't come over the scanner.

He considered postponing his study with Coltan. That thought fled away quickly when he reminded himself how desperately the kid needed someone reliable. If he lost Coltan's trust, it would be difficult to win it back. He said a quick silent prayer for God to guide them all.

After study, he would drop by the precinct and get all the details.

"You make sure you lock all the doors," Beverly instructed Natalie, "and keep all the exterior lights on. "

"Of course." She had heard this so many times before. "I promise."

"I mean it."

Natalie didn't understand the sudden urgency in her mother's voice. She decided to forgo her usual backtalk and answer instead with a wordless and sincere nod.

Taken aback, Brian wondered what his wife knew that she had not shared with him. Were there rumors of some kind going around the hospital? Were they the same rumors that had been going through the police force? They would have to find time to talk.

He felt strongly they had better start on the renovations soon.

CHAPTER 2

As Brian expected, Coltan was waiting for him in the small visiting room. He had his Bible open to the section they would be covering tonight, and his workbook was open, the pages full of his answers and thoughts in scrawled handwriting. To his right was a small notebook, and he was busy writing in that when Brian sat across from him.

"How are you doing?" Brian asked.

Coltan looked up at him. He smiled briefly as he replied, "Okay." Just as quickly, he returned his attention to the important task of recording his thoughts. This was important to him, as it helped him remember key issues in his study and afforded an outlet to express his thoughts and apply the scriptures to his own life issues.

Brian observed the writing in the notebook. Coltan had made it a habit to write his questions and thoughts in French instead of English. Although he found it curious, Brian had resisted the urge to inquire about it. He decided he would ask about it, but not yet.

"How do you feel about going home tomorrow?"

"I'm not looking forward to it." His dark blue eyes were full of sadness.

"Do they know what happened?"

"They don't care." He shrugged and added, "I'd rather they didn't know, anyway. It'd just give Richard more fuel, if you know what I mean. They showed up at the hearing, that's more than enough."

Brian recalled the hearing. Richard, the stepfather, had encouraged the judge to give the boy a good long stretch in Juvenile Hall, claiming Coltan was incorrigible and needed to learn a lesson.

The mother (a skinny woman that reminded Brian of a praying mantis) sat in silence, a curious mix of anger and detachment. Coltan had told Brian she wasn't angry he had gotten into trouble; he was always in trouble. What ticked her off was the fact she had to get out of bed so damned early to make the stupid hearing. As for her detachment, it was her way of telling Coltan she didn't really care what happened to him. She and Richard left before the proceeding concluded, after reiterating to the judge their belief he should give the boy a harsh sentence. Never once had they looked at their son, nor he at them.

Brian knew what Coltan had waiting at home. "Are you afraid?"

"No. Like I told you, he's afraid of *me*. I'm finally bigger than him—and stronger." He smirked with slight satisfaction as he remembered the moment he finally fought back and beat the piss out of a very surprised and unprepared Richard. "He hasn't touched me since."

"Would you tell me if he did?"

"Yes, sir." He pulled the workbook in front of him. "I'd like to get to the lesson. I worked hard on it. Got lots of questions, too."

He glanced down at the open notebook at Coltan's right. "I have a question."

"Yeah?"

"Why do you write your thoughts in French?"

"So the other guys can't read it. The ones that can read, anyway."

"How did you learn French?"

"Richard. He's from the South. They speak it there where he grew up. My mom speaks it, too, but not as well."

"I never knew that."

"I don't tell people."

"I'm worried about you going home."

"I'll be alright."

"Tell me. Why did you get drunk that night?"

"I lost my girl, I lost my job, and I lost my place. That's reason enough, ain't it?"

"No. That's reason to pray. You know that."

He didn't reply for a while. Brian waited. He knew that sometimes Coltan would carefully ponder before he offered an answer. Coltan looked away, thinking. Finally, he said, "I didn't think God would listen."

"Why?"

"I keep screwing up."

"We all screw up. He won't stop loving us because of that." He sensed Coltan pulling away emotionally, and he wanted to prevent that. "After all we've been through together you should know you could always talk to me. Why didn't you tell me what happened?"

"I'd like to get to the study, sir."

"I want to talk about this, first."

"I don't, sir." He spoke softly and respectfully, a manner Brian had come to recognize as Coltan's way of easing out of an uncomfortable conversation.

"Are you having thoughts about killing yourself?"

"No, sir."

"Look at me." When Coltan met his eyes, he repeated the question, "Are you having thoughts about killing yourself?"

His answer was sincere and full of conviction, "No, sir."

"I don't want to go through that again, and neither do you."

It struck a very fragile nerve, and Coltan's eyes filled with tears. He remembered the incident as if it had happened that morning. He recalled the endless hours Brian and Beverly had sat with him as he lay helpless and in pain in his hospital bed. He recalled his despair that Brian replaced with hope. The fact that he survived was a miracle in itself, and they had taken every opportunity to remind him. Now he was ashamed he had almost thrown it all away. He couldn't understand why God, Brian and Beverly had not given up on him.

Brian gave him time to pull himself together. This was not the first time Coltan faced his demons, nor would it be the last. The process of healing could often take a lifetime; he told Coltan. Coltan accepted it and tried to be patient with himself. It had been a difficult road in the beginning, and it would still be difficult. But, the young man was stronger now and understood the process and understood once he conquered one demon, another would arise to take its place until he finally defeated them all. As Brian helped him, he witnessed the slow transformation in the boy's coping strategies.

Coltan was not the same young man Brian had met almost two years ago. The boy he had written up with six speeding tickets was sullen, combative, enraged and dangerously self-destructive. The seventh time he pulled the kid over for speeding, the boy had dared him to use the cuffs. He arrogantly reminded Brian the tickets were ineffective and he'd simply pay it off the next week and continue with the same behavior. Brian accepted his challenge, but on his own terms. He demanded the keys, and Coltan handed them over with a nonchalant smirk. With a show of bravado, the boy offered his wrists for the cuffs. He never took his glaring eyes off Brian's.

"You're gonna ruin my lunch hour," Brian said. "Then there's all that damned paperwork. I hate paperwork."

Coltan shrugged. "So, gimme back my keys."

"We're going for a ride," Brian replied.

For the slightest moment, the tough, defiant eyes showed fear. The wrists were still awaiting the cuffs. "All that paperwork..." Coltan taunted, "I get to fuck up your lunch hour."

Brian never reached for his cuffs. Instead, he pocketed the keys and with minimal, but authoritative roughness, escorted the boy into the back of his patrol car. He made a u-turn and headed down the hill toward town.

"Am I being arrested, or what?" Coltan sneered.

"You're having lunch with me," Brian answered.

There came a laugh of disbelief. "What?"

"You heard me."

There was silence between them until he parked and shut off the engine at the Dairy Delight.

From the backseat, a wisecrack, "The fucking Dairy Delight? Not only are you an asshole, you're also a cheapskate."

Brian found his comments more comical than insulting. He opened the back door and gestured for him to get out. "Order whatever you want."

"I want lobster."

"Not on the menu, kid." They walked together to the window. Brian ordered burgers, fries and sodas for them. He found a table and went to it, walking ahead of the boy, testing him, half-expecting him to run.

Surprisingly, Coltan followed and joined him, took a seat across from Brian at the outdoor table. "Why aren't you arresting me?"

"Paperwork."

"Man... you must really hate paperwork."

"I don't want to find you wrapped around a tree."

"Who cares?"

"Have you ever seen the result of an argument between a motorcycle, the road, and a tree?"

The kid snorted derisively. "Gimme the lecture, *ossiffer*."

"Down at the station, we've got an archive of color photos. You might be interested in seeing them. There's one case of a guy about your age, who ran into a tree head-on. Like you, he wasn't wearing a helmet. You'd find it particularly amusing."

"How's that?"

"On impact the guy's head exploded and his brains spilled out. As is that wasn't bad enough, he also puked up his guts. Stomach, intestines, everything. Forced up his throat, squeezed up and out like you'd squeeze a tube of toothpaste. They were hanging out of what was left of his mouth and half glued to the base of the tree when I found him. He'd been there about six hours before anyone saw him and reported it. By that time, there was a trail of ants crawling up those guts and into his mouth."

"Aw... fuck you!"

"Don't believe it? I'll take you in to see the photos, tough guy." From the walkup window, the girl called out their number. Brian stood. "How about that? Our burgers are ready. I don't know about you, but I'm starving." Coltan regarded him scornfully in response, still convinced the whole story was a scare tactic. As Brian returned to the table with the food, he saw an impromptu performance of the tough guy's blatant disregard. The boy was fidgeting, drumming his fingers on the table, one knee bobbing up and down to an imaginary beat. He had no idea how ridiculous he appeared. Brian slid the burger and fries to him. "After lunch, we're going over there to see the photos."

"I got a date after lunch." He took a big bite, trying to prove the hideous accident scene had not affected his appetite.

"I really hate paperwork," Brian warned him.

"You're a real asshole."

After a trip to the station house and a detailed viewing of the accident photos archive, Brian drove Coltan back to his bike. During the entire drive, Coltan's behavior was subdued. Seeing the color photographs had at least given him something to think about, but the rebellious fire was still in his eyes. Brian had seen that fire before. He was familiar with the anger and hopelessness that lay behind it.

They stood at the side of the road next to the Harley. The kid peered at him confrontationally, and Brian knew the attempted intimidation was a ruse. He wanted to shake the little punk. He knew the photographs had produced only the most minimal impression on him, if even that. Maybe if the kid had been there to see it in glorious *Realitycolor*, it might have made a difference. It was difficult for Brian to dam his emotions and maintain a professional emotional distance. At the time, he didn't realize the boy had been studying him, analyzing the inner turmoil he thought he had concealed.

"Are we done?" Coltan's attitude had softened only a little.

"Have I wasted my time?" Brian figured he already knew the answer, but he wanted the kid to be honest with him.

"Does it hurt?"

"What?"

"The impact. What that guy did."

"How the hell would I know?"

"One good thing came out of it."

He sensed Coltan intended to push his buttons. "What?"

"The ants got a damned good meal." The fire returned to his eyes, and he was daring Brian to react as he anticipated.

His first impulse was to slap the shit out of the punk. However, he stuffed that impulse, knowing that's what the kid wanted. "Keep it in mind." He handed Coltan his keys, pressing them into his palm and closing his fingers around them.

"Who was he?" Coltan asked.

"His name was Derrick. He was my little brother."

Coltan's reaction told him he suspected this. There was a hint of sympathy in his eyes, but only for the briefest moment. There was nothing else for either of them to say. Brian returned to his patrol car and slowly drove away, leaving Coltan alone to think about it. Through the rear view mirror, he saw the boy open his hand for his keys. He saw the boy look back, puzzled.

He had found the item Brian had slipped in with the keys, a small pewter cross.

A week later, he found Coltan waiting in the precinct lot for him at the end of his shift. He had parked the Harley alongside Brian's car, and sat there straddling the seat. When they caught sight of each other, Coltan removed his helmet and hung it on the handlebar.

Brian noticed the helmet. His decided the helmet was just for show, so he said nothing about it. He leaned back against the side of his car and tried to read the boy's expression. He noticed the anger had subsided a little, but that was all he could see. Coltan regarded him stoically, and it was impossible to discern his feelings.

After a few tense moments had passed, Coltan took his hand out of his pocket and opened it to reveal the cross. "Why?"

"Why not?" Brian said.

There was distrust in his eyes. "Why?"

"Why not?" They could go on like this all night, if necessary.

Coltan studied him, tried to read Brian's intent. He noticed a subtle lingering sadness in the policeman's eyes. The deep lines on his forehead were additional indications of a battle through a time of profound grief and lingering self-blame. Coltan knew well what this was about.

When he spoke, it was flatly, a statement of truth. "Your brother did it on purpose." He didn't mean it as an attack; he meant it as an offer of truce, a way to tell Brian he understood.

Brian took it as intended. "Yes."

"Did he believe?"

"No."

"Was he like me?"

"In some ways." *Actually, in too many ways.*

"I'm not him. If you want to settle your guilt with him, go bawl on his grave."

"I've done that already. Let's talk about you."

"Fuck you..."

At that time, Brian hadn't realized what Coltan wanted to hear was that someone cared about him because he was Coltan, and not because he reminded them of a previous lost cause. So, frustrated and believing he had hit an impenetrable wall, Brian relinquished all concern and good intentions. For a second he actually chided himself for believing he could save this mess of a kid. He commended himself in at least he had made the effort. Maybe God would send someone else to finish what he had started. He turned and used the remote to unlock the car door. "See you around, kid. Try to stay out of trouble."

"Leviticus is missing."

"What?" He then turned and saw Coltan holding up a small Bible, a raggedy thing with the pages loose in what was left of the ancient peeling leather binding.

"I needed rolling papers." The boy smiled a little, appreciating the irony.

"You used Bible pages to roll cigarettes?"

"*Joints*, you jackass. Suppose I'm going to hell for that, right?"

"Why Leviticus?"

"It was boring. I like the New Testament, though. But it's hard to understand."

So, he had tried to study the New Testament. This was something Brian hadn't expected. The kid had never impressed him as someone who would read a stop sign, much less an ancient holy manuscript. He suspected God in His wisdom had inspired the kid's sudden one-eighty. In that case, he would take it and hope for the best.

"Are you asking for my help?"

"You got time?" His tone revealed an expectation of disappointment.

"I can make time."

"When?" Coltan was pleasantly surprised, but did his best not to let on.

"Now." He saw Coltan was hesitant to fully believe this. Reassuringly, he said, "Let me call home first."

"You sure?"

Brian was more than determined. "I'm sure."

So began their relationship. It was uneasy at first. Coltan was not trusting of anyone and guarded in what he shared about himself. However, once he began studying the Bible under Brian's guidance, he relaxed his guard. The young man queried him about how the ancient Scriptures applied to modern life, particularly his life, in general. After a few months, Coltan opened up about his life and his feelings about things. Still, there was much he would not reveal. Over time, with a lot of encouragement and a hefty dose of humor, Brian finally got the kid to relax a little and learn how to have fun, something Coltan had never learned in his sixteen years. He impressed Brian as someone who was battle-weary and battle-scarred, and it saddened him to see this in someone so young.

He had found the boy unexpectedly perceptive to what was happening in the world. Over time their shared fears and concerns, coupled with their love of Christ created a bond between them. The boy seemed alone, fearful, pessimistic, and greatly needed someone to care about him and guide him. He had appealed to Brian's paternal instincts and the closer and more trusting they grew of each other, the more Brian mentored and encouraged him.

However, as time went on, Coltan began to withdraw into himself. He was less willing to talk about his life and seemed preoccupied. Brian noticed Coltan's bruises and scrapes where the clothing couldn't hide them. Still, the boy refused to discuss it in depth, only alluding with a nervous laugh to an occasional fistfight. He dismissed a deep and massive fresh burn injury over his left wrist as caused by a kitchen mishap. He arrived for their next Bible study wasted on some kind of downers.

Brian recognized all the signs, but failed to convince Coltan it was safe to open up and talk about it. Coltan insisted nothing was wrong. Brian decided to give it one more week before contacting the

Child Protection Bureau to launch an investigation. The decision to delay proved a big mistake.

Their meeting place had been the outdoor tables at the Dairy Delight. Coltan had attended every scheduled Bible study faithfully, and always arrived early to grab a soda and have a smoke while he reviewed his notes. One day, he didn't show. Hours later, Brian spotted the Harley parked at the side of the road with the keys still in the ignition. The helmet and jacket lie tossed aside near it. He walked up the road one way, then backtracked and stopped at the bridge. When he looked over the side, he discovered Coltan face down on the rocks in the shallow part of the creek.

Beverly was on the team that performed the surgery to repair the broken bones and facial injuries on the left side upon which he had landed. Miraculously, no brain damage had resulted. Brian was waiting in the room when they wheeled him in from the surgical recovery ward. He couldn't believe the damage the boy had survived. The blackened bruises, scrapes and swelling obscured his facial features. The surgical team wired Coltan's shattered jaw shut. His left arm, hip and left leg was in a cast. The ribs on that side were also broken. At the foot of the bed, the catheter bag slowly filled with a mixture of urine and blood. Brian watched in horror as Beverly and the nurses hooked him up to the monitoring equipment and oxygen. The boy was unconscious and his breathing was slow and shallow.

After the nurses left the room, Beverly sat at his bedside. She took up her stethoscope and listened to his heart, which had suffered some bruising from the fall. Because of Brian, her concern for this patient was personal; she was now here on her own time.

"Will he live?" Brian asked her.

"Despite his best efforts," Bev said. "Listen, there's something you should know. The full body scan revealed a lot of old minor breaks and tissue damage. There's also external evidence, a lot of scars all over his body. Looks like it's been going on for years."

"The parents?"

"Probably. We've already filed our report. But, we can't prove who's guilty until this kid talks."

Brian felt his temper seethe. "Have the parents shown up yet?"

"They signed papers and left."

"How could you let them go?"

"The authorities will handle it." She reached across the bed and took Brian's hand, "You're too close to this kid. You stay out of it. Let the Bureau do their investigation. Right now, your job is to be here for him. He needs you here at his side."

"I'm not leaving him," Brian stated.

"I'll stay, too. With Natalie off at camp, we'll be able to take shifts here. We'll take care of him together."

"How bad is he?"

"It'll be a long recovery. He'll also need psychiatric help. No one takes a jump like that unless they're serious. If he had landed differently, he would have died. I think there were some angels around him."

"I should have reported it right away." He succumbed to tears. "I saw all the signs. He wouldn't tell me the truth."

"Even if you could have intervened this time, he would have done it later. He was serious. No matter what, he would have tried it again." She took something out of her pocket and gave it to Brian. "They found this in his hand. I think you gave it to him."

Brian took the cross from her and stared at it, thought about the scene. Coltan had parked the Harley and left it. If Coltan truly wished to kill himself, he would have done it at full speed on the bike, like Derrick.

"Do you think it could have been an accident?"

"I think it was a spontaneous decision. The railing at that bridge is too high for someone to fall accidentally. You know that, honey. He made a sudden decision and he went for it before he could change his mind."

"He had the cross in his hand..."

"He's the only one who can tell you what that was about." Beverly placed her hand on his forearm and squeezed gently. "This was not your fault."

Coltan made a sound, a child-like moan accompanied by a grimace of pain, and his right hand closed into a tight fist. Beverly pushed the button on the morphine drip connected to the IV She tenderly stroked his forehead and moved strands of hair away from his one good eye. Her gesture was undeniably maternal, full of care and giving of comfort. A tear fell from the outside corner of his eye. She wiped it away. He whimpered softly, and she unfolded his fist, took his hand and held it in hers. He wrapped his fingers around her hand. She couldn't tell if he was aware of her presence. Sometimes, the minute reactions of patients in his condition were unconscious, instinctive.

Initially, Coltan was not a cooperative patient. Upon finally waking into full consciousness, he was enraged at his failure to take his own life, and threw a violent temper tantrum. He pulled out his IV and put his one remaining good fist through some hospital equipment; that broke not only the machines, but also the thumb and three fingers on what used to be his good hand. As if that wasn't enough, in the mad throes of this tantrum, oblivious to the catheter, he tried to pull himself out of the bed and ripped the catheter out in the process. His screams of agony traveled throughout the surgical ward, and brought a team of orderlies, nurses, security guards and doctors to his bedside where they literally tackled him and applied restraints. In all the confusion, none had any idea his screams were now regarding pain and not part of his tantrum. It wasn't until Beverly got word and rushed to his side, that the blood and urine dripping on the floor from the catheter tube told her what had happened.

During that whole scene, Brian had tried to tell them about the catheter, and he begged them to forgo the restraints, but no one listened. Unable to bear the screaming, he left the room and stood helpless in the hallway. He had only been gone for a few minutes when Coltan awakened, but it was enough for him to blame himself for the scene that resulted. When he saw Beverly rush into the ward, it was as if God had sent an army of angels in the body of that one woman. He watched as she pulled the hospital personnel away from the bed, and demanded they stay back. With amazing calm and protective concern for her patient, she took full control of the situation. After assuring Coltan she would care for him, she vanquished all personnel except for one nurse. With a rapid and furious sweep of the curtains for privacy, she soothed Coltan as best she could and ordered medication, a new IV set-up, and a new catheter. As she removed the restraints, she discovered the broken thumb and fingers and ordered delivery of the portable x-ray machine. She spent the next two hours soothing him and repairing the damage, while all Brian could do was observe each movement of shadows beyond the curtain. When the nurse allowed Brian in after all this time, he found his wife holding the miserable and completely despondent boy sobbing in her arms. He knew if it hadn't been for Beverly's intervention, the other doctors would have consigned Coltan to the Psych Ward. Coltan knew this, too. In those moments, he bonded with Beverly and would trust no one else to care for him. She had stepped beyond the role of doctor and into that of mother. From that day to the day he fully recovered, Beverly spent two hours after every shift at his side, and three on her days off. That's how it went for months.

This ordeal was the second-worst thing Brian had ever endured, the death of his brother Derrick being the first. He visited Coltan throughout the following two months while Coltan underwent physical therapy at an inpatient post-op center.

In all this time, Coltan's parents had only visited the hospital once, and that was to provide insurance information and sign some papers. They had never looked in on their son, and never phoned to inquire as to his condition or progress. As much as Brian wanted to confront them, he kept his distance so as not to complicate the Child Protection Bureau's investigation.

During the investigation, Coltan steadfastly refused to implicate his parents as his abusers. Instead, he insisted his past injuries were self-inflicted or the result of accidents. Brian and Beverly found it difficult to understand his refusal to bring the perpetrators to justice. Ultimately, the Bureau closed the case; they had a backlog of other cases to investigate, and this one was a waste of their time and resources.

Eventually, Coltan told Brian the truth about his home life and the years of abuse. In the process, he revealed that many of his past injuries had indeed been self-inflicted, but he refused to explain why. He asserted his suicide attempt had nothing to do with his parents or their abuse of him, but refused to reveal what triggered it. To this day, Brian still wondered.

Coltan turned to the first page of this week's lesson. They had been studying the Gospel of John and had now reached the account of Jesus' final night on earth. Coltan had re-read the chapter six times, and had dissected Jesus' prayer in the Garden at Gethsemane line by line. He found it fascinating Jesus' main concern was for others, even though he knew his death was drawing nearer by the moment. Even though Jesus had weakened briefly and asked God to remove the cup of suffering, Coltan knew without a doubt that if God had granted him that request, Jesus would have ultimately refused it. He concluded no mere human being could ever face so agonizing a death with such courage and unselfish grace.

"I want to accept Christ as my Savior," he told Brian. "I want to do it now."

"You've already done that," Brian replied. "You don't have to renew it. It doesn't expire like a driver's license."

"By trying to kill myself I showed him I never really trusted him. If I never really trusted him, then I haven't really accepted him, have I?"

"Well, you make a good point, but—"

"I lied to him."

"No. You didn't—"

"Yeah, I did. And, here's something else, Brian. As I was flying off that bridge, you know what I told him?"

"What?"

"I told him to go fuck himself."

"Colt, you were very ill. He knows that."

"He knows I didn't believe in him. That's what it boils down to. Now, are you gonna pray with me, or what?"

Brian admired his determination. "I'll pray with you."

"I need his forgiveness. I need yours, too."

"You have our forgiveness."

"Let's pray, then. After that, I wanna get on with this study. I have a lot to share and lots of questions."

They finished the study in a little over an hour. At nine-fifteen, the overhead lights dimmed and the announcement came over the loudspeaker bedtime and lights-out would be in fifteen minutes. The early bedtime was one of many things Coltan would not miss about this place. He was looking forward to his freedom and getting away on his Harley.

"Do you need a lift home tomorrow?" Brian asked.

"I'll take the bus." He managed a smile as he added, "I'm in no hurry to get there."

"I'd like to hire you to do some carpentry work at my house."

"Carpentry?"

"The theater in Reyton gave you a glowing recommendation.

You still have friends there, you know. So, how about it? I'll pay you well."

"I don't want your money." He made it clear the offer of pay insulted him. "When do you want to start?"

"Soon. A couple of weeks. It's still in the planning stages."

"Interior or exterior?"

"Interior."

"How does Bev feel about it? I mean, about me working inside her house?"

"She's okay with it. She trusts you."

"I wouldn't."

Brian leaned across the table, addressed him confidentially. "We wouldn't trust *anyone else* with this. We're counting on *you*."

Coltan understood the nature of the project by the imperativeness in Brian's voice. "It's starting, ain't it?"

He gazed somberly into Coltan's worried eyes, "I think so."

BRIAN STOPPED BY THE station on the way home to find out about the bus crash. Just as he suspected, there was something unusual about it. A passenger had attacked the bus driver causing the bus to veer through the guardrail and sail off the overpass. Reports from survivors indicated the perpetrator seemed physically ill in addition to exhibiting strange behavior before he attacked. The perp died in the crash and his body awaited autopsy in the morning.

Brian found Natalie asleep on the couch in the living room. She always seemed to prefer to sleep downstairs when her parents were away at night. He thought it was because she felt less vulnerable downstairs; she could hear if someone was trying to break in, and the location was close to the gun safe.

A worn biography of Joan of Arc lay open upon her belly. Natalie loved reading about strong women who took no crap from anyone. Her bookcase upstairs was brimming with books about women warriors who, for better or for worse, made their mark in the world.

Brian was certain Natalie would join the Marines and rise high in the ranks.

He left her asleep on the couch and headed to the basement. It was a good time to review his blueprints for the planned renovation.

CHAPTER 3

It was mid July, and the temperatures over the season so far had been unusually cool. The weather was the topic of the day for the two elderly men sitting at one of the outdoor tables at the Dairy Delight.

Sitting within earshot, Natalie and Carolyn eavesdropped as they sipped their milkshakes. Listening in on other people's conversations was a favorite pastime of Carolyn's, and something Natalie had come to appreciate as a way to get information about things she would normally not be privy to. Today, it was just the weather.

"My dad says it's all those volcanoes going off in the South Pacific." Carolyn remarked. "He says it always changes the weather patterns around the world."

Natalie didn't reply. She watched Carolyn suck down some more milkshake. High calorie stuff like that was the last thing Carolyn needed. She was already overweight. Many times Natalie wanted to mention it to her, but didn't want to hurt her feelings. She surmised Carolyn had a mirror at home, and if she hadn't noticed her growing obesity, it was because she chose to be blind to it. Just a few years before, Carolyn was slim. When she began menstruating, her weight ballooned. Natalie was grateful she didn't have a weight problem. The worst she got from the menstruation ordeal was cramps and mood swings.

"Do you think it's the end times? My dad says it's the end times."

"No. It's not the end times. Your dad needs to relax."

Carolyn became serious. "They're selling almost everything."

"Who?"

"My parents, you idiot! I heard them talking last night. They were talking about turning everything into cash. Why would they wanna do that?" At this, she took the lid off the container and started stirring the rest of her milkshake with the straw.

"Hardly anyone uses cash anymore, unless they're doing something under the table. I bet your dad's still gambling. Maybe he owes someone and can't pay. You know they never tell us anything."

"He's even putting his antique T-Bird up for sale. Says the gas for it is too hard to find and too expensive."

"Sounds like he owes someone and they got it in for him." Natalie had been drinking too quickly and now she had brain freeze. She put her milkshake aside. "Don't worry about it. They're still planning that trip, right?"

"Yeah. I guess." At this point, Carolyn was just plain frustrated. She reached for Natalie's milkshake. "If you're not gonna finish that."

"Go ahead." She stood and pushed back the cheap plastic chair, "I'm gonna get a coffee."

"You and your coffee..." This she said while pouring the remains of her milkshake into what was left of Natalie's. Strawberry and chocolate went together well.

Natalie ordered a cup of coffee with cream and three sugars. As she got the coffee and started back to the table, she noticed the two elderly men leaving, walking over to an ancient older-than-God Cadillac painted a butt-ugly rust-orange. The taller man took the driver's seat and started it up. White smoke emitted from the tailpipe and the car trembled, made a rattling noise, and then quieted down to normal. "Cheap gas..." The diagnosis came under her breath. She rejoined Carolyn at the table, began putting the cream and sugar into the coffee. She was starting to feel chilled as she watched the Caddy turn out into the tree-lined two-lane road.

"Hey," Carolyn said, "You didn't notice."

"Notice what?"

"I got eye shadow on. What'cha think?"

She had noticed it, but didn't want to bring it up. It was a horrible shade of green that paled out Carolyn's vivid blue eyes. "I think it's a little heavy, but I'm the last one to ask."

"Heavy? Nah-uh. I think it's just right." She closed her eyes to give Natalie the opportunity to see it better and therefore change her opinion.

"Like I said, I'm the last one to ask."

She opened her eyes and looked squarely at Natalie. "Well, I like it."

"That's all that matters, then." She hunched over and sipped her coffee, relishing the warmth.

An approaching motorcycle caught her attention. She watched as the black Harley slowed and pulled in. Although he was wearing a full black helmet that covered his face, she recognized the rider by the wife-beater shirt.

Ever since the boy had moved in to their neighborhood a little over two years ago, he was a mystery to the two girls and all the neighbors. As far as Natalie could ascertain, no one knew his name. He and his parents had made no effort to mix with their neighbors, and that suited all the residents just fine. The three were the scourge of the neighborhood, rich white trash that did not belong there. Many days and nights, they hosted their druggie friends, and there was usually loud music, drunken fights and screaming arguments. The home was so chaotic even the boy himself avoided the place. Natalie and Carolyn noticed he would often disappear for days at a time, only to reappear for a few hours before disappearing again. His longest absence lasted almost a year. His most recent absence lasted five months.

The mystery surrounding the boy served as nourishment for Carolyn's imagination, and she relished those rare moments when he came home and she could spy on him from her bedroom window. She was frustrated during those times, though, because the distance between their houses made it difficult for her to get a good look at him. However, she viewed enough of him across the distance to appreciate his lean, muscular form. To be this near to him today was a special treat, indeed. Carolyn purred salaciously, "Ummm... Harley Guy. It just got a little warmer here." The milkshake forgotten, her entire focus was on the object of her adolescent lust. She stared at him, watched every movement of every tight and well-defined muscle as he dismounted the bike. The next word came as a sigh of admiration, "Damn..."

"Don't stare." Natalie said in a half-whisper.

"I can't help it." Her eyes were wide. "He's taking off the helmet. God, he's amazing."

Again, Natalie whispered, "Stop staring."

"How can you not look at him? What's wrong with you?" She was incredulous.

"I've seen his house and family."

"You know what I notice about him?"

"What?"

"He doesn't have any tattoos. You'd expect a guy like him to have tattoos."

"Why don't you ask him about it?" Natalie already knew the answer, but it was fun to razz her.

The green-shadowed eyes grew wider and focused on Natalie. "Yeah, right!" Then her gaze just as quickly returned to the boy. "He's going to the phone booth."

The phone booth was at Natalie's left. Natalie stole a glance nonchalantly. He inserted his AllCard into the slot, punched in his code, waited for card approval, removed the card, and dialed.

"You'd think with all his money he'd have a portafone." Carolyn whispered.

"Maybe he forgot to charge it." Natalie said.

"He can charge me anytime," she replied naughtily.

Natalie grinned and it took everything for her not to laugh, "Obviously."

He hadn't noticed them at all. His entire being was devoted to whatever was at the other end of the receiver. He was too far away for them to hear his voice, but they saw he was speaking. He paused, listening, and then he spoke again. He leaned against the phone box, rested his wrist against it and slowly drew his hand into a fist. His fist tightened as he listened. He spoke, paused for the reply and ruefully shook his head. His face reddened as he frowned and spoke loudly enough for the two girls to hear. His voice was angry, but at the same time plaintive, "Please!" Another pause and his jaw tensed. He slammed the receiver down and bowed his head, pounded his fist onto the box. In the next second, he shouted to himself, "Fuck!" and slapped his open hand onto the box with so much fury it caused Natalie and Carolyn to jump in their chairs. When he turned in their direction, they saw the fiery glare in his eyes.

Alarmed by the boy's dramatic behavior, Carolyn could only react as she habitually reacted to most uncomfortable situations in her life. She giggled nervously and whispered to Natalie, "Harley Guy must've got dumped..."

Natalie sent her an expression of consternation and disbelief. She wanted to admonish the girl for her insensitive behavior and comment.

Harley Guy tilted his head to one side, bored into Carolyn with his fierce penetrating glare. He then locked eyes with Natalie who was watching him with concern and sympathy, as well as a modicum of fear.

Instead of coming towards them as Natalie anticipated, the boy simply stood there for a moment. The fire in his eyes dimmed to a pathetic ember of pain. He looked away, his eyes searching the trees as if he could find the comfort he needed there. His shoulders slumped, and he looked down at the pavement, turned and walked away. He boarded his motorcycle and reached to the handlebar where he had hung his helmet. He took the helmet with one hand, then drew it to him and cradled it near his abdomen with both hands as he contemplated until he finally put on his helmet and flipped down the face shield. He sat there for a few moments before he revved up the Harley and sped out the driveway.

Natalie released a long and shaky breath. Her face felt tense, and she realized she had been watching him with an expression of genuine concern and compassion.

"Damn..." Carolyn remarked with a relieved sigh. "I thought he was gonna come over here and beat the daylights outa me!"

Natalie paid only half attention to Carolyn's remark. She cupped her hands around her coffee cup and gazed up into the trees, felt sad for the boy's despondency. Did answers grow in trees? Of course not. She knew he had simply focused on the trees as a way to collect his thoughts. Now she was doing the same.

The image of her mother came to mind, the maternal hand covering that of her maturing daughter, the words about Jesus and bringing others to Him. She thanked God she had parents who loved her.

She asked God to comfort the boy she didn't know, the boy who seemed to be carrying so much turmoil within.

WHEN NATALIE RETURNED home, she expected her father would still be sleeping, as he had to work tonight. He generally did his errands early in the morning so he could sleep by ten in order to be up by five. It surprised her to find a note taped to the coffee maker:

"Having lunch with Mom. Start dinner at 4. Love Ya. Dad."

It was highly unusual for him to be up this early and out of the house. She shrugged it off as just a case of her parents trying to steal a little quality time together.

She picked tomatoes from the garden outside the kitchen, harvested a head of lettuce and some leaves of spinach. The garden was healthy this year despite the cool weather. Her mother had insisted on installing a huge garden instead of a lawn and swimming pool. The garden was much more practical, she had said, and with food costs skyrocketing and shortages becoming the norm, it was always a good idea to be a little ahead. Dad, the champion of self-reliance, heartily agreed with her, and they worked together prepping the soil and installing the fence.

The watermelon was ripe at the farthest ends of the property. In a separate section, the corn reached for the sky. There would be pumpkins and other kinds of squash in the fall, potatoes, turnips and radishes a bit later. Peach, apricot, fig and apple trees claimed another area; orange and lemon trees still another. The citrus would be ready just around Christmas if the weather didn't turn too cold.

It would soon be time to harvest the peaches, apricots and figs. Every year her mother placed the fruit into decorative baskets and gave them to Carolyn's family and old Mr. and Mrs. Spencer across the road. Last summer, her mother had dropped off a basket at the lottery winners' house. No one had answered the door, so she had slipped in a note and left the basket at the door. They never replied, never said thanks. Beverly didn't mind; it was simply good enough to have the abundance to share. As she would say many times, "It all belongs to God."

She would can the rest of the fruit and a large amount of the vegetables. This was the one activity Natalie and her mother still did together without fail every year. Once they labeled and dated the jars, they stored them in the basement. Natalie and Carolyn used to play down there when they were little, pretending they were running a grocery store. There were never any customers, so they took turns playing customers. It was fun at first, but they soon grew bored with it and found other summer activities.

Natalie popped a cherry tomato into her mouth and strolled over to the corn. She pulled a few ready ears and dropped them into the bucket. Tonight's menu was broiled chicken, corn on the cob, and salad. With extra time to spare, she strolled to the covered rear porch where she rested on the steps.

Loud angry voices from the lottery winners' house broke the serenity. As had previously been the case, the words sounded foreign, and two male voices and one female voice overlapped. Natalie couldn't resist looking over there. She could see their weed-eaten backyard clearly; privacy fences were non-existent between properties there.

The boy rushed out the back door, crouched on the steps and lit a cigarette. From the house came more yelling, more sounds of things breaking. The boy ignored it. Suddenly, a wooden dining room chair crashed through the large bay window, sending shards of glass into the air. The boy ducked. The chair tumbled and landed close to him. He remained seated, casually smoking as if this was all banality. Even when the Squirrel on Speed slammed open the back door and confronted him, yelling something unintelligible, he maintained his cool. He simply stared up at the Squirrel, patiently waiting for him to shut-up. When the man indicated no sign of stopping, the boy stood and hotly strode to the side yard. The man tailed him, his mouth still running. Natalie heard the Harley rev, heard the sound of scattering gravel and then the sound of the bike roaring away.

In the next second, she realized something interesting about herself. As she had been watching their confrontation, she had been rooting for the boy.

The sound of her kitchen door opening to the rear porch startled her.

"Hey, girl." It was Dad.

She showed him the bucket. "Thought we'd have this with dinner."

"Good!"

"They're fighting over there again."

"I heard it." He seemed a bit concerned and mildly angry.

He went in and turned on the scanner in the kitchen. He began preparing a pot of coffee, humming to himself. Natalie thought it was, "*His Eye Is on the Sparrow*," but she couldn't be sure. Dad had no talent as a singer.

She brought the bucket in and set it on the table. A call came over the scanner, a domestic dispute in the east part of downtown. A few minutes later, a car accident. Following that, a disturbance in the emergency room at the hospital. Normal stuff.

"How's Mom doing?"

"Busy. Lots of traumas coming in. Did you hear about the private plane crash over at the airfield?"

"Uh-uh."

He started humming again as he took the chicken out of the fridge where it had been marinating overnight in a bowl. He took the plastic off the top and sniffed the poultry. Satisfied, he transferred the bird to a broiler pan and set it into the preheated oven.

In the living room, he found the remote, flicked on the tube and sat to watch the local news that was just starting. The lead story was something about additional state funding for the hospitals.

The voice of a young male police officer came over the scanner. "Ten-ninety-seven." Natalie knew the code meant, *"Arrived on scene."*

Shortly after, a woman's voice, "Dispatch. Ten-ninety-one-cee. Request animal control."

Dispatch replied, "What's your ten-twenty?"

The woman officer, "Maple at Thornton."

The young male officer came back on. "Dispatch. Ten-fifty-four."

Dead body.

Natalie was more interested in the chaos coming over the scanner. Most of that never found its way to the broadcast news unless it was a murder or kidnapping.

The male officer's voice suddenly became tense. "Uh... fifty-one-fifty." *Subject mentally ill.* "Code twenty." *Send backup.*

Reply from Dispatch, "Ten-four."

A nutcase, Natalie thought. *Now, this is getting interesting.*

Dad's voice sounded from the living room, "Don't boil the corn. Use the steamer."

How did he know she was going to boil it? He must have recognized the sound of the empty boiling pot when she set it on the stove. She put the boiling pot back in the cupboard, took out the steamer pot.

Another voice came over the scanner, this one deeper, belonging to an older man. "Dispatch. Fifty-one-fifty. Bonito Valle Hospital Emergency Room. Code twenty" *An additional nutcase and an additional call for backup.*

"Ten-four."

"Uh... ten-fifty-seven." *Firearms discharged.*

"Hey, Dad." Natalie called, "Is this a full moon?"

"Not even close."

"Lots of crazy people today."

"Yeah." He was dividing his attention between the TV and scanner.

The voice of the young male policeman who had found the dead body and had encountered a crazy person came back on. He sounded out of breath, as if he had been running. "Dispatch. Ten-thirty-five." He was ordering them to scramble the transmission so it would not transmit over the scanner.

Natalie had stopped herself from filling the steamer pot. She didn't want the sound of the running water to interfere with the drama from the scanner. Just when she turned off the water, the electricity died and everything went silent. Dad muttered something. She cussed under her breath. Now she'd never know what happened with the dead body and the crazy people.

"Don't even ask me for the hand-held," Dad entered the kitchen with a golly-gosh kind of grin on his face, "I loaned it to Griff."

"We need a battery powered backup," Natalie said.

"It's on my list."

"Sounds like there was a murder. Now I'll never know what happened."

"I'll fill you in tomorrow after my shift." He went to the utility closet, took out a battery-powered lantern, and set it on the counter. "Here... If the power doesn't come back before dark."

"Thanks." She filled the steamer pot with water and put it on the stove. "Good thing we've got gas for cooking."

"I'm going up to take a nap. By the way, they're keeping me on the eleven to seven shift for the next couple of months."

"When did you learn that?"

"This morning." He started for the staircase, but stopped and turned abruptly. "Listen, Nat. Your mom might be late again tonight. Keep your PF handy in case of emergency."

"She's on a double?"

"A lot of the doctors have been sick."

"That stuff that's going around? What the TV said?"

"They don't know yet." The frightened look in her eyes concerned him. He put his hands on her shoulders, reassurance in his voice. "Now, don't go getting all worried. Mom is fine."

"They got a fifty-one-fifty in the ER right now. Someone shooting. What if he gets away up to the surgical floor?"

"It won't happen. They're all trained to prevent that kind of situation. You know that." His private uneasiness dulled the confidence in his voice. "You might as well hold off on that steamed corn unless you want some."

"Okay."

"I'll set my alarm for eight-thirty. In the meantime, I want you to stay home."

"No problem."

He started up the stairs. He made it up six steps before he stopped again. "Oh, yeah. Write down an inventory of the food in the basement. When the lights come back on, that is."

"How come?"

"We want to keep up on it, that's all. Goodnight, Precious."

While the late afternoon rolled into evening, Natalie cleared the wind-driven dust and broken plant debris off the back and side porches. While she swept, tidied and cleaned, she noticed the smell of smoke and looked in the direction of it. A fire raged in the lower valley at the south end of town. She rested on the steps at the west side porch and tried to ascertain the location of the fire. By her best guess, it appeared to be one of the industrial buildings. There had been sirens earlier, but that sound was gone now. She figured they had all the trucks they needed at the scene. It would have been nice to have the scanner going so she could hear what was happening. She wondered if it had anything to do with the power outage.

The lottery winners' house was quiet. The dining room chair was still backrest-down in the weeds. No one had covered the broken window yet.

Just after eight o'clock, the electricity kicked on and, shortly after that, her mother returned from work completely exhausted. She gave Natalie a quick kiss on the cheek and remarked yes, she heard about the shooter in the ER—Dad had called to check on her. All she wanted to do was go to bed and sleep.

Once the food was ready, Natalie prepared two dinner plates and put them on a tray with the silverware and napkins. She poured a small glass of cabernet for Mom and a good strong cup of coffee for

Dad and put these on the tray. She took a salmon colored rose from the vase in the dining room and placed it between the plates, and then she took her gift of comfort up the stairs.

CHAPTER 4

The yard sale next door at Carolyn's house was going full speed ahead. They had put out most of their luxury items and the standard collection of knick-knacks, kitchen items and linens. Natalie found it curious they had put out furniture—good stuff—including bedroom sets, their full dining room set (fancy and flawless and looking brand new), and even their formal living room set. They were selling all their yard tools and even their riding lawn mower. It looked more like a moving sale than a standard yard sale.

Although it was a Saturday, there were few people dropping by. Most of the people there were elderly ladies and young women with toddlers in tow. There were a few younger men, rugged types, who were looking at the tools, and one middle-aged man who was eying the formal living room set.

Carolyn sat at a white folding plastic table, AllCard Reader in front of her, acting as cashier. Carolyn's mother, a short, roly-poly woman, slouched in a folding aluminum chair keeping an eye out for thieves. The father, tall, bearded and fat in the middle, was busy giving a sales pitch for his restored 1960s era Thunderbird. He had spent years restoring that car and had driven it in antique car shows. With the exorbitant insurance and gasoline costs, and with the antique car shows and auctions all but dried up in the last two years, he was ready to unload it cheap. Someone inquired about the motor home beneath the carport in the side driveway. He shook his head and declared it was not for sale.

Carolyn pressed her finger on the AllCard Transfer Reader's *Total* icon and gestured at the sparse earnings. "This really sucks.

They want everything for nothing."

Natalie asked in a whisper, "Did you ever find out why they're doing this?"

"No. They're keeping me in the dark. I know something bad's going on." She glanced around to see if anyone was within earshot. Satisfied it was safe, she leaned in close to Natalie and whispered, "Dad got drunk last night. He never gets drunk."

"Oh, Care... Natalie said sympathetically.

"This bullshit's makin' *me* wanna drink!" She seemed resigned to the idea that things might only get worse. In addition, it hurt that her parents wouldn't trust her with the truth.

"Things'll get better, Care. Just remember the Lord's watching over you. Turn it over to Him."

"I've seen Mama praying and praying. Nothing's getting better." She didn't realize her voice had gotten louder with her emotion.

"Shhh, shhh..." Natalie whispered.

"It doesn't make any sense!" Carolyn went on in hushed tones, "We're good people. My parents work hard. Yet, people like that doper white trash a few doors down get the big break. And, look what they've done with it. What the hell..."

"Shhh.., Care. C'mon, now."

"Them and their mean-ass trashy kid..." She said it as if her troubles were their fault.

"Ask your mom for a break so we can go talk."

"I can't. They said I have to be out here." She blinked back tears.

"Maybe tonight?" Natalie offered.

"Yeah. I guess."

THE TEMPERATURES HAD still not risen above the mid-seventies. As Natalie coasted her bicycle down the hill and past the Dairy Delight, the shade from the trees along the road cooled the temperature even more. She could not remember summer ever being like this. It had gotten to the point where she always carried a sweater with her whenever she went out. At the bottom of the second hill, she took a right onto the main drag into downtown and headed toward the shopping district.

Many of the businesses at the eastern edge of the valley had called it quits or uprooted to the west near the interstate. The once popular smorgasbord restaurant had folded. Further west where the interstate came through, the Sandy's sign stood proudly like a sentinel. Someone had thrown or shot something at the restaurant's sign, putting a huge crack in the middle of it. Sandy's was still open because it got the bulk of its business from the interstate and all the travelers that had to wait hours while their cars recharged at the adjoining EC station. Because of the interstate, businesses in this part of Bonito Valle were thriving. The small businesses in the original downtown in the old south end of town were slowly dying or had moved out leaving that neighborhood impoverished and crime-ridden.

She reached the *Radio Waves* store at the strip mall along the interstate and locked up her bike. She always felt uncomfortable there because of all the cameras watching her from every angle. There was even a camera above the Radio Waves front door staring at her, something the State required at every business, traffic light and streetlight, as if every citizen was a criminal. Through the window, she could see Mitchell Fenny setting up a display of batteries on sale. He saw her and waved. She waved back as she headed for the entrance below the intrusive camera.

He greeted her enthusiastically as if she was his own daughter, "Miss Danbury! How ya doin'?"

"Okay, Mitch. My dad said you had those portable scanners for me to pick up." She tried not to glance at the camera behind the checkout pointed at the front of the store.

"They're dandies, too." He went behind the counter, bent and produced four boxes and put them on the counter. "Proudly made in the United States of America!" A tall thin man in his mid-fifties, Mitch was a former Marine like her dad. Although hidden by his long-sleeved shirt, she knew he had a tattoo on one arm that said, *"Semper Fi,"* and on the other arm a tattoo of an American flag with the words, *"Born of Patriot Blood."* He was bald at the crown and all that remained of his hair was close-cropped graying hair at the sides. His mustache was already fully gray. "Your dad says you're a regular *Annie Oakley* at the shooting range these days."

Natalie grinned from ear to ear. "He told you that?"

"Sure did. He's right proud of you."

"Cool!" Natalie was still grinning. "How much do we owe you?"

He double-bagged the scanners, winked conspiratorially and whispered, "Nothin'. You gonna be able to carry these on your bike?"

"In the basket. Sure."

"Say..." He confidentially leaned across the counter, "Tell the old man Griff's got somethin' for him. He'll know what I'm talkin' about."

Griff was the guy who ran the shooting range.

She leaned into Mitchell, imitating his confidential manner. "You gonna tell me?"

Mitchell stole a glance around the store. A customer, a big hairy man in his twenties wearing a black vest was perusing the aisle near them. Mitchell whispered, "Ears." He nodded towards the man. "Y'know..."

Natalie understood. "Okey-dokey."

"Hey." Mitchell was still whispering. "You be careful goin' home. And don't go near the south end for anything. *Anything.* Things are stirrin' up down there. Scary shit goin' on."

Mitchell was a no-nonsense kind of guy, not one to spread

rumors.

"I've been hearing the calls coming over the scanner," she whispered back.

"You be safe," he said in a low volume. "Go right home." He placed the bag into her hands. "Here. Don't forget to tell him Griff got his stuff."

"Gotcha." She turned to leave, and a suspicion she'd been anticipating over the last two days came to mind. She turned back to Mitchell and asked softly, "There's gonna be riots. That's it, isn't it?"

"Your area's safe. Go on home, now." Then he said, "Hey, wait." He went over to the battery display table and took two large packs of double-A's and put them in her bag. "On the house."

Natalie thought about her brief conversation with Mitchell, his comment about the south end and about Dad getting another firearm. It finally sunk in that things were much worse than she had noticed, and her parents knew far more than they would share with her about it. She recollected the calls she heard coming over the scanner days before, weird stuff she had joked about as the result of the full moon, and then this morning's unusually frequent calls to the violent south part of town. The south end was normally quiet early in the day, and the moon had nothing to do with its predictable cycle of emergency calls. For once, she worried about the civil unrest brewing in her small hometown. Riots and crazy people shooting up hospital ER's was big city stuff. However, the ills of the country were now reaching the smaller communities, and that was probably what stressed out her mom and dad lately. Maybe Carolyn's folks were worried about the same thing. She wondered if they were planning to move away. Where do you go? Bonito Valle was about as safe a place as you could find these days, despite its current uptick of violence. Yet, she couldn't stop thinking about it, couldn't help thinking that conditions might worsen. She decided to discuss it with her mother as soon as she reached home.

The added weight of the scanners and batteries only made it more difficult to pedal up the hill. Her legs were feeling the strain as she reached the crest of the hill. The next portion of the way would be flat, and she was grateful for that. She stopped pedaling and coasted for a bit until the bike began to slow, then she started pedaling again, but was not in a hurry. The scenery was enjoyable, and traffic was light, which allowed her to hear the bird songs and the rippling water from the creek. It was God's music.

She felt the tires run over something, and there was a popping noise. She hardly noticed and continued on her way, dismissing it as gravel. After a couple of minutes, it became harder to pedal. The front tire was rubbing. She stopped the bike and looked down at the tire. It was flat.

"Shit..." she whispered, and lowered the kickstand.

It was more an inconvenience to her than a concern. She kept a tire inflator strapped to the frame under the seat. She unclipped her repair kit, opened it and sat down cross-legged next to the bike. The small can of puncture sealant weighed heavy in her hand. She shook it. There was no sound. Over time, the stuff had hardened in the can. On to Plan B. If she still had the patch kit, she'd be back on the road in no time. Had Carolyn ever returned it? It wasn't there.

There came a snapping sound, and the brush off the side of the road moved. She figured it was a small animal or a bird. The snap came again, this time louder, heavier. Almost like a person stepping on a twig. Then she heard a grunt, followed by a soft growl. Natalie tensed and stood, watching.

In the next few seconds, a motorcycle approached at a leisurely speed from behind her on the road. The noise made it impossible for her to monitor the sounds from the brush. Before she could turn to see the road, the cycle roared past her. She just caught sight of the Harley as it continued away, the rider familiar by his clothing and full black helmet. He slowed the Harley, made a u-turn and pulled up beside her.

Natalie had a fleeting recollection of Carolyn always calling him, "Harley Guy." An image from her last encounter with him at the Dairy Delight flashed in her mind. She hoped he was in a better mood today, because he obviously had decided to pull over and interact with her. Apprehension suddenly swept over her as she realized he knew she was alone and her bike was out of commission. Did he intend to take his revenge out on her for Carolyn's stupid remark that day? Maybe all he wanted to do was pull over to laugh at her and then race off. As he paused beside her and observed her through his tinted face shield, she felt her body tighten in anticipation of a conflict with him.

He turned off the engine, put the kickstand down, took off his helmet and hung it on the handlebar. The distance between them was less than three feet. This was the first time she had ever seen him up close. The rays of the sun played upon the golden-auburn highlights in his dark brown hair, the length of which rested uninhibitedly in lazy waves just below his earlobes. There was no part in the uncaring style in which he wore his hair; it simply seemed to do its own thing. With one finger, he brushed some rebellious strands away from his eyebrows along with some sweat. The length of his nose was average, non-imposing, and it crooked slightly to one side as if it had once been broken. There was a little peach fuzz on his tanned face where a mustache and beard could be in a year or so. She noticed some scars on the left side of his face. Regardless of the scarring, Natalie thought he was handsome.

His sapphire eyes regarded her concernedly, and she melted under his gaze. "You look kinda stranded. You need help?"

In contrast to the gruff and arrogant voice she heard when he was fighting with his parents, the unexpected medium pitch and gentle quality of his normal tone of voice greatly surprised her.

She feigned only minimal concern at her predicament. "My tire's flat."

He gestured at her repair kit. "What kind of tools you got?"

Her lack of preparedness embarrassed her. "Well, I slacked off and haven't looked over my supplies in a while. I guess I can just walk it home."

He rubbed his chin, thinking. "Huh..."

As he stared off into space with his thoughts, she took the opportunity to glance over his body. Scars marked his shoulders and arms. Natalie tried not to stare, resisted the urge to ask him how it happened. In the next second, she assumed the wounds were the result of fights or maybe an accident of some kind. Whatever the cause, the scars appeared old.

The sound of a car engine jolted them from their thoughts. An old red sedan raced by. The young male passengers at the front and back passenger side leaned out the open windows and howled at them. Although Natalie had only caught a glimpse of them, she was sure they were teenagers. The driver gunned the engine, and a cloud of dark gray smoke puffed out the exhaust pipe.

Harley Guy seemed to recognize them, and it was apparent they were not friends.

He looked at Natalie. She sensed he was taking note of her small, wiry frame and her tiny immature breasts that were only a little larger than training-bra size. His glance then rose to her oval face, expressive brown eyes and limp shoulder-length dark hair. He seemed to recognize her but concurrently he rubbed his chin, still gazing at her as if he was uncertain.

He worriedly cast another look at the red car getting smaller down the road, and then told her, "I'll walk with you."

She felt more nervous about him than about the guys in the red car. "You don't have to."

"I need the exercise." He referred to the Harley and patted the two-up seat, "Don't get much on this anymore."

The Harley was shiny and black, with detachable black leather saddlebags on each side. It was an impressive and beautiful machine, and by the condition of it, much loved.

"Yeah..." She began to pack up the repair kit, searched for conversation to put them both at ease. "I see you out riding a lot these days. That's a beautiful bike."

He smiled and said affectionately, "My Fatboy."

Natalie didn't know what that meant, but assumed it was something special. Having just left Mitchell's store, she thought of Mitchell and knew he'd know what a *Fatboy* was. He'd appreciate the Harley if he saw it. "As a friend of mine would say, 'it's a dandy.'"

"Is your friend moving?"

It took her a second to realize he assumed she had quoted Carolyn. "Carolyn?"

"Whatever. Looks like they're moving."

"I don't know." She noticed a perplexed expression on his face. She decided to elaborate, but did not understand why she felt compelled to do so. "The parents won't tell her anything. I think they might be having some money trouble like most people these days." She strapped the kit back in place and started walking the bike. "When my grandparents were alive, they said this was the best country in the world. There was lots of industry, jobs for everyone. Food... everything you wanted." She smiled nervously as she glanced at him. "Sorry. I don't mean to rattle on."

"No. It's okay. Go on."

"People were nice to each other, you know? Not like things are today. Now it all seems to be falling apart. I was talking with my dad's friend a while ago, and he got me to thinking about what's going on right now—y'know, stuff I usually don't pay attention to. Everybody's on edge, nobody trusts anybody. Crime, homicides and stuff, even suicides are at an all time high. It's like there's no hope anymore."

He paced her, pushing his bike along. "Yeah..."

"You know what I mean?"

"Yeah." His eyes met hers commiseratively. "Y'know," he said, "I listen to the radio late at night. People call in all the time saying the same thing. Some think it's gonna get a lot worse."

"What do *you* think?"

He raised his eyebrows as he stated, "It's gonna get a lot worse."

His candidness and knowledge surprised her. Compelled to hear more, she inquired, "How much worse?"

He was quiet, thinking about it. Finally, he said, "Worse enough that we'll be wondering how we're still here." When she, taken aback, did not respond to his reply, he offered her a quote, "*Abandon all hope, ye who enter here.*"

Her brow furrowed in both concern and wonder. "Huh?"

"It's from Dante's *Inferno*. Have you ever read it?"

"Uh-uh..." Literacy was not something she would have expected from him. He did not impress her as a bookworm. She replayed the quote in her mind. It frightened her. She glanced back at him; saw he was thinking about it too. "Maybe I *should* read it."

He half-smiled at her, and then he shrugged.

She found his pessimism creepy. The day was too beautiful for such dourness. Humorously, she teased him, "Well, aren't you a ray of sunshine!"

He laughed concurringly.

They walked a long way in silence. Natalie thought over what he said. Could he be right? She couldn't imagine what things would be like if it all got worse. Mitchell's warning about an impending riot in the south end sent shivers through her. Maybe this Harley Guy knew about it. She stole a glance at him. He was staring straight ahead, lost in thought. *A thinker,* Natalie decided. At the same time, he displayed a calmness that seemed to emanate to her and envelop her.

When they came to the Dairy Delight, Natalie said, "One more hill."

They noticed the red car parked in the lot and the four boys gathered at one table. These masterpieces of not so polite society wore *gangster* type clothing and sported abundant tattoos. Two wore silver devil head piercings just below their lower lips. Slugging down sodas and burgers, they were boisterous and messy.

One spotted Natalie and her companion and brought it to the others' attention. The scruffiest one recognized Harley Guy and hollered to him, "Hey! You pickin' 'em young these days!"

His companions howled laughter.

Harley Guy whispered to Natalie, "Just keep walking."

The mouthy scruffy one taunted him, "Hey! I'm talkin' to you!"

Natalie made the mistake of looking the punk in the eye.

"Hey!" The miscreant yelled, "Hey baby! Wanna taste a real man?" At this, he stood and pushed his pelvis forward and cupped his hands around his privates. "Taste a real man, baby!"

His buddies urged him on with more laughter, inaudible comments and waving fists.

Harley Guy abruptly stopped. "Shit..." He took a deep breath and pushed it out forcefully. His jaw tightened, and his eyes developed that fiery look Natalie had seen two weeks before at the Dairy Delight. In the same moment, he set the kickstand, turned to Natalie and said firmly, "Stay here." He shrugged one shoulder, then the other, loosening up. His posture ramrod straight and his hands folded into fists, he strode briskly and purposefully across the road.

The punk was oblivious, mocking. "You rammin' it to little girls, now?"

His muscles tensed under the *wife-beater* shirt as he quickened his pace and made a beeline for the mouthy punk. Without a word, he brought up his fist and slammed the guy's nose so hard the crack of bone and cartilage breaking echoed as blood spurted into the air.

For a good ten seconds, the bigmouth tottered, staring in shock, blood running down his mouth and chin. He toppled like a downed tree. The other boys scattered, gaping at Harley Guy in fear.

Harley Guy stood his ground. "Anyone else? Huh?"

There were no takers.

"Good!" With this, he calmly crossed the road, took the handlebars of his motorcycle, released the kickstand and started walking the bike. "One more hill."

She knew his actions were more in her defense than as a reaction to their taunting him. With that knowledge, she realized she had just witnessed a previously undiscovered aspect of Harley Guy's personality: adherence to a code of honor and an honor of all that was decent and right. "Oh, my God..." Natalie's sudden chuckling immediately lightened his mood. He laughed in response. She liked the brightness of his laughter, and the fact his teeth were not perfectly straight, just as her own were not perfectly straight. Proceeding alongside him, she remarked admiringly, "You got a punch like a canon!"

He flexed his fingers on his right hand, performed a quick visual survey for any damage.

Natalie noticed the old scars on his hand. She mused if he had been a used car, he would be so dented up no one would want to buy him. There was no telling what hidden damage existed under the hood. No wonder he was pissed off most of the time.

"Anything broken?"

"Naw."

"Does it hurt?"

"Naw." His slight grimace revealed *it sure did.*

Natalie grinned. "Remind me not to piss you off."

He grinned back and lit a cigarette.

They said nothing else the rest of the way. When they reached her house, he simply nodded and started up the Harley. She hollered *thanks* over the noise. He smiled, nodded again and flipped down his face shield. As he raced away, she noticed he was taking the road back toward town. Her curiosity about him heightened, and she realized she had forgotten to ask his name.

NATALIE FOUND HER MOTHER in the garden, hunched over a freshly dug row of fertile soil, her knees on a foam kneeling pad, a broad straw hat shielding her neck and shoulders from the sun. She set the spade aside and dropped a half-potato with sprouting roots into the hole, tenderly covered it with soil and began to dig another hole.

Natalie knelt beside her. "I picked up the scanners."

"Thank you," Beverly said.

"Is Dad sleeping?"

There was tension in her voice. "He was called in early."

"I didn't see him on the road."

"You were probably downtown by then. How's Mitchell doing?"

"Spunky as always." She took a breath in preparation to question her concerning what Mitchell said about the south side, but her mother's next comment interrupted her.

Beverly dropped another half-potato into the fresh hole and covered it. "Did I hear a motorcycle a few minutes ago?"

She didn't know why that would matter to her mom. "Yeah. He's headed into town." She thought of mentioning her walk with the mysterious *Harley Guy*, but quickly decided Mom would admonish her for associating with him.

Beverly started on a new hole. "Was there anything on the porch? A bag?"

"No." Natalie didn't wonder about it; Mom was always having stuff delivered.

Beverly set down the spade. She took a deep breath and closed her eyes, and her lips moved in a brief silent prayer.

Natalie took the spade and began to dig a new hole.

Beverly snatched the spade from her. "Let me do that."

"I want to help."

Her voice became uncharacteristically harsh. "You can help by typing up the inventory list. Your fives and eights look the same. I can't read your writing."

"Okay." Natalie tried hard to brush it off.

"Do it now." A tear fell from the corner of her eye. She continued to focus on her gardening.

"Mom...? What's going on?"

No answer.

"Why are you crying?"

Beverly stopped and wiped her tears away. She sniffed and took a deep breath.

"Mom...?"

"I need you to be very strong," she said. "Very strong."

"What is it?" Her first thought was that somebody died. Her second thought was Mom or Dad had cancer or something.

Beverly continued after she reined in her emotions, "We have to prepare. We have to be ready for what's to come. It's happening faster than we expected."

"You mean the riots and stuff?"

"The riots are just the beginning. People are murdering each other for gasoline and food. On the news this morning they said Chicago, Detroit and Los Angeles are under martial law. New York City is preparing. All the big cities are preparing. Now it's spilling over into the smaller towns. We're not safe anywhere. Do you understand?"

Natalie had not seen the news. She figured Mitch had known but didn't mention it. Her mother's revelation caused her gut to wrench.

"Yes."

Beverly didn't pause, "They're rounding up all the gangs, all the *undesirables*. Those people are disappearing. They're readying rescue stations across the country. FEMA has been quietly preparing for a year, now. They've deployed the National Guard. They're taking guns from law-abiding citizens. They'll be at our door. This is just the beginning, Nat; just the *beginning*."

"Oh, no..." Natalie found it difficult to accept this, but she knew it was the truth.

A steady stream of tears slid down Beverly's cheeks. She plunged the spade faster and harder into the soil as she worked her way down the line, still talking.

"You know that new disease that's going around?" She didn't wait for Natalie to respond, "It makes people crazy. First, they get symptoms of a stroke. Then they go into a brief coma. Then they recover. After that, they go nuts and start biting people, trying to eat them. Like cannibals. I operated on one guy that had his gut chewed up. While he was coming out of anesthesia, he tried to bite me. It took six security guards to hold him down. We've got thirty of them in quarantine now. They don't respond to medication. Nobody knows what to do with them. Nobody knows how many we don't know about yet, how many are out there on the street. Two weeks ago, one of them killed a cop, and the bastard's still out there." She tossed potato pieces into the holes, started covering them, going down the line assembly-style.

Natalie recalled the reports coming over the scanner the day the electricity went out. She remembered the young cop who had found a dead body and then had encountered a crazy person. The cop was panting from running as he ordered Dispatch to scramble the signal. Was he the murdered cop?

Beverly continued, "We'll be gathering up supplies to bunker down here. That's the plan. No sense bugging-out. The roads will be impassable. The traffic on the interstate's increasing every day. The government knows it. They're planning roadblocks. They want to transport the people into the rescue centers. Keep them there. Watch them. They know a lot will be diseased. They've got to separate the diseased ones from the healthy ones. We're not going to any rescue center, Nat. Look what happened during that hurricane last year. Look what happened when those terrorists infiltrated that nuclear power plant back east, how everybody panicked, trampled each other for space in the shelters. Thousands died trying to get there, and hundreds more died inside the shelters. They won't be able to handle everybody. The rescue centers are a death sentence."

Still crying, she wiped her nose with one gloved hand. It left a smudge of dirt above her upper lip. She gazed intently at Natalie. "Don't discuss this with anyone. Especially Carolyn."

Natalie knew Carolyn was a bigmouth. "I won't tell anyone. I promise."

"We should have started sooner, but we thought we had more time. You'll be running a lot more errands for us. With your dad and me on duty longer hours, we can't do it all ourselves. Dad's going to teach you how to drive the truck. We're not going to bother about you getting a license. It won't matter. We're working on a list of supplies. Some you'll be able to pick up on your bike. We'll need the truck to haul the rest. Colt—Coltan's going to help."

"Coltan? From Dad's Bible study? He knows about this?"

"He's a smart boy. He knows what's happening. He knows we're running out of time." She stopped working and turned to Natalie, spoke with manic rapidity. "Your dad and I have decided to take him in. We need his help. He needs us just as much. We were going to discuss it with you. We gave it a lot of thought. We know we can trust him. If your dad can't find the time to teach you the truck, Colt will do it. You can trust Colt. I promise you. You can trust him. We prayed about it. God answered. You can trust him, okay?"

"Okay..." She had never seen Mom like this. It was frightening.

Beverly spoke over her, "There's no safe place for him to go. You understand that, don't you?"

Natalie nodded, "Yeah, but Mom, I really don't know who—"

Beverly didn't hear her, but continued to speak over her, "Your father has gotten so attached to him. We can't see him surviving this alone. He needs us. You've seen what it's like. He won't have a chance. We need him, too. There's so much he can do. So, trust us, Natalie. I'm sorry there hasn't been time."

The pop of an explosion down in the valley startled them both, and they gazed out and saw smoke. Beverly's eyes widened, and Natalie could see the desperation rising there. Her attention on the smoke in the valley, she instructed Natalie, "Turn on the scanner for me. Pray for your father. Don't forget to pray for him."

"I won't."

"Go on, now."

"Mom! You're scaring me!"

She wiped fresh tears away. "I promised myself I wouldn't do this. I have to trust God. We have to trust God." She surveyed the garden. "There's so much to do! I'll finish this. Go type up that inventory. I'll be in soon."

Natalie hesitated. Mom's behavior not only scared her, it made her wonder about her sanity. This was not the calm, take-charge woman she had always admired.

Beverly snapped at her, "What are you waiting for? Go do what I tell you! Do it now, Natalie! Leave me alone!" She started crying again. "So much to do. I've got to finish this. I can't talk. Just go inside and type up that inventory. Make sure you don't forget anything. Double-check it."

Natalie stood quickly and started for the house. It was useless to try to reason with Mom when she was like this.

She called after Natalie, "Don't forget to turn on the scanner!

Pray for your father!"

CHAPTER 5

The voices from the scanner spilled into the den where Natalie was typing up the inventory list on the computer. The riot in the south end had started. Looting, fires, assaults, rapes and shootings were already in progress. Police, fire and medical personnel were on scene. A few times, she had heard Dad's voice come over, calm, assured and in charge. She imagined him in his full riot gear, bulletproof vest and helmet protecting him. She stopped typing and again prayed for him. Now, she saw God protecting him.

Her hands trembled.

The sudden ringing of the doorbell made her jump in her chair. She expected to hear her mother's voice saying she'd get the door. However, no voice came. Natalie rose and went to the door, peered through the peephole. She was surprised and felt a curious twinge of delight to see it was Harley Guy. She released the locks and opened the door.

"Is your Dad home?" he asked.

"No."

"Your mom?"

"Yeah."

He held up a large paper bag. "I got this for her."

She wondered if this was the bag her mother had mentioned. If so, what was he doing with it? "What is it?"

He met her question with exasperation. "She asked me to pick it up."

Since when did Mom ask favors from this guy? "I'll take it."

He looked past her into the house. "I need to talk to her."

She didn't know what to make of this. She turned and hollered, "Mom..." only to find her mother had stepped up behind her.

Beverly pulled open the door, pushed open the screen door. She was both happy and relieved to see him. "Colt! Come on in."

Natalie stepped back to make room. She swore she felt her heart stop for a moment. The mystery of *Coltan* finally solved.

He handed her mother the bag. "It's all there." He then turned and closed the door, locked it, turned back to Beverly, "You hanging in there?"

"As best as I can," she answered. "Come in to the kitchen. There's a fresh pot of coffee if you want."

"Thank you."

He followed her into the kitchen while Natalie remained at the door, completely dumbfounded. Beverly set the bag on the kitchen table and began taking out the contents—prescription drugs. Her interest peaking, Natalie joined them and stood there, watching.

Beverly spoke over her shoulder as she organized the drug containers by category, "Nat, get the first aid kit. The big one. Bring it here."

Natalie retrieved the kit from the utility closet.

Coltan talked while she did this. "I went to three different stores, like you said. You were right about the pharmacies being short on meds. Oak Shores is almost a ghost town. I had no trouble, though." As Natalie set the kit on the table, she saw Coltan produce her mother's AllCard from his pocket and hand it to her, saying, "I covered it."

"I didn't want you to," Beverly said.

He looked at her as if she ought to know better. "I don't need it."

Natalie read the bottles from a short distance. They were painkillers and antibiotics, all from different stores, one in Oak Shores, some prescribed to her and her mother, others to Coltan.

Coltan continued, "Make a list of everything you need. The

sooner we get them, the better. The stores are starting to run out. They said on the news delivery trucks are stranded all over the country. Others have even been hijacked. It's gettin' ugly! The sooner we get everything, the better."

Beverly was already a step ahead of him. She had opened the kit and was performing a visual inventory. "Yes. We need much more. Much more..." She addressed Coltan, "Coffee?"

"Yeah." He turned to Natalie and said, "Natalie. Right?"

"Uh-huh." She was staring at him, trying to make sense of all this.

"Did you fix your tire?"

"Not yet."

"I can do it."

She was perfectly able, and she wanted him to know it. "No. I got it."

Beverly poured a cup of coffee for him and one for herself. She brought them to the table. "Sit down. How long can you stay?"

He shrugged, watching her, observing her expression. "As long as you need."

"Cream and sugar?"

"Black's fine." He sipped it. "This is good."

"Columbian roast." There was a tender, motherly expression in her eyes as she looked at him. He smiled slightly and briefly in return. In the next moment she said apologetically to Natalie, "Oh, Natalie. Do you want some, too?"

"I'll get it." She felt mildly insulted her mom had shortly forgotten her. However, Coltan had a way of commanding attention without trying.

Beverly grabbed the pen and notepad from the counter under the old landline wall telephone, a near obsolete backup line in the event of a power-out scenario. She joined Coltan at the table and started the list. Natalie noticed Coltan seemed to be analyzing her mother, and he seemed to be worried about her. When Beverly paused to reach for her coffee cup, they noticed her hand trembling. After she took a sip, set the cup down and began to add to her list, Coltan covered her resting hand with his own hand. She stopped and peered at him inquiringly. He draped his arm around her shoulders, leaned his face close to hers, and softly spoke some words that seemed to reassure her. She simply nodded and resumed writing.

On the scanner, Dispatch was sending an ambulance to the Sunnyside Nursing Home. Another call came in a second later about a fire at the Gas/N/Charge station on Tenth Street in the south side.

"We'll need gauze, splints, bandages," Beverly read back her list. "Antacids, diarrhea meds, Tylenol, Advil, rubbing alcohol, hydrogen peroxide, batteries—all kinds—"

"Can't forget batteries." Coltan said.

"On the meds, look for the ones with the furthest expiration date. The batteries, too. We need them to last."

He nodded, "Definitely."

Dispatch came back, ordered an ambulance and additional firefighters to the gas station.

"There are crutches in the garage." She was looking up at the ceiling, thinking. "Let's see... thermometers. The new kind, but also grab some of the old-fashioned mercury types. Do they even make those, anymore?"

"I don't know," Coltan said. "But, I'll look. Uh... How about sports drinks, Pedialyte, vitamins, stuff like that?"

She smiled at him. "Excellent!" She added them to the list. "Oh," she said, "Gel pads—hot and cold compress. Sheet protectors. Butterfly sutures. Hemostat. If you go to the medical supply store, they'll have the hemostats. You know what? Get it all at the medical supply store. Forget the drug stores. Buy everything you think we'll need and everything you don't think we'll need. You might as well take the truck. Take Nat along. She's got a good head for the medical issue."

"Learned it from you," Natalie said, pleased.

"They're closed tonight," Coltan reminded Beverly.

"Tomorrow's fine." She stopped writing and gave him that motherly look Natalie had seen whenever she felt protective. "I don't want you going out anymore tonight."

"I would if you needed." He was sincere and deeply concerned for her.

"I know." That tender look was in her eyes again, and there was a subtle wordless communication of her appreciation for him. In a moment, she squinted as she always did when she was considering something, and then she cupped his face in her hands and examined his scars. "Are you still having those headaches?"

He completely accepted her intimate gesture. "No," he answered. "Once I got the broken teeth replaced that took care of it."

Natalie found their familiar behavior toward each other both odd and sweet. She wanted to know the whole story, but a strange feeling nagged her, a feeling there was something between them so unique only God could understand it.

"I'm glad that's all it was." She released him. "I want you to stay here tonight. We have two guest rooms. Your choice. You'd be very comfortable."

"Okay." He said it after a little bit of surprise and a moment's thought.

It was apparent to Natalie her mother and Coltan had already known each other for a long while. Maybe Mom had been the doctor who treated his facial injury. The rapport between them suggested a history of sorts, something that had developed over time into almost a mother-son relationship.

It occurred to Natalie her mother assumed she and Coltan were already acquainted.

Carolyn would crap her pants if she knew Harley Guy was spending the night.

There was a call for additional firefighters and paramedics at the south end.

THE FULL MOON HAD RISEN high and bright. Over the previous hour, it had taken on a pinkish tone from all the smoke in the air. Coltan was on the back porch smoking a cigarette. A pad of letter-size paper, a pencil and a measuring tape sat on the table behind him. He turned toward the house and leaned against the railing, rubbed his chin as he always did when thinking something over. His attention was now on the many windows on the lower floor. Brian was right. Even though they were double-pane shatter resistant glass, they still posed a security risk. Coltan had come up with an idea for boarding up the windows at a moment's notice. He was now done with the measurements of the east, south and west windows. The only ones left were at the front of the house at the north. Natalie had been working at the computer in the den. He wondered if she was finished yet. He thought it would be better to measure the den windows from inside when he imagined her becoming scared at the slight noise he would be making while measuring from the outside.

He decided to enjoy the last drags of his cigarette, first. In the valley the fires were still burning, sirens were still wailing. The riots hadn't caught him by surprise. He had overheard the talk a week ago from the shit-brains in the red car. He had ridden through the south end and observed the poverty-stricken residents using anything on hand to board up their windows. He saw groups of street people taking over and boarding up the vandalized abandoned houses. Drug dealing was now out in the open, the criminals confident the cops already had their hands full with more serious things. He had seen an old black man take a shotgun to a young gangster who was siphoning gas out of a car. The old man had missed, and the punk pulled out a .38 and blew the old guy away with one shot. After that, the scum casually went back to siphoning the gas. It was at that point, when Coltan decided he had seen enough to tell him how close they were to the horror that was to come. He hadn't returned to the south end since.

Beverly had provided an ashtray left over from Brian's days as a smoker. Coltan snuffed out the butt in it, having smoked the thing all the way to the filter. He made a mental note to buy a few cases of cartons of cigarettes.

Beverly came out the back door and met Coltan as he was heading that way. She was frustrated and more than a little worried. "I've been called in," she said. "I really don't want to leave Nat alone tonight."

"I said I'll stay." He hoped the reassurance in his voice would set her mind at ease.

She noticed the pad, pencil and measuring tape in his hand. "You measured the windows. Good. Brian's already got plywood and paint waiting at the lumberyard. We're not sure how much we'll need."

"I suggest getting more than we'll need. How about power tools?"

"Got them."

"We'll need heavy lumber for the basement stairs. We should get one and a quarter inch plywood for the windows."

"List everything. Tell Brian when he gets home." She placed her hand on his arm, "Oh. Don't forget to start moving some of your things in here. I think it's time."

"Yes, ma'am."

"And, Colt?"

"Yeah?"

"Natalie's up to date on what's happening. She hides it well, but I know she's scared."

"She'll be okay." He didn't know it, but he felt it.

They entered the kitchen. Beverly closed and locked the back door. "Keep all the exterior lights on. I've got to go now." She headed for the door that led from the kitchen into the garage.

"Beverly?" He waited until she turned and looked at him. "Thank you for trusting me."

COLTAN CHOSE THE LARGE guest room that had its own private bathroom attached. The guest bedroom was so large, the full size bed and two bunk beds and accompanying furniture in the room were not enough to fill all the space. Brian and Beverly used this room to host visiting missionaries back in the days before the emerging anti-religion United Earth Federation infiltrated the House and the Senate. These days, with religious attendance of every kind dwindling and missionaries increasingly under threat of violence, the two guest rooms sat empty. Knowing the history of the rooms through Brian, Coltan felt sad at their disuse, but glad to have the choice of the largest room and the privacy. This room was not only large, but also luxurious. The linens felt new, and the comforter on the full size bed was plush. He guessed it was one of those down-filled types. Whatever the filling, it was soft and warm to sit and recline on. Naturally, he found he preferred this room to his own at home. This room was clean, tidy, and quiet. The quiet was the best thing about it. At his house, there was always noise and chaos. This place was a sanctuary.

In the years before his mother's ten-dollar purchase of a lucky Quick Pick Lotto ticket, Coltan, his mother, and Richard moved around the country like Nomads. They settled in Bonito Valle six months after his mother received her lottery winnings of one and a quarter million dollars after taxes. Richard especially liked their neighborhood because it was like living in the country yet close to town. The semi-isolation of their hilltop home made it convenient to continue their drug lifestyle (purchased with and subsequently sold for old-fashioned *underground cash*) without ruffling many feathers, although they were often careless when it came to loud music and their guests' violent scuffles. The parties ended when their bank accounts shrank, and their stash of underground cash and expensive sellable items disappeared into the hands of their sticky-fingered guests. Fights ensued over the thefts, and the neighbors called the cops too many times.

As far as those visits from law enforcement went, Richard always blamed Coltan as the culprit who invited society's dregs to the house without his permission. This always infuriated Coltan (who spent the bulk of his time stoned back then), and Coltan usually struck at Richard in response, which prompted the police to haul Coltan off to Juvy for bad behavior. Eventually, Coltan avoided the home altogether and made camp in the isolated woodlands around town or in nearby towns where he drank or smoked himself to sleep.

Coltan knew from a young age he was unplanned and unwanted. His mother gave birth to him in an abandoned gas station restroom somewhere in Alabama and regarded him as a nuisance. She had never shown him any tenderness or nurturing. Before his mother won the lottery, his presence only served to guarantee a supplemental benefit deposit to her AllCard every month, and he knew that was why she tolerated him. She hooked up with Richard when Coltan was eight years old. Once Richard established himself as lover and reliable drug supplier, she barely noticed her son at all. Richard and drugs were all that mattered to her. Getting high was the goal of every day. When her fortunes smiled down upon her, the lottery winnings made that easy.

At least Coltan's mother had had the forethought to put some of the cyber money into a savings account for him. She didn't really care what he did with the money, so long as he stayed out of her hair. He knew his mother's gift of money was merely a bribe to keep him away. His absence served to bring peace to the home; Richard was mostly inclined to take out his temper and *tough love* methods on Coltan, who was annoyingly too sensitive and bookish to ever satisfy Richard's coarse image of what constituted a *real man*.

The motorcycle was the only large purchase Coltan made. The Harley was his escape.

Still, the freedom he enjoyed because of the Harley did nothing to soothe his intense loneliness. Upon first arriving as a stranger in Bonito Valle, he had sought out others like him, other boys who understood the street was sometimes safer than their own homes, other boys who shared and understood the rage that seethed in the depths of his soul. However, they were not the type of people who took kindly to someone with aspirations for a better life. He found it impossible to establish an intelligent or meaningful conversation with any of them, and his efforts sometimes resulted in him being the butt of cruel jokes or violent confrontation. Of course, he never lost a fight and put more than one in the hospital. That was the only thing that won him their respect. Consequently, he realized they were too much like what he was trying to escape. Frustrated and hopeless, he avoided cultivating any new relationships among those in his age group.

He resigned himself to the idea of a solitary existence, and did his best to ignore the longing inside for something that would give his life meaning. He was wholly convinced he didn't deserve that *something*. Because of that and everything else, he decided it was safer and easier to simply remain alone. He learned to get along on his own and even came to enjoy it, although that something to give him a reason to go on consistently eluded him.

Before he met Brian, and then during the time of Bible studies, before his suicide attempt and before he got the job in Reyton and found a studio apartment there, he only went home occasionally, and that was to shower and get a change of clothes. Now that he was back in Bonito Valle, he had returned to his old pattern. He spent most of his days at the library where he would often read one classic novel in one day's time. Sometimes, he would check out a book of poetry and spend days perusing, deciphering and digesting the verse. He spent his nights in a sleeping bag next to the river where the serenity was therapeutic and the vast starry sky made him feel closer to God.

This night in the big guest room at the Danbury house, Coltan found a Bible in the nightstand and was sitting up in bed, propped up on pillows, reading. Since Brian had reintroduced him to the Word and had studied with him, he found the Scriptures now made sense to him. Nowadays, the Word was alive and spoke directly to him. Because of this, Coltan had become aware of a gradual change deep within himself. He now felt sure his life had purpose. Even more wonderful, he had become aware of the presence of God around him.

It was a similar impression of a benevolent presence in this house that caused him to pause in his reading. He had noticed it the moment he stepped through the front door. Now, the presence was even stronger in this room. It made him feel safe and strangely peaceful. He wondered if it was Jesus.

A tapping at the door brought him out of his reverie.

He chuckled at the unlikely image in his mind of Jesus tapping at the door. "Come in."

Natalie opened the door and looked in. "I just wanted to tell you there's a new toothbrush and toothpaste in the bathroom. The towels are in the cupboard on your right."

"Thanks."

"You need anything?"

"A radio, if there's one handy." He was too comfortable to get up and retrieve his from the Harley.

"I've got an extra in my room. I'll go get it."

"Before you do that…"

She lingered at the door, not wanting to invade his space. "Yeah…?"

He noticed she hadn't combed her hair since he saw her that afternoon. She appeared exhausted. Not physically exhausted, but mentally exhausted. Her eyes showed it. "Are you okay?"

She didn't know why he would ask such a question. "Yeah."

Obviously, she had no idea her fatigue was noticeable. He closed the Bible, but used his thumb as a bookmark as he sat up at the side of the bed. "I guess you're wondering how I know your mom. She was my doctor when I… had my accident. That was about a year, maybe sixteen months ago. We've kept in touch since my recovery." He smiled subtly. "Your dad was the one who knew me first, though. You know about the studies, right?"

"Yeah. He's very proud of you."

"Really?" That made him happy. "Your parents are something real special, you know."

"I know they both think the world of you. They really do."

He looked away for a moment, embarrassed and flattered. "Well… it's mutual." When he looked back to her, he thought she seemed wary of him. It was understandable. Her mother had invited him to stay without considering Natalie's feelings, and now she was here alone with him. He knew Natalie regarded him with the same scorn and fear as the rest of the neighbors. Even earlier that day, while he accompanied her as she pushed her bike home, he could sense her unease. If her parents had ever said anything in his favor to change her opinion, it wasn't apparent at this moment. Coltan wanted to reassure her in some way. "This wasn't the way it was supposed to be. At first, I was just gonna work here." When she said nothing in response, he continued, "I was only gonna be here sometimes during the day when your dad was home. He said he told you."

"Yeah, he told me." She relaxed a little and leaned against the doorframe. "Mom finally told me today you were gonna live with us. I didn't know until tonight you're that *Coltan guy* they kept talking about. I guess they thought I knew who you were."

He looked down at the Bible in his hand, caressed the cover. He shifted his gaze to Natalie. "Do you and your dad study the Bible together?"

"When I was younger. Not anymore."

This surprised him. "How come?"

"Time."

"Do you study on your own?"

"Not much. I still believe, though. I still pray. I have faith in God, in Jesus."

He perceived she had more depth than anyone else in his age group did, and he liked that about her. She had apparently spent a lot of time contemplating the more important things in life, and that made it all the more easier to ask her his next question. "You ever feel his presence?"

"Sometimes." However, lately she had felt very much alone, and seldom read her Bible anymore. She looked away from him to the floor. "Not often enough these days."

"Why?"

"I don't know." She stared at the floor. Her past displays of temper and selfishness came to mind. "I haven't been... walking the talk lately."

"He loves you, anyway." Coltan surprised himself by saying that, and was even more surprised how completely he believed it. However, she still bowed her head in shame. He gently stated, "Hey... it's tough times."

She looked at him, her eyes dead with fatigue, and then looked away to hide her brimming tears. Until this evening, there had been no one to talk to about her growing fear and waning faith with Mom caught up in her own anxiety and Dad gone most of the time and mentally preoccupied when he was home. It hadn't occurred to her until this moment how miserable she had become. Even prayer hadn't alleviated her misery.

"I feel him in every inch of this home." He leaned forward intently, his voice barely above a whisper, "You know something else?"

"What?"

"I felt his presence in you that day at the Dairy Delight."

She remembered the phone call, remembered his anger and the pain in his eyes. She decided not to ask him about it. If he wanted her to know, he would tell her without prompting. The second element in that memory was the sympathy she felt for him, how she had prayed for him after he left. Could he have known?

Coltan, his voice soft, gentle, and full of certainty, continued, "He's with you. He's in you. Never believe otherwise."

Touched by his sincerity and tenderness, she felt remorseful she had prejudged him as hopeless trash. "I'll get you that radio."

"I won't need it tonight, after all. I think I'll read."

She turned to leave. "Goodnight, Coltan."

He smiled subtly as he told her, "You can call me *Colt*."

Natalie chuckled, felt herself relax at his invitation. "Okay... Colt."

He noticed she still seemed weary, even a little depressed beneath her smile. Her wavering faith concerned him, and once again, he wanted to reassure her. "Natalie?" When she turned back to him, he said, "Faith."

"Some days it ain't easy." She said it lightly, humorously.

Coltan could tell her volumes about his battle to trust God during his many periods of despair. The condition of the world, the growing coldness and sordidness of society, even in his own United

States of America, gave him few reasons to anticipate a happy future for himself. He was certain the disintegrating world outside their door only added to her feelings of fear, helplessness and resignation. He guessed she had spent more time worrying about it than she realized.

"Maybe you should turn off the scanner and get some sleep."

"Yeah," she said, "I was thinking the same thing. Goodnight."

CHAPTER 6

The smoke still hung in the air. Natalie observed it with a depressed sigh as she poured a cup of coffee and gazed through the kitchen window. The thermometer on the post outside gauged the temperature as sixty-five degrees. On an ordinary August day, the temperature at eight in the morning would be around eighty. Nothing was normal anymore.

Dad and Coltan were looking over a roll of blueprints Dad had spread out on the largest table on the back porch. Dad was still wearing his uniform, minus the riot gear. Coltan was wearing his usual wife-beater shirt, jeans and boots. Natalie wondered if that was all he had to wear. Then she wondered at the fact he seemed impervious to the cool temperature, especially in the shade of the porch.

Coltan took the pencil from behind his ear and made a notation on his supply list. Dad said something, and Coltan laughed, then Dad laughed. They took their coffee cups and toasted, to what, Natalie didn't know. For all she knew, they were just celebrating being men. She felt a twinge of jealousy. She reminded herself Dad was always more jovial when he was strung-out on coffee. He'd probably had three cups by now. The two of them dug in to a pink box of donuts on one of the other tables. They chose from the assortment and began to eat, Coltan being none-too neat about it, cramming a half-donut into his mouth. The crumbs stuck to his lips and chin, and some fell onto his shirt. He wiped his mouth with the back of his hand and wiped off his shirt with both hands. After chewing and swallowing, he made a remark about cops and donuts, which sent Dad into a crumb spitting fit of laughter.

She heard her mother's car enter the garage. As Beverly came in, still dressed in scrubs, Natalie continued to watch the guys through the window. They were now flinging crumbs at each other, ducking and laughing.

"Look at this," Natalie said.

Beverly came up alongside her, watched the men being men. She chuckled and said, "What a pair."

Brian said something to Coltan, and Coltan returned to the blueprints, studied them and added another notation to his list. Brian came into the kitchen and went straight to his wife. He embraced her and hugged her tightly. She returned the tightness of his embrace. He slowly said to her, "I love you." He kissed her lips three times.

Still holding him, Beverly asked, "How's it going?"

"Very well," Brian said. He looked over at Natalie. "Good morning, Precious." He parted a little from Beverly, invited his daughter into the fold, "Come hug me, you *wascowy wabbit.*" She joined the hug fest. Brian said, "My two girls... Who wants breakfast?"

"I want a bath," Beverly said. "A long hot bath with lots and lots of bubbles."

"Mmmm... honeysuckle." Brian whispered to her.

Natalie pulled away, more interested in watching Coltan through the window. He was lighting a cigarette and peering out into the valley. His stance reminded her of the fourth of July, how she stood in that same spot with her mother waiting for the fireworks to start.

"Room for two," Mom invited Dad in a low husky voice.

"That's very, very tempting." Dad said playfully.

Oh, man... Natalie said to herself, *now they're gonna get all lovey-dovey.* She tried hard not to imagine the two of them naked together in a bubble bath.

Beverly drew away from him, gazed at him with sudden concern. "Is it safe out there for the kids to pick up supplies?"

"We've managed to contain it for now." He reluctantly parted from her. "Guess I'll see where the boy's at." He went out on the porch and playfully addressed Coltan, "Hey! You're too young to smoke!" Coltan chuckled, responded with a smirk and his middle finger. Dad hollered good-naturedly, "You, too... Juvenile delinquent." To which Coltan laughed.

"That boy lights up when he laughs," Mom said, smiling.

Natalie murmured, "Yeah."

"You got the med list?"

"Uh-huh."

"I have a prescription for you to fill." She produced a slip from her pocket, "A three-month supply of Valium prescribed to me. It'll go into the kit."

Natalie knew Valium was tough to get these days. "How'd you—"

Mom interrupted her, "Don't ask." She started for the living room, turned and added, "Get some OTC antihistamines, too. I forgot to add them. Put them on the list, okay? Oh! Triple-antibiotic ointment, too; five of those. And exam gloves—all sizes."

"Okay."

"You and Colt, be careful."

"We will." Natalie glanced out the window. Dad was ruffling Coltan's hair. Coltan returned the favor, which made her father's hair stick up in limp strands and revealed a balding area at the top of his head. Coltan pointed at him and chortled. Dad laughed, embarrassed, and smoothed down his hair.

She feared Coltan would replace her in Dad's affections.

Beverly came up beside her. She knew what her daughter was thinking. "Guys like to rough-house. It's good for them. Don't worry,

Nat. As much as he loves Colt, your dad has a place in his heart that belongs to no one but you. That will never, ever, change."

NATALIE NOTICED THE yard sale was in its second day at Carolyn's as they pulled out of the driveway. There were only two customers. She realized she forgot to call Carolyn last night, and she felt bad about it. Coltan steered the truck in the opposite direction, and Natalie turned in her seat and strained to see her. Their position on the road made it impossible.

Coltan shifted the gearshift like an expert. He pushed in the cigarette lighter and took a smoke from the pack on the dash, and let it dangle from his lips as he waited for the lighter to pop.

"I don't think you can smoke in here." Natalie said.

"Your dad said it was fine." He looked straight ahead, watching the road. He had one arm draped over the steering wheel and was controlling it with his wrist. The lighter popped and he lit his cigarette. I like these old trucks. What is this—a mid-eighties model? Must be."

Natalie said, "I think so. He takes good care of it."

"They don't put lighters in cars anymore. I don't know why. Trying to keep us from smoking while driving, I guess. Controlling bastards..." He took a long drag and blew it out, then stated, "We'll hit the med supply store first."

She caught herself staring at his long tanned arms and strong hands. His arms and hands were muscular, but not bulky; he was lean. She found his arms and hands attractive, and didn't understand why. Maybe it was simply because she was attracted to the strength and protection they symbolized.

Coltan smiled and turned to her. "You know what your dad told me?"

"Uh-uh. What?"

"He told me you can kick my ass."

She laughed softly. "Dad..."

"You got suspended last year for breaking some guy's tooth."

"Yeah." She was still proud of that.

He laughed and shook his head. "Damn! And you told me you didn't want to piss *me* off!" He glanced at her again, his blue eyes full of admiration.

She chuckled

He looked back at the road, smiling. He flicked the cigarette ash out the window, took a drag. "Maybe I should have let *you* deck that guy, yesterday."

"That's okay. I enjoyed watching you do it." She became serious, "Hey... thanks for doing that."

"You're welcome." A second later, he laughed to himself. "I would've loved to have seen you punch his lights out, though. You're such a little scrap of a thing. They would've never forgotten it. He would've never lived it down. Man! That would've been good!" He began to chortle at the image of it in his mind.

Natalie found his child-like laughter amusing, and she began to laugh with him.

Her laughter fueled him, and she reminded him of Dad, the way he had a hard time stopping once he started laughing, just like this morning. Coltan roared at the recollection.

THEY FOUND ALMOST EVERYTHING they needed at the medical supply store. While they shopped there, Coltan noticed the cameras watching them from every vantage point in the place. Although he was used to them—hell, they were in every building and on every street in the country—their presence caused a knot to form in his gut. It crossed his mind that someone was watching and knew they were stocking up for an expected apocalyptic type event, and someone would stop them and question them before they left the checkout register. Coltan tried not to think about it lest he began to appear suspicious.

He hung back and observed Natalie filling the cart with medical instruments and first aid items. She seemed to know the name and purpose of each instrument. It intrigued Coltan when she told him a hemostat was a medical instrument for clamping off arteries to stop blood flow. However, Coltan recognized the instrument as the same thing his mother and Richard used to smoke the remains of a joint. Would wonders never cease? Natalie second guessed her mother and added more things to the cart, including a larger container that had capacity for much more than that of the kit at home. As an afterthought, she tossed in two compact pre-stocked portable kits meant to fit into a backpack or glove compartment. When they came to the oxygen tanks, she wondered aloud if her mom had ever considered that. Then she dismissed the idea entirely and steered into the checkout counter. Coltan double-checked the list and crossed things off; all the while knowing that the record of everything they just purchased had already entered a vast surveillance system that monitored everyone's shopping habits. The record of their subsequent purchases that day would wind up in the same place.

Natalie gave no thought to that as they swung by the drugstore for the rest of the items. Coltan suggested it would save time if they had the prescription filled while she shopped there, and he would go on to the lumberyard and retrieve her on the return trip. Before exiting the truck, Natalie covered the bags of medical supplies in the space behind the seat with a blanket. Coltan gave her a thumbs-up and a grin as he pulled away. A strange, warm feeling suddenly filled her chest.

Natalie was relieved to find there was no line at the prescription counter in the busy drugstore. She turned in her mother's prescription for Valium, found a cart and began shopping for the rest of the items they would need. She had difficulty maneuvering through and around all the people. There was desperation in the air. The shelves were almost bare in some spots. She came upon the paper goods, and realized toilet paper wasn't on the list. She put three twelve-packs of double-rolls into the bottom rack of the cart. A matronly woman impatiently elbowed her aside and grabbed the remaining four twelve-packs, stuffed two at her cart's bottom and two in the basket and, after a furtive glance at Natalie, swung the cart toward the canned goods aisle. Natalie understood the woman's anxiety. With no desire to reprimand her rudeness, Natalie remained silent. She found everything else left on the list and returned to the prescription counter, the cart full. She noted there were only two pharmacists on duty when usually there were five.

A casually dressed woman in her thirties lingered at the pharmacy counter. She was pale, sweating profusely, and one side of her face was sagging noticeably. Natalie caught some of the woman's conversation with the pharmacist as she approached.

"There's no more triple antibiotic ointment on the shelves," she was saying to the pharmacist, "Do you have something comparable in the back? I really need it." She showed her hand to the pharmacist, and Natalie stole a look at it. Peculiar marks resembling imprints of teeth circled the inflamed swollen base of the woman's thumb. Dried blood enhanced the indentations, and a bruise had formed at the site. A red line beginning at the wound followed the track of an artery up her arm. The line disappeared under the short sleeve of her shirt. "My kid bit me this morning. I think it's getting infected."

The pharmacist, an old guy who had the face of someone who has seen everything in life and then some, masked his alarm as he observed the wound. "You say your kid did this?"

"My little boy. He's been sick." Her speech slurred.

"Is he here in the store with you?"

"He's home with his dad."

The pharmacist suggested in a gentle, casual voice, "You go sit down over at those chairs. I'll check and see what we've got."

"Thank you." The woman began to cry, defeated by the weakness that continued to spread through her body. "This hurts so bad!" She trudged wearily to the waiting area and sat down heavily, closed her eyes and let the tears slide down her cheeks.

The pharmacist turned to Natalie. "I'll be with you right away." He picked up the phone and dialed 911. He listened, impatience on his face, and said in a whisper to Natalie, "It's still ringing." While waiting, he turned to the other pharmacist and told him, "Check out this young lady here." The emergency dispatcher finally answered, and the pharmacist informed her, "A suspected Vee Priority."

"What's a 'Vee Priority'?" Natalie asked him as he hung up the phone.

He replied briskly. "It gets them here faster." His attention turned to the woman, "We're checking for that ointment, ma'am."

The woman didn't reply. She slumped lopsided in the chair, sweating and silently crying.

The second pharmacist rang Natalie up. She tapped her mother's credit card on the payment reader and returned it to her jeans front pocket. Before she turned to grab the cart and head for the main checkout, she again questioned the first pharmacist. "She's having a stroke, isn't she?"

"Looks like it."

Natalie leaned closer to him. "The bites and the virus cause that. How many have you seen today?"

He scowled at her and whispered, "Go home, young lady. Finish your shopping and go home. You didn't see anything here."

It took twenty minutes to get through the checkout line. She sat down against the wall in the shade outside the store, away from the busy doors, the cart full of bags parked at her left. The ambulance finally arrived, and the paramedics wasted no time. They rushed into the store, gurney in tow. Shoppers dodged out of their way. Natalie scanned the lot for the truck. Coltan hadn't returned yet. She popped open a can of root beer and drank slowly.

She thought about what her mother said about the patients in the isolation ward, about the surgical patient who tried to bite her. They all exhibited symptoms of a stroke at first and then came out of it, only to start acting crazy. What kind of disease was that? Where did it come from? There was the fact the doctors suspected there were many more undiagnosed cases. Natalie was sure the woman in the store and her little son were two of them. Obviously, the pharmacist knew it, too.

The reverberating crack of cars colliding caused her to jerk her head up and gaze across the parking lot. Two cars had pulled out at the same time and rear-ended each other. The drivers, a rough looking red-haired woman and a tall man with a handlebar mustache, confronted each other. Their argument escalated as they blamed each other for the damage. The other shoppers noticed, but then disregarded them and continued stocking their vehicles. The woman struck the man, and the man returned the blow. In the next second, they were into a full-blown fistfight. From the tailgate of a beat-up jeep, two young guys having a beer cheered them on.

Coltan pulled up in front of her, blocking her view. Leaving the motor running, he leapt out of the truck and grabbed the cart, hurriedly started tossing the bags into a vacant space he reserved against the tailgate. Seeing this, but not understanding his haste, Natalie tossed two bags in while he got the rest in one armful and spilled them into the bed.

"It's crazy!" he exclaimed as he opened the door for her. "Get in. Hurry!"

She scrambled in while he rushed around the front and got in the driver's seat. He shifted the truck into gear and headed for the exit to the main drag. A line of cars trying to enter the freeway across from Sandy's Diner blocked the east and westbound lanes of the main road, the westbound lanes the quickest route to their neighborhood. Coltan made a u-turn and took the store lot's south exit to the frontage road that wound under the freeway a mile down.

He wiped sweat from his brow. There was fear in his eyes. "There's accidents everywhere. People are going nuts! I saw some guy chasing another guy with a shotgun. Some woman was beating the hell out of another woman with a baseball bat! There was another guy in the road by the refinery—I'm sure he was already dead—and he was on fire, and people were just crowded around him, watching! We gotta get home." He took the pack of cigarettes off the dash and tossed them into her lap. "Light me one." She did so, and got dizzy when she accidentally inhaled. He didn't notice as he took the cigarette from her. "Thanks," he said and took a drag.

"Dad said the riots had been contained."

The fear had not left his eyes as he glanced at her. "Not anymore!"

"There was a woman sick inside the store," Natalie remarked. "Her kid bit her."

He pulled into a gas station and snuffed out his cigarette, "We need gas." As he pulled up at the gas pump and hurried out of the truck, he noticed the price had gone up to twenty-sixty-three a gallon and that was just for regular. "Almost twenty-one bucks a gallon! Dirty thieves!" He remarked with unveiled sarcasm, "Look at the line for the stupid e-charger stations. They'll all be sitting there for days. And, look at the price for that: three-hundred bucks for an hour's charge. Dumb fucks..."

Natalie leaned out the window. "Did you hear what I said?"

"Yeah..." He squinted up at her as he filled the tank. "I saw the ambulance. You didn't get near her, did you?"

"Uh-uh."

"There was another one at the lumber yard. He was just starting to feel sick. I stayed away from him." His eyes took on a glint of sadness as he stated remorsefully, "I didn't know what else to do."

THAT AFTERNOON, COLTAN knocked on the door at the Spencers' house. Geneva Spencer finally wobbled to the door on her arthritic legs and swollen feet. "Hello, Coltan," she said, pushing open the screen. "Muffy's been waiting for you. She just loves you, you know."

He stepped inside. The television news was on, the volume loud. Mr. Spencer was not in his recliner. He was always there at this time of day when the news was on. Mrs. Spencer wobbled over and slowly sat down in her chair next to her husband's. She took Muffy's leash from the end table and called for the dog. Little Muffy came trotting in from a back bedroom, a white mix of poodle and terrier, wearing a pink collar. The groomer had combed Muffy's front hair up out of her eyes and had tied it with a cheerful pink ribbon. Coltan squatted, and Muffy pounced on him and covered his face with doggy kisses.

"That's my little girl," Coltan said, petting her and returning her kisses. He looked up at Geneva, asked loudly over the TV volume, "Say... how's Mr. Spencer?"

"Still sick," The old woman said. "Got that bad cough from the cancer, you know. Can't do nothin' about it."

"Does he have enough medicine?"

"Oh, yeah." She tossed Coltan the leash. "It don't do no good, though." As an afterthought, she added, "He's made his peace with God."

"Don't think that way," Coltan said.

"Oh, it's alright." She said it brightly, "We know it'll be soon.

He's ready for it. Lookin' forward to seein' the Lord." She directed her attention to Muffy and her eyes glinted with that motherly love Coltan had seen in Beverly's eyes. "You're a good girl. A good girl, ain't you? Ready for your walk with Uncle Coltan? You love Uncle Coltan, huh?" Muffy barked happily, making Coltan laugh. Geneva went on, "Yes! You do love him. You *do*."

The news anchor reporting about Hawaii perked up Geneva's ears, and she turned the volume up still higher and leaned forward in her chair to better see the screen. The station was showing file footage of Waikiki, and the anchor was mentioning something about Hawaii's Governor considering a quarantine of the islands.

"Ha!" Geneva said. She turned to Coltan. "You ever been to Hawaii?" He shook his head *no*. She went on, "You ain't missed nothin'. Hawaii sucks!"

He burst out laughing, finding it hilarious to hear this sweet old lady talk like that.

Geneva continued, "Don't waste your money."

He attached the leash to Muffy's collar, still chuckling. He knew the Spencers had traveled all around the world in their day. Of all the places they had lived, they still loved the good old *"yoo-ess-of-ay"* the most. They showed it by displaying the flag in their front yard every day of the year, and replaced it with a new one every Fourth of July. They had lost two sons and one granddaughter in three separate wars and never doubted their sacrifice was worth it.

"You take her for a good, long walk," Geneva suggested. "She's gettin' a little fat."

"You feed her too many treats," Coltan advised.

With a shrug she said, "Well, all dogs got to do is sleep, eat and shit"

He led Muffy down the steps, through the front gate and onto the sidewalk. Muffy paused at the corner of the gate and urinated. Coltan waited patiently, glancing across the road at the Danbury house. He knew Natalie was in the garage repairing her bicycle tire, and Brian and Beverly were probably just getting out of bed.

He decided to take Muffy up the hill where the two-lane road continued past the grove of trees and neat houses. He passed by his own house, and resisted looking at it. The place had been pristine two years ago when they moved in, but was now a deteriorating dump. Richard was too lazy to take care of it and refused to part with the bucks to hire a professional. His mother languidly remarked she preferred the yard return to its "wild and natural" state. They didn't even own a lawn mower. Coltan knew they were the bane of the neighborhood, and the disapproving eyes of his neighbors reminded him at every opportunity.

Once they passed by the last house, the traffic was non-existent. Few people used this route to the mountains anymore, preferring the convenience and safety of the interstate. This road became a narrow and windy pathway as it started up the foothills and into the mountain. In the winter, snow and fallen trees made it treacherous and often impassable.

For a brief time, he forgot about the lunacy of the world.

Muffy began pulling forward on the leash, trying to pick up the pace. Coltan went into a trot, and Muffy happily trotted beside him. His own dog had lived with him for six months before Richard killed it in a drunken rage for peeing on his shoes. Coltan had cried bitterly for days and vowed never to get another dog so long as Richard was still around. In the meantime, Muffy was a joyful substitute and was safely far away from Richard and his mean temper.

They veered off the road and trespassed through a gap in the barbed wire fence. Muffy knew where they were going and led the way. The sparkling rippling waters of the creek beckoned them in the waning sunlight. He let her off the leash, and they ran with abandon. Out of breath, and blaming it on smoking, he stopped and panted.

The winds had picked up again, and the air was cooling down

fast. When the wind blew straight at him, he swore he could hear its song. He threw his head back, arched his neck and chest, and let it caress him. He closed his eyes and imagined he was an eagle coasting on the breeze. He stood like that for a long time, entranced in the ecstasy of the moment.

He caught up with Muffy at their usual spot, a clear sandy area along the water. The creek was low, having suffered an unusually dry winter that year. He reclined on a rise of weedy dirt, and Muffy jumped onto his chest. He cuddled the dog, kissed her nose and said, "Did you know God created you? Yes, he did. He made you special. One of a kind." Muffy peered into his eyes and cocked her head to one side. "One of a kind," Coltan repeated. She licked his face.

He sat up and lit a cigarette. He recalled Natalie lighting his cigarette earlier that day, briefly recalled the mayhem in the valley. His stomach tightened when he wondered if they had been exposed to the mystery epidemic. However, in the hours that had passed since then, neither felt ill, and the disease was supposed to produce its initial symptoms quickly. He decided they were both safe, and hoped with all his heart that he was right.

As much as he tried to not think about what was happening in his country, even in his own town, he found himself replaying the memories of the horrors he'd seen that day. He feared what would happen to people like the Spencers, two elderly folks in failing health. How would they deal with the coming breakdown of society? They wouldn't be able to pack up and leave. Even if they could, where would they go? From the reports he'd seen, the mayhem was unfolding worldwide. He thought if they opted to stay and try to protect themselves or, at the least, stay hidden, he could help them secure their house. Ideally, the Danburys would take them in. He thought it was worth approaching Brian and Beverly with the idea.

The sun was beginning to set, and the air had grown bone-chilling cold with the wind picking up. They trudged back,

Muffy on the leash once more as they entered the road and strolled back into their neighborhood.

Across the street and one down from the Spencers, Carolyn was packing up the rejects from their yard sale. She spied Coltan and met his eyes with curiosity. He avoided her gaze and continued toward the Spencers' house.

From her rocker on the porch, Mrs. Spencer cast Carolyn an indignant glare. As Coltan led Muffy onto the porch, she remarked, "Nosy... lookin' over here like there's somethin' to see!"

"I'm sure the word's out I'm on community service for you."

"Screw that! You're a good kid. Wish you were my kid." She bent and welcomed Muffy into her lap, "Did you have a nice walk with Uncle Coltan, sweetie?"

"She sure did," Coltan said.

"Lemme sign your service sheet." The old woman gestured for it, grabbed a pen off the little wicker table beside her. "I'm gonna give you six extra hours. You didn't deserve no sentence."

"It wasn't a sentence." He took the folded sheet out of his pocket and handed it to her. She signed it and noted six extra hours. "To tell you the truth," he said, "I really have enjoyed working for you. Muffy's a great dog. Even though my time's up, I'd like to keep walking her. If it's alright with you, that is."

"You can come over any time you like." She looked away, watched Carolyn go into her house, and muttered, "Fat little shit."

"She doesn't know any better," Coltan stated.

"Henry just died. Guess it was a half-hour ago. Went in his sleep, I suppose." She was accepting of it. She even smiled a little. "Jesus got him in his arms now."

Coltan was shocked. "Mrs. Spencer, I'm sorry."

She nodded towards him, gave him back the paper. "You can call me *Gen*. The ambulance should be here soon."

"I'll stay with you."

"Nah..."

He took her hand and held it. "Will you need a ride into town?"

"I got the car. I can still drive." She smiled and patted his hand. "You go on now. He wouldn't want you to see him being brought out."

"All right, then." He took the steps slowly. He wondered how she would make it on her own. The old lady and her sweet little dog would be among the first victims when the shit hit the fan and the inevitable hordes of looters and rioters invaded this neighborhood.

He stopped to look at her once more as he closed the gate. She was rocking in the chair with Muffy on her lap, smiling serenely and softly humming a song from days long gone. Geneva caught his troubled gaze and reassuringly waved so long.

CHAPTER 7

PREPARATIONS

THE BONITO VALLE POLICE Department called all available officers to duty that night, and the hospital did the same for medical personnel. Natalie's parents were already on edge and completely exhausted. She knew they regretted having to leave their daughter at night, that they worried and felt guilty and at the same time helpless. She knew they were spending most of their spare moments in prayer. That was all anyone could do.

The kitchen clock indicated two-thirty. The full moon was visible in the right side of the window, orange hued with the smoke in the atmosphere. Coltan had propped the screen door to the back porch open, and some of the smoke scent drifted into the kitchen.

The crack of wood tossed onto wood echoed through the house. Coltan stayed busy unloading the lumber and hauling it into the basement. He had almost unloaded everything from the truck parked in the gravel along the garden. The previous day's supply run had left no room in the truck for the entire load. Coltan planned to return to the lumberyard for the rest at sunrise. He was not looking forward to another trip to the fringes of the south end.

Coltan's footsteps on the basement stairs were heavy with fatigue. He was so focused on his task he didn't notice Natalie as he went to the truck for the final load. She leaned against the doorframe and watched him as he pulled and tugged and finally freed the last planks of lumber. His clothes were dirty and ripe with sweat. There was dust and dried sweat in his hair. He grimaced with the weight as he lifted the planks and balanced them on his left shoulder.

"I can help." Natalie offered.

"I got it." He came toward her with the planks. She stepped out of his way. As he passed her, they made eye contact, and he smiled and winked to set her mind at ease. Without pausing, he bounded down the stairs and disappeared into the basement.

Natalie pulled the screen door shut, locked it, and closed the interior door and double locked it. She finished preparing their sandwiches and cut them diagonally on the plates. She tucked two small plastic bottles of orange juice into each pocket of her sweatpants and took the plates down into the basement.

Coltan sat slumped on the bottom step. He had taken off his undershirt and was wiping his face with it.

Not wanting to disturb him, but knowing he needed food, she gently settled beside him. "Here. You must be starving."

"Thanks." He set the plate on his lap and wasted no time taking the first bite. "Mmmm!" The second bite was even bigger. He ate like he hadn't seen food in days.

"Orange juice, too." She set one of the plastic bottles beside him. He grunted something that amounted to gratitude, his mouth full of tuna sandwich. He used his undershirt as a napkin, ignoring the paper napkin under his plate. She said, "I bet you're wiped out."

He nodded, chewing.

A thought crossed her mind that if she took the plate away from him at that moment, he would growl and snap at her like a starving dog. The image almost made her laugh.

He caught her expression out of the corner of his eye. "What?"

"You eat like a barbarian."

"I'm hungry!" He started in on the second half of the sandwich after gulping down some juice. The pace of his eating did not slow.

Natalie considered her appetite and realized she was not hungry. She placed half of her sandwich on his now-empty plate.

"No, no." He said through a full mouth.

"I'm not that hungry. You eat it."

"Thanks." The barbarian stuffed it into his mouth. "Good stuff." Crumbs went flying on the word "stuff." The undershirt again served as a napkin.

"I'm gonna start some laundry. Add yours to it."

"I gotta stop home and get a change." He slugged down the rest of the juice. "I hate goin' there for anything."

"I saw the chair fly out the window."

A bit embarrassed, he laughed as he blurted, "You saw that?"

She responded humorously, "Yeah. Good thing you ducked."

"It wouldn't have been my first concussion." He stood, wiped his hands on his pants. "Well... maybe they're passed out or busy screwing the shit out of each other." He saw Natalie blush. "Sorry." He leaned back against the wall, crossed his arms in front of him. "Your folks gave me a key. Are you okay with that?"

"I'm the one who had a copy made for you. I'm not always here to play doorman, you know."

"We don't know each other, and, with you being a girl and everything..."

"Mom and Dad trust you, so I trust you."

"You know I got a record."

"All I heard was something about vandalism at the park."

"I was drunk. Not that's it's an excuse."

"What else is there?"

"A fight. But, the guy dropped the charges. He knew he had it coming."

The *fight* revelation did not surprise her. "Anything else?"

"Speeding." At this, they paused and gazed at each other. It was just plain silly, and they laughed again.

COLLEEN A. PARKINSON

"Yeah," Natalie said. "You sound like a real danger to society."

He took a long drag off his cigarette, stared off in thought. After a few moments, he looked at her and smiled. "Well... guess I better get some clothes."

"Will you be back soon?"

"Yeah. Why?"

"I want to start the laundry." The real reason was she didn't want to be alone. It never bothered her before, but the riots had flared up again. Also, there was the fact that there were people wandering around who had gone crazy with that new disease. She knew she could take an intruder out with one shot, but she didn't want to be alone should the opportunity arise.

Coltan said, "Your mom was right."

"What?"

"You hide it well."

"What?"

"Fear."

"I'm not afraid. I know how to use a gun."

"I know that." He started up the stairs. His back to her, he quipped, "Just make sure you don't shoot me."

She took offence at that. "Insult me again and I just might!"

He chuckled mischievously as he reached the top step. He turned to her and said playfully, "I love a gal with a gun! Hot and spice-saaayyy!"

She threw the empty plastic bottle at him. Coltan dodged it, and it bounced off the doorjamb and tumbled back down the steps to her. He pointed at it and teasingly sniggered some more before he ran beyond her throwing range. She could still hear him chortling even after he shut the back door to the porch. His mischievous humor caused her to realize she was beginning to enjoy having him around.

COLTAN'S MOTHER WAS sprawled out on the sofa, snoring. Richard zoned in the recliner, empty beer cans around him. The house was dark except for a grouping of lit candles on the coffee table. *"Highway to Hell"* played loudly on the stereo. The place reeked of pot. Richard lit another joint and popped open another beer. If he was aware of Coltan's presence, he didn't show it. The snotbag just sat there, drinking beer and smoking pot, bobbing his head to the drumbeat. In the candlelight, Coltan caught a glimpse of a razor and the dusty remnant of a line of white powder on a mirror on the coffee table. Coltan wasn't certain if the powder was meth, cocaine, or something else. His mother and Richard used all kinds of substances and often mixed them with booze.

The end of the world would not deter them from their fun. They probably didn't have the slightest idea anything bad was happening outside their front door. These two were the perfect example of the bliss of ignorance.

Relieved Richard hadn't noticed him, Coltan bounded up the stairs and into his room. He found a duffle bag among the piles of discarded dirty clothes in his closet, and tossed it on the bed. From downstairs, *"Highway to Hell,"* repeated. Coltan longed to hear a Chopin nocturne; it calmed his nerves. He spied his disk player, a thrift store find, on the nightstand. The earphones were still attached and laying on top of it. He unplugged the unit and put it into the bag. Then he gathered his disks of Classical music (also thrift store finds) stacked haphazardly in the cubbyhole of the nightstand. He put them all with the obsolete player. He packed all the clean clothing he could find into the duffle bag. Then, recalling an invitation to attend church with the Danburys, he went to the closet and selected a couple of appropriate shirts. He looked around the room for anything else he would need and spotted his old Bible, a ragged, third-hand find at another thrift store, on the bed near his pillow. A sentimental treasure and missing the book of Leviticus, he stuffed it into the bag. He retrieved his four remaining cartons of cigarettes from under the bed and put them at the top inside the bag, filling the duffle to capacity.

Some unrecognizable *Gangsta Rap* replaced *"Highway to Hell"* downstairs. Coltan closed the door. He reclined on the unmade bed and lit a smoke. There was a list in his head of additional things to take, but he was too tired to remember much of it.

He closed his eyes to rest them. In the next minute, he dozed off. He awoke with a start at the pain of his cigarette burning his belly. With a whispered tirade of cuss words, Coltan swept the ashes away and sat forward.

Natalie awaited his return.

He blinked, took a deep breath, exhaled slowly. His body ached from all the lifting he had done in the last twenty hours. The sunrise would bring more work. Still, he was grateful he had a safe place to bunker down, and people that genuinely cared about him. It was all worth it.

He went over the list in his head. There were two more things. He found his leather jacket and gloves on the floor; they counted as one item. The second item was dear to his heart, and he was baffled why he would forget it. Perhaps he was just too tired to think straight. He opened the nightstand drawer and found it easily.

It was a tiny plastic bag, the kind gemologists use for holding small loose gems. The precious gem in this bag was a coupling of locks of Brenda's blonde hair and his brown hair. She had tied them together with a jade ribbon and placed a little note inside. The note read:

Always together. Forever.

He felt the sting of tears, and her words of assurance blurred.

Five minutes later, Coltan descended the stairs on stealthy feet into the dim candlelight from the living room. As he drew near the main floor, the increasing volume of Richard's Rap, so-called, *music* assaulted his ears. Coltan paused behind Richard's worn recliner. He could barely see the top of his tormentor's balding head tilted lazily to one side against the headrest. The head remained motionless as Coltan stopped behind the recliner. Coltan figured Richard had passed out. The boy wondered if, during all those violent episodes over all those years, Richard ever felt his bitter hatred for him. Probably not; Richard was always too loaded to feel much of anything, anything except his own anger, his own supposed suffering, never that of another's. Coltan rounded the side of the recliner and gazed at the little beast spread out like a toad awaiting dissection. The bastard was dead to the world, his gnarly bare feet askew on the footrest, a portrait of oblivious serenity. The longer Coltan gazed at him, the hotter his rage boiled.

He noticed Richard's wool-lined leather slippers on the floor beside the recliner. The sight of the slippers only reminded Coltan of another reason he despised the man. The sight and the sound of Richard beating poor little Digger to death for pissing in his shoes was burned into his memory. Although it had happened two years ago when Coltan had just turned sixteen, he had not yet grown taller or stronger than Richard. In those days, Richard consistently and brutally overpowered him. Because of that, his terror of Richard played a large part in his inability to intervene to save the dog. In the end, all Coltan could do was beg on his knees for Richard to stop, and he pleaded relentlessly until death silenced the animal's pitiful cries. Not only was the horror burned into Coltan's memory, the agony of it had seared a still-festering wound deep into his soul. Not a day went by Coltan was not reminded of the incident in some way.

At this moment, the vicious monster contentedly slumbered. It was the perfect time and the perfect opportunity to finally get even.

Coltan slung the duffle over his shoulder. He then unzipped his pants, exposed his friend *Mister Dolce* and took careful aim. Coltan emptied his bladder into Richard's expensive wool-lined leather slippers.

CHAPTER 8

The sirens wailed most of the night. With the sunrise, they had not abated. Smoke was thick in the air, and new fires had broken out in town.

Hoping for a local update, Coltan immediately turned on the radio when he entered Brian's truck and started the engine. Hearing the international news first frustrated him, but the march of dire information kept him riveted to the station:

Some fool pressed the button and launched missiles into northern Egypt. Wars, starvation and disease rampaged in Africa, Asia, Russia and South America. Power grid sabotage paralyzed parts of Europe, the Philippines and Australia. Throughout parts of Great Britain, murders, rioting and a burgeoning culture war between native Brits and immigrants gained momentum. Civil wars between the dominant majority migrant population and the small but powerful emerging United Earth Federation dominated France, Germany, Italy, Spain, Portugal and the Scandinavian countries.

Almost as a footnote, the announcement of substantiated reports from these countries of a brain-infecting virus that causes cannibalistic behavior added to the upheaval. The French called the infected homicidal carriers of the virus, "Mordant". The British immediately translated the term as meaning *Biters*, but adopted the French translation. The BBC and every British tabloid warned of "the increasing number of deadly *Trans Mordants*". The Spanish speaking nations called them, "Caníbales".

America's top stories followed after a commercial break. As Coltan expected, they began with the major story that all the big cities and cosmopolitan areas of the country were under martial law due to rioting over the crumbling economy, record high unemployment, exorbitant gas and electric car charging prices, food and supplies shortages, and race and culture clashes. Critics of the current administration charged America was swiftly becoming serfdom, and the elite wanted it that way. That only added fuel to the volatility as more Americans polled came to agree with the critics. The President ordered the National Guard to summon all inactive members to duty as reinforcements, while urging citizens to remain calm.

In other news—again, almost as a footnote—the mysterious disease, now dubbed *The Mords Maker* by the American public, achieved global pandemic status by the World Health Organization. The American government was in the process of instituting *Pandemic Protocol* to prevent further spread of the contagion.

"About time!" Coltan yelled at the radio.

The report went on to reveal scientists were studying victims of the disease and intended to roll out an effective vaccine soon. The Centers for Disease Control advised citizens to report any suspected cases immediately.

"Fat chance!" Coltan muttered. "Idiots!" He shifted the stick hard, and had to remind himself not to take out his frustration on Brian's truck.

Only two employees showed up for work at the lumberyard, and both had their hands full with desperate customers demanding all the plywood they could buy. It had taken Coltan two hours to load up the rest of the lumber order by himself. A side trip to a hardware store for fasteners, screws, extra drill bits and such had eaten away another thirty minutes because that store was also low on staff and inundated with customers. Upon leaving the store, he found five men trying to unload the lumber and paneling from the truck. He took them all on: broke one guy's arm and dislocated another guy's knee. The other three fled in their van, afraid he was exhibiting symptoms of the mords maker. At that moment, Coltan realized he must have appeared to be completely insane to them, so great was his rage and determination to save his precious cargo.

His knuckles were painful and bruised. He examined the damage and noticed his baby finger was purple and swollen. His right wrist hurt and was beginning to swell. He figured he had suffered a couple of minor sprains during the altercation, a small price to pay for saving the lumber.

He scolded himself. This would not have happened if he had remembered to go to the hardware store first.

Just when he thought he had found a shortcut through the mayhem, a gas and recharging station on fire necessitated an unexpected detour. He took the frontage road and the overpass to the east side. A glance off the overpass onto the interstate below revealed a parking lot of frustrated, road-rage intoxicated evacuees. He heard horns blaring and people yelling and screaming. He wiped sweat off his forehead and was grateful he didn't have to take the freeway.

When he pulled around the rear of the Danbury house, he saw Natalie and Beverly rush out the door toward him.

Now, what?

Beverly hugged him as he got out of the truck. "Thank God! We're so glad you're all right!"

He gave her a peck on the cheek and said, "Of course I'm all right."

She gazed at him wildly through eyes bloodshot from lack of sleep. Dried blood and vomit soiled the scrubs she wore. "We've been listening to the scanner. When we heard about all the criminals trying to hijack supplies from people, we worried about you. We prayed and prayed."

"Jeez, Bev..." The sight of her brought it home to him what she'd been going through all night and half the morning. He realized she must have left work hurriedly without bothering to change out of her soiled scrubs, and reached home only a few minutes ahead of him.

She cupped his face in her hands and looked closely at the bruises on his left cheek and jaw, and the bleeding gash on his temple. "Oh, my gosh..." She then noticed the bruises on his hands, the sprained baby finger and wrist on his right hand. "Oh, my gosh...." Her eyes full of concern, she turned to Natalie, who had been watching from the porch. "Get out the first aid kit!"

"I gotta unload this stuff." Coltan said.

"It'll wait!" Her tone of voice became low and authoritative. "You're coming inside."

"Aw... good grief! It's nothing."

"Don't argue with me." She took his arm and walked him up the steps.

He felt they were overreacting as they entered into the kitchen, noted Natalie's angry expression—anger *for* him, not *at* him—as she set the first aid kit on the table and opened it, eager to render him assistance. "Here, Mom."

Beverly sat him at the table. "Don't you move," she ordered him. "Put your right hand on the table." He did as ordered. She turned to Natalie. "Put a cold pack on that."

"Yes, ma'am." Natalie opened the cold pack and gently laid it on his hand and over his wrist. When he winced in pain, she whispered, "Sorry."

"This ain't necessary," he stated.

Beverly sternly corrected him, "*Isn't* necessary." Just to rag him, she amusedly tossed in, "Tough guy..."

"Where's Brian?" he asked.

"He's over at Griff's." Beverly unloaded the kit, set aside the necessities.

"Who's Griff?"

"He owns the shooting range," Natalie said.

"What's he doing over there?"

"Getting more firearms." Natalie replied. "Man, I hope the other guy looks worse than you. How'd this happen?"

"They were trying to steal our supplies."

"You're lucky they didn't kill you." Beverly dabbed at the bleeding cut on his temple.

Coltan pulled back. "Easy!"

She rolled her eyes and stood back a second. "Quit fussing. Big baby."

"Hey..." If she had known he took on five guys to save the lumber, she wouldn't be calling him a baby.

"Well," she said as she finished cleaning the wound. "At least it's superficial. No stitches for you today, soldier." She next examined his swollen cheekbone. "You'll have a black eye soon. A badge of honor... Huh, hotshot?" Her gently teasing smile was her way of thanking him. "Now for that hand..."

He realized it was useless to resist. For the next ten minutes, he played the role of compliant patient while Beverly examined his injuries. The entire time she did this, he noticed Natalie watched the exam procedure with great interest and seemed to be taking mental notes. Even when Beverly began to wrap his sprains, Natalie studied the entire process with the earnest curiosity of a medical student.

He thought briefly of his mother and Richard. They had never shown concern all the times he had been hurt, especially all the times Richard caused the hurt.

He appreciatively observed Beverly's face, the gentleness in her eyes. She rubbed his back and softly patted his shoulder. He saw Natalie's expression of concern and admiration for him while she put out the wrist brace and hand wrap, as if she was silently thanking him for defending her family's provisions.

These two were fussing over him as if he was in critical condition.

When Beverly finished wrapping the sprains, she bent and drew him to her, rested his cheek against her shoulder, kissed the top of his head. He felt himself blush at the unexpected motherly affection.

"You rest a while," she whispered.

AFTER DINNER, BRIAN acquainted them with the new firearms that were older military grade, and a supply of silencers. He explained the noise of gunshots would attract the hordes, both diseased and military. Therefore, they would use the silencers whenever possible. The plan was to stay hidden and quiet, which meant only shooting when necessary.

Brian knew Beverly and Natalie were crack shots. Coltan was a different story. The only gun he had ever fired was Richard's .22 revolver. He was eleven then and wanted to kill the scumbucket. He missed. Richard wrestled him to the ground, sat on his back, cocked the gun and put it to his head. He warned Coltan he'd count to three and fire the bullet into his brain. On *three*, Richard pulled the gun away and shot at the fence. The sound made Coltan deaf for a few days; the only thing he was able to hear was constant high-pitched ringing. That was the last time Coltan picked up a gun.

Brian knew it was the reason for Coltan's fear of guns. Regardless, he convinced Coltan it was imperative he mastered firearms. He arranged for Griff to open the shooting range to them during off-hours.

They discussed the reinforcement of the house. Protection of the windows took priority. Coltan disagreed with Brian's plan to install plywood over them on the exterior. He explained the weather would eventually weaken the wood and, besides that, they needed to be able to see intruders before they reached the house. Natalie countered they could keep watch from the upstairs windows. Beverly voiced her opinion that the house would always be dark with the windows boarded, and she could not tolerate living in what would feel like a cave. After much discussion, Coltan presented a plan three of them agreed to. Brian reserved his vote until he saw a prototype of Coltan's idea.

In the event someone, be they desperate refugees, criminals, or soldiers managed to infiltrate the home in search of food, weapons, or citizens to force into government "shelters", a hide-in-place plan came next. The establishment of an alternative route to the basement from the second floor was the next project. The new route would take them from the attic access room down a flight of stairs that would cut through the existing walk-in closet in Beverly's office, and on down into the basement. They would install a second wall in the back of the office closet to hide the new stairway. They would eliminate and cover with a full wall painted to match the rest of the kitchen the existing door to the basement from the kitchen and then build a small pantry closet in front of that space. On the second floor, dividing the largest guest room into two rooms, and disguising the existence of the second half of the room (which would give access to both the attic and basement) was third. Next, they would begin the conversion of the attic into secret living space with enough room for all of them. They would reserve a separate concealed space in the second floor below the attic for a small group of refugees, should the need arise. The attic would serve as living space during winter, the basement in the summer.

Exhausted, they went to bed around midnight after a dessert of watermelon.

COLTAN HAD NEVER GOTTEN over to see Mrs. Spencer that day. Very early the next day, he went to visit her.

She stared at him through the screen. "What the hell happened to your face?"

"I had a little disagreement with a thief."

"Good God, boy! And, look at that hand!" She pushed open the screen door. "I hope you put him in the hospital."

"Sure did," He knew it was more an assumption, but he didn't feel like rehashing the actual scene for her.

She was watching the morning news, the volume blasting, as always. She asked, shouting over the noise, "You know they're callin' in the National Guard? They're sayin' the firefighters can't get into Baltimore because of all the riotin'. Said it's burnin' to the ground!"

"I heard they didn't want to evacuate." Coltan shouted back. "That new disease is spreading like crazy, and the Feds are trying to herd them into rescue centers where they can separate the sick ones from the healthy population. The people swear it's just an excuse for racial cleansing."

"Racial cleansing...? Bullshit! They're rioting in the white communities, too! I heard the National Guard's been confiscatin' all our guns! That's what they're pissed about!" She turned the television off with the remote. The house felt suddenly empty in the blessed silence. "We got a government that's takin' away all our rights! When I was growin' up, Americans woulda never stood for that!" She slammed the remote down on the side table. "Evil runs the whole damn thing..."

"Aside from being pissed at the news, how are you doing?"

"My arthritis is actin' up."

"You stocked up on medicine?"

"Enough for the next month." She leaned over and called for Muffy. Muffy didn't come. "Damn... That dog don't wanna leave Henry's bed. She ain't eatin' or nothin'."

"Want me to check on her?"

"Nah..." She called for Muffy again.

There came the sound of little paws on the hardwood floor, the jingle of tags, and Muffy ambled slowly into the room.

"Hey, Muffy." Coltan said. The dog looked miserably sad. She approached Coltan and stood on her hind legs. He picked her up and cuddled her. "Poor little girl." He glanced at Geneva, who seemed equally downhearted. "Maybe a walk will perk her up."

"Take her," she said with a wave. "Makes me sad seein' her like this. Poor little baby..." Characteristically, she abruptly shifted into a different conversation, "Funeral's day after tomorrow."

"What time?"

"Eleven."

"You need a ride?"

"Nope."

"Well, I'll be sure to attend."

"You're the sweetest thing..."

The compliment embarrassed him. He didn't know why.

Geneva continued, shifting topics again, "You seen the traffic out there lately?"

It was the last thing Coltan wanted to think about. "Yeah..."

"People are crazy out there!" She sat forward and looked him straight in the eye. "The mortuary's full. Said they been busy all week. Bodies pilin' up. They promised to take good care of my Henry, though. Put him on the *fast track*." She paused and laughed. "I told them that was probably the fastest he'd moved in years!"

He had to appreciate her black sense of humor, laughing, despite the sadness.

"They said a lotta people been sick. Dyin' of this thing." She narrowed her eyes scornfully as she asked him, "Do you think they know what it is and they ain't tellin' us?"

He had the same suspicions, but he didn't want to get her fired up. He simply shrugged. Muffy licked his face. The bruises hurt.

"I think it's all the evil in the world," she said. "The evil's catchin' up to us."

It made him picture Satan walking the Earth. He pushed the image out of his mind, afraid he'd attract Satan to him just by thinking about him. He replaced the image with that of Jesus battling the demons with a mighty sword.

"There's still good in the world." He was referring to the Danburys, and sweet old Mrs. Spencer and little Muffy. He was convinced, too, Jesus was alive and well, and had not abandoned them.

"I've watched it go downhill," Geneva replied. "There used to be a time when you didn't have to lock your doors. Hell... My grandpa told me there was a time when you'd go to a gas station and they'd pump the gas for you. Wash your windows and check your oil for you, too. Check your tires and air 'em up. Good luck findin' that anymore. They gave you green stamps, too. My second great-grandmother bought this chair with green stamps." Once again, Coltan had no idea what she was talking about. "We used to buy things with cash," she continued. "Now there's no more cash. Got this damned cyber and digital money crap that you need to use an AllCard or your portafone to use. You know what's behind that, right?" She didn't wait for Coltan's answer. "That's so the sonsabitches can track everything you do, everything you buy, where you buy it, and how much of it you buy. Cash gave us privacy. There ain't no privacy anymore. They got us all tethered to them so they know everything about us. They took all our rights away by takin' over the one thing we can't do without in order to survive. Smart sonsabitches. Evil bastards. They got total control now. Got it gradually, right under our noses with all this new technology shit and made us dependent on it. That's how they did it. We ain't ever gonna be free no more." Her old eyes took on a look of regret, "I feel sorry for you kids comin' up. You'll never know the way things used to be. Glad I'm outa here soon."

He didn't want to hear her talk about all the things wrong with the world that he couldn't control, and he sure as hell didn't want to hear her talk about dying. "Well, I guess I'll take Muffy out."

She tossed him the leash. "You'll take good care of her..."

It almost sounded like a question to him. "Of course I will." He attached the leash and pushed open the screen door. "I'll give her a good run. I promise."

He took her out on the same route they always took. Once past the barbed wire fence, Coltan let her off leash and bounding happily. At least her spirits seemed to pick up. He was glad for that. He wondered if she understood what happened to Mr. Spencer.

With that thought, he remembered he had intended to talk to Brian about taking Mrs. Spencer and Muffy in when it came time to bunker down—another thing he had not done yet. He reminded himself to do that when he returned to the house. He thought Brian would be up by the time he returned.

He noticed another dog by the bushes along the creek bed. It appeared to be a small mixed breed, black and scruffy. The dog spotted Coltan and Muffy and raced towards them, barking. Muffy raced ahead to meet it, ready to play. *Alright,* Coltan thought, *Muffy's got a new friend.* The two dogs met nose to nose, sniffed each other's butts, and then met nose to nose again. With no warning, the black dog growled, bared its teeth and attacked little Muffy, went for her throat. Muffy screamed in pain and fear, that horrible high-pitched, pitiful crying that always seemed to make the air itself cringe. Coltan was off like a shot. He grabbed the black dog by the scruff of its neck and threw it as far away as he could throw with his bad arm. Muffy writhed on the ground, squealing in shock. The black dog bounded over, teeth bared and tried for a second lunge. Coltan intercepted and kicked it as hard as he could. "Get outa here!" The dog hung back, not even acknowledging Coltan's blow. Focused on Muffy, it made a third attempt. "No!" Coltan yelled. He picked up Muffy and held her to his chest, kicked at the other dog. "Get outta here!" The dog backed off and began to turn away, then turned and glared at him once more before deciding to trot off. It disappeared among the brush.

Muffy trembled and panted in his arms, her eyes filled with terror. He petted her and said comfortingly, "He's gone now. You okay?" Her panting and trembling increased. He could feel the sweat from her paw pads through his shirt. He lifted her chin to see her neck. There was a spot of blood from a minor wound. Coltan figured a little hydrogen peroxide would take care of it.

He carried her all the way home, the whole time wondering how he'd explain this to Mrs. Spencer. He had promised he would protect her. He failed.

Muffy squirmed in his arms as he climbed the steps and reached the screen door. He pulled open the door and saw Geneva sitting in her chair. He stepped in slowly, holding Muffy close and said, "Gen, we had a little trouble. I'm sorry I—" At which point, Muffy jumped out of his arms and out the door, which was ajar, and raced out the open gate. He stepped out on the porch. "Muffy!" The dog raced up the road toward the open field and the creek. "Come back! Muffy!" If the dog was intent on returning to even the score, it was suicide. He turned back, stepped inside the doorway and said to Geneva, "I'm sorry. I'll go get her. Don't worry."

Geneva Spencer did not react to Coltan's voice or Muffy's sudden escape. Her gaping eyes stared at the black television screen and her hand clutched the remote.

Coltan approached her. "Mrs. Spencer?" There was no response. He squatted in front of her and looked into her face. Her eyes stared vacantly ahead.

A bad morning had just gotten worse.

He took her almost obsolete five-year-old portafone out to the porch and called Brian.

CHAPTER 9

The ambulance attracted a crowd of curious onlookers. Natalie stood with Carolyn in Carolyn's driveway and watched as they loaded Mrs. Spencer into the back. A policeman interviewed Coltan on the porch.

"What did he do to her?" Carolyn asked.

"Nothing. He found her dead." Natalie's eyes were on Coltan. He stood against the railing, his arms folded across his chest. Shock, sadness and fear played interchangeably in his eyes. Her father wrapped his arm around Coltan's shoulders. The policeman asked Coltan a question, and Coltan nodded and stared at the steps. Brian then said something to the policeman.

"He's been over there a lot," Carolyn said. "Weird coincidence that he was there when both of them died."

Natalie had tried, but could not understand the sudden hatred Carolyn had developed for Coltan. That day at the Dairy Delight was certainly not enough to justify it. In addition, Natalie was certain she did not know the mysterious *Harley Guy* was now living at her house; so, jealousy could not have been the issue.

"He was helping them out with stuff and walking their dog." Natalie stated flatly. She watched Coltan enter the house alone while her dad and the policeman conversed.

"Did you see his face?" Carolyn asked. "Somebody beat the crap out of him. Bet he deserved it, too."

It took everything for Natalie to suppress the urge to give Carolyn a good, hard slap. She looked away and observed all the neighbors watching the show. How many of them were coming to the same conclusion as Carolyn? Yes, the Allen family was the neighborhood disgrace and, yes, they unjustifiably ostracized Coltan as white trash. It was only human to judge a fruit by the tree from which it had fallen. It didn't help that Coltan's avoidance of his neighbors, because he knew how they had prejudged him, served as a mitigating factor in their suspicion and fear of him. Natalie knew she had also wrongly judged him and she regretted it. If there had been any way to go back in time and change that she would do it in a heartbeat.

Coltan returned to the porch with a bowl of water and a separate bowl of dog food. He set it by Mrs. Spencer's rocker. He scanned the field and the tree line along the creek, hoping to catch sight of the little dog. The worry was obvious in his face, in his eyes.

"Look at that show he's putting on!" Carolyn remarked. "Trying to play the soft-hearted caring neighbor kid. What a crock! They oughta arrest him right now."

Natalie had had enough. She spun, and her words came in a low, angry whisper through clenched teeth. "You're totally wrong. You're wrong about everything. Colt is good and kind, and decent. And I'm glad he's my friend!"

"What?" She couldn't believe what she was hearing. "Since when?"

"He's better than you or me, or anybody else!"

"Since when?" Carolyn demanded.

"And, he'd never hurt anybody—especially the Spencers." The words tumbled out with hardly a breath in between, "And, for your information, he got beat up protecting me and my family! Yeah! You heard right! He doesn't deserve this from you. He doesn't deserve all your snide remarks and mean-ass looks. He doesn't deserve all the shit he's been taking from you, and me, and the neighbors, and the school, and everybody else. Do you hear me? He doesn't deserve it! And, God forgive me, I'm just as guilty as you and everybody. So, shut up!"

All Carolyn could do at this point was gaze flabbergasted at Natalie. After what seemed the longest thirty seconds in history, she finally asked, "Is that why you haven't called me?"

THE OVERCAST SIENNA-gray sky hovered ominously above the upper and lower valleys. Above the mountains, puffy black storm clouds sailed southeastward in the cool wind. Sunbeams played in the clouds as dusk settled in. A single star twinkled low in the horizon. The scent of smoke lingered in the air, though most of it had blown away with the winds. Now that the rioting had subsided, an eerie quiet settled over the valley.

Natalie put the two remaining lamb chops on the plate with the rice and corn. She neatly dabbed some homemade mint jelly over the lamb. Her father loved lamb chops with mint jelly. She and her mother always made sure there was an extra plate for Dad to reheat when he returned from his shift in the morning. This would be a welcome treat for him. She covered it carefully with a plastic plate lid and set it in the fridge with a note taped to it, *Dad! Your favorite!*

She glanced through the living room entrance as she began clearing the table. Mom and Coltan were sitting together on the couch. They were talking softly, and Mom had her Bible open on her lap. They were discussing scripture, and Coltan was full of questions and observations. All Natalie could make out was the discussion had something to do about death and why good people sometimes suffer terrible things. Coltan asked something about animals, and Mom smiled at the opportunity and began turning pages until she came to scripture that spoke about animals in Heaven. In the next moments, she was pointing out a scripture about how God cares for even the smallest sparrow. She went on to explain God blessed all animals with the ability to survive in the direst of circumstances, and that God never intended or viewed his creatures as something disposable. Each was equally important and precious to him. Each found their final destiny in the palm of his loving hand. Natalie saw Coltan bow his head, and cover his forehead and eyes with one hand. She heard clearly the words, "Richard," "why" and "suffer." The conversation continued then in whispers.

When Natalie realized she was straining to hear the rest, it occurred to her she was intruding on their privacy. She scolded herself and quit eavesdropping. Mom was being Mom, the best Mom in the world, and was using the gift God had given her—the gift to heal, physically and spiritually. Natalie thought God must have a special place in his heart for Coltan, because he had brought him to her mom and dad.

Subsequently, a disturbing thought came to her. They were giving the bulk of their love and attention to him these days ever since he came to live there. Natalie felt they were so concerned with his needs they had come to forget all about her. Why couldn't they see she needed them, too? What made him so much more important? Resentment grew inside her, resentment of all three of them. She tried to dismiss her feelings and brush them aside as umbrage based only on her own immature selfishness. Despite her best effort to quell her simmering anger, it continued to nag her.

OVER THE NEXT FEW DAYS, Coltan checked the food he left out for Muffy. Something had dined there, but Muffy herself hadn't turned up. Not one to give up hope, Coltan continued to leave food at the Spencers' porch. He stopped by Animal Control and looked for her there, then explained the situation and left a report with instructions for them to call him. He overheard two Humane

Society officers comparing notes about the number of insane vicious animals they had to euthanize on the spot, mostly dogs, raccoons, opossums, some foxes, and a number of coyotes. It made Coltan recall the black dog by the creek.

In town, life was still far from normal. Interruptions in the supply chain caused by increasing numbers of people not showing up for work either because of illness or simply bugging out meant empty shelves in the stores. Although the financially healthy had the luxury of stocking up before the shortages, the financially strapped did not. As things worsened in the poor areas throughout the country, those with no money and no transportation realized they had no choice but to bug in, and they could not do that without food and other supplies. It was the same in the south end of Bonito Valle where brazen mobs quickly stripped the shelves of what little was available and once they cleaned out the stores, they savagely turned on their neighbors and friends, and then set their sights on the prosperous sections of town. The rioting had spilled over from the south end into the center of town and crews were busy cleaning up the debris. There were many burned buildings; those that had escaped the fires had broken windows and smashed-in doors. Impassable streets in some areas necessitated meandering detours.

So far, no National Guard troops arrived in Bonito Valle. Coltan figured the big cities took priority, and he was glad for that. The military would only be a hindrance to his freedom of movement as he continued to attend to his personal business and gather more supplies.

Due to the number of impassable roads in town and the resulting detours and gas shortages, Brian and Beverly decided Coltan's Harley was the most efficient transportation for running lighter errands completed by the two teens. They set a rule Natalie could not ride on the motorcycle until she was dressed safely and properly. Coltan used the truck to take her shopping for a leather jacket and gloves, a helmet, and a pair of appropriate boots.

While in the store, it occurred to Coltan binoculars had not been on the list of must-haves in the bunker-down plan. He purchased four of the best and most expensive on the market. He also purchased four walkie-talkies and eight cases of batteries in all sizes.

Natalie accompanied him to the double funeral held for the Spencers. Only a few of the Spencer's family members attended; the rest too far away to make the trip. None of their neighbors attended.

They noticed there were many other funerals in progress. There were so many funerals, had they not come over on the Harley there would have been no place to park.

THE WINDS DIED DOWN in the early afternoon. The temperature hovered in the high seventies. They took the seldom-traveled road to the foothills under the clearest and bluest of skies.

Riding behind Coltan, she had her arms around his chest and leaned comfortably against his back. She found she was enjoying every moment alone with him. As he sped up on the straightaway, she clung tighter. She loved the feel of his body against hers, and wished their ride could last forever.

He slowed the Harley when the road became curvy and took the turnoff into Baker Creek. As they entered the little town, he obeyed the twenty-five speed limit and slowed the bike. He parked in front of a small café, and they both removed their helmets.

"Ever been here?" He asked.

"No," she replied.

"Want to go for a walk?"

"Sure!"

It was a tiny old burg settled in a small valley in the foothills. The population hovered at around eighty full-time residents, and one-hundred-fifty or so during the summer with the tourists and summer residents. This summer had seen few tourists, and most of the part-time residents who came up to their summer cabins had also stayed away. Because of this, the town was quiet and empty of the expected summer traffic. The only consistent sound was that of the roiling creek that wound between the hills into the valley below, where it continued into Bonito Valle and on into the Victorian-era railroad town of Reyton in the west.

They strolled casually, Coltan pointing out historical points of interest and sharing anecdotes about the town's history and people. Natalie was impressed with his knowledge about the place and suspected he visited here often.

When they passed by a tavern that had changed little since its origin in the 1880's, a fat, grizzled old man called out, "Coltan Allen!" When he saw what was left of Coltan's bruises, he sauntered over to him. "What in hell happened to you?"

"Defending provisions," Coltan called back.

"Atta boy! Don't take crap from nobody." He looked Natalie up and down. "Who's the pretty girl here?"

"My friend Natalie. Natalie, this is Wilton. His family's owned this place since it was first built."

Wilton grinned warmly. "Good to meet you, Natalie. This boy been behaving himself?"

"Ask *him*," Natalie replied playfully.

"Ask *him*?" The old guy chuckled and said, "He's just gonna lie his ass off. First time I saw him, ol' Riley was writin' him up a speeding ticket. Shoulda heard the story this kid tried to use to get out of it."

"Hell... At least I tried." Coltan said.

The old man winked at him confidentially. "Givin' the girl the tour?"

"Yep."

Wilton addressed Natalie, "You must be some special lady for him to share *this*."

She directed her question to both of them. "Why so?"

Coltan answered. "I'm always alone when I come here." He lit a cigarette and grinned at Wilton. "Gotta keep the place secret. My refuge from the world. Right, Wil?"

"*Our* refuge, dude." Then, to Natalie, "The kid fits right in."

Coltan noticed the many lost pet signs on the bulletin board. He turned back to Wilton, "What's with all the missing pets? Coyotes?"

"Hell if I know. They're just disappearing. No bodies found, nothin'. Just disappearing."

"How long?"

"Two weeks or so. Riley thinks it's coyotes. Ol' Bernie shot a rabid skunk yesterday by his chicken coop. At least, he thought it was rabid. Who knows?"

"The same thing's going on in Bonito Valle. Pets vanishing, I mean."

"No shit..." The old guy thought for a moment, and then said, "There's a lot of people desperate these days. I wonder if they're stealing 'em and selling 'em to that lab over in Oak Shores."

This struck at Coltan. "Oh, man..."

"Come on," Natalie interjected. "People aren't *that* desperate."

Wilton gazed at her disbelievingly. "Where you been, girl? Don't you watch the news?"

"More than I can stand," Natalie replied. "I know about the unemployment, the food shortages, the rising prices, the riots, the increasing homelessness. But, it's not that desperate."

Wilton shook his head from side to side. "Shit. There was a family over in Bonito Valle that was living on cats."

"No way," Natalie retorted. "That was just some sick rumor. It never happened."

"Not what I heard," he insisted. He looked at Coltan, "Boy, set this girl straight."

"I never heard about it." Coltan said. "I know a lot of animals have been sick. Maybe it's rabies or distemper. Animals tend to go off alone when they know they're dying."

"We ain't found no bodies up here." Wilton reiterated.

"Well," Coltan cocked his head, rubbed his chin, thinking. "I don't know."

"You two have fun today." He went back in the tavern's doorway, and turned once more to them. He addressed Coltan, "Hey... you goin' over to the diner?"

"I was thinking about it."

"Shirley'll be sorry she missed ya. She's gone to the airport to bring Lillian home. Seems that new bug goin' around hit the Bay Area. They shut down the college. Lillian said a buncha them kids died from it."

Coltan frowned with worry. "Is Lillian sick?"

"Not yet, an' Shirley's gonna make sure it stays that way. From what Lillian told her, all the hospitals are full down there, an' they've cancelled concerts an' stuff. They're tellin' folks to stay home, stay outa crowds an' all. She said a lot of the cops an' paramedics are comin' down with it, said there's been riots an' such—general anarchy. Shirley told me she wants to get Lillian outa there before they shut down the airports. It's a helluva mess!"

"I hope they get back alright..." Coltan said.

"They will." Then, to Natalie, "Keep him outa trouble."

As they walked away from the tavern, Natalie asked Coltan, "Who's Shirley?"

"She owns the café." Coltan grinned warmly. "She's a nice lady—always nice to me, even when I was drunk. I can't count the times I sobered up on her couch."

"You've been blessed with some good people," Natalie remarked. Introspectively, Coltan replied, "It took me a while to realize it."

They walked back to the café and dined on filet mignon. Coltan ordered an espresso, and Natalie a cappuccino. One thing Coltan appreciated about having money was that he could eat anything he wanted without worrying about the price. It got him to thinking about the times ahead. The days of fine dining may soon be over, and money wouldn't matter. He decided he would eat like a millionaire while the food was still available.

Natalie noticed he was conscious of his manners. Instead of the usual messy scarfing down she had seen, he was neat, chewed slowly, used his knife and fork properly, and had even placed the cloth napkin on his lap. He ate everything on his plate, and wasted no time ordering apple pie with two scoops of ice cream for dessert. A second espresso accompanied the desert. It seemed the only thing not different was his appetite.

"There's a shaded picnic area along the creek here," he said. "I'll have to show you sometime." He picked at the remains of his ice cream. "Sometimes I camp there. The locals don't care."

"So, this is where you go."

"Huh?"

"When you take off on your bike. I noticed you always took the road out this way."

"You've been watching me?" He cast a naughty smirk her way.

She blushed. "No. I just saw you a couple of times."

He laughed softly. "I was just kidding."

She laughed too. "Carolyn thought you were going off to meet up with some biker gang up here."

He almost busted his gut laughing at the idea. "That doesn't surprise me."

"She called me to say goodbye. They left this morning to go to their cabin for their annual vacation. She wanted me to go, but her parents said not this time. I used to go with them every year. This year, things are too screwed up."

"Screwed up is putting it lightly..." Coltan remarked.

Natalie nodded in agreement. "She had a million questions about you, wanted to know how we got to be friends. I told her about that day you walked with me when my tire went flat, said that's how we got acquainted. She said that was a nice thing for you to do. All I said was you *are* nice."

"That's right..." He intoned playfully. "Ruin my image."

"I would think that'd be a good thing."

He became contemplative. Finally, he said, "I kinda like it when people are scared of me. It makes me feel... safe. They don't mess with me as long as they're scared of me. Your mom made me see that."

"I heard you and Mom talking about it. She talks to you like you're an old friend, like an adult. I wish she'd talk to me like that."

"You should tell her."

She shrugged. "Her and Dad still see me as a little kid."

"You oughta give them a chance. Hell! I wish I had..." He stopped himself. It hadn't occurred to him until this moment just how much he had come to want Brian and Beverly as parental substitutes.

"They love you. They absolutely love you." She couldn't mask the resentment in her voice. As much as she liked Coltan, she still resented his sudden intrusion into her family, and resented even more the love they showed him.

Anger replaced his initial shock at her tone as he stated just above a whisper, "You've got everything I never had. You've got two fine people who love you completely. *Completely!* And, yet you're so ungrateful! If they were my parents..."

"Congratulations. They *are* your parents."

"I had no idea you felt like that." The hurt in her eyes made him feel remorseful, even though he had done nothing to cause her pain.

"We have to settle this *now*."

"I know." She felt sorry about it. "I know it's not your fault. Don't think I hate you. I don't. I like you."

"You hate sharing them." He gripped her hands tightly and spoke in a low whisper, "Listen to me. They saved my life. They reached in and lifted me out of hell. And, I'm no victim, either. I created most of that hell all by myself." He thought it through for only a few seconds before he decided it was time to show her the repugnant truth about his past. Once she saw this, she would understand the depths of her parents' love not only for him, but for her as well. He rolled up his sleeves and began to point out specific scars on the inside of his arms; he spoke slowly in a confidential whisper. "I did this all to myself. See this burn? I held a lighter there, held it there to see how long I could take the pain. These other ones: cigarettes. To see how long I could take it. This one: I stabbed myself... I pushed the blade in very slowly, deeper and deeper. I wanted to touch the bone. That was my goal. I wanted to feel it stop at the bone. I did it, too. Sick shit, right?"

"My gosh... Why?"

"I thought I deserved it. It wasn't that I enjoyed the pain. I really believed I deserved it. And, still, it wasn't enough." There was a hint of tears in his eyes, and he blinked them back. "My point is, if they had so much love to give someone like me, someone so hopelessly fucked-up as me, then, they have a bottomless well of love to give you. And they give it to you. I see it. I see how much they love you. And, your dad, he thinks you're the smartest kid in the world. He respects you. He admires you. He has all the confidence in the universe in you. So, get off your pity-shitter and thank God they love you."

Coltan sat back and rolled his sleeves down to cover the scars. He gazed at her, regretting he had revealed his shame to her, but hoping she understood.

"Mom and Dad know about that?"

"Yeah."

"Do you still want to hurt yourself sometimes?"

"No."

For Coltan to reveal this secret spoke volumes as to his trust in her. In the back of her mind, she suspected he was certain she carried something of her own that enabled her to understand and sympathize with his compulsion. How could he know she had once done something similar? She had only done it once, and that one time was enough to convince her never to do it again.

Coltan asked, "Are we good?"

"Yeah."

He gestured at the food on her plate. "Eat up." Coltan ordered another cup of coffee and another serving of pie so she wouldn't be eating alone.

As they finished their meal, a military jeep pulled up and parked in front of their window. The four soldiers, all wearing fatigues, scrambled out. As they neared, Natalie noticed there was no Army insignia on their fatigues. In place of the insignia was a strange logo that looked like the world encircled by two horizontal lines. A sickeningly bad feeling panged and then knotted into a heavy ball of foreboding in the pit of her stomach. When she glanced at Coltan, he grasped her hand. His eyes showed his distrust of the soldiers, and the warm color drained from his face.

"We should go," he said softly.

After a momentary hesitation, she replied through trembling lips, "Yeah."

The soldiers entered the restaurant through the door situated behind Natalie. Coltan casually watched them, but only for a few moments. He whispered to Natalie as she was just about to turn and look at them, "Just be cool."

The soldiers took a table along the interior wall, as Wilton's niece subbing as waitress gathered menus for them. Coltan and Natalie, stealing a glance at her, noticed her weakly veiled nervousness at the soldiers' imposing presence. The soldiers abruptly quit their hushed and intimate conversation as the girl greeted them and distributed the menus to them.

Natalie whispered to Coltan, "Those aren't National Guard."

"No," he mouthed in silent reply.

Her fear remained in her eyes as she barely breathed out the words, "What the hell?"

"Are you scared?"

"A bit." She tried to look away, but his gaze held her. She turned the question back to him, "Are you scared?"

He debated between being a stoic tough guy, and being truthful. She had already seen the evidence of the worst of his character, the violence he had done to himself. Admitting fear was a minor thing compared to that.

Finally, he answered. "Yeah."

CHAPTER 10

O ut on the back porch, the whine of the power saw had been going off and on for four hours. The racket of drilling, the crack of wood on wood, and the laughter and voices of the two men filled the few quiet moments. Sawdust covered everything.

Natalie shut the back door when she noticed some of the sawdust had blown in onto the floor. For a minute, she watched them through the window, bent over the large table, almost head to head, talking and tracing the blueprint with their index fingers. Dad appeared perplexed and shook his head. Coltan suddenly stood straight and said something, and Dad nodded and grinned. Coltan grinned back, made some kind of wise-ass comment which caused Dad to laugh. He got two cans of soda from the cooler, tossed one to Coltan. Coltan caught it in one hand and turned back to the blueprint. In addition to sawdust, the air was full of testosterone.

They had been at this for two days. Dad devoted his early mornings to rousting Coltan out of bed at seven-thirty. After a trip over to the indoor shooting range, they would return at nine to begin work on the "refurbishments," as Dad called it. Coltan called it, "The Saving Our Asses Plan." By three in the afternoon, it was bedtime for Dad, and Coltan continued the quiet work of measuring and marking countless plywood sheets, planks and boards in the basement.

Natalie took over the duty of checking the Spencer house for Muffy every four hours. In the evening, she refreshed the food and water. Muffy still had not returned.

In addition to that, she was still running the lightest errands on her bicycle. This morning she had returned to the pharmacy to fill a prescription for antibiotics and codeine for her mother. The drugs went into the growing medical kit. Stolen suture packs and other items found their way in from the hospital. Beverly atoned for this by increasing her tithe to twenty percent at church, and donating a case of beef stew and a box full of veggies from the garden to a local food pantry. Under the circumstances, she hoped God would call it even.

The attendance at church had been steadily declining. Many had left town, and many others were sick. A few had died. The previous Sunday, Beverly called an ambulance for a man she had tended to that had arrived exhibiting stroke symptoms. As the ambulance left and everyone returned to the pews, she, Brian, Natalie and Coltan exchanged knowing glances. They said nothing about it until they were in the car heading home. That was when Beverly told them the man had a human bite wound on his arm. That led to a discussion about the fate of the sick and the disposal of the dead victims of the virus: The Federal Government ordered all civil authorities to turn both the living and the dead over to Homeland Security. What happened once HS carted them off was anybody's guess.

AT THE SOUTH END OF town, Brian and Officer Tim Belco were the first on scene for a domestic disturbance call. The neighborhood was located at the industrial end of Branstead where the chronically unemployed and low-income residents lived in tiny row houses. Brian had answered many calls in this neighborhood and had gotten acquainted with many of the people in the process. He recognized most of the faces in the small crowd that had gathered outside number fifteen-sixty-two, the people drawn by the screams and sounds of things breaking. The residents moved aside and made a pathway for the two officers.

Just as Brian and Belco approached the front door, a young, obese Hispanic woman dived through the window and got caught up, partly impaled on the broken glass in the frame. Before the two policemen could reach the window, a young slightly built man raced to the woman's aid, tried to pull her the rest of the way through. Belco reached the woman next and helped the man free her. The three of them tumbled onto the sidewalk. She was bleeding from her many wounds, screaming hysterically. Brian thought he heard her wail, *"Mi bambina!"* As the officer and the young man laid the woman on her back, she began to ramble urgently in Spanish. Although Brian and Officer Belco were both fluent in Spanish, the woman was speaking too quickly and frantically for her words to make sense.

Brian recognized the young man under the lights of the porch and streetlamps. "Raul! What's she saying?"

"She said he went crazy. He killed the baby and tried to kill her."

"Is he armed?" Belco asked.

Raul asked the woman. After she answered him in a slurred and hysterically sobbing account, he translated. "She said he don't have no weapons. He's just crazy and he killed the baby. She said he bit the baby's throat, and then he bit her when she tried to stop him. He bit her all up and down her arms."

Brian cussed under his breath. He drew his weapon as Belco rose and drew his. They gazed ruefully at each other, knew what they would find inside the tiny house.

As Brian radioed for assistance, Belco turned to the crowd of onlookers below the streetlamp. "All of you get back!"

As the people drew into the shadows, a little black-haired girl wormed her way to the front of the adults to get a better look. The sirens from the approaching ambulance and police back-up diverted her attention for only a few seconds, and then she stared again at the bleeding woman on the sidewalk. She stepped forward and tugged on Brian's duty belt as he moved past her. "Is she gonna die?"

Brian bent and placed his hand on her tiny shoulder. "You stay back with the grown-ups, Rosa. Do what I say."

She backed up respectfully. "Yes, sir."

Belco kicked open the locked door with one mighty thrust of his robust leg. The escaping stench of pot stung his eyes. When no perp jumped out at him, he entered the semi-dark space with his weapon ready. Brian followed and performed a quick check of the interior. In the dim light of a single table lamp, they could see clothing, shoes, a shattered tequila bottle, a tipped amber smoking bong, fast food wrappers and soiled diapers scattered upon the worn carpet. There was no one in the living room and initially the house was silent. However, the sudden faint sound of growling directed their attention to a small bedroom at the right rear. They silenced their radios, pointed their weapons, tiptoed cautiously to the faintly illuminated open doorway of the room and peered in.

The perp sprawled in front of the toppled bassinet on the littered floor. He seemed unaware of the two officers, and continued to contentedly eat something as if it was an ear of corn and he was at a church picnic. In the near-darkness, it was difficult to tell the nature of his meal. It was not until Brian flicked up the light switch on the wall when they saw the horrifying feast.

Brian swallowed back the vomit that rushed up his throat. He struggled to shut down his churning emotions, to maintain his professional equilibrium.

Although this was Belco's fifth one of the day his gut twisted and his skin flushed lucent green. "Shit..." As of this morning, the Bonito Valle Police Department adopted a new policy for dealing with mords and, for Belco it had become almost automatic by now. He aimed and sent a bullet into the perp's forehead

The man fell forward. His baby, a naked, half-devoured little girl maybe four weeks old, tumbled out of his arms. In the eyes of the Feds, the two would be just another dead mord and victim for the HAZMAT arm of Homeland Security to collect from the morgue.

Knowing this, Brian silently mourned not only their deaths, but also the callous disregard of their humanity.

As the ambulances raced away, eighteen-year-old Mario Rodriquez sprinted from the bus stop at the end of the block. At first, he thought the police and ambulance were at his home. The welfare of his mother and his little sister Rosa fueled his panic. Once he reached the heart of the activity, he was relieved to find the authorities at Hector and Carmen's house three doors from his. He assumed it was just one more of many domestic violence calls to their squat, and he expected to see Hector led off in cuffs for the umpteenth time.

Rosa broke from the crowd the second she spotted Mario in his Bujjet Mart vest. She ran to him and exclaimed excitedly, "Hector tried to kill Carmen! The cops shot him and they took him out in a big black bag!"

Mario immediately swept her into his arms. He wanted with everything to get out of this neighborhood, get his mother and young sister away from the escalating violence. "Where's Mama?"

"She's talking to Officer Danbury." With hardly a breath, she continued, "Raul got cut when he pulled Carmen outa the window. He saved her! They took Carmen to the hospital!"

Mario wound through the dissipating crowd of jaded, but still curious, neighbors. He found his mother on the front step with Officer Brian, who he considered a friend, and immediately extended his hand to him.

They shook hands in greeting and Brian gave Rosa's curly hair an affectionate tousle. Brian noticed the sweat and fear on the boy's face, the heaving of his chest as he tried to catch his breath. Brian realized the kid had run all the way from the bus stop. "Are you okay, Mario?"

"Is it true? Did Hector try to kill her? Did you shoot him? Is he dead?"

Brian did not want to discuss it in front of the child. He suggested to Mrs. Rodriquez, "You should get Rosa inside now."

She took Rosa's hand and said, "If I remember anything else, I'll call you."

He nodded, "Thank you, ma'am." He waited until the woman and child were inside before he answered Mario's question. "Yeah, it's true. It wasn't a normal dispute, though. The man was sick."

"He got that mord maker thing?"

"Yeah."

"Who's taking care of their baby?"

"The baby's dead."

Mario grimaced with disgust and sorrow, sunk down on the step. "Aw... God..."

Brian sat down beside him. The image of the dead baby returned to his memory. He wished he could erase it. In the next moment, he thought of little Rosa. "Listen, Mario. I want you to make sure your mother keeps this place locked up, even during the day. And, for God's sake, keep Rosa inside!" Brian paused for a few moments, all the worst-case scenarios playing in his head. "Do you have any other place to go until this blows over?"

"We got our uncle over in Durham City, but we can't get there. We got no transportation, and the Army's takin' over the railroad. Besides, I gotta work. People ain't showin' up. They got me on double shifts. If I don't work, we can't make rent or food or nothing."

Brian wanted to tell him the job at Bujjet Mart would not matter. He wanted to tell him that soon—too soon—the military would man all the stores exclusively for the military. However, Brian perceived the boy was not ready to accept that. Like too many people, Mario expected the government would handle everything and return life to normal. He hated the idea of the boy, his sister and his mother so vulnerable in this situation. "Do you have a gun in the house?"

Mario hesitated. The gun was illegal.

Brian understood. "I'm not going to bust you, son. This is confidential. I want to make sure your family has some kind of protection."

He whispered it. "Mama has a gun."

"Do you have ammo?"

"Yeah. How much, I don't know. Mama keeps it hidden. She keeps it high up where Rosa can't find it."

Brian gave him his card. "If you change your mind about your uncle's house, I'll get you there. I want you to call me if you need my help. My PF number's on the back."

IN THE DEN, COLTAN secured the second roller frame around the window. He intended the upper and lower frame to serve as both a guide and holder for the plywood sheet. He had already installed a third piece that served as a block on the right hand side of the window to keep the sheet from overshooting the window's width. He double-checked the plywood sheet that would cover the window. Coltan secured the fourth frame at the left edge. It was now time to put the square u-shaped bar holders on the right and left frames. He had already assembled those, and all he had to do now was screw and bolt them into place. The battery powered hand drill and screwdriver made light work of it. Finally, all he had to do was lift the plywood panel, guide and insert it in the roller frame gutters and slide it to the right until it met the blocking frame on the right side. This part of the task was a two-person job. He called for Natalie.

She finally bounded down the stairs and into the den. "Ready?"

"Yep. This is the test model. You get that end. Lift it using the bar holder; it's easier." They worked together, positioned it into place, and slid it widthwise into the gutters of the roller frame, and then Coltan slid it to the right, shutting it. The frame on the left side attached to the panel met flush with the upper and lower frames. Next, he grabbed the long wooden board and dropped it into the holders centered at either end of the plywood panel. It fit perfectly. He tugged on it to check it. The left side gave. He realized he had forgotten to flip down the locks that fastened the left side frame to the wall. He did that, and tugged again. Satisfied, he stood back and looked it over. "Perfect," he said.

"Do you think it will hold?"

"Yeah." He went over, flipped up the locks and slid the panel to the left. The light poured back into the room. "See? All we have to do is slide it shut and lock it. That'll save lots of time. We can do the whole downstairs in less than five minutes. Every window."

"Good job." Natalie was impressed. "But, we should be protecting the windows. What if they break the window? Can't they bust through the panel, too?"

"That's why we're gonna test it; the panels I'm gonna use are one and a quarter-inch thick."

"But, it makes more sense to protect the window," Natalie stated.

"Anyone with a power screwdriver can remove the panels from the outside." He demonstrated the test panel again, showed her how the locks worked to brace the panel.

She still distrusted the idea. "Okay. Slide open the window and close the panel. I'll go out and take down the screen. We'll see how strong it is." She went outside and pulled the screen off on the right where the window slid open. He hadn't slid the panel closed yet. She popped her head inside, and saw he was picking up his pack of smokes from the desk. "Hey, you. No smoking inside."

"I know that." He slid the panel shut, covering the whole window. She heard the reinforcement board drop into the holders.

His voice came muffled through the wood. "Okay. Go ahead."

She stepped back, pivoted and karate kicked the panel. It budged, but it didn't break. She stepped back and kicked it again. It held. She kicked a third time. It splintered superficially, but it held. "That's great!" she hollered through the wood. Coltan slid the panel and grinned at her through the open window. She approached the window and leaned in, "Well done, Professor."

"Did it split at all?"

"It splintered a little."

He climbed out the window and alighted on the ground. "Let me see." He leaned in and slid the panel until he could see the splintered area. He ran his finger over it. "I was right. The thickest will do it. Okay." He slid the panel back and climbed inside, "This was a good test."

"You got enough of the thick?"

"Yeah. This was the only thinner piece—one-half inch thick for the test model." He was proud of his work but wanted her to be proud of it too. "What'cha think?"

"I think it's a winner."

"Thanks!" He lit a cigarette and hopped up, perched in the window frame. "I'll use this piece as a template for this room." He dropped out the window and strolled over to the back steps where he sat down and stretched out.

She followed him and sat beside him. "Where did you learn this stuff?"

"I worked at the theater in Reyton for a while. General carpentry, set building, stuff like that."

"That one they remodeled?"

"Yeah. They're using it for light opera and concerts like in the old days. Great place. I got to watch all the shows for free." The memory was pleasant, and it rekindled his memories of Brenda. He gazed off into the valley, thinking about her, remembering her, even the scent of her perfume.

"It was a good time for you..." Natalie assumed.

"Yeah." He released the memories and returned to the present. "I should get back to work. There's a lot of sliders to build."

"After lunch." She said it like it was an order. "Mom said to use the left over roast beef for sandwiches. How does that sound? I'll make you two. And, potato salad."

He smiled endearingly at her. "You know, Nat, you don't have to do that for me. I know how to make a sandwich."

"I thought you'd like to rest. Have another smoke, that's all."

"I don't want you to wait on me." He couldn't explain it. It simply bothered him that she was settling into a *wifey-wifey-mom* kind of role. She was more like her mother in that caring, maternal way than she would ever admit. He was used to taking care of himself. The more she doted on him, the more he wanted to shrink away. She was smothering him with kindness, that's what it was.

She sensed his mild frustration with her. She opted to give him some space if that's what he wanted. "Well," she said lightly, "I'm hungry. I'm gonna go eat."

He took her arm as she started to stand. "I didn't mean to hurt your feelings."

"You didn't." It did hurt a little, but that was because she realized she'd been acting like a fool, fawning over him while he secretly hated it. She was glad he brought it to her attention. She grinned bravely at him. "It's about time you got off your lazy ass and made your own damned food." She stood and went towards the house, saying over her shoulder, "You probably know how to cook like a European chef, anyway, for all I know."

He called after her, "If it comes in a can."

SHE PULLED BACK FROM him over the next few days. She stopped offering her help when he didn't ask for it. She stopped hovering every time he got a "boo-boo." He continued his work in the basement and out on the back porch while she designed an inventory tracking spreadsheet on the computer. She was up at one-thirty in the morning typing in the update when she felt his hand on her shoulder. She looked up at him just as he set a sandwich and a glass of milk on the desk beside her. There was a warm look in his eyes she couldn't read or describe.

"You missed desert," he said. "Thought this might do." He rolled a chair from the other desk next to hers and sat. He read the screen. "What'cha got there?"

"The inventory spreadsheet."

"Impressive," he said.

"We're pretty well stocked up. We should get more toilet paper, though."

"Yeah. Don't know how long we'll be stuck here. Good idea."

"And, plastic bags. The thick kind, for garbage. To keep the bugs and the smell out."

"Yeah..." He was glad she was putting her energy into something besides him. That's what he wanted.

She noticed he was still wearing the same dirty undershirt he had been in all day. He smelled like sawdust and sweat. At least he had washed his hands. "How are the windows coming?"

"All done." He smiled tiredly. "Your mom's gonna hate this, but we gotta start on that basement door soon."

"In the kitchen... Yeah."

"After I build the new steps and the new entry to upstairs."

"Is Dad helping with that?"

"No. I got it."

"How's it going at the shooting range?"

"Well," he began with a grin, "I can point a gun without puking now." Natalie laughed. He continued, "My aim's a lot better." He smirked and added, "With the gun, not the barf." She laughed harder, but quietly so as not to wake Mom. He chuckled and pushed the sandwich towards her. "I bet you can't wait to eat now."

She saved and closed the program and took a bite of her sandwich. After swallowing, she told him, "I've been researching those ID chips they talked about on the radio last night. Pretty scary."

Coltan had been aware of the proposed subcutaneous identification program for years. He decided not to tell her that and instead asked, "Did you bookmark it?"

"Yeah."

"I want to see it. But, eat first."

"There's also stuff about the mords. Nothing official. Just people sharing their ideas. Some posted their own experiences with people that have it, and a bunch posted videos of them attacking and the cops taking them down. *Scary*! Somebody else was talking about some new military that's supposed to replace what we've got now. You ought to see this stuff." She turned to log on.

He brushed her hand away from the computer. "Eat first."

"No. Let me log on. You've got to see this."

"Afterwards," he said sternly.

"Remember that day in Baker Creek? Those soldiers? They weren't regular army. They're part of that new military. C'mon, Colt... we saw it for ourselves."

"Hey!" He gestured at the sandwich. "Eat that before it turns into salmonella or something."

"Okay, okay. You're so bossy." She took the sandwich and milk over to the couch, where she reclined and began to eat. "My back hurts, anyway. Too much time at the computer." She took a bite and chewed it, gestured at him with the sandwich. "This is yummy. Thanks."

Natalie shut down the computer at almost five in the morning. She and Coltan viewed graphic underground video of mords wreaking havoc in Europe and Canada, as well as in America. Natalie found and shared with Coltan informative articles and talk about the chips, the new military and the mords. There was so much more to read and investigate further, but too much for one sitting. As was always the case using the Internet for research, one site led to another to another to another, *ad infinitum*. It got to the point where they couldn't focus anymore. They were exhausted.

Coltan decided to go out back for a smoke before getting a nap. The sun was just rising in the cloudless sky, and the air was crisp and cold. He heard birds waking in the trees; saw a few grubbing in the garden. A deer came out of the woods into the clearing across from the house. He watched the deer, a beautiful buck with bulbous velvet coated antlers, as it grazed on foliage and wildflowers. The world seemed so peaceful.

There came a low humming from far in the distance. As it came closer, the sound thump-thump-thumped and shook the picnic table Coltan sat on. The military chopper was flying low and then gained altitude and veered northeast. Coltan ran to the east side of the porch and watched it. He heard the screen door slam, footsteps running. Natalie came up beside him. He pointed. They watched the chopper on its journey toward the mountain. It slowed just beyond the foothills, descended and disappeared behind the distant foliage between the hills. Then, more chopper sounds from the west. Three flew over the house and followed the path of the first. Like the first one, they disappeared at the same spot.

"Do you think it's Baker Creek?" Natalie asked.

His expression was as grim as his voice, "No doubt. No doubt at all."

CHAPTER 11

They found Beverly brewing a pot of coffee when they returned to the kitchen.

"Did you see it?" Natalie asked her.

There was worry in her eyes. "I saw it."

"Four of them," Coltan said. "I think they landed at Baker Creek."

"Is it starting, Mom?"

"It's getting close. What are you two doing up at this hour?"

"Research," Natalie said.

"Research?"

"About everything that's going on with the virus and what they're doing with the mords. You know—the military, Homeland Security and all that stuff."

Coltan interjected, "There's more, though. A lot more."

"I don't want to hear it right now." She turned on Natalie, her voice angry, "Why are you wasting your time on that?" The dark circles under her eyes and the slackness of her facial muscles clearly indicated her exhaustion. Coltan noticed her trembling hands as she reached for her coffee mug. She saw Coltan noticed the tremor and said directly to him, "I want you to work as fast as you can to finish securing this place. How much is left?"

"A lot," Coltan answered hesitantly.

She demanded impatiently, "How much is *a lot*?"

"Not more than I can handle." He wished he had a magic wand to make it all materialize. Until that magic wand was in his possession, he could only rely on his physical stamina and gut determination.

"How's the hand?" she asked him.

"Okay." It still hurt like hell whenever he lifted anything.

Beverly wasn't convinced. "You have to let Brian help you. You can't do it by yourself. We're running out of time."

"What are they doing up at Baker Creek?" Coltan asked.

"I don't know," Beverly said. "A rescue center, maybe. I don't know."

"They're not regular military," Natalie said. "They're something else."

"How do you know?"

Coltan jumped in with the answer. "We saw them at Baker Creek."

Her expression softened. She poured a cup of coffee and motioned them both to join her at the table. When they were all seated, she said, "Natalie, I need you to review the supplies, all the inventory. Note what we still need, or what you think we need more of. I also want you to harvest the garden and begin on the canning. Don't forget the fruit trees."

"I can't do that without you, Mom!"

"Yes, you can."

"I'll screw it up."

"We've canned together for the last ten years. You know how to do it."

"I'll screw it up," Natalie repeated.

"No, you won't."

Natalie took a breath for another round of protests. Coltan nudged her and shot her a stern look.

"Nat," Beverly said. "You can do this. You *have to* do this. I'm depending on you."

Natalie surrendered and stared down at the tabletop. She didn't feel competent, not at all. It was too important a task. If she messed up, the food would be worthless. They would starve because of her. She didn't want the responsibility. Not by herself. Not without her mother.

Beverly continued to address her, "That also means we need more jars. We also need three times as many lids, wax and seals. Put it on a list. You know where I keep the household card. Make a list and buy the rest of the supplies today. *Today*, Nat."

"I can't carry it all on my bike."

Beverly looked at Coltan. "Would there be time to take her sometime today?"

"Yeah," he answered with certainty. Natalie looked at him doubtfully. He tried to ignore her, and said to Beverly, "We'll figure it out."

"There's a store close by that carries it all."

"Okay," Coltan responded. "What else? Let's get this planned out."

"Are there any more supplies *you* need?" She was trying not to scream at the whole overwhelming mess. The conflict was in her voice, the slight trembling of her lips before she spoke, the fear in her eyes.

"No. We've got everything." Coltan said this as reassuringly as he could. "We're waiting on the chemical toilet to be delivered. It should be here any day, now."

"I'll grab more medical supplies." Beverly said this almost to herself, as if she was thinking. She asked Natalie, "Do we have enough bleach?"

"Two gallons."

"Get six more."

"Okay." She couldn't think why they required so much bleach.

"Large water containers. The kind with the spigots."

"Got four already."

"Get six more."

"Okay." She was still gazing at the tabletop, utterly overwhelmed and afraid.

"You should be writing this down."

Natalie looked up at her, her eyes blazing. "I got the spreadsheet. I can remember six gallons of bleach and six large water containers with spigots. I can remember the fucking jars and lids and wax."

Before Beverly could stop herself, she delivered the hard backhanded slap as a reflex. Natalie reeled back, her cheek stinging and her eyes tearing. Coltan pulled back from the table, stared at Beverly in disbelief. Without a word, Natalie slowly stood. Her jaw was set taunt in anger and tears of humiliation began to spill down her cheeks. She restrained her rage, left the kitchen. Beverly and Coltan heard the desk chair in the den roll back, the keyboard drawer slam open, and the click of the button on the computer.

Coltan murmured respectfully and barely above a whisper, "Ma'am..."

"She doesn't use that language with me." Beverly looked up at the ceiling. "Father, forgive me for hurting my daughter." She looked again at Coltan. "I need her to pull it together. We all do. She's been slacking off too much, these days." She took her coffee cup over to the sink and poured the whole thing into her travel mug. She grabbed her purse and laptop off the counter and headed for the door to the garage. "I have to get to work. Thanks for your help, Colt. You're a good boy."

Coltan seethed at the injustice he witnessed. Obviously, Beverly knew nothing about all the hours Natalie put into the spreadsheet, and the many short errands she had run on her bike to pick up the small, light items they would need. She didn't know Natalie had been tending the garden and doing all the cooking and cleaning. If she had known all that, she would have understood Natalie's frustration. Regardless, it kindled Coltan's anger when Beverly backhanded her. No one had been around to protect him when he was the target. He would not let this happen to Natalie. He would protect her, even if it meant invoking Beverly's wrath. He blocked her from opening the door to the garage.

"Bev..."

"I have to go."

"You shouldn't have hit her."

She looked away from him, "I forgot that you—"

"This isn't about me. You have no idea how hard she's been working. She's hardly had any sleep, and I don't know how she does it all. One thing I *do* know is she's scared to death. She needs your love, not the back of your hand."

Beverly regretted her actions, but she knew from experience Natalie would reject her apology. She knew from experience Natalie needed time to cool down. They both needed time to cool down.

"I have to go, Colt."

He moved aside, wishing she would look at him. "You stepped on *her* last nerve, too."

She turned away and set her coffee, purse and laptop on the counter. Of all the roles Beverly performed in her life, motherhood was the toughest, and she saw herself as a complete failure in that role. Immersed in her shame and frustration, she began to cry helplessly and bitterly.

Coltan placed his hand on her shoulder, and she turned to him and buried her face in his chest. This was something new to him, and he didn't know how to handle it. He utilized his *when in doubt* method and muttered humorously, "Damned women..."

Through her tears, she giggled appreciatively at his awkward comment. She pulled back from him and wiped her tears. "Thank you."

He handed Beverly her purse, coffee and laptop and opened the door for her. After she left, he stood there for a few minutes, evaluated the situation. He didn't know whether to try to comfort

Natalie or leave her alone to cool off. He felt no matter what action or inaction he took, it would be wrong.

A crash accompanied by the breaking of glass from the den startled him. Coltan crossed through the living room cautiously and leaned in the doorway to the den. Natalie had thrown a lamp across the room. She had thrown it against the fireplace mantle, and the impact had not only broken the lamp, but everything on the mantle as well and left a dent with a jagged scar at the edge of the mantle. The lamp lay in pieces, some on the brick, the rest on the carpet.

She stood with her back to the window, her eyes searching the interior of the room for something else to break—preferably, something her mother valued. She was trembling from head to toe, her face almost purple with rage.

"Nat..."

She spun and faced him. "Fuck off!"

"You can break everything in this room, and you won't feel any better. I *know*."

She charged out the entranceway, shoving him with one arm against the bookcase on her way out. She shoved him with such fury she sent him flying backwards off his feet. He fell against the solid oak shelves where a few of the books shook loose and tumbled to the floor. Coltan followed the books to the carpet. He sat there sprawled in a sitting position for a few moments, amazed and appalled by her display of temper. It did not help his frayed nerves, either, when she slammed the back door.

As soon as Brian came home, Coltan told him what happened. Brian found Natalie sitting in the farthest corner of the garden, sulking to herself and smoking one of Coltan's cigarettes. Coltan stole glances as he set the planks for the basement steps on the outside table for sawing. He was relieved to see Brian did not admonish Natalie for smoking. It surprised Coltan when Natalie gave the smoke to her father, and he took a puff. They sat in the dirt

154

together for a long time, talking and sharing the cigarette.

And, so the day went. The three of them worked together to get ahead on the preparations. Brian took Natalie for the supplies. They were gone longer than it should have taken, and Coltan assumed they had gone to lunch for some father-daughter quality time. Maybe he took her to the shooting range to release her pent-up hostility. As long as things calmed down, that's all that mattered. The afternoon saw Natalie harvesting the garden, and Brian and Coltan working together on the basement steps and the new basement entrance from the second floor.

IN THE VALLEY, THE mords were increasing in number. In the south end of Bonito Valle, the poor and the homeless armed themselves for the coming onslaught. They were the first ones to figure it out, and the first ones to realize the situation provided an opportunity to "clean house." While the mords, posing the most immediate danger, were priority, the pimps, the bangers, the drug dealers and the drug addicts were second on the list the south side populace marked for extermination. The South-Enders were ready for war.

Elsewhere in the valley, the mostly apathetic, self-absorbed and preoccupied populace finally realized the horror unfolding in their neighborhoods and work places was potentially more perilous than the tattered economy, the rise in violent crime, the gradual loss of privacy and personal liberties and then the resulting riots. Now there was an additional enemy to contend with and, while many opted to flee from the populated areas, many opted to bunker down to protect their homes and families.

At the Bujjet Mart along the freeway where the south side met the central area of town, frantic customers scurried about and filled shopping carts beyond capacity. Over in the tools and hardware section, Mario Rodriquez worked overtime to restock the shelves with rapidly diminishing must-haves that included Chinese and African-made power tools, hand tools, batteries and portable radios. The cheap plywood panels and shelving was already gone, and the customers yelled at him as if it was his fault. To make matters worse, a majority of his fellow employees stopped showing up for work, and this tripled Mario's responsibilities. Finally fed up and shaking from the stress, Mario took temporary refuge in the massive stock room.

He noticed someone had left the key in the padlock on the door to the electrical access space. The sight of it inspired him to re-evaluate his last-resort plan to bunker with Mama and Rosa inside that space between the walls, should their home become unsafe. The frantic behavior of the shoppers at his store and the increasing violence in his neighborhood convinced him his back-up plan was a good idea and he should take this opportunity to secure the space. He looked around and saw he was alone save for the surveillance camera that faced the loading dock doors and pivoted to view the sales floor entrance. Security was too overwhelmed out on the sales floor with shoplifters and fistfights; they would not return to the surveillance monitors for at least another day. Under normal conditions, they seldom paid much attention to the monitors, anyway. The boy grabbed the stepladder and climbed up beside the camera, took his box cutter out of his pocket and severed the connection.

Quickly, he returned to the electrical access door, unlocked the padlock and took a second look inside. There was enough room. With the rest of his coworkers busy with the mayhem on the sales floor, it was the perfect time to toss his emergency supplies in there. He hurried to a corner where he had concealed his stash inside a giant cardboard box marked, *"defective – for return."* In a rushed frenzy, he removed the box and tossed the stowed sleeping bags, food and two cases of water into the access space. The final items were a large first-aid kit, two battery powered camp lanterns, a radio and extra batteries, a twelve-pack of toilet paper, a box of heavy-duty plastic trash bags, a bucket, and a new toilet seat. He threw it all in there, replaced the padlock, locked it and put the key in his pocket.

WHILE ON A RETURN TRIP to the garden, Natalie saw six additional military helicopters. This time, they were heading for Reyton. She wondered if they were planning on using the railroad to move people into the rescue centers. The vacant land in the foothills at Reyton's north end would be a logical place for them to set up the centers. The trains went right through there. The more she thought about it, the more she thought she was right.

BEVERLY BROUGHT HOME supper from the Dairy Delight and some *oops, it musta fell into my pockets* items from the hospital. Over the last few days, she had managed to incrementally steal additional medical supplies, and today's booty found their way into the extra clothing duffle she kept in her locker. She felt no guilt about it. There was talk the military would take over the hospital, and they would restock it with official *yoo-ess-gover-ment* medical supplies purchased with her tax dollars.

As Brian removed the duffle from the trunk, he urged Beverly to open up a dialogue with Natalie, settle their spat and smooth things over. Upon return to the kitchen, she saw Natalie was still canning fruit and had taken up all the counter space with the supplies. Beverly set the food bags on the kitchen table. She glanced at Natalie and saw her daughter purposely avoided acknowledging her. Beverly feared an apology would only result in another confrontation.

Brian transferred the medical supplies into the bin and slid it back into the utility closet. He nodded at Beverly, silently encouraged her to speak with Natalie.

Beverly placed her arm around Natalie's shoulders. "You're doing a great job. I'm sorry about this morning. I didn't realize how hard you've been working, how tired you must be."

"Same here," Natalie mumbled.

"We're short-staffed at the hospital. I have to go right back." The hammering from Coltan's efforts in the basement reminded her how close they were to the inevitable. Impatiently, she turned her daughter to face her. "Listen, Nat... We can't waste time quarreling. Things have gotten really bad. The casualties are stacking up in the morgue. My last patient was a homeless guy who told me the homeless community's been eliminating the sick in their groups. That means there are at least a hundred, maybe two hundred or more, contagious corpses out there. It means anyone who comes into contact with them will be infected. It means those newly infected will be out there spreading the virus. The virus has mutated. It spreads faster now."

"What about the vaccine the news reported?"

"There is no vaccine. There's nothing to stop this. We're running out of time. Please, Natalie, please put your anger aside. Forgive me for hitting you. Forgive me, and let's put it behind us. I love you and I want you to be safe. I want us all to be safe."

"It's all forgiven." She hugged her mother for a long moment, grateful Mom had taken the time to address her with the truth as an adult. "I love you, Mom." In the same moment, she imagined the chaotic and dangerous scenario at Bonito Valle Community Hospital, all the injured and infected in the ER and exam rooms, all the infected employees who did not yet know they were infected and doomed. Natalie wished her mother did not have to return there.

"Be careful at the hospital."

Beverly kissed her cheek, reluctantly released her. "I have to go now."

Brian accompanied Beverly out to the garage, and they paused beside her car. "It came over the scanner the military's taken over all the gas and charging stations. There's been some altercations with civilians over it, some shootings. You be careful, Bev. It's getting desperate. There are gangs hijacking cars. You got your firearm handy?"

"Always. Don't worry about me. Make sure Natalie keeps the house locked up." Beverly's eyes watered, and she stifled a sob. "I wish I didn't have to go back!"

He tenderly stroked her face and kissed her. In the next instant, he embraced her. "Same here."

AFTER NATALIE FINISHED canning all the fruit and the jars were cooling on the counter, she decided to take a break. She put on her sweater, grabbed her portafone and went out on the back steps of the porch while Dad and Coltan ate burgers and fries in the basement. Coltan had left a half-finished cigarette in the ashtray. Natalie took it and lit it with the matches she had stashed in her pocket. She sat down and smoked, and felt tired. The soreness in her feet, legs and back only added to her fatigue.

Many concerns floated through her mind and, besides the immediate issues at home, she worried about Carolyn. Carolyn had promised to call or message her as soon as she arrived at her family's cabin. The promised call had not come, nor had the message. Natalie's subsequent calls and messages to her remained unanswered. It was not normal for Carolyn to be incommunicado. Natalie tried Carolyn's PF number again only to reach her voice mail again. She chose not to leave a message this time and instead tried their cabin number. No answer.

In a while, Coltan joined her on the steps. As usual, he was all sawdust and sweat. He lit an after dinner cigarette and gazed out into the valley where streetlights and traffic lights competed with the lights of the hospital to sweeten the view.

"Spare one?" Natalie asked.

He said, "I wish I had never started smoking. Why do you want to start?"

She ran her hands through her hair, shook the strands through her fingers and let it all fall wherever it landed. She looked at him with sad eyes. "Let me have a drag."

"Jeez..." He relented and gave her the cigarette. "Don't blame me when you're sucking on an oxygen tank."

She took a drag and lamented, "I can't get hold of Carolyn. She promised to call." After that, she stared sullenly off into the distance. Coltan's silence indicated he shared her concern for Carolyn's safety. He put his arm around her shoulders, pulled her to him and gently kissed her forehead. She didn't move away. Instead, she froze, unsure how to react. Finally, she asked, "What did you do that for?"

He had not moved, either. His lips were still close to her forehead. When he whispered back, his breath tickled her skin, "I felt you needed it." He took the cigarette from her fingers, bent and looked into her face, his own face close to hers. Still whispering, he told her, "Carolyn's okay. We'll all get through this."

She felt her eyes sting, and tried to look away. He gently turned her face to him. He wouldn't let her hide. There was hopelessness in her face and in her eyes. It seemed like something was dying inside her. He knew that feeling well and now he felt it from her.

Natalie realized she was beginning to soften, and she did not want to cry in his arms. She reinforced her emotional wall and changed the subject. "How's it going down there?"

"Good," he said. "We got the upstairs floor to saw over the stairway. We're gonna do that tomorrow. The stairs are pretty much done." Something came to mind and he smiled. "Hey... Did you know they have wine down there?"

She nodded. "Uh-huh."

"Shelves of it. I didn't know your parents drank."

"They have it with dinner sometimes."

The sound of a helicopter in the distance drew their attention. They squinted and strained to watch its course in the night sky.

"Heading for Reyton." Natalie remarked.

"What?" He could not disguise the alarm that gripped him.

"There were a bunch earlier. Reyton's got the open space and the railroad. Think about it."

This greatly disturbed him, "Aw, man..."

"You got friends there?"

"Yeah." At this, he stood, watched the sky over the valley. She stood also, studied the alarm and worry on his face. She noticed, too, he was clenching and unclenching his fists. His breathing quickened. Without another word, he turned abruptly on the step and raced up onto the porch and into the kitchen. As the screen door slammed, she caught sight of him briefly, bounding with panicked urgency down the basement stairs.

DOWN IN THE BASEMENT, it took everything for Brian to calm him down as Coltan spilled the story about Brenda. He wanted to take the Harley to Reyton that very moment to snatch her away from her overbearing parents. Her parents hated him and forbid their daughter to see him again after his arrest for assault. They knew the true story, the reason Coltan had beaten the man, but they only believed their own perception that Coltan had a short fuse and was dangerous. Now, Brenda was trapped there in Reyton without him to protect her from the coming horrors.

"That's why I gotta go *now*," he told Brian. "Before it's too late!"

"And, then what?" Brian asked.

"I want to get her out of there!"

"And, then what?" Brian asked again. "Bring her here?"

"She could help," Coltan said. "There's a lot she can do. She'd pull her own weight. She would." He was at the pleading point by now, everything else in his life forgotten.

"What if her parents won't let her go?" Brian waved Coltan over to join him on the bottom step. "What will you do? Kidnap her?"

"If I have to!" Coltan refused to sit, but stood swaying from side to side like a caged lion.

"No," Brian said, using his *Sensible Dad* tone of voice. "You can't kidnap her."

"Yeah, I can!"

"What if she doesn't want to go? Have you thought of that?"

"She loves me. I love her." The pleading evolved into desperation, "She'll go with me. I know she will."

"And, what about her parents?" Brian suggested patiently. "Have you thought about what it would do to them if she left them at a time like this?"

"Screw them!"

"Son..." He knew well what being in love did to make a man feel invincible. He knew also the primal, hard-wired need to protect the one he loved. He understood it well. However, Coltan had not considered how it would affect everyone else involved. "A father and mother will fight to the death to protect their daughter. If you go up there like *this*, they'll have you arrested. Then what? Don't forget, you're eighteen now. No more Juvy. You're stuck in jail while all hell breaks loose. Stuck in jail, alone, away from those who love you. Is that what you want?"

He bowed his head. "No..."

"Think it through, Son." He put his arm around his shoulders. "What you might gain and what you could lose."

The words came softly and with persistence, "I love her."

"And, *we* love *you*." In the next second, Coltan gazed at him with surprise. In the second after that, his expression changed to one of doubt. Brian told him sternly, "You're part of our family now. What does it take to convince you?"

"I..." All he could do was sit there and stammer. In all the time he had spent with the Danburys, it never crossed his mind they had adopted him as their own. He had never dared to entertain even the hint of such an idea.

"Did you think our plan was to work you to death and then throw you out the door?"

"No, Sir. I never thought about it. I don't know. I... I guess I've made it a habit not to expect anything. Nothing ever worked out—mostly my own damned fault."

"Well..." Brian said, "That's rather an insult to us—and you—don't you think?"

He stared at his boots, a wave of conflicting thoughts and emotions splashing around in his mind. He finally said, "I didn't mean that. It's just what I've come to expect. " He stopped himself there, feeling anything else he said would only come out as confusing to both himself and Brian.

"Wait until morning. Cool off. Think it through." Brian was not aware how tightly he was holding on to Coltan. However, he was fully aware of how much he had come to love the boy, to consider him as his own son, even. The possibility of losing him now was unthinkable. He could feel Coltan trembling, and said, "I know you'll still want to see her. You'll want to know she's safe. That's fine. But, keep your head. Don't do anything that will get you arrested. If you end up in jail, and it all breaks loose before I can come get you...

Think about that. I don't want to lose you. *We* don't want to lose you."

"I guess I can be pretty stupid sometimes."

Brian smiled, "No. You're the brave knight who will go through hell and back to save his beloved maiden."

"You'd do the same for Bev."

"Yeah."

Natalie appeared at the top of the stairs. She saw them and called down, "Everything okay?"

"Yes, Precious."

"There's two burgers left. You want them?"

"We'll get them in a while." He then turned and saw her. Her posture was that of an exhausted and frazzled old lady. It hurt him to see her that way. "I want you to go to bed and get a good night's sleep."

"Colt?" she said, "Are you okay?"

"Yeah," he answered. "Get some sleep."

Brian met her up at the basement doorway. "Crisis averted," he whispered. "You need some sleep."

"So do you." She glanced down at Coltan, then again to her father. "What happened?"

"He's alright."

"What happened?"

"He's worried about someone. That's all."

"Who?"

"Natalie... Stop. Stop right now. Let him be. No more questions."

She still wanted to know, but respected her father's decision to protect whatever confidence Coltan had shared. Instead of pursuing it further, she asked, "You gonna get some sleep?"

"In a while." He hugged her tightly and wished he could somehow erase all the terrible events unfolding in the world. He'd lost a lot of sleep worrying for her safety if something happened to him. He had also spent a lot of time in prayer after losing that sleep, placing it all into God's hands, remembering the promise God made that he would protect his own. It was now Brian's habit to discuss it all with God every time he laid his head down. Sleep came easier, and his dreams were often about angels. He wanted angels to surround his daughter at all times. "I love you so much," he said earnestly.

"I love you, too, Dad."

When she left them, Brian returned downstairs. Coltan had been watching them from the bottom step, and he realized how fiercely Brian loved his daughter.

"Let's call it a night," Brian told him. "How about we get a few hours and set our alarms for, say, four o'clock?"

"Sounds okay."

"Promise me you won't take off tonight."

"I promise."

"You sure?"

"Yes, Sir. I thought about what you said." He stood, and added, "I can't promise I'll get any sleep, though."

"Talk to God about it after you lie down. You'll sleep."

Coltan decided that was good advice. "Okay." They started up the stairs together. "And, Sir?" Brian looked at him and Coltan continued, "About Natalie..."

"Yeah?"

"I'll be here for her."

CHAPTER 12

At six-thirty in the morning, Natalie awoke to the whine of an electric saw coming from Coltan's room. She threw on a pair of old jeans and a tee shirt and padded barefooted toward the noise.

Her dad was sawing through the wall on the left side of the large room. The saw grunted and made a grinding sound when it met the stud and began to slice it. He had already cut the other side of the section. The wall was starting to tip over him, and Natalie feared it would break and fall on him. She sprinted and braced the piece. He noticed her out of the corner of his eye and finished. After he shut the saw off, they eased the section down together.

He took off the protective glasses. "Good morning."

"You should have waited for Colt." She turned to leave, "I'll go get him."

"He's gone right now." That stopped her. He continued, "He went to Reyton."

"For how long?"

"He'll be back in a few hours." He handed her the sledgehammer, "Want to take out your frustrations?"

"I'd love to!" It was heavy in her eager hands.

"Go on the other side there and hammer out the drywall."

She grinned mischievously. He responded by offering her the safety glasses, which she took and put on.

NOTHING SEEMED AMISS in the small town of Reyton. The

commuters who worked in Bonito Valle headed eastbound to catch the two-lane road that led to the freeway. The locals were opening up shop. Coltan was careful to mind the speed limit as he rolled into town, knowing the Reyton police were ticket-happy, and he didn't want the hassle. Going slower also afforded him the opportunity to check things out for anything unusual.

He spotted the theater on his right, a place of many happy memories, most of them to do with *her*. Besides the railroad history, this theater was the town of Reyton's other claim to fame. As the only local showplace that consistently booked well-known entertainers, it attracted audiences from all over the area and beyond. The marquee announced a performance by a country western star he'd heard of, the show scheduled for Friday and Saturday nights. During the off-season The Reyton Historical Theater Guild booked local musicians and artists. At Christmastime, the Reyton Concert Orchestra opened the holiday season with a four-performance weekend show right after Thanksgiving, and then the local production of *The Nutcracker* performed until the weekend before Christmas.

This was where he met her a few days before Thanksgiving the previous year. He was on the set-building crew for the Reyton Concert Orchestra's show. She had shown up the week before opening night every morning promptly at ten to rehearse at the grand piano. The crew liked to listen to her play as they worked, even though most of them hated that kind of music. However, Coltan was enraptured, especially when she rehearsed the Chopin and Rachmaninoff pieces. At the time, he had never heard Classical music before, and he found it spoke to his soul in a way nothing else had ever done. He stopped going out for his cigarette break with the guys, preferring to stay and listen to the marvelous sounds from her piano. It was on the third day when she noticed he had stayed to listen. When they finally spoke, she had confided to him she was a nervous wreck, that this was her first featured performance with the orchestra in public. She wanted to rehearse there instead of at home because she wanted to become accustomed to the feel of the place. She hoped her familiarity with the energy of the building would help calm her nerves. He found himself full of questions about the music, about her.

On the fifth day, he took her to dinner at the swankest place in town; he even purchased a suit for the occasion. It was during that meal when his ignorance of table manners became apparent. Even the purpose of the cloth napkin eluded him and he set it aside with the thought it was there only as table decor. Mom and Richard had never bothered with napkins, and he had always wiped his mouth on his arm or his tee shirt. To his delight, Brenda viewed his lack of sophistication as charming. To spare him further embarrassment, she discretely guided him.

She found him adorable, and was impressed with his sincere appreciation of the music and her talent. In addition to music, she had many interests. The more she expressed these to Coltan, the more they found they had in common. The things they did not have in common didn't matter. She said he made her feel like a real person, instead of a marketable commodity, which is how she thought her parents saw her.

On opening night, he was with her in the wings as the musicians were taking their places on the stage. Her knees were shaking, and her hands were sweating. He told her if she performed anything like he had heard her rehearse, she would have the audience in the palm of her hand. Following her first flawless solo just before intermission, she received a standing ovation. When the curtain came down, she bounded over to him and embraced him, laughing and crying at the same time. At the end of the show, she received another standing ovation during the curtain call.

It was the first time in his life he had experienced the complete joy of overflowing pride and happiness for another human being. It felt incredible.

He met her parents for the first time that night after the show. It was then he discovered they had lived ten years in France before returning to America. They had looked down their noses at him as he conversed with them in his *Louisiana French*, and made it a point not to invite him along for the after show dinner. He knew then it would be an uphill battle to gain their trust and respect.

Brenda met with him whenever she had the free time. Usually, it was for coffee, lunch, or dinner. Sometimes it was enough just to stroll through the snow together. It wasn't long before they retired to his small apartment now and then. He found her fascinating, exciting and adventurous, and their lovemaking lasted for hours. Their lovemaking even took place over sumptuous meals in fancy restaurants, with foreplay consisting of sexual longings and intentions whispered in French across the table. She didn't care that he lagged behind her in age by two years. He had the soul of a mature man, she had told him. She didn't care about his background. What mattered was the fact he was reaching beyond it.

He slowed the Harley as he neared the intersection of Main and Boyd. At the railroad station at the right side of the road, soldiers transferred cargo from boxcars to covered trucks. It dismayed him to find Natalie's suspicions correct.

When the oncoming traffic cleared, he took the left onto Boyd. This took him into the residential district, but there were also some small boutique type stores and a coffee shop. The coffee shop held memories, too. He decided to slow below the speed limit to get a good look at everything.

The first thing he noticed was the four police cars and two ambulances near the front entrance. A large pane of shattered glass at the entrance side of the restaurant spilled sharp glistening fragments into the street. Coltan surmised someone had either fallen or been thrown through the glass. The paramedics were loading someone into the ambulance, the body covered with a sheet, the blood seeping through. He pulled over at this point and watched from the other side of the road, the engine still running. He saw the second gurney emerge. The patient on this gurney was alive, but was a bloody mess and appeared to be having a seizure.

Nothing could have prepared Coltan for the next thing that happened.

The patient on the gurney, a man, bolted upright, grabbed the closest paramedic, and bit through the side of his face, tearing off a slab of skin and tissue. Two of the policeman raced over, pulled the chewing man off, and subdued him while the second paramedic and one of the paramedics from the first crew strapped the patient down. The bitten paramedic held the spurting side of his face while succumbing to hysterics. A minute after that, two military jeeps pulled up and blocked Coltan's view as a third ambulance arrived.

It was after that when Coltan noticed the line of cars, the drivers jockeying to be first out of the parking lot, their faces pale, their eyes wild with panic and their mouths agape with shock. When the lead car pulled out and turned to go in the opposite direction, Coltan noticed what appeared to be fresh blood smeared around the handle of the driver's side door.

He had seen enough. He sped out onto the road and reached Magnolia Avenue in two minutes. There he made a left. It was a quiet upscale neighborhood with wide streets and large houses sporting broad, neatly manicured lawns and old oak and maple trees. There wasn't a single magnolia tree in sight.

Flowers bordered the walkways and the driveway of Brenda's house. The flowers were overgrown and full of ugly spent blooms; that was the first thing Coltan noted as he slowed the Harley and pulled into the driveway. He then saw the gardener had not arrived to mow the expansive overgrown lawn. Coltan knew Brenda's appearances-obsessed mother would have never neglected the landscaping, and this struck him as a bad omen. He shut the engine off and put the kickstand down, took off his helmet. He listened. The only sounds were birds chirping and sirens in the distance. Ordinarily, dogs would be howling at the sirens, but there were no sounds from any dogs at all. He returned his attention to the house, expected to see the maid appear inquisitively at the big bay window, but no hand parted the curtains. He kept his radar up as he walked to the door and rang the bell. There came no answer. He knocked, listened and waited, knocked again, listened and waited some more. With justified curiosity, he lifted the mail slot cover and peered inside. There were scattered sales flyers and envelopes on the custom imported floor tiles. Beyond the foyer, the dark, regally furnished home seemed to mourn the absence of life-affirming energy.

An image came to his mind of the parents dead, victims of mords, and Brenda hiding, possibly injured, somewhere in the house. The image made his stomach twist inside him and his heart race with consternation.

He hurried back to the Harley and gazed up at her bedroom window above the huge garage. The closed curtains blocked his view of the interior. He called for her. Called again and again. No answer. No sign of life. It occurred to him to look around the side of the house where the driveway wound toward the back of the garage. Their motor home was gone.

His stomach twisted again inside him, and he felt his entire body suddenly flush with heat. As the birds sang and more sirens screamed through the air, he bent and vomited at the base of the hibiscus bush.

WORKING TOGETHER, BRIAN and Natalie demolished what remained of the wall that separated Coltan's room from the smaller room that served as access from the hallway to the attic. They planned to eliminate the door that led to this room from the hallway. Brian had unfolded the attic stairs from the ceiling weeks ago, and the bottom step rested on the wood paneled floor four feet from the hallway entrance door. The vast attic itself had a finished floor, and had served as storage for a few off-season items and discarded furniture.

Brian saw Coltan had already installed the sliding panels on the windows of the attic. He checked them out, sliding them all back and forth. They moved smoothly and quietly. He was impressed with Coltan's work. He pointed to a far corner and told Natalie, "The chemical toilet will go here, with a wall for privacy, of course. If the plumbing goes to hell or we can't get down to the second floor for any reason, we'll use it then." He strolled over to another wall. "Over here we're going to install a storage closet for all the provisions, mostly the paper items. But during the winter, we can store a good share of the boxed and canned goods here. They'll go back down to the basement in summer."

"Okay..." He hadn't asked Natalie for her opinion, so she offered none. It bothered her immensely their refuge and the impending situation that would require it was this close to becoming a reality.

He moved to a wall with a window on the north side as he told her, "This area over here will be walled-off for privacy as a room for your mother and me. You and Colt will share the main room, which will double as common area for all of us." He saw the disapproving expression on her face. "We have to make sacrifices, Nat. You can change clothes down in the access room. It'll be a lot bigger. Or, you can use the storage room to change. I'll try to find a screen of some kind to separate your sleeping areas. You'll still have some privacy. The bathroom in Colt's room will be the bathroom for all of us down there."

"Okay." It was all she could say. Then a thought, "How long do you think we'll be up here?"

"I don't know." His expression was apologetic. "There's a rumor that a group of Christians have been working on a refuge up in the mountains. I've been trying to find out if it's true. Mitchell said he heard about it, too, so he's working on it. If it turns out to be true, Mitch will give me the coordinates, and we'll head up there right away. However, if the Feds block the roads, or if winter comes before we get the info we'll have to wait until it's safe to travel. Till then, we'll bunker down here."

"What if it doesn't exist? We can't live like this forever."

"I don't know. All we can do is put this in God's hands."

For the first time in her life, Natalie distrusted her father. His plan was half-cocked at best. As far as putting it in God's hands—she didn't trust that either. Where was God in all of this? Why wasn't he stopping it?

"Dad... please. Tell me what you *do* know... About what's happening out there."

"The infected are the most immediate danger," he answered. "There are more of them every day. Once the infected are eliminated, then we'll have the military to contend with."

"You know about it. You know they're not our army anymore."

"I don't know who they are. I don't know where they came from or who they're working for."

"Why isn't our government stopping them?"

"They're part of our government now."

"What?"

"Our president and all our elected officials stopped working for America years ago," he said. "They serve only as a façade to keep the masses ignorant and complacent."

"Have they been chipped already?"

He was surprised she had heard about the covert program. It was only last week when Beverly discovered the proof of the government's biometric Residence, Education, Financial, Employment, Health and Location Program, also known as REFEHL and pronounced *Reffel*. Up until recently, the general public resisted implantation, although many had embraced it as a necessity as well as a convenience in the conduction of their day-to-day activities, especially commerce. The inventers of the REFEHL chip touted it as hack proof.

Now, in response to the mord maker virus epidemic, the Feds had delivered a batch of "vaccine" to all medical facilities. The vaccines arrived preloaded in special syringes, and every hospital and clinic came under order to open vaccination stations to the public. During a rare lull, Beverly had suspiciously checked a dozen of the vaccines under a microscope. Every one contained nothing but distilled water and a tiny REFEHL chip.

"Did your mother tell you about that?"

"I heard about it on one of those radio shows Colt listens to. There was also something on the Internet, but it's been pulled since then. So... is it true? Have the government guys been chipped?"

"Yeah."

"And, we're next. That's why we have to hide." There was a subtle glint of rage in her eyes, the same as he had seen in rape victims. She then said, "The Beast has been here all along."

"For maybe about twelve decades," he responded. "Putting it all into place secretly and gradually. Using human nature as the fuel to fire its engine, gaining converts to its way of thinking without them even realizing it."

"Why didn't somebody notice?"

"You know how a plant grows. If you sit and watch it every second of every day, you never see it growing. That's because it's growing so slowly, we can't see it. Remember those films where they show a plant's growth in fast-forward? It's easy to see it grow, then. Right?" She nodded, and he continued, "It's full grown now."

His portafone rang. He recognized the number, and answered. After listening to the caller he asked, "Did you talk to her?" The reply drew his sympathy. "I'm sorry. Okay. Be careful. See you soon." He flipped it shut and replaced it on his belt. "Colt's on his way."

"Who did he go to see?"

"A friend."

"Who?" She could be annoyingly inquisitive.

"It's Colt's business, not yours."

She glanced down at the floor, and then she went to one of the windows and peered out. It was another clear and cool day, and a little breezy. She longed to be reliving that pleasant day with Coltan in Baker Creek. On the other hand, she wanted to stop time and live only in that moment when he pulled her close and kissed her forehead, gazing at her with those dark blue eyes full of love and care. The memory faded quickly as she realized, with sickening clarity, she had misread his affection toward her. Someone else claimed his heart. Whoever she was, Natalie hated her.

Her dour expression and suddenly slumped shoulders told him what he hoped was not true, but he asked her anyway, "Are you falling for him?"

"No," she said quickly. "I like him okay. He's not my type."

He forgave her dishonesty. In an odd way, he was grateful, as his daughter had never before shown interest in boys. Additionally, her lack of interest in her femininity, her lack of interest in all the things girls her age were normally interested in sometimes concerned him. On the other hand, he realized her feelings for Coltan could pose a problem. In all the time Coltan had spent with her, Brian had never seen him behave in any way toward her other than as a friend. He did not seem interested in her as anything other than a friend. He wondered if Coltan perhaps had said or done something Natalie had misinterpreted. They had spent a lot of time together, much of it alone with each other. Something might have occurred, something

Natalie mistook for romantic interest. It made him regret he and Beverly had not discussed these things with her.

"Natalie," he said. "Talk to me?"

"About what?"

Her innocent act didn't fool him. Brian approached the subject gently and supportively. "Him. You like him. You like him a lot, don't you?"

Her cheeks flushed red. The sudden lump in her throat trapped her confession.

He sighed and wished Beverly was home. This was something more appropriate for Beverly to handle. But she had never handled much of anything when it came to Natalie's issues. Perhaps that was the root of the problem.

His portafone rang again. The police department summoned him back to work.

"What about Mom?" Natalie asked. "When's she coming home?"

"I'm not sure. They've also got her covering the ER. It's getting bad there." Wishing he had used the word "busy" instead of "bad," he tried to soften her resulting fear, "They've added extra security guards. She's safe. She'll be home later."

He secretly doubted Beverly would come home soon. Although the hospital was the front line, it also seemed to be Bev's escape from the problems at home. It was easier for her to deal with trauma patients than the emotional trauma her daughter was experiencing. Additionally, he and Bev had been seeing little of each other lately. They were becoming strangers. They used their bed only for sleep, the both of them too exhausted to make the effort. He missed her and longed for things to return to normal.

AFTER HER FATHER LEFT, Natalie gathered up the pieces of drywall and deposited them in the giant bin they rented for the construction refuse. It took three trips. She had no idea drywall was so heavy. After that, she went over to the Spencers' porch and checked on Muffy's food and water. The food was gone, and the water was low. She refilled both, calling for Muffy in the process. The dog never showed.

After brewing a fresh pot of coffee, she started on more of the canning. It would be the vegetables today, and she would start with the string beans.

As the string beans cooled in their jars on the counter, she decided to go out on the back porch for a break. She sat down on the bottom step and lit a cigarette she had stolen from Coltan the night before. She found she enjoyed smoking, and it no longer made her feel dizzy. The sensation of the smoke hitting the back of her throat was pleasurable, and she now thought she understood why people enjoyed the habit.

She heard barking from the clearing in front of the woods way off in the distance. It sounded like a small dog. She stood and looked, but it was too far to see well enough. The barking came again, this time accompanied by that of other dogs. She trudged quickly through the yard toward the gully that separated the clearing from her property line. When she reached the edge of the gully she squinted and scanned the area. A small white something moved in the low dry grass. It jumped up, and she saw another dog, a black one that was a little bit larger than Muffy. They seemed to be playing. She called out, "Muffy!" The dog ignored her and kept playing. Again she called out, "Muffy! Muffy, come here." Both dogs ceased and looked at her, their noses twitching, smelling the air. "Come here, Muffy. Come home." They stayed frozen, both dogs watching her. In a moment, many other dogs emerged from the woods, their eyes on her. They all looked thin and dirty. The black dog turned and ran back to them. It stood with the pack and watched her. Then Muffy turned and joined the pack, and they all returned into the woods. "So, that's where she is." Natalie stood there for a long time watching the woods and enjoying her cigarette.

She thought Coltan would be relieved to know the little dog was still alive.

The wind picked up, and it made the screen door back at the porch slam shut. She remembered closing it, and thought she must not have latched it. She snuffed out the cigarette in the dirt and returned to the house. There was too much to do today to waste time chasing after Muffy. Besides that, after two cups of coffee, she had to pee.

She locked the screen door, went into the living room and started up the stairs. It startled her and stopped her midway when something fell and broke in the den next to the staircase. She turned and looked, taking two steps down in the process.

Her first thought was Coltan had returned. However, she had not heard his motorcycle.

What followed gave no time for a second thought.

A man emerged from the den. His face was familiar, but she couldn't place him. He was an old man, tall and thin, with wild gray hair sticking up in all directions. His clothing was torn and dirty. Her eyes widened and her heart quickened as she saw the dried blood on his shirt. It was a lot of blood. There was some blood still at the corners of his lips and on his chin. His hands were blood stained. His eyes, dead of emotion, met hers. His lips curled up, and he growled softly.

She fought panic and slowly took two backward steps up. She didn't take her eyes off his.

He slowly made a half-circle to the foot of the staircase; his eyes still pinned on hers. The growl became louder, and only paused when he licked his lips and took a deep breath.

She glanced quickly at the locked gun safe in the living room. She couldn't get to the key hidden in the bookcase. For a moment, she was angry with Dad for not allowing her to keep a gun in her room. That would have been easy to get. It was then she remembered Dad always kept a second gun in his room on the nightstand at his side of the bed. She looked back at the intruder and wondered if she could outrun him.

Her heart pounded. She feared the man could hear it. Her breathing quickened, and she could feel herself shaking. Again, she willed herself not to panic, knowing panic was her enemy, even as this mord was her enemy. The adrenalin kicked in against her best efforts to suppress it. She dashed up the stairs and into her parents' room, rolled on the bed to her Dad's side, and found the gun next to the landline phone. In one move, she grabbed the phone and the gun and crouched between the bed and the wall. She released the safety and pulled back the hammer. Watching the doorway, she dialed 911 and waited for the operator. It rang twice before Dispatch picked up.

"Nine-one-one. What is your emergency?"

"I got a mord in the house!" she whispered.

"A what?"

"One of the infected!"

"Alright, ma'am. Stay calm..."

"Listen to me!" Natalie hissed, "I'm alone in the house. He's in here. Coming up the stairs. I'm armed."

"Do you have a way out?"

"No! Sonofabitch! Get somebody here now!"

"Don't hang up. Help's coming. Stay on the line with me."

The man's footsteps drew closer. She set the receiver on the floor. He moved slowly, his eyes darting about, searching the hallway. He tilted his head and sniffed the air. He found her scent and turned toward the doorway of the room. She bolted to her knees, rested her forearms on the mattress and took aim as he started toward her.

She fired. The bullet hit him precisely in his heart. He stood for a moment, staring at her, and then he put his hand slowly to his heart. Fresh blood spurted and then a consistent vertical flow down his shirt spread to the waistband of his pants. He fell to his knees, and then he fell sideways onto the carpeted floor of the hallway.

She waited, panting with fear, expecting him to get up. Her hands trembled as she tightened her grip around the gun. She was determined to shoot him again if he moved. But he didn't move, didn't make a sound, didn't appear to be breathing.

From the receiver on the floor, the Dispatch operator questioned, "Ma'am? Ma'am? Pick up. Ma'am?"

Her eyes riveted to the dead man on the floor, she picked up the receiver and spoke into it. She had to catch her breath before she replied, and even then the words came out labored, "I just shot him."

"Is he still alive?"

"I don't think so." She heard the Harley pull in, and at the same time heard sirens.

"They should be there in a minute. Are you alright?"

"Yes." *Not really.*

The garage door rolled up, making a groan, and the Harley was loud in the empty garage as it pulled in. She heard the engine cut out and the garage door descend. In the next second, she tried to remember if she had seen a second mord come out of the den. She couldn't remember. The fear gripped her there may be another one in the house, and Coltan was on his way in.

Dispatch came back, "Ma'am?"

She heard the garage door to the kitchen open and shut. She heard Coltan's steps on the floor, then much quieter when he reached the carpet. Dispatch would have to wait.

"Colt?" She found it hard to yell with any volume due to her distressed respiration.

"Natalie?"

"Mord," she yelled as loud as she could. "There's a mord up here. There might be another one down there. Be careful!"

The sirens were louder, nearer.

"Ma'am?"

She ignored the operator as Coltan bounded up the stairs. She couldn't see him, but she could hear him. "Be careful!" she yelled again.

Coltan appeared clutching the poker from the fireplace in both hands. He backed up against the wall when he saw the dead man lying there in a pool of blood. A strong odor arose from the body, a strange pungent combination of rot-soaked earth and the metallic odor of raw blood.

"He's dead," Natalie said. "I shot him."

Coltan looked across at her half-draped over the side of the bed with the gun trained on the doorway. Her face was ashen, her eyes big.

"The police are there." Dispatch again, "Ma'am?"

Natalie picked up the receiver and spoke into it, "Thank you."

"Is there someone else in the house?"

"Yes. My friend just got here. We're alright."

The dispatcher advised her, "Officers are pulling up. Please set your weapon down."

Natalie set the landline back in the cradle. She would keep her gun ready although she knew it was procedure to set it aside.

Police cars accompanied by an ambulance sped to a stop at the curb in front of the house. The sirens ceased.

Coltan reminded her, "Put the gun down, Nat."

"No. There might be another one. Move back here with me."

He joined her, but remained standing so the cops would clearly see him and not shoot him.

She heard a key in the front door. At first, she wondered why the police would have a key to her house. It took a second for her to realize her father had answered the call and raced to the scene.

His voice made her feel strangely relieved. She found herself fighting tears, not wanting to reveal her fear now that it was all over. "Up here, Dad! Colt's with me."

He raced up the staircase and stopped at the entrance to his room. He gazed with disbelief at the body on the floor. There came three other policemen behind him, all with guns drawn, just as he had done. His gaze went to Natalie. She had not moved.

He soothingly advised her, "Lay the gun on the mattress, Natalie. It's all done."

She rested the gun upon the bed and released her grip, raised her hands so the officers entering would see she was unarmed.

She had killed her first mord.

It then occurred to her she still had to pee.

CHAPTER 13

A HAZMAT crew arrived swiftly to remove the body. They cut away and removed the blood-saturated section of carpet and padding, and they sprayed a disinfectant on the wood underneath. After they left, Brian threw a thick old rug over the spot.

Although Natalie vehemently denied being afraid, Brian had enough experience with crime victims to know different, and he knew his daughter well enough to know she wasn't the tough soldier she tried to evoke. He knew he wasn't made of steel, either. Until this mord thing hit, he had only shot his gun once in all his years on the force. The affects of that haunted his psyche to this day. With that in mind, he gave her a Valium to soothe her nerves.

After a four-hour break to be with Natalie, Brian returned to work. He left a message at the hospital for Beverly, but she still had not called by the time he resumed patrol. He was at once angry with her and worried about her. It was not like her to ignore the family's need for her, especially under these circumstances. Maybe they had not given her the message. He decided he would stop at the hospital when he got a little down time between calls.

By late that afternoon, Coltan replaced all the screen doors with security doors. Once he locked everything up tight and double-checked the downstairs windows reinforced with the sliders, he entered Natalie's room to check on her. She was out cold, the Valium doing its job well. He knew the chill would set in soon with the sunset. He unfolded a blanket he found in the linen closet and covered her with it.

As the night unfolded, he answered two calls from Brian

inquiring about Natalie. The second call came from the hospital where he had briefly spoken with Beverly. The hospital was a madhouse, now woefully understaffed, and Bev would not be home tonight, either. She had sent along a message via Brian, sending her love to him and Natalie. There was no reminder to lock the doors. Brian knew Coltan needed no reminding.

Coltan was so busy working the night seemed to race by. He completed the flip-up door to the basement in the floor of the attic access room. Exhaustion setting in, he managed to half-finish installing the new wall that would separate that room from his bedroom, the big bedroom with a full size bed and a bunk bed. Walling off the attic access room decreased the space in his room by a quarter or so, but he thought it worked out okay.

The ongoing lack of sleep and today's drama only added to his physical fatigue from all the hard labor of the construction work. His hands were sore and blistered. The sprained wrist still hadn't completely healed, and it was bothering him, too. He had swigged enough water to fill a reservoir and he had sweated it all out, not needing to urinate even once.

Coltan sat at the edge of the full size bed and took his boots off. His eyes were closing, and he thought a nap would be a good idea. He was still too hot from all the exercise to want the comforter, so he rolled it up and put it at the end of the bed. He turned over and looked at his gun on the nightstand. He took it and set it beside his pillow. It made him feel secure.

He worried about Brenda. Was she safe? Where and why had she and her family gone? Had they gone on vacation and ended up trapped somewhere because of the violence? Had they suddenly decided to evacuate, like so many others? He prayed for her, prayed for her parents, too. Brenda was his last thought as he drifted to sleep.

When he awoke at sunrise, he found Natalie slumbering in the lower unit of the bunk bed. He had not heard her enter the room during the night, and concluded he must have slept hard. He then scolded himself for sleeping so long. As tired as he felt, he knew he could not curl up under the covers safe in the arms of Morpheus, where Natalie seemed to be.

He wondered why she had chosen to sleep in here, and concluded it was probably because she had awakened and felt alone and frightened. He had left the light on in the room. Most likely, she had come to talk with him and had found him asleep. Still under the effects of the sedative, she probably decided to sleep there, finding the presence of another human being a comfort. He noticed, too, she had not extinguished the light.

Quietly, so as not to disturb her, he went barefooted downstairs that was dark because of the sliders covering the windows. He thought about sliding them open, and decided against it. With him spending most of his time upstairs now, the house was too vulnerable. He flipped on a lamp in the living room and the switch for the overhead light in the kitchen. After starting a pot of coffee, he went out back for a smoke, taking the gun with him. No mord was going to catch him unprepared.

He peered far across the yard into the woods beyond. Had Natalie been right about Muffy? He listened to all the sounds in the air. All he heard was sirens, wind, birds and some dogs howling in the distance. None of the dogs sounded like Muffy. He thought it was time to let go and stop leaving food on the Spencers' porch. It was doubtful Muffy was the one eating it, anyway.

During his second cup of coffee and third smoke, Natalie joined him. They were both wearing the same clothes from the previous day, having slept in them. Her hair was tangled and matted. She didn't seem to give it a thought. She set her coffee on the step and asked for a cigarette.

"I told you no," he said. "And, quit stealing them."

"Sorry."

"My ass." Her halfhearted apology meant nothing to him. She looked a mess, stunk of perspiration, and he found himself being frustrated with her. When it came to grooming, she was about as conscientious as a three-year old.

She avoided his gaze and, with a sullen sigh, stared off into the distance. There was something about her hair, her posture, and the hint of ever-present hurt and anger in her eyes that reminded him—painfully—of someone else he had known. He tried to will the recollection away, tried to suppress the memory of the girl. However, he could never forget her face, her eyes full of rage, accusing him, hating him.

Coltan locked the memory away and focused on the present. "I'm gonna try to finish the upstairs today."

"I have to finish the canning."

They sat quietly for a few minutes, immersed in their own thoughts, battling demons both real and imagined.

Finally, Natalie asked, "Have you heard from Dad?"

"Not since about three this morning."

"He should be home soon."

Coltan thought Brian would insist on helping with the rest of the construction. The backbreaking work and lack of sleep was already taking its toll on Coltan. He couldn't imagine how Brian could keep going at this pace and maintain his position on the police force where he had to be sharp as a tack mentally as well as physically. It wasn't possible. He made a decision at that moment to finish as much of the work as possible this morning. If Brian insisted on helping, he would flatly refuse his help, even if it meant a quarrel.

Then Natalie asked, "What about Mom?"

"She's stuck at the hospital. She knows what happened yesterday. She said to tell you she loves you." He gathered the coffee cup and the gun, and stood. "Let's go in. Come in with me. I want to lock the back door."

"You think there's more mords around?"

"I'm sure of it."

She took her coffee and walked with him. "Did you see any in Reyton?"

"Yeah."

"How many?"

"Two. No telling how many I didn't see."

"Is your friend—" She caught herself. "Are your friends okay?"

He didn't notice, and held the door for her. "I guess." He anticipated her next question. "They were gone. The motor home was gone. I guess they took off."

"I'm sorry, Colt."

He locked the door. "For what?"

"That you don't know for sure."

"I gotta get to work. By the way, you were right about the military. They're setting up camp there."

Her concern at this moment was mords. "Are you keeping the gun?"

"Yeah."

"I'm gonna get mine out of the safe. You'll be upstairs while I'm down here. It makes sense that we're both armed."

"Definitely."

Around noon, Natalie had finished canning the corn and was starting on the beets and carrots when her dad entered the kitchen. He reacted to her bright smile with a mixed expression of concern and sadness. She had no idea her haggard appearance, exhausted posture and rank body odor made him worry that she was beginning to buckle under the stress.

Despite that, he smiled back at her and drew her to him in a tight hug. "How's my girl?"

"I'm fine, Dad." Her cheek pressed uncomfortably against his overgrowth of stubble, and she could feel the bulletproof vest beneath his uniform that made his body feel rigid. His deodorant antiperspirant had worn off hours ago, an indication he had suffered through an unusually stressful shift. She felt compelled to comfort him and assure him his home was still his sanctuary.

"We've got everything under control here. You go right to bed."

"Have you had any rest, Nat?"

"Some." She smiled again. "I'm doing fine. You go get some sleep."

He hesitated as if mulling things over before he asked, "Where's Colt?"

She pointed with her thumb at the ceiling. He said nothing else, just turned away and headed up the stairs. She noticed as he turned he had a paper bag in his hand. She figured it was more hardware. In the next minute, she could hear their voices, but not their words. The hum of the drill resumed and then stopped. She heard Coltan say loudly and humorously, "Absolutely not!" After that, she heard their laughter. She did not expect the laughter. It made her happy to hear them laugh. She continued working, comforted by the joy in their voices.

AT BONITO VALLE COMMUNITY Hospital, Beverly was examining and treating a girl of about thirteen years of age. Like Natalie, she had long dark hair, but this girl's hair was curly to the point of being almost frizzy. The girl was half reclined on the gurney in the exam room, dressed in a hospital gown. Blood was seeping through where the hem of her gown met the injury on her upper right leg.

Beverly removed the bloodied dressing the paramedics applied to the gaping wound. It looked to her that something ripped away the layers of flesh. Although she already knew the answer, she still asked her patient, "How did this happen?"

"One of them bit me!" The girl was crying. "Oh... it hurts. It hurts bad!"

"I'm going to take care of that right now, hon." She stepped over to the head of the bed to lower it. "I need you to sit up for a second here while I lower the headrest." The girl sat up slowly, in a lot of pain. Her blood pooled on the sheet and the back of her gown. Beverly parted the gown where it tied in the back. Dirt and gravel clung to the wounds on the girl's deeply scraped back. "What on earth...?"

"One had my hair and was dragging me. And the other one was chasing, trying to get me, too, and she jumped on my leg and bit me, and the other one was still pulling!"

The thought came to Beverly then of Natalie's long hair. In the next moment, the echoing pop of a gunshot startled her. Even though it had become routine over the past thirty hours, she still found herself jumping whenever the soldiers shot a mord that was too far-gone, and just plain dangerous.

The girl also jumped. "What was that? Did they shoot someone?"

"We're safe here," Beverly said. "Security's on top of it." She purposely used the term *security* instead of *soldiers*. The soldiers' presence only added to the tension, and the patients were frightened enough already.

Beverly tried not to think about what would happen to the girl. She knew the isolation ward would be her next stop, and from there, some reps from the CDC would transport her off somewhere. The hospital staff still didn't know where the infected were being taken.

She lowered the headrest, putting the gurney into a flat position, and eased the girl down carefully, "I'm sorry this hurts your back, hon. I'll inject a painkiller for your leg and your back. Okay?" The girl said nothing. Beverly could tell by her eyes and her pale clammy skin that she was going into shock.

The girl whispered and moaned woozily, "They had me by my hair... oh... God..."

BEVERLY WAS RELIEVED to find her car had not been vandalized or stolen. She locked the door and retrieved her handgun from the glove compartment. Her route out of the hospital would take her along the edge of the south end and then through the center of town. After what she had seen, she was taking no chances.

As she drove home with her handgun on her lap, Beverly could not stop thinking about the longhaired girl. It could have been Natalie on that gurney, and the possibility of it becoming reality filled her with dread. When Brian came by and told her what had happened at home, she was relieved to know Natalie had not panicked and kept enough sense to grab the firearm and use it. But, what if there was another assailant and no firearm nearby? She knew there was little she could do from the hospital to protect her in the event of such an attack. However, she knew there was one thing she could do to increase her chances of escape and survival, should it ever come to that.

On a normal day, in a normal life, Beverly would have stopped to offer assistance to the two accident victims in their crumpled cars at the intersection. Today she simply drove around the lone police officer directing traffic around the mess and kept going until she had to stop for the red at the next intersection.

While waiting for the light to change, she tried to fight the effects of the amphetamines and coffee that had kept her going over the last three days. She didn't want to arrive home shaking and stammering like one of the many addicts she had seen. A glass of wine would be good, maybe two, or even three. That would calm her down. Maybe she would be able to sleep. That would be an added benefit. She thought she had forgotten what sleep felt like.

A loud thump at her side caused her to jerk and glance over just in time to see a man's face and his hand reaching through the open window to release the door lock. He was a rotund young Hispanic man about Coltan's age. His eyes were desperate. Beverly slammed his hand with her left to stop him from reaching the lock control. In the same moment, she took the gun off her lap with her right hand and cocked it.

He shrieked as he tugged on the door handle and reached in for the lock, "I'm takin' your car, bitch!"

She pointed the gun, a .357 magnum, at his face. "Reconsider!"

"Fuck!" He backed off, scared.

This told her he was unarmed. He would have already had a gun pulled and would have shot her by now. The light turned green. She pressed the accelerator hard and sped off, rolling up the window in the process.

It was odd to her she was not the least bit frightened.

She found her daughter at the kitchen table, bent over a sheet of adhesive labels, writing the date and the name of the vegetables for the canning jars. There were at least forty jars of all sizes filled with carrot slices and pickled beets spread out on the counters, drying on towels. She knew it was the right decision to turn the job over to Natalie. Despite Natalie's protestations of perceived ineptness, the girl had proven herself quite capable.

Natalie looked up at her, said brightly, "Hi, Mom." She resumed writing on the labels, her head down.

Beverly was surprised to find Natalie so calm as if nothing unusual had happened. "You were very brave yesterday. I'm proud of you."

There was the hint of a smile when Natalie glanced at her. "One shot."

"So I heard." She noticed Natalie's gun on the table, and was glad she had thought of it and was keeping it close. At the same time, it bothered her Natalie seemed to feel no remorse over killing another human being. "You know," she began cautiously, "Your father once shot a suspect that pulled a gun on him. Even though it was self-defense, he never really got over it. He still prays for him, and he prays for himself, too. How do you feel about that 'one shot,' about killing that man?"

Natalie stopped writing and replied after some thought, "Once I got over being scared, I felt terrible about it. That guy used to stop by the Dairy Delight. Him and his friend would pull up in that ugly old orange Caddy. Me and Carolyn used to laugh at that car, it was so ugly. I don't even know if the guy had a family. If he did... well... I'm sorry, Mom. I didn't know what else to do. He was gonna kill me. I did what I had to do. I can't take it back."

The girl suddenly gazed at her as if she was seeing something hideous. Beverly didn't understand why. "What's wrong?" She had no idea she was trembling, that her face was pale, her brown eyes bloodshot and the pupils dilated. Her hair, which she had fastened into a ponytail, had come loose, and the bottle-blonde strands dangled limply around her face and shoulders. She reeked of perspiration and hospital odors.

"You need some rest, Mom. Don't worry. Everything's on track. I've been working hard on the canning. The shelves are filling up downstairs."

Beverly motioned at all the jars. "You did a great job, Nat. I knew you would."

"I'd reserve judgment until we taste it and don't die of food poisoning."

"Stop it, you." She was trying her best to offer encouragement, "I know you did it right."

It was then Beverly noticed the darkness throughout the rest of the house. The plywood sliders protecting the windows blocked the sunlight. On a normal day, under normal conditions, the rooms would be bright with the light of the sun. Today, the only illumination came from the kitchen light and a lamp in the living room.

The drill upstairs made noise and then wound down to a stop. "The kid's still at it?" Beverly asked.

"Relentlessly. He's working on the supply room, now, up in the attic."

"We'll have to start moving the supplies up there." Beverly was talking more to herself than Natalie.

"We'll take care of that."

Beverly looked across the room at the door that led from the kitchen to the basement. "I thought they would have done that door by now."

"Not enough time," Natalie replied. "We decided the attic should come first. Colt's gonna disguise this entrance down here with a cabinet. He'll attach it to the wall to hide the door. We'll stock it with some canned goods and stuff for appearances. Will that work?"

"I guess." She was not sure about anything, anymore.

"It'll work. We also figured if someone broke in, if they weren't a mord, they'd probably be someone looking for food. We figured if they found the food down here they wouldn't bother with the rest of the house. At least, we'd be feeding somebody."

Beverly gazed at her daughter and briefly remembered the little girl who liked to sit with her as she styled her hair and applied makeup in the morning. In those days, they had a solid mother-daughter relationship. They enjoyed lunches in the tea room across from the beauty parlor where Beverly got pedicures. Natalie had sat quietly watching, fascinated by the procedure, asking why and how about everything while the nail polish dried. Sometimes she wanted to hear again her mother's experience as a contestant in the Miss Pine County competition. After the story, Natalie always told her with the utmost certainty, "You should have won, Mom. You're the nicest and the most beautiful!" The conversation sometimes turned to men, Natalie dreaming about what her future husband would be like, and already planning their number of children. They strolled through stores and sampled the new perfumes and lipsticks together.

It seemed like it happened a thousand years ago. Over the last two years, the only perfume Natalie wore was her own natural scent. Lipstick, or even gloss for that matter, was too much trouble to maintain. She wore simple, comfortable clothing and didn't care for frilly accessories. Half the time she didn't even bother wearing a bra. Her hands were scarred, the fingernails close-cropped and unadorned. She noticed Natalie hadn't combed her hair for days, and she had developed a terrible body odor. When had her daughter stopped caring?

She gently stroked her daughter's hair. It was dirty and had become oily. Her fingers caught in the tangles, and she pictured the monsters using the knots for a secure grip as they dragged her to Who-Knows-Where. The image made her cringe inwardly. It took a lot of effort to control her voice. She said softly, with a benign smile, "It's all tangled."

"So is yours."

"I'm going to get a shower and a nap. You need one, too. A shower, that is."

"When I'm done." She was unconcerned.

"You have to take a shower and wash your hair, Natalie."

"I will."

"When?"

"When I'm done here."

"You stink!"

"I do?" Natalie was mortified. "Is it bad?"

"Horrible!" Beverly softened when she saw the embarrassment on Natalie's face. "I'm telling you this because I love you. Please take better care of yourself. The canning can wait for an hour."

"As soon as I finish this batch. I promise."

She knew it was pointless to nag about it. Natalie had a habit of shutting down. It seemed to happen less often with Brian. "Is Dad home?"

"He's sleeping."

"I'm off tonight. I hope he is, too."

"He has to go in."

Beverly responded with a sigh of disappointment. She was hoping they could have a little time to talk, maybe some intimate time together. It had been so long. Just two hours of normalcy. It was a small thing to ask. Instead, it would be another night alone, another night of cool bare sheets at his side of the bed. She missed his touch and the sweet whispers afterward, those moments when they lay in each other's arms exhausted and deliciously satisfied. How she missed it. How she missed him.

She poured a glass of rosé and took it with her upstairs. The rug in the hallway across from their bedroom door caused her to pause. This was where the mord had met his death. The spot still smelled of disinfectant, and the odor made her think of the hospital and all the mordants and their victims. How long would it be before there were more of them than *normal* people? Her stomach clenched as the longhaired girl in the ER came to mind.

Tonight, she would cut Natalie's hair, and then her own.

After her shower, she went naked into the bed and curled up under the covers beside Brian. He was on his side, facing her, his breathing soft and rhythmic as he slept. She kissed his cheek and rested her head on his shoulder. She breathed in his scent, and it still excited her, even now after all these years. So what if he had gotten a little paunchy and his hair was thinning. She smiled at the memory of teasing him, kissing the growing bald spot at the top of his head, purring into his ear, "You're still my Galahad." It always embarrassed him and made him giggle. However, she knew it made him feel like the young, virile man she had married; the slim, handsome young man who lifted her with muscular arms and covered her with kisses and loving sentiments. In her eyes, he was still that same man.

She fell asleep, and was sad and disappointed to find him gone when she awakened hours later.

CHAPTER 14

When Beverly entered the kitchen early that evening, she found Coltan loading the dishwasher. She noticed his clothing, the apparent uniform he always wore: the sleeveless undershirt and denim jeans. The clothing seemed painted onto his skin, exposing every ripple of every muscle, the fine grace of his young and healthy form. He had his back to her, and she caught herself taking in the view, and enjoying the view. Brian had looked just like that when she had first met him. In her brief reverie, Beverly recalled the sensation of his taunt rippled belly beneath the light, passionate caresses of her fingertips, how the firmness of his body excited her. For a millisecond, the memory became a fantasy, the imagined transference of sensual affection from her husband's body to that of the attractive young man in her kitchen. She felt her face get warm. She quickly looked away, felt ashamed of her lustful thoughts and the arousal that welled up within. To make matters worse, she had lately begun to consider Coltan as her son, and her sexual attraction to him, although momentary, seemed hideously incestuous. That was enough to kill any remaining desire for him. Immediately, she reprimanded herself and secretly prayed for forgiveness.

"Feel better, Nat?" He was closing the dishwasher, and had not turned around.

Beverly recovered her composure. "I couldn't answer for her."

He made a quarter-turn, glanced over his shoulder at her and smiled warmly. "Hi, Bev." He switched on the dishwasher, and it hummed so softly they could barely hear it. "I thought you were

Natalie."

"Where is she?"

"She's finally in the shower." He poured a cup of coffee and brought it to her. He pulled a chair out at the kitchen table and wordlessly invited her to sit.

Although he seemed content, she sensed turmoil within him. "Are you doing alright, Colt?"

"Yeah. How are *you* doing?"

"Better, now that I've had some sleep." She gazed at the coffee cup. Coffee was the last thing she wanted.

He seemed to read her mind. "I can get you something else."

"There's wine in the fridge. I really still need to wind down."

She resisted the urge to follow him with her eyes as he removed the cup and emptied it in the sink. Instead, she glanced around the kitchen, then around the house. The place was dark and depressing with the sliders shut. The only sunlight came through the security screen door protecting the kitchen to rear porch door that Coltan had left open for fresh air. The security door had a window on it, and he had installed a vertical slider of thick plywood over the interior side of the glass. She could see it through the reflection on the exterior of the glass as it sat open against the edge of the counter.

He poured her a glass of wine and brought it to her. "There you go."

"Has Natalie been okay?"

"A champ. Really. I don't know how she does it." He wanted to discuss Natalie's depression, but was uncertain how to introduce the subject. He took a stab at it, anyway. "You two must've talked."

Beverly smiled slightly. "About our little altercation?"

"Among other things."

She was too tired for guessing games. "Cut the bullcrap, Colt."

One of the things Coltan loved about Beverly was her forthrightness. He plunged ahead. "She's been pretty depressed.

Along with that, she hasn't been... her hygiene..."

"We just talked about it. She didn't realize how bad it had gotten."

"Are you off tonight?"

"Yes, thank God!"

"Maybe you and her should do something special together. Just the two of you." His uncertainty about butting in to their family dynamics was obvious in his nervous tone of voice, "Not that I know anything about... Ma'am... I like her a lot, and I hate to see her like this. I know you hate it, too. Maybe it's not my place..."

"It's alright, Colt." She slugged down the wine and set the empty glass away from her. Her eyes filled with tears. "It's been difficult between us, ever since she hit puberty."

"With all that's happening she needs you more than she realizes. She needs *you*, Bev. She needs her mother." He added apologetically, "I'm sorry. It's none of my business."

Beverly understood and was grateful for Coltan's desire to intervene on Natalie's behalf. The scars on his face and body reminded her every day what he had survived. It was in moments like this her awe of him returned in that he had cultivated not bitterness, but compassion for others, as a result of his suffering. Equal to that, she appreciated his intelligence, strength, humor and his persistent efforts to better himself in every possible way. Her heart suddenly filled with her love for him, and she took his face in her hands and gazed lovingly into his eyes. "You're our family, Colt. Your home is here with us. You have an equal say. We love you."

She sensed turmoil under his flattered and appreciative smile. She also sensed his reticence and thus decided not to pursue the matter. Whatever was bothering him, he would eventually discuss it with her.

For now, one other matter needed settling and Beverly found Natalie in her room freshly showered and dressed in clean clothing.

The girl had not bothered to comb her hair; she had simply dried it with a towel and allowed it to fall where it wished. At least, it was a start.

She brought Natalie into the master bedroom where they reclined together on the bed and Beverly held her as she used to when Natalie was small. They discussed their concerns and fears about the looming crises. They had girl talk that made them both laugh and cry. In the end, the mother and daughter realized they had more in common now that the younger had reached the threshold of maturity.

In a while, they cut each other's hair, and Beverly introduced her daughter to her first salon-style facial. She rubbed fragranced lotion on Natalie's arms and legs, in the process giving a short lecture about the importance of skin care. Even though the world was going to hell, a little personal pampering did wonders to make a girl feel better, no matter how dire the circumstances. They had another laugh over that.

UP IN THE ATTIC, COLTAN enjoyed the sound of their laughter. When Beverly came up with a soda for him, she seemed relieved of a burden.

"She's okay?" he asked.

"She's missing Carolyn, worried about her. Besides that, she's been worried about everything else, and she's exhausted. She told me something else, something I never knew before. She told me she thinks she's ugly." Beverly shook her head solemnly. "Damned kids... all the years of teasing. I didn't know it was that bad!"

"I think she's pretty." Until the words spilled out, Coltan had not realized just how attractive she was to him. What he found most attractive about Natalie was the fact she was the polar opposite of all the painted self-absorbed girls in her age group. "And, as far as substance goes, she's got it far over all those other girls!"

"Thank you for being so kind. Thank you for caring for her." At that moment, she was looking at him as if he was the most wonderful person in the world. Her eyes were full of happiness and thanks.

He wanted to tell her he didn't deserve her gratitude.

After she went downstairs, he continued with the work in the attic storage room. He had installed the shelving frames today after measuring and re-measuring to make certain he got it right the first time. The shelves sat in a neat stack a short distance outside the entrance of the room. Leaning against the wall beside that room was the old door from his bedroom he had decided to reuse up here. He had already removed the attic access door from the hallway. That door he recycled by using it for Brian's and Bev's room up here. Down below, he had torn out the old doorframe in the wall between the hallway and the attic stairs access, filled the empty space with sheetrock, and then reinforced that entire wall with a second layer of sheetrock. The only thing left to do there was to cover it with paneling to make it look like it had been that way forever. He had already installed the new wall in his room with a secret access door that now served as their new entrance. He planned to disguise it with the rest of the paneling. Next on the list, he would install the steel reinforced door at the entrance from the hallway to his bedroom. He also had plans to install two bolt locks and three barricade bars for that door, just for extra protection. The cabinet to conceal the original basement door from the kitchen would be his final project.

He sat on the floor in the storage room and rested against the wall, reviewed his work. It made him feel better that it was all almost done. He sat there for a while, taking a break, finishing the soda Bev had brought up to him. At least the stuff was loaded with caffeine. It would help him stay awake to continue working long into the next morning.

He listened to a radio call-in show as he worked. Most of the calls concerned the increasing numbers of mordants and the increasing numbers of military troops in the big cities. Civil disobedience, general widespread panic, looting and chaos were now the norm in most places. The military had begun evacuations and were escorting people by the busload and trainload to rescue centers. Some of the callers shared reports from the suburbs and smaller towns that the same scenarios were popping up there, as well. Then, another caller, whose brother was in the military, stated his brother told him the military was bombing cruise ships at sea due to breakouts of the mord virus. All this made Coltan fear they were almost out of time.

The radio broadcast went into a commercial break at the end of the hour. The first commercial was a plea for monetary donations to the Rape Crisis Center. It was the last thing he wanted to hear about. It brought the memory back, and his gut suddenly panged sickeningly.

He was fifteen then, and had met her at a campsite gathering of other street kids. It was a small group of people like him, and there was always drugs and booze available. Most of the girls and many of the boys picked up cash through prostitution. Coltan had not been one of them. Instead, he found odd jobs around the area, determined that it would never get so bad he would have to sell his body to keep food in his belly and drugs in his pocket.

She had only been with them for one day, a pasty-skin waif who was trying to escape a bad home life and liked to get high. It had been a real party that night—everyone was stoned. The higher she got, the friendlier she got, cuddling and kissing and putting her hands on him. He liked the attention, loved the arousal and hated her for being such a stupid and disgusting little slut. When things started to get hot and heavy, she decided she didn't want to go any further. He saw the others had all paired-up and were either making out or screwing. He thought this little prick-teaser had no right to deny him. She had started it, and he was determined to finish it, just to teach her a lesson.

This was the way he thought and felt in those days. He had decided long before then that human beings were innately evil and deserved all the bad they got. He viewed himself that way, too. His mother and Richard had beaten this reality into him for ten years.

And, here she was, gazing at him with innocent, apologetic eyes, and a pathetic need for tender humane love. She didn't deserve it, just as he didn't deserve it.

He pinned her down on his sleeping bag, pinned her under his body. He tore the waistband of her pants and pushed them down below her knees. He intended to give it to her, give it to her until she couldn't stand. It was an act of brutality perpetrated by a sadistic monster, the monster he used to be back in his Days of Rage. He took his rage and savagely poured it into her, ignoring her cries of pain, even covering her mouth to silence her. Still pinning her with his body, he warned her he was far from finished with her. And, when it was all over, he felt his rage dissipate. He rolled beside her and surveyed her, surveyed the damage. He saw the blood mixed with his semen had pooled onto the sleeping bag in the space between her legs. The girl was shocked and helpless, curled up, sobbing, and moaning in agony, her hands protecting the painful place he had invaded with the vicious force of a crazed animal.

He could never forget the girl afterwards, the hatred in her eyes at his betrayal. At that moment, at the sight of her like that, at the realization of what *it* had done, Coltan incarcerated the monster. Months later, he saw her by chance from a distance, saw what it had done to her, how it had changed her appearance and behavior.

His shame and regret spilled down his face in hot tears as he sat there against the wall in the storage room. He accepted he could not undo the damage. In addition, he knew she could never identify him as the monster. They were strangers who had gotten high together, and she was too brain-fried to remember his face. However, his conscience would convict him for the rest of his life, and the clarity of the memory of her curled up and crying, protecting her body from further violation, would punish him all his days.

Perhaps by the grace of God, it served as a catalyst to change his behavior and his treatment of other people—girls, in particular. Although he had changed his ways and was working still to atone for the wreckage in his wake, the pain of his guilt would always be a constant companion.

Not knowing about this incident in Coltan's life, Brian had assured him Jesus had already paid the price of his sins for him. At this moment Coltan was convinced that no price, no action of atonement, could ever repay the damage he had done to an innocent life. He was as much a murderer as all the guilty sitting on death row. You can't buy back a human life. However, Jesus had done just that. He purchased Coltan's life. He wondered how Jesus could possibly pay for what he, Coltan, had done. He then saw Jesus suffering the stripes on his behalf, saw each agonizing contact of hammer to nail being meant for him. Then he tried to imagine the unimaginable pain, the pain he deserved and should have received. He wanted to take it away from Jesus so he could feel it himself, because he deserved every second of it, every agonizing second, until it killed him and sent him to hell where he rightly belonged. But, Jesus had already taken it and would not give it back. Why would he want to do that, anyway? Why would Jesus want to save this monster, this scum, this sorry and miserable waste of human life?

He surrendered to his remorse, bent his head and cried silently. He cried so hard everything around him ceased to exist, no buildings, no sounds, nothing. His entire awareness swallowed by his grief and shame, his shoulders quivered with each wave of quiet, painful sobs. He couldn't stop.

His awareness gradually returned with the slight weight of a gentle hand upon his shoulder. Even then, he couldn't raise his head, couldn't stop the wave of tears, self-hate and shame. Someone pulled him and held him close, and his body weakened in the comfort of it. He became aware of a subtle scent of flowers, the warmth of her body pressed to his. She said nothing. She made no sound at all. He still couldn't stem the tide of emotions, and surrendered further, allowed it to overwhelm him until there was nothing left.

CHAPTER 15

B rian took it upon himself to build the cabinet that would cover the basement door and access from the kitchen. Secured to the wall, it completely covered the wall and the door. Natalie brought up the canned and packaged goods they had set aside to fill this cabinet. They worked together stocking it, and even added a few cleaning products in the lower shelves to make it look official. He shut the cabinet doors and looked it over. It would do.

He went up to check on Coltan's progress. Coltan had already installed the paneling on the wall that faced the hallway. There wasn't the slightest evidence that a door had ever been there. It looked just like a wall, as he intended. Beverly had just finished hanging a painting there, and was moving a small table under it. On the floor were some pretty knick-knacks for the table, and a fake bamboo tree that would stand in the corner where the wall met the short wall next to the staircase. He watched her set it all up. The result appeared perfectly innocent and cheerful.

She stood back and examined her work from a distance, pleased. Brian reached for her hand, and they held hands for a moment. They kissed and hugged, and tried not to think about the imminent dreadful dawn.

In the basement, Natalie swept up the sawdust and hung up all the tools on the far wall. The basement was a fully enclosed windowless area that ran the length and width of the main floor upstairs. Brian and Coltan had moved the freezer against the wall closest to the new attic access panel they had mounted in the ceiling at the top of the stairs. She lifted the freezer's lid and checked the meat and poultry. She wondered if they would have electricity long enough to eat it all.

After another glance around the basement, Natalie took the stairs up, pushed open the access panel and entered the access room from where she climbed the retractable stairs up into the attic. Everything was in place there. She and her mother had worked together to make the space habitable and homey. She had helped her mother bring up the new twin size mattresses for her and Coltan, and they brought up the new queen size mattress and box spring and placed it on the floor in the separate room for the two adults. All their original bedding remained in the downstairs bedrooms so as not to elicit suspicion from anyone who broke into the downstairs quarters. The lower spaces had to appear as if the people living there had evacuated.

Beverly had purchased four extra twin-size mattresses and had stacked them neatly against a wall in the main attic room. These were reserved for any refugees deemed safe for inclusion in their hideaway. Beverly was certain they had enough food should that situation arise.

Coltan had earlier set sleeping bags and pillows on his and Natalie's mattresses, and then unpacked and tested a few combination electric/battery-powered lamps and found them in good working order. The oil-filled space heater would keep them warm. They even had a small refrigerator and microwave oven. A tabletop propane stove and a couple of electric hot plates would serve for other cooking when they required it. A small television with satellite access sat in a corner. Coltan had put a radio by his mattress. In another area were firearms and ammunition, and emergency backpacks pre-stocked in the event of emergency bug-out. Ten fire extinguishers hung on another wall, convenient and ready for rapid service. The extra scanners were there too, one plugged in, ready for them. Four new walkie-talkies sat near the wall of her parents' room. Stacked by the storage room door were the many boxes of canned and packaged foods, paper goods, batteries, extra blankets and everything else they had purchased to stock this space. The rolling first-aid cart would go in there, too. The only thing left to do was to put away the goods in the storage closet. Natalie and Coltan decided they would quietly do that job tonight while her parents slept.

Satisfied with the attic set-up, Natalie left the space and knocked on the access panel to Coltan's room. He pushed it open and, with a smile of welcome, motioned her in. He was on the floor, installing the last sheet of panel to that wall. He had chosen a type of faux pine paneling that would camouflage the entrance to the attic access room. On the other side of the room, he had replaced the door that led from his bedroom to the hallway with a steel-reinforced door that he could lock and barricade from inside the room. Coltan had already installed the barricade materials. The iron bars lay conveniently on the floor next to the door to secure the door as soon as everyone was safely in this room and on their way to the attic.

"You did one helluva job," Natalie remarked.

He smiled at her as he pressed the panel against the glue on the wall, "Thanks." She watched him add some thin reinforcing nails to the panels. He used the nail gun, going down the line quickly, each nail perfectly aligned. The job looked like a professional had done it. He stood and walked back a few paces, turned and viewed it from a distance.

"It's perfect." Natalie said, "You'd never know there's an access panel there. You really got some talent. You know that?"

"It's just stuff I learned working at the theater." He brushed it off as if it was nothing. He was too tired to pat himself on the back. She had been up all night, as well, and appeared as tired as he felt. He took her hand and guided her over to the bed, where they reclined together, propped up against the pillows, his arms around her. It was nice and cozy, and they both needed the respite.

She felt something poking against her spine, and she shifted and removed her gun from its place tucked inside the rear waistband of her jeans. She turned over and set it on the nightstand next to his as he watched, amused. The two guns sitting side-by-side seemed to belong together.

"Bonnie and Clyde," she said.

"Bonnie and Clyde?"

"That's what we'll name them."

He giggled like a little kid, "You want to name our guns?"

"Why not? Mom named hers *Brutus*."

This elicited a fit of chuckling from him. "Aw... man... that's too funny!"

She laughed, too. "What?"

"That's too funny, man... That's just too funny." It took him a minute to let his soft laughter die down.

Natalie said hesitantly, "I have a question for you. Why did you replace your bedroom door with that heavy one?"

"In case mords break in. I can barricade it. Our only access to the attic is through this room."

She thought about it and murmured, "Oh. That makes sense."

He smiled again at her and stroked her hair, now clean and soft. It smelled nice, too, some kind of floral scent. He liked her short hair. The style flattered her, accentuated her eyes and the shape of her face. He encouraged her to rest her cheek against his shoulder, and he held her to him. He loved holding her. It seemed as natural to him now as it would have if they had known each other forever.

Natalie closed her eyes for a few moments, enjoying his tenderness and the love she felt for him.

She had maintained her discretion about his meltdown the night before, and she never asked him what it was about. She assured him as he slowly recovered his composure, "No one else will ever know." She had no idea how much those words reassured him. Since then, they found it easier to be this close. The episode had created an unspoken, mutually acknowledged intimacy between them.

"Can I tell you a secret?" Natalie asked.

"Yeah."

"I think Mom and Dad are wrong."

"About what?"

"Staying here. Hiding. We should have gotten out while the going was good."

"And go where?"

"I don't know."

"That's why we have to stay here. At least, we've got all we need here." He stated as she puffed out a breath of silent uneasiness combined with a subtle side-to-side nod of her head. "We'll be okay."

"For how long? We can't stay hidden forever. What kind of a life is that?"

"Your dad told me there's supposed to be a safe area somewhere. Once we find out where, we'll be out of here."

"He told me that, too. But he doesn't even know for sure if it's real. We can't count on that, Colt. We can't."

"We have to."

"Even if that place is real, how are we gonna find out where it is? And, if we do find out, how are we gonna get there safely after all the roads are blocked and the military's watching everybody? They're already preventing people from traveling in most parts of the country. They're already forcing people into those *rescue centers*. Did you know they shut down all the airports today? They've taken over the railroads and busses, too. Even all the ships. They've taken over all the cruise ships and are leading them back to port. They said a lot of people on them are sick. Did you hear about all that?"

"I heard it on the radio this morning." He quickly decided not to tell her about the caller that reported the military had actually obliterated the cruise ships at sea to prevent them from docking.

Instead, Coltan focused on Natalie's conflict about bugging-in. "That tells me even if we found out today where the safe area is it's already too late to go for it—at least, until things quiet down. We have to trust your parents, Nat."

"I think they're wrong."

"If I thought they were wrong, do you think I'd be busting my ass to reinforce this place? Look... I know you're scared. I am, too. We have to make the best of things. We have to have faith that God's looking out for us."

"I don't think there's a God, anymore."

"What?" This took him by surprise and troubled him.

"The God I was raised to believe in is a kind and loving God. A kind and loving God would not allow all this. He wouldn't allow some disease that makes people turn into cannibals. From what the Bible says, that kind of thing is detestable to him."

"Yeah, but if you remember the history there, there was a time when people starved. And, during that time, some people ate their own kids. Do you remember reading about that?"

"No."

"It's there. I'll have to find it and show you. When that happened, God allowed it. I don't know why. But, eventually, he took care of it and righted things. He took care of his people." Coltan searched her expression for some hint of relief from her worry, but found none. He told her sternly, "Do *not* lose your faith! Don't let the bad guys win. That's what they want. That's what *he* wants. If you lose your faith, *he* wins. Think about it!" She shook her head, still nagged by doubt. This only made him more persistent. "I don't know what's gonna happen to us. If something bad happens, and they find us... Our faith may be the only thing we have left. They've already taken away our rights and our freedom. Are you going to let them take away your faith, too?" She did not respond. He sighed tiredly and rested his head against the pillow. "You need to get back in the Word. Now, more than ever."

"Don't tell them about this."

"That's up to you, not me." He closed his eyes and relaxed. "I'm so tired..."

She rested her head against his shoulder again and closed her eyes. "Me, too. Thank you, Colt."

"For what?" he whispered.

"For being my friend."

He held her a bit tighter; his way of telling her the feeling was mutual. "You're my friend, too." His next words trailed off humorously, "You scrawny little, bad-tempered tomboy."

"You're a bossy shithead..." she retorted lazily, teasing him.

"I love you, too," he replied in a whisper. His arms relaxed around her as he faded into sleep.

WHILE BEV TENDED TO the steaks in the broiler, Brian came up to tell them dinner would be ready soon. He looked first for Natalie in her room. Finding she was not there, he figured she was probably helping Coltan install the paneling in his room. He crossed to the door and found it wide open.

The kids were asleep in each other's arms. At once, he thought the sight of them like this was endearingly cute and, at once, he was gravely concerned. His first thought was that they were simply tired out and had dozed off while talking. His second thought, and it bothered him, was that they might have been making out. However, their clothing appeared undisturbed, and Coltan had wrapped his arms around her in a protective, innocent manner. Still, the sight worried him. They would be living in close quarters and the possibility and opportunity for further intimacy between them now was apparent.

He decided it was time to have a talk with Coltan.

Beverly called from the top of the stairs, "It's ready, hon."

He turned, put his index finger in front of his pursed lips and motioned for her to come and see. When she came up beside him, he pointed as he put his arm around her.

She gazed at the sight and, with a smile, murmured, "Aw... look at that."

"What do we do?" he queried softly.

"About what?" she whispered back.

"You know what I mean, Bev." This time it was a little bit louder.

"Was the door closed?"

"No. It was wide open. I give them that."

"It's perfectly innocent." She was still whispering.

He lowered his voice. "It can go beyond innocent."

"Let them love each other."

"Do you realize what that means?"

"Sweetheart," she whispered. "Do you realize what kind of a world they will be growing up in? Do you realize how difficult it is, even now, for them? They'll need each other."

"Our daughter is not ready for that kind of relationship, and neither is he."

Beverly countered, "We don't even know if they've done anything."

"He's a boy, Beverly. That's all they think about at his age."

"If you really believed that about him, you wouldn't have brought him here."

She was correct, of course. Coltan had never impressed him as one of those immature boys who lusted after girls. It had always seemed to him Coltan had too many serious problems to be wasting his energy on getting a quick lay.

Moreover, by what he had observed of Coltan and Natalie together, Coltan always treated Natalie with respect. He had seen

Coltan put his arm around her a few times, but that had always been when Natalie was ready to blow a fuse over something. For now, it seemed their relationship was one of close friendship.

But that still didn't answer the question of what would happen in the near future, with them all locked up and hiding together. He was certain the inevitable would happen, no matter what.

His response now came in a hoarse, forced whisper. "But, Beverly! What if they do take this further? And, they will! She'll get pregnant. We can't have a baby around in a situation like this!"

"She won't get pregnant. I brought home something that will prevent that."

"What?" He thought of birth control pills. It occurred to him also that she said she had already brought them home. If that was the case, Beverly was throwing away all the Christian precepts they had been instilling in their daughter all these years. She would be, in effect, telling Natalie it was perfectly fine to sleep with boys.

She motioned Brian to follow her to the top stair where they sat. The conversation continued in whispers. "At the hospital I learned something that scared the hell out of me. The mords can smell blood—especially menstrual blood. It attracts them. Most of their initial victims have been women and pubescent girls. Now I know why. I will not let Natalie be in that kind of danger if I can prevent it." Brian began to ask a question, but Beverly stopped him and continued. "There is a drug the military uses. They give it to their female troops when they're going out into the field. One injection stops the menstrual cycle for one year. I got some from the hospital. I was going to tell Natalie after dinner, and we're both going to use it."

"Bev!"

"We have to do it. How can you not see that?"

Protecting their lives was one thing, and that made perfect sense. But the drug was also a contraceptive, and Natalie would know that. He stole a glance back at the doorway of Coltan's room. The kids were still asleep. He turned again to Beverly. "What about the issue of premarital sex? It's not like we'd be able to run out and get a pastor for them!"

"Even if we find a way to separate them somehow, they'll still find a way to be together. You know that, and I know that. I say we ask them to consider all the ramifications if they decide to go any further. I say we *gently* encourage them to practice self-control until they're absolutely sure."

"That's like giving permission."

"Under the circumstances, do you think a just and loving God will condemn them?"

"Well, he sure won't be happy about it."

"With everything else going on, I don't think a couple of young adults in a loving, monogamous, committed, although unmarried, sexual relationship is going to be that big a deal to him. Our God understands us. He sees our hearts. He sees *their* love for each other in *their* hearts. I say, if and when the time comes, let them bring it to God, and then take it from there."

"Well, I'm going to talk to Colt."

"And I'll talk to Natalie." She thought for a moment, and decided it was time to bring up one more concern. "And, what if something happens to us? Tell me you haven't thought about that. They'll need each other even more. They have to stay together! In order to survive, they have to stay together. They won't survive any other way. You know that, as well as I do." After another pause that gave him no time to think or respond, she said, "If it's true they're falling for each other, well... I'm glad it's Colt. He'll take good care of her. I know that."

Brian was more at peace with the idea, being she put it *that way*. It was something about Coltan of which he had always been certain.

218

AFTER DINNER, BEVERLY sat with Natalie on her bed, the both of them propped up against the pillows. She cuddled her daughter, something she had come to miss over the last two years when Natalie had begun to grow increasingly emotionally distant. She was grateful for the second chance to bond with her, especially now when they needed each other more than ever.

Beverly explained to Natalie the mordants' attraction to menstruating women, and she injected herself and Natalie with the menstrual cessation drug. Their discussion of something so intimate and shared presented the perfect opportunity for her to bring up the subject of Natalie's relationship with Coltan.

It took some gentle prodding on Beverly's part, but Natalie finally confided her true feelings for Coltan and her jealousy of the girl in Reyton who had claimed his heart. Natalie's honesty opened the way for Beverly to discuss her concerns about their upcoming seclusion in the attic.

"Okay, Mom. I know where this is going." She placed two fingers over her mother's lips when she began to interrupt. "You want to make sure Colt and I don't *do it*, if we get to that point. I've got to be honest with you—I can't promise I'd say no. All he has to do is look at me, and I melt. I can't help it."

Beverly smiled understandingly. "You've got it bad."

"Sure do." Natalie returned her smile, glad her mother understood. "I can make one promise to you. If things ever go that way, and they may not, we'll pray about it. And, if you know Colt, and I guess you've known him a lot longer than I have—praying about it would be the first thing he'd want to do. Right?"

Beverly thought about it for a few moments. She remembered the defiant and miserable young man she first met two years ago. The memory was as clear as if it had happened yesterday, all the hours in surgery trying to repair the damage he had done to himself, the two times she had to shock his failed heart to bring him back to life, and how he had fought her efforts to save him because he had no will to live. She contrasted that memory with the courteous and Spirit-led young adult she knew today. A fleeting memory also came of a recent moment when he had unconsciously addressed her as "Mom," and he never realized it. Their relationship had grown and evolved much over that brief time. Thinking back further, she recalled how it had made him smile when she addressed him as "son" a few times.

Finally, she decided, "Yeah. He would pray. That's what he'd do."

Natalie saw her mother seemed relieved. However, she had wondered about something for a long time, and hoped Mom would give her an honest answer. "How did Colt get all those scars on his face? And all the other ones on his body?" When Mom hesitated to answer, Natalie said, "I never asked him. But, one day he showed me the ones he did to himself, and he said you knew about them."

"He told you about that?"

"He sure did. I never asked him about the rest, though. I don't think he wants to talk about it. So, I'm asking you."

"The ones on his face and some of the ones on his body happened when he fell off a bridge."

"Fell?" She knew better. Coltan was not clumsy or careless.

"Good grief, Natalie! You really should ask him yourself." She hugged Natalie closer. "I don't feel right talking about this. He's been through a lot. That's all I can tell you."

"They beat him, didn't they?"

"Natalie..."

"Mom, I've seen stuff over there. Ever since they moved in. I heard the yelling. A lot of times I heard sounds like someone was being hit. I remember when they first moved in, hearing things late at night. One night, the sound of their little puppy screaming woke me up. Remember that puppy? They had it in the back yard, and Colt spent a lot of time out there with it. That was the only time he ever looked happy. Then, all of a sudden, it disappeared one day."

The dog's mysterious absence brought to mind a recollection she had long buried, "And, there's something else, something I never told anyone."

Beverly had never seen this much hurt and compassion in Natalie's eyes. Whatever it was Natalie had to confide was something traumatic. She sat up and worriedly searched her daughter's face. "Tell me what you saw."

"I was out in the garden, and I heard crying from their yard. It was the most painful type of crying I ever heard in my life. So, I snuck closer to where the sound was coming from—the doghouse over there. And... you know, this was back when Colt was smaller than he is now... He was curled up in that doghouse just crying and crying. And then, his dad came out with the dog's leash—you know, the kind with the chain—and he dragged Colt out of there by one leg and sat on his back and just started whipping him with it. And, he kept hitting him with it, and there was blood. His shirt had blood all over it. And, Colt kept trying to protect his head, and his dad was hitting his hands with the chain and... finally, Colt stopped crying. But his dad wouldn't stop hitting him. And, there was so much blood... I ran away and hid in the corn, and I saw his dad drag him into the house by one leg. Colt wasn't moving. That's what I saw."

"Why didn't you tell us?"

"I think I might've fainted, because I woke up in the corn and couldn't remember what I was doing there. All I could remember was coming out to pick some tomatoes for dinner—nothing after that for a long time."

"My God..." Beverly whispered forlornly, her sadness not only for Coltan, but also for Natalie who had witnessed the abuse.

Natalie fought back tears of anger. "How can someone do that to a kid? Or, to anyone?"

To Beverly it was just another frustratingly incurable disease. "No one really knows."

OUT ON THE BACK PORCH, Brian set a freshly brewed cup of coffee before Coltan as he sat at the small table having a smoke and looking out over the valley. Coltan thanked him, and Brian joined him there. He motioned to Coltan for a cigarette. Coltan slid the pack across to him.

"Thought you quit," Coltan teased.

"I did." He lit up and took a deep, satisfying drag, "... Mostly."

Coltan knew Brian well enough to recognize when something was bothering him. "What's on your mind?"

Two matters concerned him. He decided to begin with what he judged the most pressing. Brian considered the security of all four of them when it came time to bunker down. Their AllCards and portafones contained built-in tracking technology that would alert the authorities about their hiding place.

"I don't want the cards or the PFs anywhere near our house. We'll have to destroy them out on the road," Brian began. "We'll do it on the west side of the frontage road that connects to the southbound freeway entrance. That way, if some authority finds the pieces—which they will because the tracking chip is so tiny it's indestructible—they'll figure we were heading south. You'll follow me in the truck, because I plan to ditch my car in the little forest area along the freeway. We'll do it the night we bug in when the traffic's lighter."

"What about Bev's car?"

"I'll have to discuss that with her. I didn't think about all this until a few minutes ago."

"How soon are we bugging in?"

Brian took a deep breath as he thought about it. Finally, he replied, "The day after tomorrow."

"Why not tonight?"

The reason for his hesitancy hinged on the fact he had not discussed with Beverly yet his desire to bring little Rosa, her mother and her brother Mario into their shelter. This was another thing he hadn't thought about until a few minutes prior.

He told Coltan, "There's a woman with two kids—one age seven, the other seventeen—on the south side with no transportation and nowhere truly safe to go, anyway. I want to bring them here with us, but I need Bev's okay, plus yours and Nat's."

"That's fine with me," Coltan said. "I'm sure it'll be okay with Bev and Nat."

"I'm not so sure about Nat."

"You're the head of this family. What you decide goes. We've got enough for three more. Natalie—if she's against it—will get used to the idea." Coltan then noted the increasing concern on Brian's face as the man paused in silent introspection. "What else, Brian? What is it?"

"You and Natalie." He noticed Coltan had placed his handgun on the table, so he took his own out of his holster and set it beside it.

Coltan saw this and joked, "Whoa! What are you gonna do? Shoot me? I didn't do anything!"

Brian began to laugh, which made Coltan laugh. There were few things Brian loved more than seeing Coltan laugh. He remembered the days when laughter did not exist for him. Things had changed so much in two years.

"I want to talk to you about my daughter," Brian said seriously.

Coltan jested, "Well, you already told me she can kick my ass. I totally believe you."

"This is serious, son."

"It's serious, huh?" When Brian nodded, Coltan said, "And, you bring me coffee instead of a beer. What kind of dad are you?"

"The best kind. The kind of dad who loves you both."

"Aw, jeez..." This was too serious. Coltan had a suspicion, but he didn't want to bring it up. This was *Dad's* job.

After twenty minutes of discussion, the only thing Brian was certain of was the fact Coltan had no idea Natalie had developed feelings beyond friendship for him. Coltan's assurances he would not encourage or seek a sexual relationship with her left him uncertain. A lifetime of experience told Brian that Coltan would not be able to honor that promise. No healthy young man could deny himself that pleasure for long, especially under their inevitable living situation. The matter remained unsettled, and this frustrated both men.

The sound of leaves and twigs cracking in the brush beyond the garden path startled them. At the same moment, the two men grabbed their weapons and bolted up. They watched, listened and waited. The sound came again, closer. Finally, an opossum ambled into the light carrying a load of dry leaves with her tail. She saw them and froze.

Brian and Coltan glanced at each other. They had assumed the exact same positions, and were a mirror image of each other.

"Possum," Coltan whispered. "I don't know about you, but I don't shoot animals."

Brian stifled a laugh and slowly sat down.

Coltan also sat slowly so as not to scare the opossum. "It's okay," he whispered to it, "You go ahead. We won't hurt you."

The opossum stayed frozen, unsure what to do. Fainting was not the best solution. She had a nest to build, and wanted to get to it before some fellow critters claimed the best spots.

"You're okay," Coltan whispered. "Go on. You're okay."

The animal stared at him. Then, as if thinking it over and deciding it was safe, the creature tottered off as Coltan and Brian watched.

Brian had thought he'd seen everything, but Coltan's way with animals was something extraordinary. More important, however, was the fact Coltan had remained alert to danger even when distracted by their conversation. It made him reconsider what really worried him.

He lit a second cigarette and thought it over. Beverly had brought up the possibility that she, or Brian or both of them could die during this time of peril. What would happen to Natalie and Coltan then? The real issue was not unrequited love or premarital sex. The real issue was their safety and survival in the absence of the two adults they loved and trusted. This was his real worry.

Although Coltan had not realized it, in the last few minutes he had proven his courage and reliability, and had set Brian's mind at ease. Beverly had been correct all along.

"You know I love you like you're my own son," Brian told him.

At first, Coltan didn't know what to say. However, he had known this for a long time. Brian didn't have to tell him. After a moment, Coltan mumbled, "Yes, sir. Thank you." An awkward silence between them followed. Coltan thought back to all the trouble he had caused Brian in the early days, and all the sharp-tongued cruel things he had said just to test his patience and sincerity. Brian had never failed him, no matter what Coltan had thrown his way. "I'm sorry for all the grief I caused you. Everything I said, too—about your brother and stuff. I didn't mean any of it."

Brian nodded subtly. "I know." He fell into contemplative silence, and Colton did the same. They smoked their cigarettes, listened to the faint drone of traffic and sirens rising from the valley. Finally, Brian said, "If something happens to me and, God forbid, Bev—I want you to take care of Natalie."

Coltan insisted, "Nothing's gonna happen to you."

"God willing," Brian said.

"Or Bev!" Coltan added.

"Right," he replied. "However, Bev was the one who brought it up. It would be irresponsible for us not to consider the possibility." He plunged ahead when Coltan fell stubbornly silent, "Natalie puts up a good front. The brave soldier, that's her. But, I know she won't make it alone. She's too young, too vulnerable. Protect her, Colt."

Coltan answered automatically and firmly, "Of course I will." Yet, he felt a need to alleviate Brian's worry. He humorously considered Natalie's tough, brave spirit. "Hell... she'll be protecting me!"

Brian laughed softly. "You'll be protecting each other."

"I suppose." Coltan didn't want to dwell on tragic possibilities. Facing the future without Brian and Beverly at his side was unimaginable. He tried to convince himself that the likelihood of such a loss was improbable. But the reality of the dangers inherent in Brian and Beverly's professions validated the opposite scenario Brian had presented. His confidence nullified, Coltan silently cried out to God to keep them safe.

As if reading his mind, Brian ended their discussion with prayer, and they retired to their beds. Exhausted, Coltan was out the moment his head met the pillow, and he didn't awaken until well into the next afternoon.

CHAPTER 16

IT HITS THE FAN

A CALLER ON THE RADIO said a friend told her the high-security Internet search engine company he works for now requires REFEHL chips for all its employees. Still another reported accepting the chip as a condition of employment at a Communications conglomerate. Someone else said the chipping for employment was nothing new; companies had been doing that for years.

Regarding a hotter topic, the next caller asserted a clandestine group called the *United Earth Federation* had manufactured the "Mordant Virus" (as the news media referred to it) as a means to reduce the population worldwide. This caller also insisted the Centers for Disease Control and the World Health Organization had been complicit in the manufacture of the virus. In the following hour, four more callers reported sightings of increasing numbers of mords, many whom they recognized as neighbors and co-workers. In the hour after that, a hospital orderly living in Los Angeles reported the military was systematically executing mords who had arrived at area hospitals. Military troops had taken control of the San Francisco Bay Area and all of Southern California, and they were to shoot all looters and mordants on sight. Unfortunately, they shot and killed a large number of innocent people, and the numbers were going up.

A caller from Compton reported that in East Los Angeles, police had teamed with the military to round up and kill all remaining known gang members and all suspected gang members. According to other callers from around the country, the same thing was happening in all the major cosmopolitan areas of the United States of America.

Another caller, who said he worked at San Quentin Prison, insisted many of the inmates had been disappearing. He went on to say some received parole early (supposedly) and others had been "transferred to another facility." The number of new inmates entering the prison was down to zero that month, which was unprecedented.

Roadblocks had gone up in the Denver, Colorado area, and military personnel were manning them to prevent any more citizens from fleeing into the mountains. Other troops rounded up one neighborhood at a time for transport to the rescue centers somewhere in the vicinity. Reports from other parts of the country told of the same scenario, but the reports were sketchy, at best.

Some guy calling from Toledo stated the mords were actually aliens from outer space who intended to exterminate all humans and take over the planet, and that aliens actually run all world governments, beginning with the incident at Roswell, New Mexico back in the nineteen-forties.

Coltan had been listening to all this while he reinforced the wall between his room and the attic access room. He had also installed four iron brackets at the left and right sides of the wall's hidden door on the interior of the attic access room. He had set four iron bars aside on the floor against the wall, ready to be set in place when the time came.

The work was finished.

He had just sat on his bed and reached for his new Bible when the explosion rocked the neighborhood and lit up the night sky outside his window. He heard shouts from the other bedrooms, hurried footsteps, more shouts. After his initial startled reaction, he looked out the window and saw the refinery in the lower valley was on fire.

Natalie rushed through the open doorway to his room. "Did you hear that?"

"Yeah!" He didn't take his eyes off the fire down below.

She joined him there and looked out, almost nudging him aside to get a better view. "It's the refinery," she said. The orange glow of the fire played shadows on their faces.

From his radio on the nightstand, someone was talking about the Antichrist. He leaned over and shut it off. It was scaring the hell out of him, and he didn't want Natalie to hear it. The scene they were witnessing with their own eyes was bad enough.

No sooner had he silenced the radio, another series of smaller explosions rattled the house.

"Oh, no..." Natalie said slowly, sorrowfully.

The refinery explosion had sent flaming debris into the weigh station along the freeway and a passing pickup truck loaded with hay bales erupted as the giant embers landed in the hay. In his sudden panic, the driver veered across the lanes. The rolling conflagration caused drivers to hit their brakes, and the vehicles dominoed into each other as the pickup truck sideswiped the center divider rail then flipped and came to rest with its tires pointing at the black sky. A motor home collided with the rear of the hay truck, accordioned into it by the vehicles behind it. The motor home exploded. Other vehicles trying to avoid the mess collided, flipped over and sailed across the lanes. Some of those exploded when they crashed into an overturned propane truck. That vehicle quickly detonated.

Coltan turned away from the sight, tried not to picture the doomed people trapped inside the burning wreckage.

At the same moment, a whining reverberation drew Natalie's attention to the south end just in time to see a small private airplane spiral into a low-rent apartment house. That place exploded into a massive fireball.

"Good God!" Natalie gasped.

Portafones rang in her parents' room. Natalie and Coltan knew what the ringing meant. She shifted her gaze from the window to him. The look in her eyes almost broke his heart.

Brian entered Coltan's room a minute later with his robe on. They faced him expectantly.

"They're calling in the whole Force," he told them. "Mom's got to go to the hospital."

"Please don't!" Natalie pleaded, "Don't go in!"

"We have to!"

"Why?"

"They need us."

"*We* need you!"

"We both took an oath, Nat." His gaze went to Coltan, and he silently reminded Coltan of his responsibility should they not return. Coltan nodded subtly. It was affirmation enough, and Natalie hadn't seen their silent communication. He returned to the master bedroom to dress.

Natalie slowly and despondently seated herself at the edge of Coltan's bed. "They can't go..." She said it so softly he almost couldn't hear her.

"They have to go."

"They don't have to. The others won't."

"Yeah, they will."

"Most of them have already skipped town with their families." In the next breath, she added, "Or they're hiding with their families. Like us."

He closed the curtain over the window to shut out the glow of the fires. It wasn't enough, for the curtains were thin and the glow showed through the fabric.

Before they left for duty, Brian and Beverly hugged them and tried to reassure them they'd return by noon, maybe a little later, depending on the conditions. They reminded them to keep their portafones and guns handy and to monitor the scanner. Also, they were to double-check the batteries in their flashlights and keep them handy in case the power went out. Coltan assured them he had already checked his that evening. Natalie promised to do so right away.

Overhead, the thumping of helicopter blades shook the house. Natalie looked outside her bedroom window and saw most of the neighbors in the street watching the whirlybirds and the commotion in the valley below. Voices drifted up as the neighbors compared notes, suspicions and rumors. By this time, the whine of sirens joined the cacophony of copter sounds, along with the soft roar of car engines starting.

She heard the garage door fall shut and watched as Mom and Dad pulled their cars out of the driveway and raced off into the valley. The fear and grief rose in her as she thought it might be the last time she would ever see them again.

Coltan appeared beside her and watched, too. He was confident they would return.

She sunk down against the window frame, slid to the floor and sat there. He sat down beside her and held her hand.

"God... protect them," she whispered.

BONITO VALLE COMMUNITY Hospital was overwhelmed with casualties. One copter after another deposited more incoming on the roof, and the ambulance bay was loaded with ambulances pulling in with additional patients and out to retrieve more. In addition to this, citizens were transporting victims in their own cars. The parking lot had filled up quickly, and the cars were now lining the streets and filling the parking lots of businesses surrounding the hospital.

Beverly found a space in the strip mall lot one block away. She had tucked Brutus into the rear waistband of her trousers. No way was she going anywhere without it now. She could see many people running through the streets. Some were trying to carry injured to the emergency room. She was grateful for the illumination of the streetlights as she made her way to the corner, and then across the street toward the west side entrance. She kept her eyes and ears open as she approached the locked employee entrance. She used her keycard and punched in her numbers. The door popped open a little, and she pulled it open enough to enter the building, then turned and made certain it latched closed.

Although this hallway seemed fairly quiet, she could hear the chaos of a multitude of voices talking, shouting, screaming and crying from the floor below. Above, a voice over the intercom system paged doctors, nurses and lab personnel. Sirens blared steadily. All together, it sounded like a bizarre symphony.

A young intern she recognized dashed madly toward the employee door. There was three days worth of stubble on his pale and wet face. His eyes were wild, his clothing soaked in sweat. She threw herself against the wall as he brushed past her, jostling her. She breathed in the stench of the breeze he created in his haste. It was the worst kind of perspiration odor, the kind produced by outright terror. He slipped his key card into the reader, frantically punched in his numbers, and barely waited for the door to pop open when he made his exit. As she watched him through the glass door, she saw him fling his keycard into the bushes beside the door, and he sped his pace to a jog as he did this, and then he ran.

She took the corridor on the left and approached the surgical wing. She grabbed her doctor's coat and stethoscope from her locker and put it on, then deposited her purse and Brutus in there and locked it. The desk clerk informed her they needed her in the emergency room. She asked how many surgeries were in progress. The clerk answered, "Only two." How can that be? The question nagged at her as she descended the stairs to the main floor.

A security guard at the ER unit employee check-in reviewed her identification tag and let her through. Soldiers watched the chaos, some standing guard, and some assisting by pushing gurneys carrying patients into the isolation ward. Beverly had counted seven loaded gurneys headed for the isolation ward by the time she carded and punched in for entrance to the emergency unit. On instinct, she turned and looked once more as she pulled open the door and saw a team dressed in HAZMAT suits enter the isolation ward. She paused, holding the door ajar and continued watching. Two more HAZMAT teams exited the room, pushing two gurneys that held a stack of four dead on each, the bodies covered by transparent heavyweight plastic sheeting.

She tasted the bile that traveled up her throat. She swallowed hard and entered the emergency unit, mentally preparing herself for the mayhem she expected to find.

A nurse stumbled against the wall, crying and holding one bloody hand with the other. The blood spurted onto her chest and soiled her uniform. Beverly grabbed a discarded rubber tourniquet off a lab tray and ran to her.

"He bit me!" The trembling nurse's eyes were wide with shock and her breathing rapid. "*Bit me!*"

Beverly tied the tourniquet tightly around the woman's wrist and examined what she could see through all the blood. The woman was missing three fingers and had a deep bite that covered both the palm and back of her hand.

Behind Beverly, a deep male voice ordered, "Step aside, Doctor!" Beverly swung around to face him. The soldier had a grim, stern, almost hostile expression on his face. Again, he ordered, "Step aside, *now!*" He was pointing his rifle at the injured nurse.

Beverly noticed the rifle had a silencer, and it struck her this soldier had probably killed many of the infected patients already this night. She also realized someone in charge of this man had planned for this type of scenario and had supplied all his troops with silencers.

He raised his arm halfway and motioned Beverly aside, his eyes still riveted on the stricken nurse.

"You can't!" Beverly exclaimed.

"Please..." the nurse begged, "I've got three little kids at home!"

The soldier grabbed Beverly's arm and wrenched her alongside him. In the next second, he threw her to the floor. He had not taken his eyes off the nurse as he did this. He aimed and fired. The bullet struck the woman in the middle of her forehead. She made a gagging sound and, with her eyes fixed disbelievingly on the soldier, she sunk to the floor in a sprawled out sitting position.

The soldier then spoke into a radio attached to his lapel, "Pick up Primary at ER Two."

Doctors and nurses were darting about frantically, many colliding as they tried to pass each other. If any of them had seen the soldier kill the nurse, and some must have, none gave any indication.

More requests for personnel crackled over the intercom. The patients in the waiting room were fighting because of the overcrowding and confusion. Their fights were now spilling into the treatment area, and security had their hands full. The receptionist was crying. There came a crash in the ambulance bay, and a fragment of red brake light plastic skipped across the hallway floor along with the shattered shards of glass.

Someone near the bay screamed, "Watch out! Watch out! Watch out!"

There came another crash, and the light of a sudden fire filled the bay hallway. The soldier looked in that direction, raised his weapon upright and rested it against his right shoulder. He stood there for a moment, watching stoically. He made his decision and walked briskly toward the ambulance bay, his posture erect and ready.

Beverly startled at the sound as she tried to scramble off the floor. When she finally got to her feet, all she could do was gaze at the scene in horror. Gradually, she became aware her hands felt stiff and sticky. She looked at them and saw the nurse's blood. In her rush to treat the woman, she had forgotten gloves.

In the women's room, she scrubbed and scrubbed her hands with a disposable brush full of antiseptic soap to clean under her fingernails and into the skin crevices. The noises from outside invaded this space, too. Even the running hot water couldn't mask it.

Her lips moved in silent, desperate prayer as she rinsed and scrubbed some more.

She wanted to go home.

COLTAN HAD MOVED THE scanner from the kitchen into the living room where he and Natalie had decided to spend the night. Emergency services closed the interstate to all northbound traffic. Dispatch was having difficulty attending to all the calls coming in. Besides the many fires in the refinery area, the interstate and the south end, other calls were coming in regarding murders, roving gangs of looters, multi-car accidents and mordants.

He and Natalie placed their portafones, flashlights and guns on the coffee table. They listened silently to the drama in the valley. Occasionally, they would hear a copter overhead. The sound no longer alarmed them. They had accepted it as part of the entire scenario.

Now and then, they would hear her father's voice come over on the scanner. His voice sounded calm. In the previous hour, they heard him speaking with Dispatch, and they could hear another voice yelling in the background, "Hey-hey-hey-hey! Don't touch that body!" But Brian Danbury's voice retained that professionally cool tone that was common to all officers jaded by years of seeing the worst of everything as he requested medical services support. However, in the last thirty minutes, they had not heard his voice at all.

Natalie was resting on her side under a blanket on the sofa. At the end of the sofa where she had laid her head, Coltan sat on the floor, leaning his back against the armrest of the sofa. Natalie placed her hand on Coltan's shoulder, and then slid her palm down and across where she caressed his upper chest. He shifted to one side, leaned his head back and looked at her.

"He's okay," Coltan said.

BRIAN CAME TO WITH a splitting headache. His first instinct was to place his hand on the painful injury to his head. The blood there was still warm and wet, and had streamed over his eyelids. He wiped the blood from his eyes as best he could and tried to focus. He felt a great deal of painful pressure in his left side and easily found the cause. The door had been pushed in, the armrest forced against his ribs. He blurrily saw through the shattered side window something big and white with red on top. He strained to see it. An ambulance had crashed into his patrol car. He could not see anyone at the wheel of the rig.

In his patrol car, the airbag had deployed and had since deflated. The cracked windshield looked like a massive spider web, the lines going off in many directions. A light pole rested part way over the hood, the rest of it leaning upon the lightbar on the roof of his vehicle, denting the roof in over the dashboard. He unbuckled his seatbelt, leaned painfully sideways and craned his neck to speak into the transmitter on his lapel.

The word came out as a groan, "Dispatch..."

No reply.

"Dispatch..." He pulled his lapel up to better see the small transmitter. It was cracked and wet with blood. He pressed the button and tried again, "Dispatch..."

The computer on the console was also smashed. And then he saw why. The right side of his car had crashed against and partially into a building. Large slabs of brick and concrete, plus some heavy rebar had broken through the window there on impact and had fallen into the car, hitting the computer. It had also broken the rack that supported his rifle. The rifle was displaced, the point of it aiming at his face. He raised his right arm and shifted it away from him, using his forearm and wrist.

His chest was painful and he was having trouble breathing. He knew it was because one or maybe more of his ribs had been broken and had pierced his left lung. The lung was filling with blood; this he could tell by the gurgling sound that accompanied each effort to take in a breath.

He coughed up blood. He coughed up a lot of blood, each uncontrollable and undeniable effort producing agonizing spasms from his broken ribcage. There came no relief as more blood oozed into his lung and demanded exit, torturously rattling his shattered ribs as he helplessly coughed another shower of slimy maroon excretion upon the deflated airbag and steering wheel.

Dispatch would get the signal his car had been involved in an accident. He knew another car and an ambulance would be there promptly. Maybe they were on their way this very minute.

An image in his head of Mario and little Rosa Rodriquez replaced his thoughts about Dispatch. Their image prompted his memory, and he remembered he had been on his way to check on them when the ambulance slammed into his car. Regardless of his injuries and trapped in his patrol car, Brian prayed first for the Rodriquez family, and then he prayed for his own family and himself. He concluded his prayers not with *Amen*, but with a rattling cough that sent more spray upon the airbag and a subsequent trickle of blood down his chin.

Through the constant ringing in his ears, he could hear a scuffle outside the car. There was a scream—a man—and the man trying to run but having trouble staying on his feet. Someone was chasing the man, catching up to him. They both came into the stream of the headlights from the police car. Brian saw the man fleeing was a paramedic. The person chasing him, he couldn't tell. However, the pursuer was growling like a rabid dog. The paramedic fell again, and this time he didn't get up. The pursuer was upon him, tearing at him.

Brian lost consciousness at that moment.

THE VOICE ON THE SCANNER caused Coltan to shudder inexplicably:

"Car seven. Eleven-eighty-three, Tenth at Branstead. Ten-fifty-three."

Natalie lifted her head and stared at the scanner.

"What does that mean?" Coltan asked.

"A vehicle accident. Officer down."

"It's not him," Coltan said quickly.

"We haven't heard him in over an hour."

Coltan repeated insistently, "It isn't him."

She didn't reply, instead she prayed silently.

Twenty minutes later, the officer responding to the call reported in. "Can't get through! Perimeter blocked by subjects and civilians!" His voice suddenly became shrill, "Jesus! They're on me! Request backup!" Immediately, there came the sound of screams, growling, a gunshot, a crash and the crush of metal, followed by more screams. Then the screams stopped, and the only other sound was growling and the wet, disgusting sound of smacking and chewing.

Coltan switched off the scanner. He turned to Natalie, determination in his eyes. "It wasn't him!"

She held herself and rocked back and forth. She prayed harder than she had ever prayed in her life.

MARIO RODRIQUEZ HAD worked into the early morning restocking what little was left at Bujjet Mart and raced out still wearing his Bujjet Mart vest to catch the final bus. He got to the stop in time and as he waited, he wondered about the many helicopters above the valley, and the wailing sirens in all directions. After thirty minutes had passed it was obvious the bus would never arrive. His gut twisting with increasing anxiety, Mario began the ten-mile trek home in the darkness. As he neared the edges of the south end, the increased presence of police, paramedics and all their lights and incessant sirens told him something catastrophic was occurring and he was approaching the center of hell on earth. Gunshots echoed, so many he could not tell from where. He quickened his pace, but did not run because, if he ran, he would attract police attention. The cops would only delay him. At worst, they would arrest him for RWH, *Running While Hispanic*. By the time he got two miles into the south end, he had seen seven mords feasting on their victims. One half mile further, a pack of five spotted him and chased him as he dashed around traffic accidents, stalled cars, and partially devoured corpses. He lost them when he fought his way through a terrified crowd that rushed toward him and the mords shifted their focus to that stampeding buffet.

IN SURGERY, THE ASSISTANT slapped a third hemostat into Beverly's hand. She clamped off the femoral artery and the assistant suctioned the remaining blood to better reveal the wound. The fascia was a shredded mess, and slivers and loose pieces of bone were visible.

From the moment the patient was out on the table, she had her doubts because of the absence of abrasions. "They say this was a motorcycle accident?" Beverly asked no one in particular.

Doctor Schneider the head surgeon picked at the mess, examining the white and gray slivers of splintered bone matter inside the wound. Something caught his attention.

"Whoa. What's this?" He glanced up at the assistant. "Rat Tooth Forceps." She slapped it into his hand, and he used it to extract the matter in question. He held it close under the light and scrutinized it. "That's an incisor!"

Beverly examined the tooth as the doctor held it under the light with the forceps. The presence of the tooth explained the torn off flap of skin and muscle, and the crushed, splintered tibia.

Schneider ordered the anesthetist, "Shut off the oxygen. Give him full anesthesia."

The anesthetist regarded him questioningly, "Doctor?"

"You heard me."

"You'll be killing the patient!" Beverly protested.

"What does a broken human tooth inside an avulsion tell you, Doctor Danbury? Well, I'll tell you. This man is infected, and there's nothing we can do for him."

"We can't kill him!"

"There's no other choice."

She stepped back, "Doctor Schneider, I can't be a part of this."

"You're excused, Doctor. Step out."

In the changing room outside the operating room, she stripped off her protective glasses and deposited them into the hazardous waste bin. She then pulled off the mask and headscarf and dropped those in. Blood—infected blood—stained her surgical apron, surgical gloves and shoe mitts. She removed these things carefully, the apron and gloves in a combined move. As an added precaution, she decided to dispose of the scrubs with the hazardous waste, too. She removed her bra and underwear and entered the shower room. When the water was hot enough, she stepped in and scrubbed herself head-to-toe with the disinfecting soap. She stood under the water for a long time, crying and questioning God.

THE VOICES ON THE SCANNER droned on, a senseless drone of numbers and coded commands that were nothing but a foreign language to Coltan.

He had been praying for Brian. He was certain God would protect him, and was protecting him at that moment. However, Coltan found his faith ebbing and flowing with the difficult waiting and the not knowing. It was driving him crazy. If this had been happening two years ago, he would have slugged down a twelve-pack by now, and would have smoked a couple of joints, too. Tonight, he coped through prayer.

Natalie had been silent for the last few hours. She was refusing to speak, or she was unable to speak; he didn't know. She stayed curled up on the sofa, curled up under a blanket with her knees drawn against her chest. It frightened Coltan to see her like this, and he didn't know what to do to console her.

CHAPTER 17

The doorbell awakened him.

He opened his eyes and glanced backwards at the sofa to see Natalie. She was still there, sitting in her curled up position, her eyes staring across at the staircase.

The voices still came over the scanner, indicating the mayhem had not died down. He wanted to unplug the damned thing.

The doorbell rang again.

"I'll get it," he said, rising to his feet.

"It's them," she offered dreadfully, "...to tell us he's dead."

"No." That thought never crossed his mind.

He went to the door and looked through the peephole. He didn't recognize the balding man with a mustache and wearing glasses. "Who is it?" he shouted.

"Mitch!"

Coltan addressed Natalie, "You know someone named Mitch?"

"Dad's Marine buddy. A family friend." She sat up, expecting Mitch had come to deliver the bad news.

Coltan unlocked the door and pulled it open.

"Who are you?" Mitch asked him.

"I'm Coltan."

"Oh, yeah. The one he adopted." Coltan didn't understand this at first. He suddenly realized that maybe Brian had adopted him, in a sense. Mitch raised his hand and displayed a folded piece of paper, "Got this for Brian. He home yet?"

"No."

"When's he comin' back?"

"I don't know. We haven't heard him on the scanner."

"You sure?" Mitch said.

"We've been monitoring all night."

"I thought I heard him around five this morning," Mitch responded.

Natalie shot off the sofa and ran to the door. "You heard him?"

"Sounded like him." He paused, and then added, "Well, there was a lotta voices. But I thought I heard him. Where's your ma, girl?"

"The hospital." The hope she had recaptured momentarily for her father faded again. Mitch had heard wrong. She had listened all night and had not heard Dad's voice after the last time just before two o'clock.

She unlocked the security door and pushed it open. "Come in."

"I gotta go." He offered the paper to her. "Give this to your dad. He'll know what it is."

She took it. "Thanks, Mitch."

He turned to go down the steps, but he stopped instead and turned back to them. "The shit's hittin' the fan. Hittin' it everywhere. Y'all be safe."

"You too," Natalie said.

They watched him get into his jeep and drive off.

Coltan closed and locked the doors. Natalie unfolded the paper. "What is it?" he asked.

"The coordinates." She stared at them. "It's real."

"What's real?"

"The refuge. Christians. In the mountains."

"The one your dad talked about."

"It's real…"

"THE ARMY'S EVACUATING Reyton and Oak Shores," the

nurse told Beverly. "My folks are there."

"When did they start?"

"Last night." She gave Beverly the clipboard. "Curtain three."

"Why are we charting on paper?"

"The system's down. All the techs have split."

A gunshot rang out from the waiting room.

The nurse remarked over the resulting screams from there, "Another mord, I guess."

"Are they still coming in? The wounded, I mean."

"They're spilling into the parking lot."

"God help us," Beverly said.

The nurse cocked her head and smirked. "God? The only thing that'll help me right now is a couple of stiff drinks!"

"Don't give up your faith..." Beverly began.

"God has left the universe, honey. Get used to it." With that, she turned and walked away.

COLTAN MADE TOAST AND slathered it with lots of butter and cinnamon sugar. He gave up on the idea of encouraging Natalie to eat. She had returned to the sofa and the scanner.

Out in the back, the sun's first rays peeked above the mountains and the birds were singing happily. The air was cold, and the winds were beginning to pick up. In the valley, the refinery was a black, smoking hulk, and he could see a large black smear at that part of the interstate that had also caught fire. Being too far away to see the details, he imagined the lanes littered with wrecked and burned cars and burned and dead people. He noticed some new fires had broken out in the downtown area, the impoverished south end, and a high-dollar subdivision on the far west side.

Sirens wailed from everywhere.

Military choppers had multiplied in the airspace over the valley. Some were heading for Reyton, and a few were destined for the small airport at the north end of Bonito Valle. The first of two giant transport planes prepped for a landing there ahead of the choppers.

They were preparing to evacuate the people and escort them to the rescue centers. Coltan wondered how much time they had before the soldiers were at their door.

His next thought was about Baker Creek. Over the past days, he had seen only one more copter fly over that way. What were they doing there? It was too small and too hilly to be a logical place for a rescue center. The only possible explanation was that they were setting up some kind of satellite base there.

He leaned forward on the railing, rested his weight on his hands. Here was a clear view of the back yard of his former home. The toppled dining room chair remained legs-up in the dry weeds like a dead animal in full-fledged rigor mortis. He noticed someone had duct taped a large piece of cardboard over the broken window. Most likely, it was Richard's work. Richard repaired everything with duct tape. A fleeting thought came that maybe they missed him. No, they didn't miss him. They probably hadn't even noticed he had left home for good. The thought of it pained him.

The security door latched loudly enough that Coltan heard it and spun around. Natalie's fatigue was evident in her face as she approached him. "Can I have a smoke?"

He took one from the pack, gave it to her and offered her a light. She took a deep drag and gazed out at the weed-eaten yard across the way.

"They should die," she stated.

"What?" It was the last thing he expected her to say.

"Good people are dying. And then there's people like them... going on their merry way." She shot a look at him, her eyes angry. "I've seen the scars on you, Colt."

"I've hurt people, too," he said.

"No more." She took another drag and glanced around. The neighborhood was quiet and lifeless, as if deserted. "I turned the scanner off."

"He might be at the hospital."

"Mom would've called."

"Maybe she doesn't know yet."

"They would have told her."

"It's hectic there. They're probably all so busy there hasn't been time. Or, maybe the message got lost or something."

"I felt him beside me." She said it in almost a whisper.

He refused to believe it. "You imagined it." Regardless, the tears ran down her cheeks. He couldn't handle her grief. "Don't!"

She sniffled and let her tears continue their course. The full impact of it hadn't hit her, yet. The initial shock was only now starting to dissipate.

"Don't..." Coltan said, his voice bitter, "Don't! Don't you dare cry! Don't!"

She raged at him incredulously. "You shut up!"

He couldn't take this. It was too much. He began to walk away, wanting to escape her grief. She took his wrist and stopped him, and she stood there for a moment, pleading with her eyes. He placed his hand on her shoulder, tried to think. His throat felt tight. She leaned into him and rested her forehead against his chest. He put his arms around her.

AFTER HOPPING A FENCE and taking a shortcut onto Branstead through the parking lot of a defunct bottling plant, Mario had arrived just in time to see Rosa tear toward him on the sidewalk in hysterical screaming terror. Her tearful description of the horror that caused her to flee their tiny house convinced him they had no choice but to run for their lives. She shut her eyes and sobbed on his shoulder as he carried her, screamed in terror each time he dodged one of the many mords that had formerly been their neighbors and friends. There was smoke in the air from all the buildings on fire, and he could scarcely see, much less breathe. Screams and gunshots rang in their ears. Once he reached the main drag of Tenth Street with her, he glanced behind him and then to each side, scanned every dark cavity between buildings, and every recessed doorway.

Unlike the area they had just fled, this part of the hood was eerily desolate and silent. Through the smoke, the dawning sun cast a hazy ginger light upon the eastern sides of the buildings, and the murky glow only added to the ethereal atmosphere.

The little girl in his arms was barefooted and wearing only a flannel nightgown that was damp with her perspiration. Her tears and sweat pasted her long black curls to her face. A bite wound on her buttocks bled through her underwear, and the growing stain saturated her nightgown. Her blood oozed in a slow stream down his arm.

Mario paused barely long enough to catch his breath before he raced onward in search of anyone sane and compassionate enough to give them a ride out of there. The boy spotted the half-devoured corpse that still wore the bloody shredded remains of a paramedic's uniform; he spotted it just in time to not trip over it. He sprinted over the dead man, and his action caused the girl to jostle painfully in the cradle of his arms. She cried out in pain, began to sob.

"Shhh... Rosa, shhh. They'll hear you. *Silencio, por favor.*" He did not look at her; his eyes were riveted on the squad car a short distance ahead, the passenger side of the vehicle imbedded in the wall of an insurance company storefront. An ambulance that had crashed into the cop's ride crumbled the driver's side of the patrol car. The squad car's windshield was shattered, held together by a spider web pattern of cracks. He could make out the still figure of a person in the driver's seat, but could not tell if it was a man or a woman, a cop or a desperate civilian. Mario knew the car was useless, and expected the driver was dead. However, if no one had beaten him to it, there would be a gun inside, and Mario desperately needed a weapon. The boy slowed to a stop and tenderly unloaded the little girl onto the hood of the wrecked police car.

She rolled onto her knees and reached for him. "No, Mario! Don't let go! Pick me up!"

He scrambled easily onto the hood with her. "I'm not goin' anywhere. Be quiet. Shhh."

He kicked at the broken windshield until it finally gave way and a crackled sheet of the glass bent into the seat on the passenger side. He leaned in and reached for the rifle. His eyes darted to the policeman lying motionless behind the crumpled steering wheel, covered chin to chest with dried blood. Mario recognized Officer Brian Danbury, and his heart fell heavily in sorrow. The boy reconsidered his assumption the man was dead, and he hopefully listened for breathing. There was no sound. Leaning further in, he lightly shook the officer's arm, called out his name in an effort to rouse him. No response. The arm was stiff and cold. Mario solemnly accepted the truth and said a quick prayer concluding with the Sign of the Cross for the kind policeman.

The peril of his situation returned to him and he remembered what had brought him into the police car in the first place. He spied the gun in the holster. Even though Mario felt a twinge of guilt about it, he released the snap and removed the firearm, found it fully loaded, and tucked it down the front of his pants. He then leaned back out a little, took the rifle and backed out on his knees onto the hood. A quick check proved the rifle was also fully loaded. With a vague sense of empowerment, he hopped down onto the littered sidewalk and retrieved little Rosa with his free arm.

Something growled behind them. Mario turned and faced the assailant who had followed them for six blocks. There was blood on her mouth and down the front of her blue nylon nightgown. Her bare feet badly cut from the litter of glass and other debris on the sidewalk left smeared footprints on the cement. Her sliced open right foot caused her to limp with each step forward. With her eyes pinned on him and the girl, she tripped and fell across a dislodged shaft of rebar that protruded from the broken building.

"Mama, no!" Rosa screamed. "No, Mama, no!"

Mario slowly lowered the hysterical child to the pavement. She clutched his vest with both her tiny brown hands as she ducked behind him for safety.

Mario pumped the rifle and aimed at his mother as she stumbled to her feet. Her eyes were vacant of the love that once filled them. She peered at the boy like a starving child would a hot, fresh pizza. The woman licked her lips, growled, and bared her broken, bloodstained teeth.

"I'm sorry, Mama..." Mario pulled the trigger. The bullet skimmed the left side of her head. The shot did not bring her down. She took another step forward. Mario pumped a second time, blinked away the blur of his tears and held his breath to steady his shaking hands. "Forgive me, God..." The second shot pierced the center of her forehead. This time, she fell forward onto her face. He cringed at the *thwack* sound as her head met the pavement. A miserable sob escaped his throat.

Rosa whimpered and buried her face in the back of Mario's vest. He turned quickly, picked her up with one strong arm and carried her with him to the ambulance that had crashed into the squad car. He found no paramedics or patient in the rig, but there was a lot of blood and signs of a violent struggle in the rear compartment.

Rosa thumped her fists upon his shoulder blades. "Mario! There's a man!"

He turned with her still in his arms and saw the ravaged remains of one of the paramedics in the intersection about ten feet away. The sight caused his gut to threaten to purge. Rosa's shivering reminded him to regain his senses and get them both out of there. Mario lifted the girl into the front seat and climbed in after her. He ripped away the remnants of the deflated airbag and reached for the key in the ignition. He prayed as he turned the key. The vehicle shuddered to a start. Rotating red light illuminated the street and buildings, and the siren wailed loudly and unexpectedly. He searched for the siren off switch, but could not find it in the confusion and desperation of the moment. After some consideration, the boy decided it was just as well. The siren would make it easier to cut through the inevitable mass of traffic ahead. Once he found the headlights control, he shifted into reverse and the rig came loose from the side of the police car with a groaning sound as he pressed the accelerator. The separation spilled a shower of broken headlight plastic onto the street.

He looked reassuringly at his little passenger who had covered her ears against all the noise. As he shifted into drive, he began to roll up his window. "Roll up your window and lock your door," he told Rosa. She obeyed immediately and without comment. "Put on your seatbelt." She obeyed again, wiped her tears, and looked up at him for further instruction. He tried to smile at her, but every muscle in his face froze with the terrifying reality of their predicament. Mario hoped his love and promise—no—*determination* of his protection showed plainly in his eyes as he gazed at her. "I'll get us somewhere safe."

Rosa covered her ears again, sniffled and stared down at her cut and dirty bare feet that hung limply over the edge of the big seat. For some reason she did not understand, her feet did not hurt anymore. They seemed to stare back at her as if they belonged to someone else. Now that she took the time to think about it, only one of her injuries hurt, and it throbbed with burning pain. She shifted her position to take her weight off the oozing bite on her butt cheek. Her blood rolled into the gutter of the upholstery where the seat met the backrest.

She gazed appreciatively at her big brother as he stared ahead and floored the accelerator. Rosa recognized the glaze of deep thought in his eyes. He was praying. He was probably praying for Mama. She joined him and prayed silently for her mother, and then she prayed for God's protection. As she prayed, she kept her gaze on Mario, confident he would get them to safety.

"WE CAN GO OVER TO THE hospital," Coltan said.

"It's too dangerous." Natalie had managed to pull herself together for the moment.

"We can call the hospital. How about if we call the station? Someone there could tell us something."

"I've been trying. The service is out on both the PF and the land line."

"Screw it! We're goin' over to the hospital." To him, it was better than sitting around waiting for information. He still didn't believe anything serious had happened to Brian, and he wanted to prove it to Natalie.

She considered the idea insane. "No! You heard the scanner! We'll never make it!"

The desperate cries of a woman emerging at the crest of the incline along the gully overlapped Natalie's words. The woman was pulling a little boy with her. They were running, at least she was running, the boy was stumbling and falling as she half-dragged him to keep up with her.

"*Run!*" the woman screamed. "*Run!*"

The boy fell again and began to wail and cry.

She grabbed him, pulled him up by one arm and started running again, this time trying to carry him. Her face was frantic and panicked.

"Over here!" Coltan called.

The woman glanced their way and veered toward the porch, followed the path between the gardens. At the ridge of the gully, four men and two women scrambled up behind her. It wasn't until they got closer when Natalie and Coltan saw the blood on their clothing, heard the growling, saw their twisted faces. Their eyes were riveted on the woman and child. She stumbled and dropped the boy. The child got to his feet, but fell again flat on his face and lay there splayed in the gravel. The woman stopped and stooped to retrieve him. The mords tackled her.

Coltan moved to aid the woman and child. He had only taken three steps when Natalie pounced on him and forced him face down onto the wood of the porch. He hit his head and saw stars. He tried to escape her weight on him and the solid grip of her arms locked around his waist.

She shouted at him, "No! It's too late!"

"Lemme up!" he screamed back, struggling to free himself.

"It's too late! You can't help them!" She looked up and saw two of the pack had noticed them, alerted by their shouting and struggle. She tried to pull him up on his feet, "We gotta go in! We gotta go in *now*!"

"I gotta help them," Coltan yelled, wrestling her off of him.

She tugged at him with both hands. "They're after *us*!"

He raised his head quickly. Through the remaining veil of stars, he saw two of the mords racing toward them. They were almost at the bottom step. He allowed Natalie to pull him up, and they ran for the doors. He pushed her in front of him, and she yanked open the security door and stepped into the kitchen. He was a step behind her and entered. The mords had reached the door, and Coltan leaned out and got a grip on the security door, kicked the lead one back, and pulled the security door shut and locked it. The mords pressed their faces against it, beat on it with their bloodied hands. He shut the interior door and locked it, and then he slammed the slider down on the small window.

They continued to pound on the door.

Coltan stood there panting. He reached behind him, reached for the gun he thought he had tucked in the rear waistband. It was not there.

"The guns... the guns...!" It came in labored, almost panicked, breaths.

He rushed into the living room and saw Natalie snatch them off the table, along with the portafones. She tossed one of the guns to Coltan.

The pounding continued.

She yelled, "Grab the flashlights!"

He walked backward and took them off the coffee table, his eyes still watching for the anticipated intrusion.

Natalie tried her portafone. She got a recording, shut it off and told Coltan, "No service!"

"Okay, okay, okay... We gotta get upstairs. Go now!" He was inching his way back into the kitchen, and she couldn't understand why.

"What are you doing?"

"There's no bread," he explained.

Pounding. Growling. Snarling. The noise of outdoor furniture overturned. They heard more shouts and screams coming from other directions outside.

"What?" She couldn't understand why a loaf of bread was so important.

He reached across the breakfast bar and grabbed the loaf of

bread off the counter. He turned to her and gave her a shove forward. "Go! *Go!*" When he reached the bottom of the staircase, he glanced around to make certain she had not opened any of the sliders. Those he could see all appeared intact.

Violent pounding rattled the front door, and the window in the den shattered. The slider there made a cracking sound, but it held. He quickly went to the front door and looked out the peephole to an invasion.

Natalie descended a couple of steps. She gazed hopefully at the front door. "Mom?"

"No." Coltan ran to her and took her hand, pulled her the rest of the way up the stairs. They dived into his room, and Coltan closed the door, locked it and placed the reinforcement bars across it.

Natalie, already at the secret access door, glanced back and saw he was starting to follow. But suddenly he stopped and went back to his bed and opened the nightstand drawer.

"Colt! Come on!"

He took something out of the drawer, something enclosed in a black leather case. "Gotta have this. Can't leave it behind." In a second, he was behind her and they both entered the access room. They stopped and dropped the bars across the door together. He glanced at the retractable staircase. "Up. Go."

She was already ahead of him.

They were safe now, up in the attic.

He set the bread down and let the flashlights drop from under one arm. Out of breath, he sat there on the floor, waiting for his heart to slow. The gun in his hand caught his eye, and he reset the hammer and carefully laid the gun on the floor. He held the black leather case on his lap, stared at it as if it was the most important and precious thing in the world.

Natalie finally realized it was his Bible.

She pulled the staircase up and locked it in place. Adrenaline rushed through her in overload. "I can't believe we forgot our guns!" she said. "If we had brought them out—"

"No..." Coltan mumbled.

"We could've taken them on, killed them. We could've."

"No..." Coltan said it again, softly.

"We could've!" She slapped her palm to her forehead, "I forgot everything Dad taught me. All that time... what an idiot. What was I thinking? How could I forget such a simple thing? One simple thing!"

Coltan got to his feet and gently laid his Bible on his mattress.

He then moved cautiously to the north window and peered out. It looked like an invasion. Many of the frantic people were hurt and some were bleeding. The horde overtook the ones who were seriously hurt. The able-bodied were banging on doors, searching for help and refuge, while some of the mords followed after them to—

He didn't want to think it.

The assailants were of different ages and mixed ethnicities. Where would such a mix of people come from all at once? It seemed to him, they had to be part of a group who may have been traveling together.

An idea came to him, and he checked the south side window. The road a short way below was the only east-west route through town from this area. The city bus route ended at the Dairy Delight where it dropped off the remaining eastbound riders. It then picked up the passengers waiting there to go west into town, stopping once more at the transfer site at Main to pick up those transferring from the old downtown. The route crossed over the gully first, then the interstate, and then entered the heart of the shopping district in the west side.

He shifted his position so he could get a better view through the trees and brush. Sure enough, there was a city bus toppled on its side in the gully. He was certain some mords were among the passengers. One or more may have caused the initial accident, and from there all hell broke loose.

Down in the street the screaming escalated. Gunshots rang out as the panicked refugees and the mords crashed their way into private homes. A carjacker commandeered a subcompact and flung the driver, a woman, into the street. He drove away as two of the horde covered her.

Coltan looked away. Her screams told him more than he wanted to know.

Behind him, Natalie grabbed a rifle and loaded it. She fiercely engaged the pump and stationed herself at another window. She slid the glass open and took aim at a mord.

The sound of the pump action diverted Coltan's attention to her. It frightened him to see how quickly she had gone from scared girl to *Commando Natalie.* Maybe she was somehow trying to prove to her father all his training had not been in vain. The splitting pop of the rifle hurt his ears and caused him to cringe.

The target dropped in the middle of the street. Adrenaline flowing through her veins, and satisfaction empowering her, Natalie pumped it again, took aim at another one and fired. The bullet pierced the man's forehead, and he went down. She peered around for her next target, a teenage girl she recognized from school. The girl, her bloody mouth twisted in a snarl and blood staining the front of her tee shirt, was dragging a toddler across a lawn at the other side of the street, dragging him by one leg. The child's mother already overcome by two other predators was as good as dead already. The child was screaming in terror, screaming for his mother. Natalie waited until the girl raised her head just enough for the child to be clear of the shot when it came. The head came up, the girl glancing around for potential scavengers. Natalie fired. The bullet entered the base of her skull. She fell on top of the child.

Coltan confronted her at the window "Your father said *defense only!*"

A man dressed in nothing except boxer shorts emerged from his house and shot dead another mord who had zeroed in on the toddler trapped under the body of his attacker. He ran to the toddler and threw the dead girl off, picked up the child and carried him like a sack of potatoes into the house. As he slammed the door, another mord crashed against it and began to pound.

Natalie pumped the rifle again. "I'm defending *them!*"

"How can you possibly tell the infected from the injured?" He yelled back.

Her tone of voice was sarcastic and insulting. "The infected are chasing the injured down and biting them!" She spotted one more that had an elderly woman by her hair and was trying to bring her down. Natalie shot and missed. Pumping the rifle again, she admonished Coltan, her eyes still on her target. "You made me miss!"

The next shot hit the spot. Out of the corner of her eye, she saw another figure dash toward the woman. She shifted in the window, pumped the rifle again. Just when she was ready to pull the trigger, she saw it was a bloodstain-free middle-aged woman rushing to the old lady's aid. Natalie took a quick, deep breath and expelled it. *That was a close one.*

They heard the crack of other gunshots from all directions. Natalie realized many of her neighbors were armed. Although surprised, it gave her comfort to know this.

She scanned the area in front and then at both sides as far as she could see. There were no more ambulatory mords. Some of the armed men finished off those still breathing. However, many of the injured most likely suffered from their bites. That was not good.

The gunfire gradually ceased, and people began to step cautiously out of their homes and out from behind bushes and parked cars. Voices broke the sudden silence, all speaking and shouting at once. A few approached the injured to offer aid. Natalie saw a woman make a call on her portafone.

"Good luck..." Natalie remarked sarcastically.

The woman's face went from fear, to disbelief, and then into a scowl. Natalie heard her loudly exclaim, "The fucking phones are out!"

A man with a portafone to his ear called out to her, "I got a signal!" In the next second, he was talking on the phone.

Coltan reconsidered his idea of where the mords came from. There were too many of them to all be on that bus. However, his mind was overwhelmed with everything else to expend energy solving that mystery.

His first concern was Natalie inundated with adrenalin from their battle, and he thought she might start to get careless. He wanted to get the rifle out of her hands before she shot him by accident.

Natalie pulled away from the window and slid to the floor. The adrenaline was still racing through her body, but she was beginning to calm down. She noticed Coltan staring down at her. "What?"

"Is it over?"

"Looks like it."

"I mean *you*."

"What?" She hadn't the slightest idea what he meant.

He squatted in front of her and snatched the rifle out of her hand.

She couldn't understand his anger at her and she resented him taking her weapon.

"Give it back..." she commanded softly.

"Calm down."

"I am calm." She reached for it, and he swung it out of her reach.

Coltan assumed she didn't realize she was panting. Her eyes were full of confusion and desperation. He held her gaze and repeated in a soft, soothing voice, "Calm down. Breathe slowly. Calm down."

"Give me the rifle."

"Calm down..." He crouched in front of her, watched her, and waited for her to understand.

She looked away. "There was a baby," she whispered. "I had to save it."

"Did you?"

"Yes."

Sirens wailed from far away. The din of voices shouting and chattering excitedly overlapped the heartrending sobbing and wailing outside the open window.

Coltan tried to shut out the sounds. "We're okay," he told her.

She continued to look around the room as she recovered from the adrenalin rush. She spotted the loaf of bread on the floor by the folded staircase. What was that about, anyway? Her gaze went from it to Coltan. "You thought you could defend yourself with a loaf of bread?"

Now he was confused. "What?"

"You grabbed a loaf of bread."

He vaguely recalled it. The reason escaped him. "I don't know. I don't know why I grabbed it."

A smile slowly formed, and she began to laugh softly. "What the hell, Colt..."

It was rather funny. He chuckled a little at himself, but at the same time it was plain to him she had dismissed all previous assumptions of him as the cool, calm, protective type. He had exposed his fear, weakness and carelessness that he had spent years hiding under male bravado. He felt humiliation rise in him at that moment.

"Please... Don't laugh at me."

"I'm not laughing at you."

"Yes, you are."

"No. It's okay. We panicked. We both panicked. We have to learn from it."

He put the rifle into her hands, stood and went to the window that faced the front. Looking out, he said to her, "We should help them."

Sirens came closer, but were still far away.

She replied, "They don't need us."

"So the plan is we sit up here and save our own asses?"

Natalie knew every person down there the mords had bitten would soon turn into insatiable predators they would have to kill. She didn't want to confront that. She didn't want to explain it to the neighbors who were, right at that moment, congregating and organizing to deal with the injured and swap theories about their attackers. They had no idea the mord maker virus was only one facet of the diabolical monster that sought to enslave them. She didn't want to tell them the army, or whoever, was planning to round them up like cattle and whisk them away somewhere for God Knows What. She didn't want to tell them their own government had ceased to exist, replaced by a force of evil. She didn't want to tell them the evil drew its power from the evil within their hearts. They would never believe it, anyway. Even if they did believe it, they were powerless to defeat that evil. They all deserved this. They had brought it upon themselves. *They* became *We* as she acknowledged the evil within herself and admitted her own culpability.

Coltan couldn't see that. It was no use trying to explain it to him. He would choose to believe he could rescue them. He would choose to believe there was still something worth saving. She found it odd there was an ember of confidence inside him for the goodness of people to win over evil. It was odd because he had experienced the worst of humanity most of his life. If anything, he should be the one who felt it was all not worth saving.

Coltan considered the events of the previous hours and the stress they were under had gotten to them both. He felt their momentary lapse of sanity was justified, but now he wanted them to regain control of the situation. He knelt in front of her, addressed her calmly, his voice sympathetic and encouraging. "We should go out and help."

She regarded those beautiful dark blue eyes that peered into her soul. She contemplated the gentleness of his face. How could he be so benevolent after all he had gone through? It seemed the compassion in his heart had only strengthened even though they had tried to beat it out of him. At this moment, he was offering his compassion to her. She wanted none of it. She didn't feel worthy of it.

Instead, the basest of human needs overwhelmed her. She felt the heat of his body merge with hers, and she wanted more of that. She wanted to touch him. She wanted to taste him. She wanted him to cover her and conquer her, take her far away to that place where nothing else existed.

She pressed her lips against his and pulled him to her, clinging tightly, forcing his lips to open and accept her. After his initial surprise, he reciprocated, wrapping his arms around her and pulling her tight against him. For many long moments, she held his face to hers, kissing him, tasting him, desiring to draw his entire being into her own. She grazed over his body with her hands, pushing her own body tighter against his, her hands moving to and exploring forbidden places. The smoothness of his skin and the tightness of his body excited her even more, and she wanted to claim him forever as her own.

Although he had not expected this from her, he found it difficult to deny her. Her touch was arousing him, and the impulse to surrender was strong. Yet, he knew it was wrong. It was nothing but desperation and raw physical lust, a side effect of adrenaline-fed terror and the high of surviving their brush with death. Common sense and strength of spirit prevailed, and he pushed her away, gripping her arms tightly.

He looked away from her and caught his breath. "We can't do this."

Fully driven by this sudden and powerful need for him, she attempted to push herself into him once more. His arms stiffened and prevented her from doing so.

"Don't," he whispered. "This isn't what you want."

"You don't know anything." She tried to push into him again.

His hands tightened around her arms, squeezing so tight it hurt her. She didn't mind the pain; it wasn't that bad. She glared at him, her eyes suddenly challenging, daring him to squeeze just a little tighter. He sensed she was deriving some kind of strange pleasure from this confrontation. It sickened him to know this. It sickened him because the ghost of the Monster told him she wanted more, and he should give it to her. He was more afraid of the Monster than anything else in all of Creation. He wanted it to stay dead, and he willed it back to the grave. He was determined it would not claim another victim, especially Natalie. Coltan shoved her against the wall and held her there at arms' length for her own safety.

"Stay there..." The words came through clenched teeth.

His shut his eyes tightly, and began talking to himself. The only audible words she could understand were, *no, dead, stay, God, Jesus, Father, help me, kill it, kill it, protect her, protect...* The rest was mumbling. She slowly realized her behavior had triggered some kind of battle within him. She had caused him profound pain. Her guilt rose quickly, and she ached for redemption. She wanted to erase what she had done to him—and to herself. Her desire for him faded away, and she backed down, mortified.

"I'm so sorry," she whispered. "I don't know why I did that." When he failed to respond she continued, this time pleading, "Colt, please... I'm so sorry. I'm sorry."

He finally looked at her, and she saw the pain there. He made no attempt to hide it. "You don't want to do this." Although his voice was gentle, it was clearly a warning.

"Okay..."

He finally released her, and he backed away, creating a safe distance between them. He avoided her worried and penitent gaze. She had apologized enough.

It appeared to her he was trying to recover, attempting to emerge from that tumultuous place inside him. She thought she heard him whisper, "Forgive me."

"I'm sorry," she said. "Please..."

"Just stay there." He hoped she understood he was only trying to protect her. After a long breath and another moment to recuperate, he stood and told her, "I'm going out there to help." He found his handgun and tucked it into his waistband.

She stayed there and watched him unlock and lower the staircase and descend. She heard him remove the bars from the barricaded door below, heard the door push open and then close. Regret welled up in her, and she could not understand why she had behaved in such a way.

It scared her to her core when she thought he did not intend to return.

CHAPTER 18

Coltan opened the first aid kit from the kitchen and handed a woman a roll of gauze, some dressing pads and tape. He found the gloves and gave those to her, as well. "Put these gloves on first. Don't get any of the blood on your hands. Use a stack of the pads directly on the wound and put pressure on it. When the bleeding slows or stops, wrap it snugly. Make sure she keeps it elevated." He gazed down at the patient, a little girl of about seven, judging by the missing front teeth, "You're gonna be okay, little one. This lady's gonna help you."

"Where's Mommy?" The girl asked weakly.

He didn't know what to tell her. Finally, he repeated, "This lady's gonna help you."

He stood and looked around at the many injured and the people who had bravely come out to render aid. Their street looked like a war zone, with houses damaged, cars dented, doors and windows smashed. There were bullet holes on some of the houses and vehicles. A few people were resting on the manicured lawns, silently awaiting the ambulances, too stunned to do anything else. In contrast to these were the seriously wounded. Many were going into shock and some were hysterical. Coltan didn't know what to do for those people. He noticed, too, the dead remained where they had died. Either no one had thought to, or someone had decided not to, move the bodies. If it was the latter, it was a wise choice. The dead were ripe with contagion and, therefore, a major hazard. Dealing with the dead was HAZMAT's job. Perhaps, someone else knew it and warned the others.

A man was wrapping his leg below the knee with his own belt, attempting to stem the bleeding. He called to Coltan, "Young man! Young man. Give me some of those dressings."

Coltan went and knelt beside him. Seeing the man's bloodied hands, he didn't offer him gloves. He gave the man a stack of pads and pressure dressings, all the while observing him for signs of shock. The man seemed to be doing okay.

"You hanging in there, sir?" Coltan asked.

"Yeah." The man took the dressings. He suddenly recognized Coltan. "You're the Allen boy, aren't you?"

"Yes, sir." Whether that was good or bad, he no longer cared.

The man seemed uncomfortable at first, and Coltan figured it was because the man had long ago dismissed him as a troublemaker and a loser. A smile crossed the man's face. "I'm Mister O'Gallegher. I teach Biology."

"I never took your class, Sir."

"You never showed up, you mean."

Coltan smiled guiltily. "I guess."

"You're doing a good job here." He grimaced and began to dress his wound. "I can't believe the sonofabitch bit me! You go on, son. There's worse off than me."

As he moved on to the next patient, Coltan saw two armed men, one at each end of the street, standing guard. They were communicating via walkie-talkies. An elderly woman tended to a casualty on the lawn one house up. This woman had brought out her own first aid kit fully stocked for field trauma. He surmised she had probably been a nurse, possibly an army nurse, in her day. A young couple came across the street with a case of bottled water and started passing them out. Someone else was offering blankets.

The neighbors had organized quickly. It made him feel that if they all got together they could beat this thing; prevent what was coming next, even.

As he expected, his mother and Richard were nowhere in sight. He figured they were most likely still passed out from another night of partying. In a way, he was glad they weren't there. If they had been there, they would have singled him out, and Richard would have started running his mouth, telling everyone how proud he was of *my boy*. Coltan didn't need the humiliation on top of everything else.

The sirens grew louder, and finally the first of two ambulances crested the hill. Coltan saw the lights before the ambulance came into view. The armed man at that end of the street waved them down and pointed to the wounded ahead. Coltan heard a woman moan loudly, "It's about time!"

Once the EMTs began to take over, Coltan decided he had done all he could. He stopped to see Mister O'Gallegher on his way back to the house.

"How are you doing, Mister O'Gallegher?"

His face had paled considerably, and he was sweating and trembling. "I'm doing okay," he answered. "Don't know for how long, though."

Although Coltan knew the man was infected, he feigned ignorance. "Sir?"

He patted the gauze-wrapped wound, "I know what this means. You know it, too. I saw it on your face when you handed me the bandages."

"I'm sorry. I truly am."

"I guess I should have gotten that vaccine." He shrugged hopelessly. "Thank you for helping me."

"Yes, sir. You're welcome." He gently patted the man's shoulder as he stood to leave.

He saw Natalie standing in the front doorway as he crossed the road. He wondered how long she had been there.

"Where are the police?" she asked.

"How would I know?" For a moment, he had forgotten about

Brian. He realized his insensitivity and told her, "They'll be here soon, I'm sure."

"I hope Dad's on the call." She had seesawed back to hope.

"Me, too." He then saw the handprint shaped bruises on her arms. He wondered how he would explain it to Brian. She noticed, and hid them with her hands. He started to say, "I never meant to..."

She interrupted him, "Let's forget about it."

"Your folks will see."

"One of the mords grabbed me." It was a logical cover.

"Let's go in."

"I'm gonna wait for Dad."

"I'll wait with you." He wearily settled on the top step.

The police arrived ten minutes later, and Natalie intercepted them as they exited their two cars. They had no answers for her. Frustrated and morose, she returned to the house and her place on the sofa. Coltan closed and locked the door and watched her as she wrapped herself in the blanket.

Gunshots rang out. She flinched at the noise, trembled at the screams and pleas as more gunshots followed.

Coltan knelt in front of her. "A lot of our neighbors were bitten, Nat. They're doing what they have to do to protect the rest of us, and maybe it's not just the cops doing the shooting. People are getting to know how and how fast this shit spreads. We're safe in here."

"I got Bonnie," Natalie murmured shakily. "I'm only worried about Dad." Almost as an afterthought, she advised him, "You should keep Clyde with you at all times. Don't worry about me. I'm just gonna stay here and listen for Dad."

He decided to give her some space, but to be near in case she needed him.

THE DREADFUL DAWN

"THERE'S MORE ON THE way," the nurse told Beverly.

Beverly was completing the wrapping of a small boy's broken arm. "How many?"

"Lots. From a subdivision at the east side."

Immediately, she thought of home. "Which subdivision?"

"Hell if I know. It came over the scanner, along with twenty other calls." After a moment, she added, "I don't know how they keep up."

Beverly helped the boy down off the table. The boy's mother rose from her chair and took the boy's hand. Beverly said to her, "It's only a temporary splint. He'll have to see another doctor in a few days. The desk clerk will give you the referral."

"Thank you," the woman said. Shaking with fear, she instructed the boy, "Tell the doctor thank you, honey."

He looked up at her with big round eyes. "Thank you, dock-it-ter."

"Feel better now?" She asked him.

"Uh-huh."

As they left, Beverly removed the x-ray from the viewer and shut off the light. She put the x-ray with the boy's chart and handed it to the nurse. "Don't ever cuss in front of my patients. I'm taking a ten minute break."

She called home from the break room. The telephone service, both PF and landline, was still out in that area. She wavered between worry and her faith that God was protecting them. She tried to call Brian and got his voice mail. She left a message and hoped he'd call her soon.

The door opened, and one of the soldiers entered. She recognized him as the soldier who had executed the nurse bitten by one of the infected, the nurse with three little kids at home. He seemed like a heartless killing machine, the worst kind of soldier. The man frightened her. He poured coffee into two small Styrofoam cups and offered her one of them.

She took it, masking her fear.

He just stood there, analyzing her. He was a tall, solid man in his forties. His coloring and facial features indicated a racial mixture of Black and Asian.

"I heard what you said about faith," he said. "I saw you praying."

She couldn't recall it. The night, the day, the hours and the endless stream of patients had blurred into an impenetrable mass.

When she didn't reply, he slipped his fingers under his collar and produced a necklace with a gold cross. He smiled reassuringly, nodded once. In the next move, he removed a card the size of a business card from his back pocket and handed it to her. She accepted it wordlessly and read it. The card contained handwritten numbers, longitude and latitude.

He said just above a whisper, "I'm one of the good guys."

After what she had seen, she doubted it. Referring to the card, she asked, "What is this?"

"The nearest safe place. Get your family there as soon as possible." His expression softened, and his eyes were full of concern for her. "Don't let them take you to the rescue centers. There's evil there."

"I know about it," she said.

"You do?"

"You know about the chips?"

"I know about it all." He sipped his coffee, and then said, "They're already injecting the refugees at the rescue centers—*vaccinations*—you know. That batch of vaccine your hospital just got—it's the same thing."

"Who are you?"

"James. I'm with the other army."

"Other army?"

"The Army of Christ. There are a lot of us. We're fighting the evil." With one finger, he tapped the card in her hand. "You'll be safe there."

The soldier quickly tucked his cross under his collar as another doctor entered the room.

The bearded young man appeared disheveled, his scrubs wet with his sweat, his stethoscope askew around his neck and his ID tag crooked. "Is it morning or afternoon?" It was less a question than a statement about the crisis and the endless stream of casualties.

"Late morning, I think." Beverly answered.

"Some asshole is out in the lot trying to convert the sinners to Jesus." He shook his head and laughed derisively. "They always crawl out of the woodwork in times like this."

James faked a smile. "They certainly do."

"We're all doomed!" The doctor laughed again to himself and poured a cup of coffee. He took a long sip and made a face of disgust. "This coffee tastes like shit."

THIS TIME, COLTAN REMEMBERED to tuck Clyde into his waistband before going outside. It wasn't as frightening in the sunlight, and he felt certain no mord was going to surprise him. After what he had witnessed, he was beginning to figure out their M.O. Excepting a few stragglers, they seemed to gather and hunt in packs, like wolves. Their hunting behavior was also similar to that of wild animals: they stayed low to the ground, identified prey by scent, and they used the element of surprise to attack their victims. The worst thing about this comparison was that, like wild animals, they ate their prey. Coltan pondered further, and a dreadful possibility occurred to him. Would the mords mate? Would they mate and reproduce, as all animals do? If so, their offspring would be just like them. *And they would go forth and multiply, and desolate the earth.*

271

He shuddered both inwardly and outwardly at the thought.

No one as yet had offered an explanation as to the origin of the disease. From what little he had seen on the news, it had sprung up all at once in many areas of the world and had spread from there. To him it seemed as if someone had simply planted the mords among the populace and then sat back to see what would happen.

Also, there was the new military. Where had they come from? Who was their leader? Why wasn't anyone talking about that? Their actions produced another puzzle. If they were the bad guys, why did they eliminate the mords on sight? Was it a ploy to gain the trust and dependency of the people? Or, had some higher-up decided there were simply too many now, and they wanted to control the population before the numbers got out of hand?

The more he thought about everything, the more confusing it became. His brain was simply too exhausted and overloaded to deal with any more. He relegated it to the *Deal With Later* file, and lit a smoke.

He walked the wraparound porch and checked all the sliders for damage. They were all okay, even the one in the den where the window had been smashed. He tried to remember if there were any more plywood sheets left. If so, he could cover the broken window from the outside as added protection. He recalled the thinner sheet he had used as a test model. That would do. It was still somewhere in the basement.

He finished his smoke and thought it best to tell Natalie. The noise of him hammering in the nails might make her think the mords had returned. And, then she would shoot him. He didn't want that. She was already turning into a basket case, worrying about her dad, worrying about her mom. Worrying about everything.

He found her where he had left her.

"I'm gonna cover the den window with some plywood."

She had turned the scanner back on and was listening for her dad's voice. There was no response from her. He didn't know if she was paying any attention to him.

"I'm going outside to cover the window." When she didn't respond, he asked, "Have you heard your dad?"

She shook her head.

"Have you tried your phone again?"

Again, she shook her head. "Still out."

Knowing the Danburys had the forethought to keep a connection to the archaic and almost obsolete landline technology as a grid-down backup, he tried the wall phone in the kitchen and heard no dial tone. Not too gently, he hung up the receiver. He unhooked his portafone from his belt and tried that in case the service had returned. It was dead. A black screen. No power. He realized it was dead because it needed charging and he suspected Natalie's PF was dead for the same reason. He found Natalie's PF charger in her room and set about charging their phones through an unused outlet behind one of the nightstands.

While there, he took the opportunity to peer through her window that faced the front of the house for a neighborhood update. It looked like an abandoned war zone. He noticed the armed men who had been on watch earlier were now absent. Coltan hoped they had simply gone on break. However, the absence of both men told him they had decided the danger had passed. Coltan thought that was a big mistake.

The sunlight was fading, and it would be dark soon. Even with the exterior lights, Coltan felt it was too dangerous to be out there hammering at night, knowing the noise would attract any mords who might be in the area. He found the plywood sheet in the basement and went to work.

He was hammering in the final nail at twilight when the copter sounds drew his attention. Looking up from that vantage point on the front porch, he only caught sight of the tail of the craft as it flew over the house and headed northeast. With the hammer still in his hand, he walked quickly to the northeast side and watched to see where it was going. He lost sight of it when it descended behind a row of hills. He waited for a while to see if it would ascend again, but it did not.

The noise of more copters diverted his attention. He saw a multitude over the city and surrounding areas. They were now black against the horizon, their flashing lights the only guide to count their number and see their locations. Many were descending, and others followed.

What the hell...? Coltan wondered. The only thing that made sense was they were National Guard arriving in Bonito Valle. The thought of it left him conflicted.

AS NURSES PREPPED HER next patient for surgery, Beverly tried again to phone the kids and Brian. Service was still out at home and on the PFs there. Her call to Brian only brought her again to his voicemail. This worried her. He would have at least left a message with the clerk or on her portafone. After some trepidation followed by prayer, she convinced herself the phone service was the culprit, and her family was fine.

There was an emergency appendectomy waiting, and she had to get to it.

IT WAS JUST AFTER MIDNIGHT when Natalie and Coltan heard a car pull up and the ringing doorbell shortly after. Coltan closed his Bible and set it on the side table. He looked at Natalie to see if she would move to get the door. She simply sat there, anticipating bad news.

Coltan looked through the peephole in the door and saw two police officers, a man and a woman. He felt the weight of sudden dread plummet to the pit of his stomach. He opened the door slowly.

THE AMBULANCE PUKED antifreeze onto the pavement as Mario steered the smoking, failing vehicle to rest under an overpass on the frontage road a mile short of Bujjet Mart. Horns blared indignantly and impatiently, and the line of vehicles the ailing ambulance had delayed sped up and passed by. The drivers had no intent to stop to render assistance. All they wanted was to get the hell out of Dodge.

That's all Mario wanted, too, but the endless detours, wrecks and traffic jams only served to stretch a normal twenty-minute drive to Bujjet Mart into eight hours. Three minutes into their escape, the emergency lights and siren short-circuited. As a result, the ambulance was now just another vehicle on the road and the cars ahead no longer gave way. He had passed by nine accidents (to the confusion and dismay of the few police present), and nearly got flagged down at another. If it had not been for the crush of traffic and a lucky big rig spill that caused a pile-up behind him, the officer in pursuit would have caught him. Along the way after that, the ambulance stalled four times, and each of those times mords attacked the rig. During the last stall, Mario spent some of his ammo on the most aggressive ones who had tried to tip the rig. In all of this, he endured Rosa's screams and hysterical tears. Now, the rig was dead forever, and Rosa was too ill to scream anymore.

As Mario shut off the engine and extinguished the lights, Rosa wiped her tears and weakly turned her head to him. "What are we gonna do now?"

COLTAN JOINED NATALIE at the sofa after the officers drove away. He had no words of comfort to offer. He had no experience with this kind of thing. When she looked at him, there was serenity in her face he had not expected to see. The initial tears she had shed were now drying on her cheeks, and no fresh tears fell to replace them. He couldn't understand this.

"Now we know," she said.

"Yeah." He searched for more words, but couldn't find any.

"I know how much you love him." She was offering encouragement for him to express his grief. "He loves you, too. You know that, I'm sure."

"Yeah..." He rubbed his forehead, his eyes downcast. The thought of losing Brian overwhelmed him, and he refused to feel his grief. It didn't seem real. It couldn't be real. Maybe they had made a mistake and the dead cop wasn't Brian, but someone else. Yet, he knew they didn't make mistakes about stuff like that. Still, a part of him refused to fully believe it. He refused to accept it, and he shut off his emotional response to that small part of him that did believe and accept the fact his father figure would not be coming home. He refused to picture what his life would be like without this man who had sacrificed so much of his free time and effort to save this miserable wretch of a kid who had given up all hope.

Natalie took his hand in hers and wrapped her arm around him. The fresh tears that ran down her cheeks were not for herself, or for her father, but for Coltan.

Coltan remained strong. He knew Natalie would need him, now more than ever. He felt he had to stay strong for her, and considered how Brian would handle this. The answer came swiftly. "We should pray for him. And your mom, too."

CHAPTER 19

Beverly checked for messages and found none. She dialed Natalie and Brian's PF's, then Coltan's and then the house landline. Service was still out on the east and south sides of town. She swallowed her growing fear. Brian would have checked on the kids by now. If anything had been wrong, he would have gotten a message to her. Still, she needed reassurance he was safe, and she dialed the precinct direct. All lines were busy.

The word came that more casualties were awaiting care, but the ER staff had it covered and wouldn't need her right away. So far, no new emergencies required surgery. She took the opportunity to follow-up on her post-op patients, both from the last twenty-four hours and two days before. All seemed to be doing well.

While visiting her patients' rooms, she noticed the televisions were all off. A patient complained the cable was out. Beverly knew it was not out. The staff in the surgical office suites had been watching the news coverage every chance they got. Most likely, the nursing staff disconnected the cable for the rooms to protect the patients from the bad news outside.

No sooner had she finished her rounds and was on her way to try the phone again, when two patients arrived by ambulance, both victims of a nasty head-on collision with a big rig hauling bulldozers. She scrubbed in for the most seriously injured, a young woman with multiple internal injuries and a broken hip, crushed sternum and pelvis. This one would take hours, and they were short four surgeons.

She considered popping one more amphetamine. Alertness was essential. However, too much of a good thing presented the potential to wire her up too much to think straight. She ultimately dismissed the idea as too risky.

Silent prayer accompanied the routine of scrubbing in. It was the first thing she always turned to, and it was all she had left.

WHILE NATALIE RESTED, Coltan went to the attic and grabbed the binoculars. He scanned the valley, tried to view the activities in different areas. The blanket of smoke made it impossible.

Natalie was browning hamburger on low heat when Coltan returned downstairs. The aroma brought his appetite back, and he sat down on a stool at the breakfast counter and watched her. He noticed she had set Bonnie on the counter, so he placed Clyde at its side. They had food, water, safe shelter, and they had guns and ammo. Maybe tomorrow they would have phone service again.

He refused to think about the two people who were absent. He refused to think about the fact that one would never return. He was not ready to feel the loss and the grief, so he stuffed that all away where it would not surface until he was able to deal with it.

She tossed him a small yellow onion and put him to work chopping it. A glance at his work told her he had never done anything close to this before. The result of his effort was sloppy, and she excused his inexperience and instead appreciated his willingness to learn. To encourage him, she took two tomatoes out of the bowl and rolled them over to him. "We'll need these, too."

"What are we making?"

"Burritos. No beans. I don't like beans in them. Lots of shredded cheddar cheese—that's what I like. And, sour cream. How'd you like to make the salsa?"

"I don't know how."

She smiled. "I'll teach you."

"Okay." At least they were doing something. It beat sitting around worrying about everything. He wiped his hands on his pants, and just sat there for a minute, watching her. She was a different person at this moment, far different from what he had seen over the past day and night. He couldn't understand how she could suddenly be so calm. Moreover, he felt she was caring for him, protecting him. He thought he should be protecting and caring for her. "I want to ask you something."

"My dad is at peace. He's with Jesus. He's safe there. Is that what you want to know?"

"Sort of."

"I don't want to mourn him." She added spices and some of the chopped onion to the hamburger. "He would want me to stay strong, especially in this situation. I can mourn later."

"Jeez, Natalie..."

"That's Jesus' name in vain."

"I didn't know that."

"Now you do." She shut off the burner and sat down beside him, began to cut the remaining tomato. Unexpectedly, she kissed his cheek. "I'm sorry for what I did earlier."

"What?"

"Up in the attic."

"Don't worry about it."

"I'm not like that."

"I know."

"Thanks for not staying mad at me."

"I wasn't mad at you. I was..." he couldn't think how to describe it, and he didn't want to tell her about it, anyway.

She sensed this. "You don't have to explain anything, Colt."

After supper, Coltan washed everything by hand and Natalie dried it all and put it away. She handed him the towel to dry his hands. "We forgot all about boxing up the spices."

"Boxing them up?"

"For upstairs."

He didn't want to think about the attic. He had been enjoying their dinner and her company. It was a moment of domestic normality. In a way, it gave him a glimpse into what their future could be if only things returned to normal.

This moment reminded him of a similar moment during his Reyton days when he and Brenda prepared flavored cappuccinos in the tiny kitchen of his studio apartment. He had felt that same longing for a domestic coupling then. Lately, Brenda had been on his mind. Coltan had been remembering their relationship and the circumstances that led to their breakup. Long before his altercation with the drunk who had tried to kiss her, Coltan had been aware their romance was drawing to a close. Brenda had made it clear their relationship would end once she left for New York City to pursue her career; she did not want him to build his life around hers. He had fought that, but he always knew she was right. It would have to end someday. She had made him feel... disposable. Secretly, he had felt that way all of his life, and it hurt that she inadvertently verified and magnified his lack of self-worth.

Now he was ready to put her memory and their relationship behind him.

Natalie went to turn away to take down the spices. Looking back, he remembered that day he walked her home, that first time they had seen each other up close, the first time they talked. That initial meeting had been awkward, and he recalled she seemed wary of him then. Things had changed since that day, and he was happy she liked him, still liked him in spite of his many imperfections. He realized then how much he had come to adore her, adore her not in a fascinated way as with Brenda, but in a deep, appreciative and even desiring way. He took her hand, drew her to him, and gently held her. He wanted to express his growing love for her, but found he couldn't find the words without sounding corny, and didn't feel this was the right time. So, he continued to embrace her and enjoy the closeness and the comfort. It was so different with her. Yes, the physical attraction was there. But there was something else that was more profound. Perhaps it was the emotional closeness and their unspoken mutual understanding of each other's needs, wants, weaknesses, and strengths. He still wasn't certain if that was all of it. It still felt to him as if there was something more.

At first, his gesture surprised her. Just as quickly, she accepted his loving embrace and settled into the security of his arms around her. He could feel her heartbeat, and the warmth of her body pressing against his. He wished time would stand still. For the first time in days, they ignored the terrors outside the door, if only for that moment. In that blessed moment they were safe together, safe from every bad thing the world wanted to throw at them. It was as if their embrace had created some kind of force field that surrounded them and shielded them in that place of safety.

He tilted her face up to see her, to touch her face, caress her skin. She was so beautiful in his eyes, and he couldn't believe he had never seen her this way before. He kissed her gently, kissed her face, kissed her lips. He did this not with physical passion. The passion that fueled these kisses were from a place of purity within his soul, that place where only the kind and the good and the right were born, that place where the well of purest love overflowed.

IT WAS JUST BEFORE dawn when Beverly released her patient to the recovery room. The girl had come through the complicated surgery well enough, but a tough road lay ahead for her. Beverly tried not to think about that, considering what was happening outside the hospital walls. In many ways, the effects of the emergency had, in fact, found their way into the hospital. Besides the obvious increase in patients, fewer staff had shown up for work. They were down to almost thirty percent of their usual staff. It was impossible to keep the place running and provide care to the patients.

She was completely exhausted. It was time for someone else to battle through an unplanned seventy-two hour shift. All she wanted now was the comfort of her family and the snug, warm comfort of her bed.

After informing the desk she was going home, she stopped by her locker and grabbed her purse. She was too tired to change clothes. As soon as she saw her bed awaiting her, everything would come off and she would slide under the comfy sheets and into a pleasingly oblivious slumber.

As she passed the desk to leave, the substitute clerk called to her, "Doctor Danbury! You have a message."

"From who?"

"A police officer."

Beverly assumed it was Brian. She felt relieved. "When did it come in?"

"About an hour ago. You were still in surgery. I'm sorry."

"Well, let me have it."

It was a note from an Officer Farnsworth, asking her to come by the precinct. She vaguely remembered Officer Farnsworth as a blonde, square-shaped female officer, one of only four women on the force. For a few moments, the part about coming to the precinct had escaped her. Maybe it was her brain trying to block out the reception of bad news. After a third reading, it was all clear. She felt it in her gut, and her next feeling was a wish to avoid the inevitable completely.

The inevitable meant he was more than just hurt. She knew if he had been *just hurt*, he would have been here at the hospital, and someone would have told her.

A bright light stung her eyes, and nothingness followed.

THEY BROUGHT THE SPICES and all the herb plants up to the attic. Natalie set the herb plants on a platter on the floor to catch the light from the south window. She saw Coltan watching out the east window with binoculars. She assumed he was scanning for mords.

"Anything interesting?"

The only traffic on the old road leading to the eastern mountains was a battered pick-up truck with a camper shell. Coltan silently wished them good luck on their journey. He brought the binoculars down. "I thought I saw something over towards the woods, but I think it was probably a deer."

"Did you see any dogs? Remember? About Muffy?"

"I haven't seen any dogs. None at all."

"That's weird."

"Out in that far corner of the garden... Are those solar panels?"

"Yeah... for the well. We have well water. The pump's solar."

"We won't lose water, then."

"Not likely."

"That's one less worry."

"We have to treat the water with chemicals, though. Once in a while."

Something out there caught his eye. He brought up the binoculars. "Ten o'clock."

"What?"

The color had drained from his face. He gave her the binoculars. "Look over there."

Five mords, all of them men, the day's growth of stubble on their faces stained with blood and dirt.

"Oh, no..."

"I've got to warn the neighbors."

"You can't go out there."

He took Clyde from his front waistband, "I can handle it."

They heard pounding, glass breaking, growls and screams. It was all coming from the north side at the front of the house. Natalie beat him to the window. She couldn't count how many there were. They had come out of nowhere like cockroaches. An infestation. They swarmed the neighborhood.

She felt Coltan standing behind her, watching over her shoulder. "Still think you can handle it?"

"Shit..." That was as plain an answer as he could muster.

MARIO HAD TREATED AND bandaged Rosa's wounds and carried her wrapped in a blanket from the ambulance. He found a safe spot for them to rest in the tall dry weeds under a clump of trees on the down slope of a hill that overlooked the Bujjet Mart building.

From this surveillance perch, they watched on their bellies in silent horror as a small group of soldiers executed the looters they had rounded up and detained at the front of the store. Once that was done, the soldiers took their turn at the merchandise and began to fill their vehicles and two helicopters. The soldiers were so busy with this they failed to notice the group of bitten, bleeding, armed-to-the-teeth civilians that watched them from the cover of an overturned delivery rig near the loading dock.

"How are we gonna get in there?" Rosa whispered.

Mario draped his arm across her shoulders and scooted closer to her side. He observed the armed civilians who were patiently spying on the soldiers who had paused to partake of some stolen hard liquor. "We'll wait."

"WE HAVE TO STAY CALM, this time." Natalie went to the rifles and grabbed her favorite. The ammo was right there, and she started loading. "Better load up, Colt."

He took the rifle from the floor next to his mattress. He had loaded it last night, but he double-checked, just to make sure. All good. His next thought was a question: Would it be murder in God's eyes?

"We're locked up down there, aren't we?"

"Yep."

"Maybe you should reinforce the access door."

"Good idea."

He dashed down the retractable stairs and went into the access room. As he bent to drop the bars into place, he remembered he had left his bedroom door open. He went in there quickly and closed and barricaded that door, then returned to the access room and barricaded that entrance. As soon as he reached the attic floor, he retracted the staircase and pull-chain and locked it in place.

In the meantime, Natalie had been picking off mords. By the time he reached the north window, he saw six had gone down.

"Ammo!" she ordered.

He slid the box over to her. She crouched below the window and began reloading. He took down all the firearms and started loading them in procession, inserting the magazines into the military rifles and loading bullets for the rest.

A bullet pierced the north window right above Natalie's head and imbedded itself in the south wall. She whispered thanks to God for the good timing. She shouted to Coltan, "Stay low! Our neighbors are lousy shots!"

Coltan checked the south window after sliding the platter of herbs to the far wall, out of the way. It was clear on that side. The east window told another story. There were well over one hundred. They were breaking off into smaller packs and splitting in different directions. Their main objective was his neighborhood and the larger subdivision down the hill.

The tumult of all the gunshots, screams, growls and things breaking assaulted him to the center of his being. He glanced at Natalie. She was half-sitting in the open window, binoculars hanging from her neck, calculating, aiming, and then firing. He couldn't recall seeing when or how she got the binoculars, and her coolness amazed him. He turned his attention back to the east window. A pack of mords had broken down the door of the Spencer house. They were pushing and jostling each other to get in. He thought of the Spencers and was glad they were gone. At his former home, Coltan saw three had broke in the back door and one had pulled the cardboard off the shattered window and was hanging half-in and half-out. He thought he heard a shot from there, but he wasn't sure until he saw the mord in the window fall out. The thing crumpled and remained motionless on the wide concrete step outside the door. It crossed Coltan's mind that Richard was finally making good use of his .22.

Oddly, he didn't think about his mother.

He aimed at a lone mord creeping around the side of the Danbury house. His first shot missed. The man looked up at him, made eye contact and snarled. Coltan almost backed away from the window when he started to charge toward the wall, but he kept his head and aimed again, this time holding his breath. The bullet went into the man's chest, and he fell. Coltan let loose a second shot, just to make certain.

There was no turning back, now. He silently asked God to forgive him.

Natalie shifted her attention to the west window and was now perched there. She aimed and fired, but there was no shot. She dove for the ammo box on the floor by the north window and started reloading. Coltan saw this when he turned to check on her. He slid two loaded military rifles to the west window so she'd have them.

"There's military in the valley," she hollered. "Looks like they got their hands full down there."

He ran to the west window, staying low. When he reached the window, she jumped down, crouched and pulled on his shirt to urge him to crouch down also. "What?" he asked.

"We can't let them see us."

"Well, what are we supposed to do? We can't let all those people die out there!"

"Shhh... Stay down and just listen for a while. We need to catch our breath, anyway."

"How close are they?"

"Two truckloads coming up the hill. The rest are stuck below, surrounded. They gotta dig in and fight."

"Are they ours?"

"What do you mean *ours*?"

"Are they National Guard, Marines—what?"

"No. They're the other ones. I saw the insignia on one of the jeeps." She raised the binoculars hanging around her neck. "These help a lot." Emerging among the other noises was the sound of heavy engines. "They're here." She motioned him to follow her to the wall at the side of the storage room. They sat there on the floor against the wall. "We might as well let them do the fighting. Save our ammo."

WHEN BEVERLY REGAINED consciousness, her first sensation was a cold breeze drifting up her nose. She opened her eyes and recognized the ceiling. Looking around, she realized she was on a gurney in the hallway of the surgical ward. The oxygen mask was more an annoyance than anything, and she removed it and sat up slowly.

She gradually became aware of the noise, a medium-pitched blaring that pulsated throughout the hospital. Voices yelled instructions and questions. Doors slammed and latched.

Nurses, lab technicians, orderlies and security personnel scurried to and fro, desperately frightened, but still in control. It took another few seconds to realize the blaring was the alarm system, and the hospital was in lock-down.

She sat up at the edge of the gurney and grabbed the arm of a nurse who was running past her. "What's going on?"

"They're in!"

"Who's in?"

"Them! The whole first floor is overrun!"

"What?"

"The mordants! They're attacking. The ER's a bloodbath! They're trying to work their way up here!"

Just then, a patient wheeled himself into the hallway, inquiring. The nurse broke away from Beverly to calm the patient and escort him back to his room.

Her first thought was her daughter. She had to get home to her. Her feet hit the floor, and she felt woozy and steadied herself at the edge of the gurney. She immediately saw someone had sealed shut the automatic doors that led to the main hallway. She knew the button on the wall there would release the lock and open the door. With that as her goal, she grabbed her purse off the gurney and hurried to the doors, her right hand extended to push the button.

A security guard raced over and blocked her path. "You have to stay here, Doctor."

"I'm going home!"

"No way, Doctor. You're staying here."

She backed away from the doors, turned away from the guard

and took Brutus out of her purse. She spun around and pointed Brutus at the guard. "Get out of my way."

Although the guard was armed, he made no attempt to reach for his weapon. Instead, he tried to reason with her. "Calm down, now. Think it over. The hallway is gonna be crawling with those... *diseased* in another minute. You won't make it out alive."

"Move!"

"Lady... think about it."

"My daughter needs me!"

"Your daughter needs you to stay alive for her!"

"Get out of my way. I will fire if I have to!"

He had still not reached for his weapon. "Do you think you can just walk through them? Do you think you'll even make it to your car?"

"Yes, I do. We're wasting time. Push the damned button and let me out of here."

He took a long look through the windows on the door, and then he stepped off to the side and pushed the button. "Your funeral, Doc."

The doors popped open with a slap and a whirring sound.

She took a step forward. "Get away from the doors."

He stepped back a few feet.

"Farther!"

"Jesus Christ, lady!"

"Shut up!" She ran forward, watching him. "Back off!"

He acquiescently drew up his hands.

She made it into the hallway and dashed straight ahead to the employee entrance. Her hands were shaking as she dug into her purse for her key card. She found it and punched out. The door opened and she raced down the steps and into the early morning sunlight, tucking the key card quickly into her purse. She held Brutus in ready mode and dashed frantically through the panicked pedestrians fleeing the monsters. At the corner, she didn't wait for the light; a quick glance told her the intersection was safe enough. She sprinted across to the strip mall lot just ahead, dodging two cars in the process. Not taking her eyes off the lot and her car sitting at the end of a parking row, she dug into her purse again and found her keys. She pressed the button on the remote and heard the door lock click, saw the headlights flash. In less than a minute, she had thrown herself into her car and locked the door. She tossed her purse onto the passenger seat and turned over the engine. In another minute, she was out of the parking lot and heading for home.

The streets were teeming with traffic, both in cars and on foot. Sirens blared from every direction. She veered around collisions and people, her mind on the only thing that now mattered to her: her daughter.

As she took the corner at Rivercrest that would take her to the frontage road, her right front headlight collided with a woman who was running. She slammed on the brake and stared at the body wearing a nurse's bloodied uniform sprawled and convulsing on the hood. The nurse's head came up, a face misshapen by torn hanging flesh and a leaking hole where her nose used to be. She snarled at Beverly, and in the next move tackled the windshield and began to pound on it. Beverly backed up and then slammed on the brake. The crazed nurse rolled part way off. She put it back into drive, and slammed on the brakes again. The nurse tumbled off. Beverly tightened her grip on the steering wheel, floored the gas pedal, felt first the front and then rear tires bounce over the woman's body.

Monica... her name was Monica. Nice kid, and really knew her stuff. First month with us, Beverly recalled as she sped away. *God, I hope she's dead...*

CHAPTER 20

Natalie and Coltan stayed low and stole a look through the north window. The soldiers were swarming, firing at the mords and hitting many civilians in the process. Over off the west side, two military trucks slammed to a stop and numerous soldiers scrambled out the back, weapons ready. It wasn't more than a few seconds when the mords went for them. The soldiers began firing, firing at everyone. It crossed Natalie's mind the soldiers did not seem prepared for this onslaught, as the mords caught them by surprise the moment the trucks halted. To make matters worse, they were shooting at everyone, as if someone gave them orders to simply wipe out the whole neighborhood to stop the spread of the disease and resulting violence.

Coltan hissed through his teeth, "They're killing everyone! Everyone!"

"Don't let them see you." She moved to the south window.

He followed her. "Hell, no!"

A monstrous vehicle that looked like a cross between a transport truck and a Humvee popped up over the ridge along the gully, its tires aloft before it finally landed just inside the property line. The vehicle sped through the garden, spewing gravel, dirt and plants. It mowed down the fence on the south side, mowed over what was left of the vegetable garden and finally bolted to a stop after flattening the north fence.

"Mom won't like that at all," Natalie said softly.

Coltan cast her an incredulous glance. "Of all the things we have to deal with..."

A group of mords made it onto the back porch. They pounded on the door and broke the windows. Soldiers turned and opened fire. More infected attacked them from behind and tackled them, bringing some of them down. Soldiers behind the monsters opened fire. Some of the bullets went right through the assailants and lodged into the soldiers they were trying to protect. Those soldiers went down, most of them dead, but a few were still alive and screamed profanities at their comrades.

The rear door of the Humvee lowered and became a ramp when it touched ground. A small tank drove out of it and, at a slow to moderate speed, headed straight to the back yard of Coltan's house. From there, it drove up the side yard, taking the garbage bin with it for a few feet, and emerged on the street at the north.

Both struck with curiosity, and more than a little fear, Natalie and Coltan returned to the north window. They reached it just in time to hear the explosion and see the bomb, or whatever it was that blew out of this thing, blast through a mass of infected and their victims. Bodies flew and spewed blood, tissue and charred bits of clothing and bone into the air. A splatter of blood struck the window and caused Natalie and Coltan to hit the floor.

Coltan stayed put on his stomach on the floor and covered his head. He was shaking, despite his best effort to rein in his fear. He glanced sideways at Natalie beside him. She stared at him wide-eyed, also on her stomach. They ducked again when a couple of bullets crashed through the window and then through the south window.

Coltan saw a vision of himself covering the holes with duct tape later.

Natalie crawled along the floor and retrieved as many firearms as she could carry.

"What are you doing?" Coltan asked.

"I think some got in downstairs."

"They can't get up here!"

Now she was shaking. "The soldiers can!"

"You're gonna take on the military? That's crazy! You can't do it!"

They both heard a familiar engine sound and the squeal of tires braking hard in the driveway. Natalie raced to the window, Coltan not far behind her.

"Mom!" Natalie screamed.

So many mords covered her car they completely blocked the interior.

Beverly shot at them through the windshield. Many fell off, and others replaced them. The windshield weakened by the shots began to shatter ever so slowly, cracks spider webbing across the glass.

She threw it into reverse and backed out, hitting a few behind the car in the process. She turned out without looking, relying only on years of imbedded memory and habit. Once in the street, she floored it and raced around the west side of the house to the back. More infected dived onto the hood and hung on. She couldn't see anything except bloodied bodies and twisted faces in front of her through the cracked surface of the blood-smeared windshield.

All around her she could hear the rat-a-tat-tat of gunfire, could smell the odor of spent ammunition, fire and burning oil, and she could feel the shaking and pummeling her vehicle was suffering from the horde of infected riding along.

Natalie and Coltan ran to the south side, just in time to see Beverly's car fishtail around the corner of the house and slam into the side of the Humvee. The crash was earsplitting. Natalie screamed for her mother.

Coltan, on desperate impulse, ran to the retractable stairs and started to unlock them. The only thought in his mind at that moment was to reach Beverly and bring her up there to safety. He didn't know how he would do it; he didn't bother to think that far yet. All he knew was he had to save her.

An ear-shattering explosion caused them to hit the floor again. Suddenly, Natalie shot up, screaming hysterically and pounding on the window with her fists. Coltan half-stood and hurried to her, his first objective to get her away from the windows before the soldiers discovered her. When he reached her at the window, he learned the reason for her hysteria.

The soldiers had pumped a hail of bullets at the car, trying to kill the predators that were clinging to it. In the process, someone shot through the gas tank. The explosion they heard and felt was Beverly's car—with Beverly still in it. Flames engulfed the car. A second explosion rocked the burning vehicle. Flaming shards of glass, metal and tire flew into the air and landed in different areas of the yard and gardens.

Coltan seized Natalie by her waist and half-carried, half-dragged, her into the interior of the room. She fought him, screaming and kicking her feet at him. "Mom! Mom! No! Mom! Oh, God! No!" He put his hand over her mouth and pushed her face-first onto the nearest mattress, used his body weight to keep her there. She continued to scream through his hand.

"Natalie! Natalie!" He said to her, "You gotta be quiet. They'll hear you!"

"No..." She screamed the muffled reply, her tears flowing over his hand.

"You gotta be quiet!" He braced himself over her, embraced her with one arm and held her to him. "You gotta be quiet. We can't let them find us!"

"Mom...!"

"I know. I know. You gotta be quiet."

She squirmed beneath him, freed one arm and elbowed him in his right side. He ignored the pain and held her tighter. She tried to free her legs to kick at him, and he used his own legs to subdue her.

Although his hand was tight as a vice over her mouth, she still managed to get the word, "No!" out, and it came as a wail.

"Shhh, shhh, shhh. Quiet. There's nothing we can do. She's with God, now."

Natalie protested angrily, "*Mmmprh Gowad!*"

"Shhh... quiet."

She finally surrendered, weeping. After a minute or so, he cautiously removed his hand from her mouth, at first keeping it close in case she began to scream again. She didn't scream anymore. She sobbed and sobbed and moaned words he could not understand. He remained over her, covering her with his body, and wrapped both his arms around her and held her while she dissolved into helpless, angry tears.

It took another hour for the battle to die down outside. The gunfire, voices and other mayhem gradually faded to quiet. The last sounds Coltan heard from there was a voice that said, "We done all we can here. Move out," and the roar of engines starting and pulling away. After that, there were no sounds except Natalie's sobs and her bitter whispered curses at God.

Very slowly and gently, he released his arms from around her and sat up, relieving her of his weight. She remained curled up there, trembling and breathing hard. He rubbed her back in an attempt to calm her. She didn't respond to him, didn't speak, and didn't move. She just lay there curled up, trembling and breathing fast. Helpless to do anything for her, he sat there and watched her for a long time. Finally, without looking at him, or anything, she rolled over on her side and managed to sit up. He lifted her face to look at her. She was pale and drenched with sweat. She seemed to be trying to focus her eyes, but was having a difficult time getting her brain and body to work in unison. One arm moved heavily, pushing him away from her. He didn't resist, instead allowing her to do what she wanted. After a few seconds, she crawled on her hands and knees over to a corner and, still trembling, curled up there against the wall, her face half-pressed to the wood. She hugged the wall as if she wished to merge into it and disappear.

He didn't know what he could do for her. In all of his life, he had never felt so utterly incompetent and lost. To add to all of this came the worry she might not ever come out of it. What would he do then? He couldn't think about it. His brain wanted to go into hibernation.

He could smell the odor from the still-smoldering car in the yard. He went to the window and saw it, a black, smoking mess with charred bodies melted to the hood and roof. Beyond the shattered driver's side window sat another charred form, unrecognizable as the sweet woman who had been his surrogate mother for just a short time.

It impressed him as strange when he realized he felt no emotion at the gruesome sight.

He distracted himself with picking up the mess on the floor, sweeping up the spent shells and broken glass, and replacing the plants to their spot by the south window. He gathered all the weapons, reloaded them, and carefully put them away. When done, he surveyed the room and remembered he and Natalie had never finished stocking the rest of their provisions into the storage room.

When he completed that task, he checked on Natalie. She had not changed her position, was still trembling and seemed to be semi-conscious. He knelt beside her, drew her away from the wall and looked into her pale sweating face. He talked to her, tried to soothe her, and got no response. He held her for a while and wondered what to do. He recalled her father giving her a Valium the day she killed her first mord. That seemed to work then. However, she had not been in the extreme emotional condition she exhibited now. He went to the medical bin and found the drawer with the medications. He decided to give her two Valiums and brought them to her with a Styrofoam cup of water. She resisted at first, spit them out when he gently placed them in her mouth. More forceful on his second try, he ordered her to drink the water and swallow the pills. She seemed to hear him this time. Once she had swallowed the pills, she retreated again into the corner, faced and hugged the wall. He decided to leave her like that until the medication took effect.

Outside in all directions the neighborhood was silent. There wasn't even the flutter of a single bird. Everything was stone silent. A couple of trees were seared, but had not caught fire. Bodies and parts of bodies lie strewn all over. There were so many bodies littering the street, one could not pass without having to step over and around them. Bullet holes pockmarked houses and vehicles. The doors had been broken down in all the homes, and every one had smashed windows.

Coltan wondered how their refuge held up. He listened for sounds in the house below and heard nothing. Summoning his courage, he quietly unlocked the staircase and let it down slowly and carefully so as not to make a sound. Once it was down, he listened again. Silence. He stepped down a few steps, bent and looked. The access door was still secure. Very carefully and gently, he lifted the bars and set them aside. He pushed the access door open just enough to where he could view the barricaded door that led from his room to the hallway. It was intact. Relieved, he backed himself into the access room and barricaded the hidden entrance. He felt anxious and wanted to return to the safety of the attic. As soon as he retracted and locked the staircase in place, he checked again on Natalie.

She was now limp against the wall. He tenderly pulled her away from it and let her rest against him for a minute. Her breathing had slowed, and the trembling and sweating had finally subsided. Her eyes half-closed, she murmured something he couldn't understand. He stood and pulled her up into his arms, lifted her and carried her over to her mattress on the floor. He laid her on the sleeping bag and adjusted the pillow under her head. There was no indication she was aware of anything. It occurred to him her sweat-dampened clothing would take a while to dry. She would be cold in the interim. He took an extra sleeping bag, opened it fully and covered her. After removing her shoes, he tucked the sleeping bag around her and watched her sleep.

When his own fatigue finally set in, he pushed his mattress alongside hers, and dozed fitfully.

MOST OF THE SOLDIERS were inebriated and exhausted by the time they loaded the last of their Bujjet Mart bounty into their vehicles. They had just boarded for departure when the White Springs College bus veered through the guardrail and sailed down the hill into the lot where it rolled and settled on its side.

The soldiers, luckily not in the bus's path, accelerated their rides and sped out of the parking lot.

The bus's engine sputtered and gray smoke belched from the exhaust pipe as twenty or so mords emerged slowly and painfully out the broken windows. Those seriously injured simply fell headfirst to the pavement where they helplessly crumbled. The ones that remained ambulatory sniffed the air and detected the odor of the doomed civilians near the loading dock, most of whom had succumbed to their bites and were feasting on the bodies of the ones who had become comatose. The mords from the bus approached the group and fought them for the spoils.

Weak, thirsty and frustrated, Mario despondently rested on his back in the tall weeds. Beside him, Rosa slept deeply, oblivious to their newest threat. He gazed up at the gray dusk sky, the stars obliterated by the thick smoke. He shivered in the cold and wondered how much longer it would be before they could make it into the shelter inside the store. There was not enough ammo in the revolver and the rifle to take out the enemy. He had no choice but to wait and hope the monsters would get their fill and move on.

Mario curled against his sister. A children's song played in his head, and he began to sing it to Rosa in a whispered voice, *"Jesus loves me, this I know... For the Bible tells me so..."* He stopped then, afraid his voice might carry.

He prayed the wind would not come up and carry their scent to the predators below.

CHAPTER 21

SHELTER

COLTAN WAS DREAMING about a flock of birds chirping in a tree. He was trying to climb the branches to join the birds safely up high away from the monsters below, but kept falling to the dirt. He couldn't see the monsters, but he knew they were there. The birds fluttered above, chirping as if encouraging him. If he could make it up there, they would protect him. He tried again, and the sunlight blinded him. The flock chirped louder.

Awakening, he opened his eyes slowly. The sun in the east window cast its light across his face, hurting his eyes. He closed his eyes and turned over, listened to the birdsong. Memories of the previous day played in fragments. The image of Beverly's car aflame caused him to open his eyes again. He focused on the wall and pushed the disturbing memory away. Another thought came: Natalie.

He sat up and peered at her. She had turned over during the night and was now facing him. She breathed slowly, still asleep. Her tears and sweat dried on her face and had left a salty white residue in streaks on her skin. A swollen bruise formed over her temple. He surmised she must have inflicted it upon herself when she had sought refuge in the corner against the wall. She seemed peaceful, and he decided to let her sleep.

As he took a sponge bath in the bathroom in the access room

below, the thought occurred to him to check the main floor for damage. However, if some of the sliders had failed, there may be mords lurking about, sniffing the air, following the trail of scent, waiting outside his bedroom door. That was enough to make him reconsider. He was unashamedly too frightened to go down there. It could wait. The next hours he would spend attending to his own and Natalie's immediate needs.

Upon return to the attic with a towel, a washcloth and a small bucket of hot water, he saw she had not changed position. He didn't want to awaken her, but he felt a need to tend to her in some small way. He gently shifted her onto her back, and pressed the warm damp washcloth to her face to absorb the salty residue of tears and sweat. Her eyes opened slowly and she looked at him, seemed to study him. She weakly murmured something. He hushed her and continued cleaning her. She pressed her hand over his as he dabbed at her cheek.

"Mom..."

"Shhh..."

"Go out and play?" Her eyes peered into his inquisitively.

"Not today," he told her, his voice soft.

"Car... fire..." She looked away, scanned the room. "Mom...?"

It was overwhelming and incomprehensible to Coltan how God had let this happen. His eyes blurred with tears. He allowed them to fall and slide down his cheeks. Anger and sadness welled up in him and he surrendered to it.

She reached up and felt the tears on his face. "Colt...?"

Not answering, he submerged the washcloth into the bucket and then rung it out. He folded it and laid it over her forehead.

Her eyes suddenly filled with certainty, she stared at him. "Dead..."

"Shhh..."

"Dead... dead..."

It struck him she was referring to the condition of each parent. *Mom's dead. Dad's dead.*

Her hesitant acceptance emerged as a soft, plaintive moan.

"Shhh..." He feared she would dissolve into hysteria again. He caressed her face, stroked her hair and tenderly kissed her.

Her eyes closed and her body slowly went limp. She would escape the horrible truth for a while longer, and he was grateful for that.

The next half hour he spent in tearful prayer. He prayed for everybody, even the mords.

ROSA DEVELOPED A HIGH fever during the night. Mario stayed awake and monitored her condition, worried not so much about her fever as about her stillness. In the light of dawn, she appeared to be in a semi-comatose state. Mario wished he had some water to give her, even as his own thirst begged relief.

The store's timed exterior lights cast eerie moving shadows upon the pavement and the loading dock. A dozen mords wandered away from the parking lot and headed toward the center of Bonito Valle. Near the overturned college bus, the injured mords who could not walk crawled or pulled themselves toward the loading dock to battle the able-bodied monsters that were still feasting on the leftover scraps of human remains.

Mario checked his ammo. There were two in the pistol and one left in the shotgun. He thought it best to wait a while longer. If, in the meantime, the mords detected his scent, he would use the two shots in the pistol for Rosa and himself.

THE LOCAL STATIONS were off the air, as were almost all the cable/satellite networks. SWNS (*Satellite World News* Service) was still broadcasting from Charleston. They ran video of the violence across the country, footage of troops escorting evacuees and refugees into busses, some other video showing the same activity at a train station. The people were in shock, carrying children and sparse belongings; some had nothing but the clothes on their backs. Many had injuries. Another video showed a soldier taking a cat from a young woman. The soldier handed the cat over to a man wearing an ASPCA jacket. The man was trying to reassure the sobbing woman her cat would be in safe hands. A voiceover explained animal rescue groups secured all pets in cages for transport in a separate boxcar for reunion with owners at the assorted rescue camps.

Later, three scientists interviewed and questioned about the mysterious disease that had turned law-abiding citizens into cannibalistic maniacs ultimately could offer no explanation for the phenomenon. They only offered theories and reassurances they were *working on it*, and a vaccination program in the works appeared "promising."

A Presidential news conference only told Coltan what he had already anticipated. The President urged the people to cooperate fully with the military and accompany them to the rescue centers. Coltan thought it interesting the President called them rescue *centers* while SWNS referred to them as rescue *camps*. The word *"centers"* carried a more benign connotation, thus reassuring and placating the masses that the government only had their best interests at heart. When a reporter inquired pointedly about the rumors of REFEHL chip implantation at the "centers," the President calmly stated no such program existed. Another reporter asked about the vaccination program. The president stated the vaccinations, although experimental at first, had proven successful and would protect those citizens who had been found free of the disease. The same reporter asked if the vaccinations were mandatory. The President replied in the affirmative. The POTUS, searching the room for a friendly face, ignored an inquiry as to what would happen to those who refused the vaccine. Another reporter pounced on this and inquired if the vaccinations could cure those already infected. The President answered, "Inconclusive at this time." Another reporter inquired as to the fate of those infected. Before the President answered, two men in suits and wearing transmitters in their ears whispered to the President and escorted him away from the podium. The Press Secretary stepped up and announced succinctly, "No further questions." Of course, the press bombarded him with overlapping inquiries. He ignored them and briskly left the staging area.

Coltan found it curious, but predictable. SWNS never mentioned or questioned the unexplained origin of the disease during their coverage. However, callers on the talk radio programs still broadcasting offered their own theories, from extraterrestrials and Middle Eastern terrorists, to proponents of the New World Order. Predictably again, the hosts of these programs dismissed as nonsense the existence of a group of elites working to decrease the population in preparation of a New World Order.

Coltan knew the only radio program that considered all theories and didn't humiliate their callers was the one he listened to in the middle of the night. That program came out of Montana and originated from its own independent broadcast facility with a super-powerful transmitter that reached most of the northern hemisphere. They hosted guests considered on the fringes by most of the general population: educated men and women who observed the goings-on behind the scenes in government and world politics, and knew the real score. They told their listeners all the things the Elites-owned mainstream news media could not reveal. He would listen to that program tonight, as he did most nights.

He shut off the television and took a look out the north window.

Flies congregated over and inside the wounds of the corpses below. Their buzzing filled the air. Coltan considered the flies, considered their offspring hatching from inside the wounds of the infected bodies. They would spread the disease everywhere they visited. Coltan thought about the bullet holes in the windows. The flies would find these entrances and then enter the attic. He had to cover these holes to prevent that. The only least-noticeable thing he could think of was clear tape. He found a roll and began the task of finding and sealing each hole. It was a *Richard* kind of solution, but it worked well enough for the time being.

LATE IN THE AFTERNOON, the ambulatory mords gradually wandered away from Bujjet Mart, and only the injured ones remained near the loading dock. Some had passed out from their injuries. Those still conscious were weak and moved slowly. Mario decided he could easily get around them, reach the back door and get inside with Rosa.

He gathered her into his arms and stood slowly, slung the shotgun over his shoulder. It was now or never.

COLTAN BREWED COFFEE and enjoyed a smoke. Natalie mumbled something in her sleep. He reclined beside her and sipped his coffee. She was better off asleep, he told himself, and wished he could sleep, too. However, there was a lot to think about, a lot to consider to ensure their anonymity and safety. So, as much as his body wanted to relax, his mind kept him occupied. His thoughts and fears tumbled around in his brain, and he selected only a few for consideration.

The bodies would begin to stink and decay rapidly, even with the cool temperatures. He knew it was not possible for him to remove and burn or bury them. There were simply too many and they were highly contagious. He wondered if someone would send HAZMAT out to do the job. If so: when? It may take days or a week or more. He searched the rolling medical bin for masks and mentholated ointment. The masks would protect them somewhat from any air-born contaminants, and the menthol odor from a dab of mentholated ointment above the upper lip would cover the stench from the rotting corpses. He found both and decided that would have to do.

Coltan saw on the television the military was returning to some of the devastated areas in search of survivors. He had seen HAZMAT in the background. This indicated the Military would accompany the HAZMAT crews if and when they arrived in his neighborhood. If the authorities discovered them, it would mean a trip to the camps. He was determined to prevent this.

He considered the sliders on the windows. If he used them to cover the windows, it would most likely indicate to the soldiers someone was living in the attic. Covering the windows would be no good. It was bad enough the downstairs windows were covered. If the soldiers decided to break in and search the house, he hoped they would only search as far as the second floor.

This thought caused him to reconsider how he had secured his bedroom door. He pictured the soldiers trying his bedroom door and finding it locked and barricaded. That would definitely give them away. He and Brian had never considered that. They had only thought about safety and keeping the mords at bay. He would have to remove the barricade on the door and leave the door unlocked, perhaps even open. He considered the hidden entrance to the attic access room: He disguised it well enough that they wouldn't discover it unless they were specifically looking for it. Additionally, the barriers inside the entrance would prevent them from pushing it open. Even if someone leaned back against it, the panel would remain solidly flush with the rest of the wall.

There were hand tools in the storage room, and he thought about stealing away for a short time to remedy that problem. Unfortunately, the sun was setting. If he tried to work down there now, he would have to turn on a light. He had not installed a slider on his bedroom window. He had intended that as the last thing, but had forgotten about it. Someone might see the light and know someone occupied the house. The risk was too great. He would have to put it off until tomorrow and work in the sunlight. He wasn't comfortable with that idea, but decided there was nothing else he could do.

Coltan also took into consideration Natalie's fragile emotional and mental state. There was no telling how she would react if she awoke to find herself alone. This convinced him to remain and be near her when she awakened.

Almost as if she sensed his presence, Natalie opened her eyes.

"Hey..." he whispered.

"Thirsty." Her voice was weak.

"I'll get you some water." He brought it to her. She tried to sit up, but was having difficulty on her own. He helped her and rested her against him. Her hands were trembling too much to hold the cup. He kept it and placed the rim against her lips. She drank slowly. "You got a bad bump on your head," he told her.

"Hurts."

"I'll bet."

"You prayed with me," she whispered hoarsely.

"Yeah."

"Dad told you thanks." She seemed to be lingering in a partial dream state.

"He did?"

"Mom, too."

He thought she had dreamed it, so he simply nodded and offered her more water.

"I know they're at peace. But I'm not."

"I know."

"Are *you* alright?"

"I guess." He wasn't, and he knew it.

She knew it, too. "We'll get through this."

"We have to." What other choice was there?

She drifted back to sleep. Coltan laid her down and covered her with the sleeping bag.

While she slept, Coltan went down to the access room where he used a straight head screwdriver to remove the shells of their portafones. He pried apart the innards, removed the memory cards, crushed the cards and works into tiny pieces with the screwdriver handle, and flushed the fragments in small increments down the toilet. He flushed the toilet three more times to ensure the pieces journeyed into the sewer. Confident he had destroyed or at least sent the tracking technology far away, he returned to the attic.

The moon sent its weak ghostly light through the window and pasted the shadow of the window frame with its pale white circular wisp dead center upon Natalie's sleeping bag. The image impressed him as beautiful and surreal, and, in a strange way, inviting. For a moment, he fantasized sinking into it as one would a pool of warm clear water.

He wearily settled beside Natalie and draped his arm across her waist. He wasn't sure if the physical contact was for her sense of security or his.

CHAPTER 22

The wind came up during the night and accelerated over a few hours to almost gale force. It intruded into their dreams and awakened them for a while. By the time the sun began to send its initial light above the edge of the horizon, the wind weakened and they drifted back into sleep.

It wasn't long before they awakened again at the same time.

Natalie wished someone would turn off the wind machine so she could get a good uninterrupted sleep. Wearily, and only one-quarter awake, she turned to Coltan and cuddled against him, her cheek against his chest. He wrapped his arm around her and dozed off again, until the voices outside caused them to open their eyes and lift their heads.

It was still mostly dark in the attic, so their strongest sense at this moment was their sense of hearing. What they heard they immediately interpreted as threatening.

The voices all seemed to be shouting at once. The noise of engines, heavy machinery and smaller vehicles accompanied the voices. Aside from the sounds, there was the scent of smoke. It was faint, as if from a distance away.

Coltan was first up, and he tiptoed over to the east window. Far out in the field where he used to walk Muffy, bulldozers and trenchers were digging a large pit. He could barely discern the figures of men working there, and decided to find his binoculars.

Natalie crouched at the north window, peeking carefully from a low corner of it. She saw military vehicles and personnel, also the HAZMAT teams and a few HAZMAT trucks on the street. The

HAZMAT teams were collecting the bodies and depositing them into what appeared to be a skip loader. Once the scoop at the front of the loader was full, the workers unceremoniously deposited the partially devoured corpses and that of their dead predators into one of many dump trucks parked at the end of the street.

Across the street, fully armed and dressed in protective battlefield body armor, soldiers were entering the houses.

*Trouble...*Natalie thought.

Coltan moved to the south window and saw the same scenario playing on the north side. The only difference was a group of HAZMAT personnel crowded around the cooling charred remains of Beverly's car. They seemed to be discussing a plan of action for peeling the melted bodies off the metal. One of them opened the door and removed Beverly's charred remains into the scoop at the front of the skip loader. At the same time, some others added their finds to what would soon fill the scoop to capacity. He stole a glance at Natalie at the north window and was glad she had not witnessed this.

Ducking, he went to her. "We better stay low and very, *very* quiet."

"The soldiers are checking the houses." She moved away from the window and sat with her back pressed against the wall. "They'll be coming here."

It filled him with dread. "I know."

"They'll find us."

"We'll pray that they don't."

"God doesn't listen anymore."

"Yeah, he does. You gotta believe it, Nat. Just believe it." He took both her hands in his, "Jesus promised that if two or more pray in his name, he would be there with them. We'll pray together."

It was then Coltan recalled he had forgotten to open his bedroom door. He considered rushing down to open it, but reconsidered with the disturbing thought of soldiers entering the house before he could return to the attic. He didn't tell Natalie about the door, but he silently relegated their safety to God as he tightened his trembling hands around Natalie's as they began to pray.

AT THE SAME MOMENT, James was praying silently for God to keep any survivors there hidden from the military and their HAZMAT teams.

After the two-day siege at the hospital ended, and they rounded up all personnel and patients for safe transport to the rescue camps, his superior reassigned him to the suburban cleanup and rescue teams. In all the rush and confusion, no one in charge had bothered to scan the soldiers for their REFEHL. The head honchos simply pointed at soldiers randomly and ordered them into transport trucks.

Sitting in the back with the others, he glanced over faces, hoping to recognize a fellow member of the secret *Army of Christ*, but there were none familiar to him. He stayed quiet and listened to the chatter among the men and women, listened for useful information. But all he heard was the sharing of stories about their battles against the mords and all the poor victims they had to execute on the spot to prevent further spread of the disease. Someone laughed derisively and said the dead had at least got the easiest end of the deal; the living had to go on fighting.

Intermittently, he wondered about the fate of the Christian woman doctor he talked to in the break room at the hospital. He had looked for her during the siege, but never found her. He hoped she made it out alive and found her way back to her husband and kids.

The population of Christians and many other religious sects had gradually dwindled to minority status over the past two decades.

Infighting, greed, sex scandals and all manner of moral decay inside the hierarchies of most denominations had soured the general population's trust of religious leaders and the Church. Even those who remained in attendance in synagogues, shrines and temples observed the same moral corruption. As a result, most abandoned their spiritual beliefs out of sheer disillusion, and those with no religion stubbornly resisted the efforts of the few believers left to lead them to Jesus or Buddha or Mohammed, or any of the other high profile "spiritual dudes." As history attests, spiritual apathy leads to hopelessness of the soul, and the last seven years had seen an increase in hedonism, all manner of self-destructive behavior, and a live-for-today mentality. The motto of the decade was, *Tomorrow is promised to no one.*

Still, many privately retained their spiritual beliefs, and all interpreted the signs of the times as the *Beginning of the End.*

This was the world in which James grew up. Like the majority, he had gone blithely along with the program. Then one day, a woman he worked for introduced him to the Gospels of Christ. He studied further and found it fulfilled that empty space inside him that had always yearned for something of substance. This was the substance. He studied with the woman for years until her death at the hands of a street gang member she had been working to save. At her funeral, he silently told her he would carry on her work. He had been keeping that promise ever since. The work culminated in the establishment of The Army of Christ and the secret work of building secluded refuges in preparation for the Time of the Beast.

The time was now.

He concluded his prayer to God and thanked Him for His protection.

The trucks dumped their first of many loads into the large pit in the open field away from the neighborhood. A special team ignited the fire low in the pit. They doused the corpses with fire accelerator, and each flaming body lit up the new ones dumped over them. Truck after truck returned to dump their load from all the surrounding housing developments in the hillside area.

Around noon, the air grew bitterly cold. Storm clouds and a hazy layer of smoke obscured the sky.

James received orders to check another house, a fine two-story house with what appeared from ground level to be a shallow windowed attic. It was the only house in this neighborhood with windows covered from the inside by massive sheets of plywood. From his view at ground level, it appeared they had neglected to cover the four attic windows, and James assumed it was because the attic was an unused space and always had been. James reckoned the homeowners had prepared for what was coming and had done their best to protect their property, but the idea of them installing the plywood sheets inside the windows instead of outside struck him as asinine and bassackwards. He hoped they had decided to bug-out like a lot of folks had done. He didn't want to find anyone hiding there. He didn't want to be the guy that would have no other choice but to turn them over to the military. He would have no other choice because any other action would blow his cover.

They partnered him with Shaunnessy, who he disliked. The guy was a screw-up and a gung-ho killer. James remembered too well the glee Shaunnessy took in executing the infected; it was just plain perverted. James figured he would find a way to keep Shaunnessy off his back, give him a little side job of some kind, like searching the cupboards for food to steal or something like that. Anything to keep him occupied so James could identify, reassure and protect from further discovery any survivors who may be taking refuge in the place.

He prayed silently again as he and Shaunnessy circled the three-quarter wraparound porch for a weak door or window to use as entry. All the lower windows were broken, but the plywood had held, and the locked security doors only sported a few dents and scratches. They found a cracked panel in one of the living room windows and bashed it in with their tools. As was always the case, James climbed in first and called out, his weapon pointed and ready.

The house was silent.

Shaunnessy climbed through and yelled out, "I want a beer, assholes!"

"Shut up!" James hissed.

The place was too dark to see anything well. James found a light switch on the wall and flipped it up. The floor lamp in one corner came on.

"You check the bottom floor. I'll get up top," James told Shaunnessy. "If the bottom's clear, how 'bout you check around for some food. I'm starvin.'"

"If you find some women up there that ain't sick, I'm starvin' for that."

"Me too, brother..." It was the farthest thing from his mind, but it pacified the idiot.

James found the light switch for the stairway and upper hallway and turned the lights on. He climbed the stairs quietly and cautiously. *So far, so good.* At the top of the stairs, he had the choice of going left or right. He chose right. The bedroom doors were open on that end. He kept his rifle ready and listened for the faintest sound.

He found the light switch for the room at the end of the hall. It was a girl's room, obvious by the décor and the discarded bra and socks on the unmade twin size bed, a Bible and a tube of perfumed body lotion on the bureau. He found nothing under the bed. He checked the half-open closet and found only clothing, shoes and an empty overnight bag. James decided it was pointless to check the drawers in the bureau and nightstands, decided it was invasive, as well; he drew the line when it came to invading people's privacy. The next room appeared to be a guest room, as it was sparsely furnished and the bed neatly made, and he noticed the room lacked any personal type items. A check of the closet revealed it was empty except for a floral comforter set still wrapped in its original packaging. Another room was a bathroom. He noticed a lone toothbrush in the holder and a tube of toothpaste on the counter along with a pump bottle of liquid soap. Towels hung neatly on the bars, a full roll of toilet paper on the roller... nothing unusual. He opened the white accordion doors along the hallway wall near the bathroom and revealed a tidy linen closet. He closed the doors snugly. He backtracked and turned off all the lights in the rooms he had already checked.

This led him back to the center of the hallway at the top of the stairs. He spied a closed door at the end of the hall and, kiddy-corner to its right another room with an open door.

He heard Shaunnessy rummaging around in what sounded like a drawer downstairs. James peered down the stairs and saw Shaunnessy emerge from a room at the left side.

"Whad'ja find?" James whispered down to him.

"Nothin."

"Go check the kitchen."

"No women yet?"

"Naw..."

James waited until Shaunnessy was out of view. He waited a moment longer and listened while the idiot opened cupboards and drawers in the kitchen. He heard the refrigerator door open. That would keep him occupied for a few minutes.

James continued on and approached the open door to the right of the room with the closed door. He entered the room and switched on the light. It was a big room, a master suite with its own bathroom and walk-in closets. He checked carefully, slowly—and felt a little unhinged—because he could feel a presence in the room. However, after a thorough investigation, the bedroom, bathroom and walk-in closets held no living creature of any kind. He still felt the presence, though, and it caused the hair on the back of his neck to tickle him. He shivered and tried to shrug it off. It was then he noticed the photograph of a man, woman and a young girl. The girl had her mother's eyes. He recognized the woman as the doctor he had spoken with at the hospital, the Christian doctor. Now he understood why he felt a presence. James paused for a moment and contemplated the energy. The presence impressed him as benevolent. He wondered if it was an angel.

Downstairs, Shaunnessy noisily dug into the pantry closet.

Next, James headed for the room kiddy-corner to the master bedroom. He approached the closed door cautiously. He ran his hand over it, found it cold. It was colder than a wood door would be. He surmised it was one of those steel-reinforced doors. Now, why would one room have a door like that? He gently turned the doorknob and found it locked. He pressed against the door. It was solidly plumb and not giving an inch.

He knew what this meant.

After listening for Shaunnessy's activity and now confident the screwball was busy chowing down on some food, James removed a card from his back pocket and a pen from his waist pack. He wrote the coordinates on the card and drew a fish symbol so the hiding occupants would understand he was a friend and they were safe for today. He shoved the card under the door and returned downstairs.

"The place is clear," he told Shaunnessy.

Shaunnessy tossed him an old wrinkled apple and a tomato, "This place smells like Mexican food. Notice that?"

"Now that you mention it."

"Nothin' upstairs?"

"Nothin'. Looks like they packed up and split."

"Yeah. The gun safe's empty, too. Lock and load and hit the road! They're probably dead on the interstate with all the others."

Shaunnessy patted his pack with both hands. "Found some chili-con-carne, canned spaghetti, some tuna, a box of crackers, and a bottle of peanuts. The rest is veggies. There's some canned fruit if you want it. Over there in that pantry."

"Yeah. I'll take a can of fruit..." It was for show. "Let's go, man."

"You gotta see the Harley first."

"Harley?"

"In the garage, man. Hot cherry, I tell ya! Couldn't find the key, though."

"You think you're gonna just ride off into the sunset on it? Hell, they won't let you get two feet on that thing."

"I can still dream, man... Go take a look at it."

"No, I'll pass. Are there any other vehicles in there?"

"Just the bike. There's a truck out back, though—what's left of it."

"Let's go, then."

Shaunnessy went for the back door.

"No," James said, "They might come back when this blows over. They went to a lot of trouble to secure this place. Leave it all locked up. We'll go out the way we came in."

After they exited through the window, James did his best to reset the plywood in the frame. It was flimsy, but it would lessen the chance of a wandering infected noticing the weak spot and getting in. He felt it was the least he could do for whoever was hiding in that room.

The only survivor the other troops found and apprehended was a skinny guy with a .22 and a motor mouth full of rotten teeth who surrendered peacefully. They found his wife shot dead in the living room and dumped her body with the others in the pit.

The troops and HAZMAT wrapped up their work by two o'clock and were all out of there by three.

Up in the attic, Natalie and Coltan breathed a sigh of relief. They prayed in thanks.

So did James.

THE ONLY SOUND THEY could hear was a faint mechanical noise coming from the field. Coltan knelt at the east window with his binoculars. He saw a small crew of men and three bulldozers at the smoking pit. They were using the bulldozers to dump soil into the pit to bury the remains and smother the fire. Coltan anticipated the crew would stay around for a few hours to verify the fire was completely out.

Natalie peeked out the south window to see what they had done. She tried to resist it, but her first inclination was to look across at her mother's burned-up car. As much as everything decent and respectful in her dissuaded her from focusing on it, she looked anyway and discovered they removed her mother's charred corpse.

"They took her away..."

Coltan turned to her. "What?"

Her eyes filled with tears. "They took Mom."

He moved between her and the window, and physically turned her away from the sight. "I didn't want you to see that. Don't look at it."

"I wanted to..." She was starting to fall apart again. "How could they do that? She was my mother!"

With tormenting persistence, the memory of her mother's death returned again. Natalie prayed it was a quick death, hoped even that she had died before the explosion. Still, no amount of imagining would soothe the pain of her loss or erase the evil that brought it about. She thought it ironic both Mom and Dad died alone in their vehicles. That recollection brought to her heart the pain of losing her father, too. They had both died with no opportunity to say goodbye to each other or to her. She had not had the opportunity to tell them how much she loved them. It pained her even more when she realized she never had the chance to apologize for every wrong thing she ever did or said to hurt them.

The cruel finality of it was more than she could endure.

She tried to be brave and tried to will the tears away, but they fell, regardless. Her body shook with each uncontrollable sob. The loss of control angered her. It angered her because she had tried to hold it all back, tried so hard to be strong, and she wasn't strong.

Racked by the painful waves of sobs, she wrapped her arms around her middle and bent forward to ease the discomfort. If only she could stem the onslaught and fold her grief inward. She tried to speak and only got out the words, "I can't..." before the rest ran together unintelligibly. She only made it halfway to her mattress on the floor before she collapsed to her knees. Her upper body folded under its own power as she held her stomach and sobbed into the floor.

Coltan cradled her with one arm while he retrieved the sleeping bag with the other and wrapped it around her. He could see no logical explanation for wanting to bundle her like this. It only felt like the right thing to do for her. He went with his instinct, and lifted her onto his lap and wrapped his arms around her, held her to him protectively as if she was his child.

"Go with it," he whispered to her. "Cry as long and as hard as you need. I'm right here. I'm with you."

Somewhere within the crashing resurgences of grief, the sensation of the sleeping bag enveloping her tightly in warmth, plus the strength and tenderness of the arms that cradled her enabled her to surrender fully. Time ceased to exist. Her mind closed itself off to everything except the pain of loss and the fiery horror that kept replaying like a tape on endless loop. It was making her crazy, and she wanted to scream. She tried to scream, only to find her voice had abandoned her. Her body convulsed with each fresh wave, and she was not aware of the trembling that increased with the resultant physical exhaustion. There came from deep inside silent screams to God, silent pleas for relief from the ordeal, relief from the memory of her mother aflame in the burning wreckage. However, the voice that cried out in desperate prayer was not her own, but that of another being inside her soul. An unexpected calmness slowly grew within her and pushed the remainder of the shock and horror away; pushed it far away to some place outside her body and mind. The warmth tightened around her and the strong tender arms held her securely. His heart was racing and its gallop pounded against her cheek. Briefly, something resembling consciousness returned to her. It became easier to breathe, and the gasping sobs subsided. Her respiration gradually slowed and she became aware of the heaviness and weakness of her body. As she slumped powerlessly into the cradle that lovingly shielded her, Coltan's heartbeat against her cheek slowed to a lulling rhythm of calm. She drifted into sleep after a long while, exhausted.

He rested beside her and continued to hold her. His desire to protect her only grew stronger.

It was in the quiet stillness of those moments when Coltan sensed a presence with them. He recognized it as the same entity he had felt before in the house. Whoever or whatever it was filled the space around them, and he felt amazingly calm and safe in its energy. A gentle hand reassuringly pressed his shoulder, and he knew it was not his imagination. The Being was real, and it was communicating to him in its own way.

"I don't know what to do for her," Coltan whispered.

The pressure on his shoulder weighed slightly heavier, and then he felt it caress his skin from his shoulder to his fingers.

"Heal her," he whispered. "Please... I don't know what to do."

There came the feather-light sensation of breath against his cheek, and with it the scent of roses. From within and without, a voice spoke softly, and it sounded as if it spoke through a waterfall:

"Don't be afraid..."

He closed his eyes and drank in the scent. Something covered him, something exquisitely warm and comforting. He felt it cover Natalie also.

Coltan could hardly speak, and his voice came below a whisper, "Yeshua...?"

"Don't be afraid..."

CHAPTER 23

H e awoke with the light of dawn and the songs of birds. Natalie was his first thought, and she was dead asleep beside him. His own sleep pattern had been sporadic and disturbed by nightmares over the past couple of weeks. Last night he slept deeply and the dreams he could remember had to do with swimming, swimming leisurely in a large green lake of placid waters. He felt thoroughly rested for the first time in over two weeks.

While the coffee brewed, he switched on the television and caught the news. It was the same old thing, people evacuating, talking heads discussing the mord maker virus, Homeland Security recruiting personnel for their FEMA branch to man the rescue camps and assist with transport. The Red Cross had set up interim centers for refugees, and those centers acted not only as relief centers, but also as point of first contact and safe locations for the refugees to await military transport to the big camps. The same scenario played in the rest of the world.

Coltan had missed the last four nights' broadcast of the radio program from Montana. He wondered if there was any more information about the new military and emerging new world government. The last he had heard, someone had mentioned there were actually two factions who posed a threat: the world government hierarchy, and a renegade group that had been responsible for unleashing the mord maker virus. During the report from that caller, the station lost its transmitter power and was off the air for the rest of the night.

Frustrated with the lack of new information via the television, he thumbed the power button on the remote and decided instead to continue his Bible study where he and Brian had left off. Appropriately, the lesson plan for this month was the book of Job, and today would be his first lesson in the series. He sat at the small round table and opened the workbook and his personal journal. He always kept his Bible zipped safely in its leather case, and he opened the case carefully and removed the sacred Book. It had been a gift from Brian, an indexed NIV/NKJV Parallel Study Bible, bound in black genuine leather. Brian had ordered it inscribed with Coltan's full name in handsome gold letters at the right bottom corner: *Charles Coltan Allen.*

Brian had written a note on the presentation page, "My dear son Coltan: May God bless you, strengthen you and comfort you throughout your days. Always remember how precious you are to Him... and to me. All my love, Brian." He had included a card that contained personal notes from him and Beverly that offered words of love, praise and encouragement. Coltan had read the card and the notes over and over again the days after he had received this gift. Over the last four days he had been unable to read the notes again, not for lack of time or opportunity, but for the simple reason his heart was broken with grief and it was too painful to drink in their sentiments. Someday his heart would mend and he would once again be able to appreciate their words with joy and remember these wonderful saviors without tears. However, that day was still far away.

As was his usual practice, he bent his head and opened the study in prayer. He especially asked God to care for Brian and Beverly this day, and interceded again on Natalie's behalf. His worry over Natalie had lightened much since the night before. He knew Jesus—or the angel, or whoever the presence was—had kept its promise to protect and heal her. For the first time in a long time, he felt peace in his heart.

Natalie awakened. She sat up quietly and watched Coltan pray.

He had propped his elbows on the table and rested his forehead upon his clasped hands as he settled into private and intimate communion with God. His expression was one of earnest submission. Natalie saw something else and at first, she dismissed it as an optical illusion. However, she stared and contemplated the pale mist of light that surrounded him. The longer he sat and prayed, the more refulgent the mist until it seemed to emanate from within him as well as from without. As he slowly emerged from his prayer, the light subsided. She had never seen this before, and she had watched many people pray. None had this light about them. Could this be the *Shechina Glory* she had heard and read about but had never witnessed?

Coltan felt her attention on him. He turned and looked at her and was puzzled by her expression. "Okay?" he asked.

She snapped out of her daze. "Good morning."

He went and sat with her. "How'd you sleep? Feel better?"

"Yeah." She noticed his eyes were clear and bright, brighter than she had ever seen. On impulse, she took his face in her hands and gently kissed his forehead.

He smiled. "What was that for?"

"I wanted to."

He put his arms around her and held her tightly. "I've been so worried about you."

"I'm okay." She reciprocated, and then pulled away a bit. She didn't want to interrupt his sacred journey with God. "Go back to your study. Go on."

"You want some coffee?"

"I'll get it. Go study."

Coltan held her hand for a moment, analyzing her expression and general condition. She seemed calm and rested, although still somewhat weak. He kissed her hand and stood. "Take it easy today."

"I'm fine. I feel better. I do."

He thought of telling her about the entity last night, and then decided this didn't seem like the right time. After another glance at her, he returned to the table and his studying.

She poured herself a cup of coffee and refilled his. Over his shoulder, she noticed the lesson subject. "How à propos," she said.

"That's French," he remarked. "Did you know that?"

"Uh-uh. I just heard Mom say it a few times. It's French, huh?"

"Yeah."

"It means 'appropriate,' right?"

"Yeah." *Close enough.*

"You study. I'm gonna crack open a window and have a smoke with my coffee."

She took her cup to the west window and slid the glass open a little. The odor of smoke and burnt chemicals still hung in the air. She ignored it while she lit her cigarette and reclined against the wall below the window. This was the perfect spot to observe Coltan as he studied. He had fallen back into it easily and was now completely absorbed in it. She watched him read, watched him as he paused with a thought and then wrote the thought in his journal. A part of her was curious about the journal, but another part of her respected his privacy. That part won out.

The sight of him studying made her think about Dad. He would be so pleased to see Coltan continuing from where they had left off. She wondered if her father had ever realized what a gift he had brought her through Coltan. Coltan had helped her keep her sanity over the past weeks, and now she couldn't picture being without him. They belonged together; of this she was certain.

They ate peanut butter and jelly sandwiches for breakfast and finished the pot of coffee. Although Coltan had survived the last two days on potato chips and trail mix, Natalie had not had a thing to eat until this morning. He made it his mission to encourage her to take better care of herself.

Of the many subjects they discussed, their most immediate concern regarded the condition of the house. Had the infected or the soldiers left the house unprotected? Had the security doors held? How many of the sliders have failed? They both assumed every window on the lower floor was shattered. Up in the attic they were safe. However, Natalie had not prepared well for living up there. Most of her clothing was still down in her room—her books, too. She wanted her books, especially her Bible. She also wanted to retrieve a photo of her parents to keep with her at all times.

And ... she wanted a bath. She wanted a long relaxing bath with mountains of bubbles and scoops of scented bath salts and fragranced oils. She wanted to shave and slather on lotion and feel like a girl. It never mattered before, but now that it was such a luxury, it became more desirable.

In addition, (she wouldn't admit this to herself) she wanted to be attractive and feminine for Coltan.

After a perimeter check through the attic windows with the binoculars, they armed themselves with Bonnie and Clyde equipped with silencers, and carefully made their way into Coltan's old room. Coltan listened at the door and heard nothing. He lay down on his stomach on the floor and sniffed the air coming through the thin gap under the door. There was no odor resembling that of the infected; they smelled like they hadn't bathed in a month and their clothing reeked of earth and blood—it was a distinct stench.

He gathered into a sitting position against the door and whispered, "I think it's all clear."

She spotted what looked like a business card on the floor next to the hinge corner of the door. "What's that?"

He took it and read it. With a smile, he gave it to her. "We got friends on the outside."

She recognized the numbers as the same coordinates Mitch had delivered. It gave her enormous comfort when she noticed the fish symbol drawn next to the numbers.

"It had to have been one of the soldiers," she mused.

"All right, then," he replied, still whispering. "Let's open this door. Got your gun ready?"

"Yep."

Very quietly and slowly, he removed the bars and unlocked the door. Natalie saw his hands were shaking. He knew this, and took a deep breath to steady his nerves. Soundlessly, he turned the doorknob and drew the door open only enough to peek out through one eye.

"I think we're okay," he whispered.

"Wait." She moved to the latch side of the doorframe, leaned against the wall and readied her weapon, aiming just in case something was waiting for them. She nodded at Coltan. "Okay."

He eased the door open. The hallway was clear. However, Brian and Bev's room was kiddy-corner to his, and their door was open. He gestured at the open door.

"I got it," Natalie said softly. "Ready your weapon."

His mouth was dry. He took another breath and licked his lips, pointed the weapon. The trembling of the barrel revealed his fear.

"Stop shaking," Natalie whispered.

"I can't," Coltan whispered back.

"Remember that day you socked that guy for me? You weren't scared then. I know you weren't scared. You can do this, Colt. Don't let your imagination feed fear into you." She saw him lick his lips again, saw the doubt in his eyes. "Colt, you're an ass-kicker. You've always been an ass-kicker. You can do this."

"Alright, alright..." He tried to push his fears aside, but the image of a horde of infected suddenly springing upon them played in his head like a horror movie. This was not the same thing as taking on some loud-mouthed punk in the parking lot of the Dairy Delight.

She thought he might pass out right there and then. She shook her head, glared at him and hissed, "Coltan! I need you! Get your shit straight! Now!"

He gritted his teeth, angry at his cowardice, and even angrier Natalie saw him as a coward. She was calm, prepared and alert. *Commando Natalie.* He was a nervous wreck. It was both frustrating and humiliating.

This was taking too long. Natalie made a decision and went for it. She pivoted and entered her parents' room, weapon aimed and ready, her eyes darting around the space. A thorough search revealed no bogymen. The master suite was clear.

The sound of a thud came from the hallway near Coltan's room. An image of him fainting and hitting the floor came to mind, then a second image of a mord knocking something over. She hurried, stepping softly to the doorway and pointed her weapon in the direction of the noise. Coltan steadied a vase he had knocked over on the table against the false wall. He gazed at her, embarrassed and apologetic. She couldn't help it; he looked so silly, she had to smile and giggle silently.

He didn't take that well. His eyes suddenly blazed, and he set his jaw in *that way* she had seen at the Dairy Delight when he broke the punk's nose. Now, that was what she wanted to see—that fire in his eyes. His humiliation had finally overcome his fear, and his male ego took over. The tough ass-kicker she admired returned for a visit. It was about time.

She returned his searing gaze. "That's more like it..."

He gripped the weapon tightly, aimed and stepped forward. The confident and powerful stride of a courageous warrior replaced his fearful shaking. She allowed it when he used one arm to gently push her behind him. This was his show, now. She followed along, two steps behind him, but still beside him. He pointed at her and directed her to check her room while he checked the main bathroom and the second guest room. She obeyed, appreciating his courage and leadership.

The upstairs was clear.

He started down the stairs, his eyes moving in every direction, his weapon pointed. Once at the bottom, he flipped on the wall switch for the overhead lights, took a left into the den, while Natalie veered right and checked first her mother's office, and then the family room beyond.

All clear.

They regrouped at the base of the stairs.

"The sliders held," Coltan said. "Did you check the kitchen yet?"

"Not yet."

"I got it." He went for it, found it ransacked but clear of the intruders, then checked the formal dining room beyond and found it to be clear, as well. "We're good," he announced.

She met him at the kitchen entrance with a grin of admiration.

He stood in front of her. "What?"

"Ass-kicker..." She stood on tiptoes and embraced him, and kissed him fully and passionately on his lips. "Now, that's what I wanted to see!" she told him.

He pulled her against him, his lips close to hers. "Commando..." He held her to him and kissed her, kissed her for a long time. She made no effort to break away, and her reciprocation encouraged him even more.

The task of reinforcing the damaged sliders finally came to mind, and he reluctantly released her.

"I want more of that later," she purred.

He tried not to anticipate *later*. The anticipation would only serve to make Mister Dolce rise to attention, and he did not want that to happen. Not only would it be embarrassing, it would make it impossible to keep his mind on his work.

She understood. Her physical responses were, thankfully, not as obvious as his. However, she admitted to herself she wanted to feel something besides grief and fear, and the possibility of sinning was of no consequence to her anymore. Maybe she would reconsider that later when they both calmed down.

They chose rooms and examined the sliders. Aside from bullet holes in many of them, the only one compromised was in the living room. Coltan retrieved hand tools and wood remnants from the basement and went about reinforcing it. He also brought up a can of wood filler putty to use for plugging the bullet holes. That way, if they came down at night and needed to put on the lights, it wouldn't show from the outside.

It occurred to him they should have carried the walkie-talkies. With him down on the main floor and her upstairs, they could warn each other of impending danger. He made a mental note to prepare the squawkers and use them next time. For the time being, God had given them a reprieve from any immediate danger, and they would put it to good use.

WHILE HE WORKED, NATALIE gathered her personal items and brought them to the attic. She set the photo of herself with Mom and Dad next to her mattress. The clothing and books she piled on the stack of extra mattresses for sorting later.

However, she extracted her Bible from the pile of books and then went to her mattress and sat. She opened it and was glad the precious something she sought was still there: a photograph of Coltan she snapped on the sly one day when he was out on the back porch having a smoke break and reading his Bible. He always seemed so at peace when he was reading, and the expression on his face at that time revealed what she identified as the real person behind the tough guy persona. Desiring to preserve his unguarded true self, she retrieved her digital camera and secretly observed him, waited for just the right moment, the camera set for a close-up shot. He looked up from the pages of his Bible, contemplating a verse, or maybe recalling a moment in his life the Scripture rekindled. He had been facing a little bit away from her at that second, and she clearly saw the contemplation and reverence in those beautiful dark blue eyes. In that moment, the hardness he had worked years to project had vanished, replaced by an angelic tenderness. She took the shot—captured his true spirit—and he had never known it. Hours later, when she had time alone, she printed the photo and trimmed it to size. She gave the treasured keepsake a permanent home between the pages of her Bible. In all the weeks that had passed since then, she had never told him about the photograph; it was her own personal treasure, and she would look at it often, trace the contours of his face with her fingers, and say a prayer for him. She would love him forever.

Her recollection of the day and night before was still hazy, but she remembered with deep love and appreciation how he had cradled her and offered her the emotional safety to express her grief. She wondered if he realized what a comfort he had been to her. Had he realized then the depths of her need for him and the gratitude she had been unable to express? Did he understand and accept how completely she trusted him? Did he know without a doubt how profoundly she loved him?

She kissed her fingers and placed the kiss on his lips. As she replaced the photo and closed her Bible, she slowly emerged from her reverie.

As planned, she took a long hot bath. In that hour of solitude in the soothing heat of the lavender scented water she let her armor dissolve and allowed herself the luxury of another cry. After a while, she surrendered to her physical exhaustion, closed her eyes and dozed. She dreamed she was floating in a lake surrounded by lush trees and grasses. The water was placid and warm and the color of an emerald. An invisible presence floated alongside her. In her dream, she knew the presence loved her unconditionally and would always be at her side.

COLTAN FINISHED REINFORCING the living room slider. He then triple-checked the others and plugged the bullet holes with wood putty. While doing so, he listened carefully for any sounds from outside that would indicate company. Except for the birds and the occasional rustle of wind, it was quiet. He stole outside through the back door and locked the security door behind him with the key for Natalie's safety. A quick and cautious survey of the windows confirmed his expectation they were all broken. The glass littered the entire porch, and overturned and damaged furniture and planters added to the mess. He would have immediately set about cleaning it up if things had been normal, but their circumstances were far from normal—even dangerous. Coltan opted to leave it all as it was to make it appear as if no one was home and would probably never come home.

Upon return to the rear of the house, the south side, he got a close-up look at what remained of Beverly's car. The sight of it sitting as a monument of sorts to her death would only repeatedly remind Natalie of that horrific scene. He wished he could make it disappear. It would be no good if he covered it with a tarp; that action would arouse suspicion should the soldiers return.

He pulled up a chair by the door and lit a smoke. The lingering odors of the past warfare had finally dissipated, and the air was cold. Black storm clouds rode the wind high up in the atmosphere. The few leaves remaining on the trees quivered in the breeze. Coltan expected winter would make an early appearance this year and it would be especially brutal, for the summer had meandered through with unseasonably cold temperatures, and this autumn was unusually brisk for the area. Fresh snow already dusted the mountain peaks.

It was too late and too risky to try to make it to the safe zone. They would have to wait until spring or early summer. In the meantime, they had enough food, water and ammunition to keep them healthy and safe. As long as the electricity held, they would have refrigeration and heat. If the house stayed secure, and the mords, inevitable looters and any other threats stayed away, they could even spend some time downstairs, just to keep their sanity.

His gaze wandered to the backyard of his old house. From the spot where he sat, he could not see the house, only a corner of the yard. The chair Richard hurled through the window was still there only it was now in a different position. He thought about his mother and Richard and wondered if they had survived. The day before when the military and HAZMAT came through to search for survivors and dispose of all the corpses, Coltan had stayed away from the windows to avoid discovery. If his mother and Richard had survived, the soldiers would have found them and taken them away. It confused him and filled him with conflicting emotions when he realized he did care about them, he did care, after all. He asked himself why he cared. All of his life they had been nothing but a source of misery to him. Why should he care? If God was nudging him to forgive them, he was not yet ready. He tried not to dwell on it. The memories made him angry.

Natalie returned downstairs dressed in clean clothes. She saw the kitchen door was open, and she could see Coltan through the security door. She unlocked it and opened it.

"Hey you..." she called softly.

He turned and saw her short hair was still damp, though it looked like she had towel-dried it. He smelled the scent of lavender.

He snubbed out the cigarette and met her at the doorway. "Hey. Feel better?"

"Lots better. I was thinking about cooking some dinner for us."

"I wonder if the smell would attract company." It was a reasonable concern.

"Maybe. Have you seen anyone?"

"No one."

"How are the windows?"

"Trashed."

"Well... Let's lock up and bring some stuff from the fridge up to the attic. There's still juice and milk, and stuff. We should use it. There's also some potpies in the freezer. I could microwave those. Use up the salad, too. Might as well not waste it. I'll fix us dinner while you get a shower."

"Sounds like a good plan." He entered and locked both doors.

"And, Colt?"

"Yeah?"

"You did great today. I knew you would."

OVER ON THE FAR SOUTH side of Bonito Valle, HAZMAT tossed more of the increasing number of corpses into the pit across from the sewage treatment plant. The military continued to round-up survivors and confiscate all weapons. A small group of resistors had taken refuge in the basement of a church, refusing to surrender their arms. Following orders, Shaunnessy tossed a few grenades down the steps and ran for cover.

James piled the confiscated weapons into the back of a truck. The explosions from the church rattled his nerves. The faceless servants of the Evil One were fast losing their patience with all resistors. Throughout that morning, he had seen soldiers coldly apprehend and execute resistors. In order to prevent distrust and quash any further rebellion among the civilians, they assured the people they were only executing the infected discovered among them. It worked for the time being, and the Civs cooperated.

The rain fell faster and heavier and the winds picked up. James loaded the last of the confiscated weapons and took a moment to peer at the black clouds moving in.

God help us...

CHAPTER 24

In the electrical access space between the stockroom and the sales floor at the Bonito Valle Bujjet Mart, Mario Rodriquez sat on the concrete floor against a corner of the wall. Little Rosa lay in his arms, her wet face resting against his blood stained shirt and torn Bujjet Mart vest. Mario had not been able to awaken her. He looked down at her, pressed his hand to her forehead, found it to be disturbingly ice cold. Yet, she was still breathing—he could hear it, could feel it. He tucked her sleeping bag tightly around her, and then he opened a second and draped it over himself.

His blood dripped on the nylon material, and he wiped at it fussily. At the exterior rear of the building three mords had managed to sink their teeth into him as he struggled with the keys to unlock the employee door to the stockroom. Rosa also suffered another bite in the process. Now, Mario could feel the fever begin in his own body, could feel the unrelenting burning pain travel through his body from every bite wound. He was weakening and had suffered some short episodes of delirium over the last hour.

He knew what would follow, what they would become.

He kissed Rosa's cold, wet forehead. She did not respond to his kiss or his gentle touch as he caressed her icy cheek. Her body felt cold against his skin through his vest and shirt. The coolness of her little body nestled into his made him shiver. Yet, she did not shiver. She simply lay there limp and silent, her breathing slow and labored. Mario wondered how long it would take for the disease to reach her brain and turn her into a ravaging animal. He could not picture her as a mord, and he was glad his imagination refused to conjure up the image. Perhaps it was his love for her that suppressed his imagination or maybe it was God's mercy, or maybe it was both. However, he was too frightened and angry to be grateful for the dimming of his mind.

He directed his anger at God for not intervening to save them—or the rest of humanity, for that matter. What kind of compassionate God sits on the sidelines and watches while everything turns to shit? Mario no longer trusted God to take action. He only trusted himself to do what he had to do.

Everything in his soul screamed at him to prevent the inevitable, to end Rosa's suffering before she joined the hordes of the predatory infected. To Mario, it was the most loving thing he could do for her.

His body now seemed out of his control, and it broke into a violent fit of shivering accompanied by a drenching cold sweat. The pain of his wounds increased rapidly to the point where the burning was unbearable. He could no longer move his legs. To add to his misery, his eyesight was beginning to fail. He wanted his own suffering to be over, wanted to end his own life before the disease gave him a new life as a cannibalistic menace.

Mario decided he had wasted enough time. He kissed Rosa once more and reached for Officer Danbury's gun at his side. The weapon felt extremely heavy in his hand, much heavier than it did that morning. With much difficulty, he raised it and attempted to cock it. His thumb was too weak to draw it back; it took both hands to finally set it. He leaned Rosa's head against his shoulder and pressed the point of the barrel to the little girl's temple. It brought him a small measure of comfort to know she would not feel the bullet pierce her brain, and she would not know he had done it. He tried to press the trigger, but his finger would not respond to his brain's commands. He persisted, focused on his fingers, attempted to will all his remaining strength there. It was just no good, no matter the amount of effort. The paralysis that had already deadened his legs had begun to spread to the rest of his body. His arms weakened further, and he could not fight it. In the next few seconds, his arms became numb—not the pins and needles kind of numb, but the kind of numbness that happens when the brain no longer recognizes its appendages.

Mario realized it was too late.

"Rosa..." he whispered weakly and disconsolately.

His strength and control now gone, Mario's hand slowly slid down to his side. His fingers slackened and fell open. The gun gently tumbled onto the floor as he gradually lost consciousness.

JAMES SLIPPED AWAY from the troops the moment he saw an opportunity. He had gathered all the intelligence he could from observing and listening to both the troops and their leaders. It was now time to make his way back into the mountains to the hidden Alpha Base Headquarters. He entered a storm drain entrance off the spillway and followed his map toward the east end of town. From there, he would emerge at a narrow arm of the river, and then swim across and pick up another storm drain route. He'd take a nap underground, and then climb up top at dusk and hike through the bushy foothills where he had parked and camouflaged the stolen and de-chipped military jeep.

The information he had gathered was sparse, but it would give the Army of Christ enough to begin planning for the anticipated battle in mid-summer. He hoped the others had been successful collecting and transporting additional weapons and medical supplies. They would need everything they could get their hands on.

The safe zones had been in the planning stages for ten years and, as the group amassed more and more dedicated members, they spent the last eight years on construction and disaster supplies, all on donations and with volunteer labor. James's safe zone, Alpha Base, was the first completed and was located inside a massive complex of lava tubes on land he inherited in the mountains of northeastern California. As of this day there were thirty communes scattered across the continental United States, one in Hawaii and two in Alaska.

James had spent the last fifteen years taking careful note of the decreased morality around the world that coincided with the increased technological advances. As was true before, and is still true today, technology could serve for good or evil. The invention of the Radio Frequency Identification—RFID—chip, and the later Residence, Education, Financial, Employment, Health and Location—REFEHL—chip was at the top of the list of technologies that could easily be exploited. The more James researched the technology, the higher the red flags rose, and those red flags convinced him of the imminence of the birth pangs preceding the Time of Troubles. The barely noticed surveillance cameras and microphones on every street corner and traffic light; televisions, computers and handheld gadgets that tracked one's every interest, purchasing habits, source and amount of income, and one's precise location at all times; the increasing hopelessness and apathy of the population (especially the young); the emerging global military force; past pandemics and now the mord maker virus pandemic; the camps and the chip-spiked fake vaccinations convinced him the *Time* was now.

The jeep started up on the second try, and it bounced up the incline and onto the crumbling narrow blacktop. This was the least traveled and most forgotten route up the mountain. In the old days, it had served as an alternate route for logging trucks until the completion of the interstate. However, it was one of many obscure routes the Army of Christ used to bring supplies to Alpha Base, their refuge and headquarters. Their traffic had consistently escaped detection from the air because of the overgrowth of tall pines and unruly brush. To James it was another example of how God used his creation for the safety and survival of his own.

He saw movement up ahead through the beam of the headlights. At first, he thought it was a deer, so he slowed down. The last thing he needed was a collision with one of those— he'd end up having to hike the remaining twenty miles. As he neared the point where he first saw the movement, something red caught his eye at the side of the road. He came to a stop about fourteen feet behind it. It looked like a jacket, and then it moved. He grabbed his rifle, cocked it and aimed.

"Please!" A girl's voice, weak and frantic. "They didn't get me. Please!"

"Let me see your face!" James hollered.

She looked up from her crouched position. Her face was pale and dirty. However, there was no trace of blood, no telltale signs of a recent meal of human flesh. "Please!" She screamed, "They're looking for me! Help me!"

"Stand up!" he ordered.

She stood on weak, wobbly legs. James noticed she was overweight, but her baggy clothing indicated she weighed a lot more before her ordeal. "Please!" she pleaded.

"Move towards me. *Slowly!*" He balanced the rifle in one hand while he retrieved the chip scanner with the other. When she reached the front of the jeep, he ordered her to stop. He locked the brake, got out and approached her. "Are you chipped?" he asked.

She didn't know what that meant. "What?"

He scanned her from a distance. She was clean.

"You been bit?"

"No! I've been running. I saw what he did to Mom. We ran and ran until she got sick. I ran away from her. I ran away. Please! Help me! They're gonna find me!"

"You said, 'we ran.' Who's with you?"

"Just me and Mom ran—from *Dad*. Then Mom got sick. I knew what was gonna happen to her, so I ran. I ran by myself. Please, Mister. They're tracking me!"

"Where's your mother?"

"Back there somewhere." In frustration, she screamed as if he was her last chance, "Help me!"

He walked over to her and escorted her to the jeep, helped her in. She was trembling from head to toe and completely exhausted. She reeked of dirt, sweat and urine. Once she settled into the seat, James wasted no time getting them both out of there.

"I'm so thirsty," she said.

He offered her his water bottle from the console. She opened it and gulped down the entire contents, spilling a lot of it down her chin and throat.

"How long you been out there?" he asked.

"A week, maybe. I don't know. We were attacked at a rest stop on our way to our cabin. We didn't know how bad it was at the time. Then Dad started getting sicker and sicker and Mom had to drive. I was in the back and couldn't see what was happening."

"In the back?"

"Our motor home. We tried to find help, but no one would help us. We couldn't find a hospital. The traffic was so bad, accidents and stuff, we couldn't find our way around. No one would help us. We took the wrong road and ended up on this side of the mountain. And, Dad was getting sicker and sicker. We ran out of gas. We tried to call out for help, but we couldn't get a signal." She covered her mouth and began sobbing. "God! Oh, God...!"

"You calm down, now..." James said. "You're safe now."

"Where are you going?"

"A safe place."

"Please... I gotta get back to Bonito Valle."

"Bonito Valle's gone."

"What do you mean 'gone'?"

He decided to spare her the gory details. "It's been evacuated."

"Evacuated?" She stared at him, completely confused.

"Do you have any idea what's been happening?"

"An epidemic. Something about an epidemic. I don't know."

"Well, girl," he said, "Bonito Valle's the last place you want to be."

"My best friend lives there." Her bottom lip trembled and fresh tears fell down her face. "Was she evacuated, too?"

"Most likely." He saw the tears, and his heart went out to her. "She's probably safe. Most people got out safe."

"Were you there?"

"Yeah. That's how I know most people got out safe."

"Did you see the neighborhood on the east side? The one up the hill? The one by the east range of the mountain?"

"I saw a lot of neighborhoods. I couldn't tell you."

"Their house had a big garden. Big! Her mom gave us baskets of veggies every summer. We used to play in the garden when we were little. Their house was the only one with a huge garden in the back yard. We had a lotta fun playing there."

He thought back, vaguely recalling a house with a large garden, but the image blurred as other images of other homes in countless subdivisions scrambled to the forefront. The many houses they ordered him to check all converged into one mass of houses that all looked alike and melted into each other. He couldn't trust his memory.

"Where are we going?" She had forgotten she had already asked that question.

"A safe place," he answered. "With good, kind people who'll take good care of you."

"Your family?"

"Yes." He considered them his family.

"Are you a soldier?"

"Yes."

"Are you on leave?"

"Yeah." He didn't know what else to say.

She was quiet for a minute, but only a minute. She bundled her jacket around her and sunk back into the seat. "They're still out there. I hope they don't find us."

"They won't," James told her. "You just try to relax and get a little rest. We'll be there soon."

"Where are we going?"

James sighed tiredly.

NATALIE HAD DINNER waiting when Coltan returned to the attic after his shower. She draped an old tablecloth over the small round table. She neatly stacked his study materials off to the side to make room for their plates, silverware and wine glasses. A quick trip down to the basement gave her the idea for the wine while she was in pursuit of the tablecloth. She had chosen the best Merlot and thought there was no logical reason why it wouldn't be okay to have a little wine with dinner.

Coltan was not expecting anything like this. It impressed him that she had spontaneously prepared a romantic dinner for two. The only thing missing was candles. He noticed the wine glasses, and he wasn't sure how he felt about that. He also wasn't sure about the whole *romantic dinner* idea. Did she think they were going to play house now?

She noted his ambivalence. "Is this okay?"

"Wow..." It was all he could say without hurting her feelings.

She realized then she had done something wrong. Yet, she was angrier with him than with herself. "For all we know we might die tomorrow! What's wrong with having a nice dinner along with a nice table setting? What's wrong with that?"

"Nothing."

"What's wrong with it?"

"Nothing."

"Is it the wine?"

"Well... I don't know."

"Do you have a problem with alcohol? Is that it?"

"No."

"So, what's the problem?" She really didn't get it. After giving him more than enough time to respond, she finally said, "Okay, fine. If you want to be a little turd about everything, I can eat by myself, and you can go down into the basement and park yourself on the steps. Don't forget to take a dirty undershirt for a napkin."

He understood she was referring to that night on the steps in the basement when he scarfed down tuna sandwiches and used his undershirt to wipe his mouth. She had told him he ate like a barbarian. The memory caused him to laugh.

She indignantly demanded, "What?"

"You're banishing the barbarian to the basement!" He couldn't help it.

"Damned right." She began to laugh, too.

His ambivalence turned to appreciation. He pulled out the chair for her and motioned her to sit. She began to sit, but wondered if he planned to do something silly like pull the chair out from under her. When she paused, he said, "Madam..." She sat and he pushed her chair close to the table. Then he sat.

He saw she had already uncorked the wine to let it "breathe." Well, she certainly knew something about wine. He hefted the bottle and checked the label. "Merlot. Hmmm, let's see here. We got beef potpies, salad, bread and Merlot. Good combination. Good choice of wine."

"My parents do—*did*—let me have wine with dinner sometimes.

If that's what you're worried about. And... I'll have you know," she went on, "I slaved all day on those pot pies. So, you better appreciate it!"

"Yes, dear." He played along, "And, I'm so exhausted from plowing the back forty." He poured her glass first, then his own. Lifting his glass for a toast he said, "Tomorrow, we may die."

They toasted to that.

MARIO TOOK ROSA'S HAND and led her out of the Bujjet Mart stockroom and out to the deserted rear of the building. They were hungry, and both sniffed the air to pick up the scent of a living, breathing meal. The only aromas that filled the air were the odors of decaying corpses, vehicle exhaust and some rotting garbage near the dumpsters. Noises assaulted their ears from near and far, noises of machinery, gunfire, barking dogs and the faint voices of men and women. They sniffed the air again. The humans were too far away.

Mario took into account the noises of gunfire, and he sensed the humans were armed and hunting for him and the little girl. A vague flash of memory showed the child on his lap with a picture book. A second flash showed her laughing, which stirred a strong feeling of love for her and his compulsion to protect her from the humans with the guns and the noisy, growling machines.

Overhead, a helicopter puttered, and its searchlight swept over the vacant lot to his right. Mario jerked the little girl to his side and took cover behind one of the pallets of flattened cardboard boxes. He watched the helicopter veer away and cast its light northwestward where it followed the ribbon of interstate. The girl bared her teeth and growled at the giant black insect with the big bright eye.

Although it was pitch black with the absence of electrical power to light the loading docks, Mario could see clearly across the lot as if it was noontime. He wanted to escape this place, escape without their predators' detection. But... how? The entire massive square of pavement around the building was wide open to the sky, wide open for the things in the air to spot them.

He scanned the pavement again, recalling there was something, some way to get under the pavement.

It began to rain. He remembered rain. He remembered the time it rained so hard the store flooded because the storm drains clogged.

He grinned then, and a low rumble of satisfaction rolled up his throat. He tightened his grip of the girl's hand, tugged on it to get her attention. When she looked up at him inquiringly, he grunted and pointed at the manhole cover. She smiled and nodded.

END OF BOOK 1

A Bunch of Words From the Author:

CLAIMING DESTINATION's first incarnation was as a novel I began writing in early 2006 and completed in 2009. The original version completed in 2009 ended with a subtle hint about the future of one particular little girl to end the story on a hopeful note. I then submitted the first draft copies to eleven test readers for their opinions and suggestions. Overall they loved the story (said it was "a page-turner"). Overwhelmingly, they wanted a sequel!

I shelved the original CLAIMING DESTINATION for another year before I decided to revise it as a book series. This entailed dividing the original novel and introducing additional characters and their experiences in the outside world. That outside world was a real horror show, as any good Dystopian/Apocalyptic story should portray.

However, by 2011 network television jumped on the Dystopian/Apocalyptic bandwagon, thus saturating viewers with every type of disaster scenario imaginable, including alien invasions, grid down events, and the Zombie Apocalypse (admirably presented as the venerable "The Walking Dead" series, among others). With so many television shows (and movies) touching on a similar theme as my CLAIMING DESTINATION series, I descended into a major depression and again shelved my work after I completed Book 5 of CLAIMING DESTINATION because I felt no one would be interested in what I, an unknown author, had to offer—especially with a genre already overdone.

Yet, there are underlying themes in CLAIMING DESTINATION that make it unique in this genre.

One aspect of CLAIMING DESTINATION that makes it a challenge to impress the traditional publishing industry and readers is my mixture of Christianity and Horror within the main dystopian setting. The principal characters are realistically imperfect Christians with their share of secret sins. Some of them behave like downright beasts when the situation calls for it. Yet, they try to maintain their belief in a loving God who answers prayers, even as society and the world in general is imploding as the evil slowly takes root and then spreads throughout the globe. They ask, Where is God and why isn't he doing something to stop this? The answer to that question is simple: human beings have brought it upon themselves. God gave us free will to do the right thing or the wrong thing, and humans seem more adept at doing the wrong thing, which brings me to the second subject in this mixture: Horror.

Yes, there is horror, as in blood and guts horror. There's gore, lots of gore. It's the kind of stuff that will turn your stomach and make you question the sanity of the author who wrote this twisted tale. There is cruelty and death, betrayal and apathy—scenarios you wouldn't find in the average Christian-themed novel, *unless you're an avid Bible reader*. The Bible is full of terrible scenarios highlighting the worst of Man.

In 2021, a friend convinced me to finish this damned series because he wanted to read how it ends after I left him hanging at the end of Book 5 when I threw in the towel. So, in 2022 I wrote the final book in the series, sent it to him with a thank you for inspiring me and hoping he would be satisfied with the end. (Yes, he liked it.) Now, he has convinced me to publish the whole package. I love this guy who won't allow me to quit!

I hope Book One in this series has made you hungry for the rest of this futuristic (but not too far into the future) saga of a world gone hopelessly mad, and I hope you like it enough to tell your friends.

Thank you for reading Book One
of
my seven-book
<u>Claiming Destination Series</u>
*Independent authors rely on reviews
to spread the word about their works.
If you enjoyed this book (or hated it),
please leave an online review
where you purchased it.
If you would like to contact me directly, you can reach me here:*
On Facebook: Colleen A Parkinson, Author
My Blog Page: https://thefinesthat.jimdoweb.com

While the entire planet descends into madness, things get
downright dangerous for Natalie, Coltan, little Rosa and her
brother Mario, and all the others you met in Book 1.
(Warning: Not for the squeamish!)
Their story continues in the remaining six books of this series:
BOOK 2: FLIGHT OF the Destined
Book 3: Isa
Book 4: The Bitter Fruit
Book 5: To Move a Mountain
Book 6: Mister Death Shadow
Book 7: Desitus

Also by Colleen A. Parkinson

Claiming Destination
The Dreadful Dawn
Flight of the Destined
Isa
The Bitter Fruit
To Move a Mountain
Mister Death Shadow
Desitus

Standalone
Beneath This Hallowed Ground

www.ingramcontent.com/pod-product-compliance
Lightning Source LLC
Chambersburg PA
CBHW070841260626
47170CB00007B/2455